"How long have I been here?"

"I found you three morns past."

Did he mean she'd been in this place for three full days? The realization made Nadine shudder. If that were true, then by now her parents were probably buried.

A heavy weight settled in Nadine's heart. They were gone forever now, and she hadn't had even the chance of saying goodbye.

She stifled a sob but couldn't prevent a lone tear from rolling down her cheek. "Has anybody come looking for me?"

"Nay. No one has come for you."

Nadine closed her eyes for a moment. She threaded one hand slowly through her hair, pushed a strand behind one ear, then let her hand fall into her lap. A deep loneliness took hold of her and she could no longer hold the sobs at bay or the tears that flowed freely down her face.

With one fluid movement he moved to her side and sat on the edge of her bed. With his thumb he wiped away her tears.

Surprised, Nadine stared as he took her hand into his huge one and placed her palm against his chest. The intimate gesture puzzled her. The sudden heat of his skin burned her hand, and the strong pulsating of his heart misled the steady melancholic rhythm of hers. . . .

A PERFECT LOVE

Sandra Landry

JOVE BOOKS, NEW YORK

IN MEMORIUM
Dedicated to the loving memory of my father, José Maschette.
A great storyteller in his own right.

TIME PASSAGES is a registered trademark of Penguin Putnam Inc.

A Jove Book / published by arrangement with
the author

PRINTING HISTORY
Jove edition / August 2000

The Penguin Putnam Inc. World Wide Web site address is
http://www.penguinputnam.com

ISBN: 0-515-12885-6

A JOVE BOOK®
Jove Books are published by The Berkley Publishing Group,
a division of Penguin Putnam Inc.,
375 Hudson Street, New York, New York 10014.
JOVE and the ''J'' design
are trademarks belonging to Penguin Putnam Inc.

PRINTED IN THE UNITED STATES OF AMERICA

10 9 8 7 6 5 4 3 2 1

Prologue

"'Tis YOUR DUTY to beget heirs."

The words hit Faulk like a pounding mallet betwixt his shoulder blades. He pivoted to face his father. " 'Tis a duty I shall fulfill when the time comes." Naught would dissuade him from departing Whitecastle on the morrow.

"The time is now." Warren Brookstone advanced toward his son. "God saw fit to grant me only one son, and now 'tis your duty to carry on our name. Putting your life at risk, traipsing after the newly crowned King of England is not the way to accomplish that."

Balling up his fists, Faulk controlled the rising frustration. His sire would never understand his need to leave England and all the haunting memories behind. Lord Warren was a man whose honor had never been besmirched, whose duties he had never failed, whose father he had never disappointed.

Faulk carried all those failures upon his shoulders.

"We have spoken of this, Father. In battle I shall prove myself deserving of our name, and of these." Faulk pointed to the golden spurs he received last summer when he was knighted at the age of ten and eight. He had been so proud. And so had his father.

How could one incredibly stupid mistake wipe all that joy away?

Lord Warren gripped his son's shoulders. They were of a similar height, both well above six feet. Their gazes locked in a clash of wills. "You can prove your worth right here at Whitecastle. Heed my words, Son."

As you did not heed them before.

The unspoken reminder shamed Faulk. He averted his gaze and disengaged himself from his father's grip. He had brought dishonor upon himself when he had wedded Elizabeth against his father's objections. Had shamed his family when he had behaved like a gullible, lovesick fool and fallen for her lies.

And then the terrible truth . . . Her deathbed confession as her blood and her unborn child's mingled in the bedding while life slipped away. Her betrayal. The child that was never his.

Pain washed over Faulk. If he lived a thousand years he would never forget that moment. Nor would he ever allow his heart to rule him again.

His father was right. Marriage was a contract, a means to an end. Love should never be a part of it.

Taking a deep breath, Faulk faced his sire. "I vow to make you proud of me. I vow to fulfill my duty and beget an heir for the continuation of our line. Choose a befitting wife for me, Father, and I shall wed her."

Lord Warren's face split into a pleased smile. "I have just the lady in mind. Her beauty is reputed to be beyond words, and she is the daughter of a good friend of mine. I shall speak with—"

"I shall wed her," Faulk interrupted. "Upon my return from the Crusades." Only when he had proved his mettle would he fulfill his duty to his father.

His father's pleased grin turned into a frown of resignation. "Very well, Son. 'Twill be as you wish." Sidestepping Faulk, Lord Warren walked out of the bedchamber.

The crown of trees shaded the forenoon sun as Faulk followed the trail to the beach where he usually went in times of trouble. And these were certainly troublesome times for him. Once again he would defy his father's wishes, yet this time Faulk was certain his decision was wise. On the morrow, at dawn, he would depart for Londontown, where King Richard gathered his forces, and leave behind Whitecastle and his haunting memories.

Immersed in his thoughts, Faulk failed to notice the old woman until he was upon her. Her sudden appearance scared his horse, and it reared in response.

"Trying to get yourself killed?" Faulk thundered as he controlled his mount, barely avoiding trampling the woman.

"I but wait for you, my lord." Her mouth moved, but the sound seemed to surround her instead of coming from her. Her impossibly wrinkled face suggested advanced years, yet her hair held no hint of gray, falling unbound in dark waves to her knees.

A sudden memory jabbed Faulk. *The witch.* She had not changed much since his childhood, at least as much as he could remember. He had seen her only one time, when as a child he had ventured into the forest to steal a look at the mysterious healer.

He thought her dead by now. Evidently the old hag was still around, but what could she want with him? Did she even know who he was?

"I had a vision that concerns you, my Lord Faulk," the woman said, as if reading his mind.

The word *vision* almost made Faulk laugh. Almost. In his present mood, laughing was beyond him. He dismissed her words. He had no intention of relying on visions to forge his future.

"Spare me your empty visions." He urged his horse forward, but the witch refused to budge, forcing him to stop lest he trampled her.

Her impudent boldness—or heedless foolishness, he could not quite decide—puzzled Faulk. Best let her speak her mind and begone. "Do you trick me, you shall pay dearly."

"I trick you not, my lord, for I possess the knowledge that shall heal your bleeding heart."

The pain of betrayal and besmirched honor spread over him like a disease. He would allow no one to speak of his shame. "Cease your rumbling immediately. Begone from my sight."

"Please, my lord, heed my words." She stepped closer, heedless of the danger. "I can give you hope, for I have seen the future. A golden vision of beauty shall come to you through the water, and when she comes, you shall know 'tis her without a doubt for she bears the mark of the rose. The brightness of the sun shines on her hair, and her golden eyes shall bewitch your heart."

"I need not your counsel to find women, old hag," he spat.

"Aye, my lord, but this lady is special. Only she can bear you healthy sons. Your line shall not die with you."

Sons. The reminder unleashed his shame anew.

"Yet to keep her you must find love in your heart," the witch continued, "for love is the uniting thread betwixt you."

Love, Faulk quietly grumbled. Love would never again be part of his life. Yet, something in the ancient face stirred an unwanted feeling of hope inside of him. A feeling he swiftly crushed.

In utter aggravation Faulk lifted his gaze to the sky as the witch prophesied the last words.

"Heed my warning. As she comes through the water, so can the water take her away."

With a scant retort at the tip of his lips, Faulk returned his gaze to the woman, but the witch was nowhere to be seen.

Scrutinizing the area, he found no signs of her presence and for a moment doubted her very existence. Yet her words remained with him, within him, and though he vowed to forget the incident altogether, he doubted he ever would.

ENGLAND
SIX YEARS LATER

"*Sacré Coeur*," Nadine du Monte muttered, stopping her pacing and sitting down. "If I ever get out of this dark little hovel alive, I shall never again enter another confining place for the rest of my life."

For weeks she had been kept prisoner in this isolated little hut, somewhere near the English coast. She only knew she was in England because she had once overheard her captors muttering about their dislike of being on English soil. The one-room hovel had no windows, and the lone burning candle on top of the little table cast off more shadow than light.

She had always disliked darkness, Nadine thought as she diligently consumed her unappetizing meal of black bread and ale, but lately she had grown to detest it.

Yet, this eve, she welcomed it.

Every so often, Benoit, her captor, left her at his underling's care for a few hours during the night. Nadine had no idea of where he went or what he did, and she cared not. All she needed to know was that he would leave again this eve.

And this time she would be ready.

Under her thin pallet Nadine hid a small knife she had managed to steal from Severine, the underling. She knew

better than to try to best the two men with it, though she
was well versed in the use of a knife as a weapon. Nay,
she would use it to free herself and flee from this wretched
captivity.

"Finish your supper, and get into bed."

Benoit's sudden entrance startled Nadine. She darted a
furtive look at him, but recognized the order for what 'twas.
Benoit was a man of few words, and Severine was incapable of uttering any at all, and she had learned to read
their moods quickly. They had not treated her cruelly thus
far, yet there was naught charitable in keeping her against
her will.

"I am finished." Nadine pushed the small table away
from her. The sooner he secured her, the sooner he would
leave, and the sooner she could attempt her escape.

Benoit tied her hands to the front of her body—a con-
cession she obtained only after incessant complaint—then
he pushed her down on the hard pallet. She lay on her back
as he tied her feet and covered her with a thin blanket. She
hated the position, but said naught.

"Give Severine no grief," Benoit warned before leaving
the hut. "He might be slow, but he is not stupid. He knows
the punishment if he lets you escape."

Nadine dismissed the admonition. She had already tried
pleading with Severine, judging him to be the weaker of
the two, but little good it did her. He had turned deaf ears
to her pleas.

Nay, Nadine had no intention of pleading anymore. Time
had come for some action on her part. She had waited long
enough for her papa to rescue her, though she was certain
he was using every means at his disposal to locate her. Her
fate was in her hands, and Nadine was determined to save
herself. After all, she had put herself in this situation; she
should be the one to extricate herself from it.

She listened to the sounds from outside to ascertain
whether Benoit had already gone and Severine had settled

down for the night. When all she heard was silence, Nadine scooped herself to the edge of the pallet. She twisted to her side, taking immense care not to uncover herself, and groped underneath the thin mattress for the knife.

For a moment she panicked, worrying she had hid it too well, then relief washed over her as she felt the blade's handle betwixt her fingers. Now all she had to do was cut the ties without shredding her hands to pieces.

Falling back on the pallet, she held firmly to the knife and began her work. As the blade slowly cut through the rope, it tightened around her wrists. Her hands began to cramp. She bit her lips and prayed 'twould not take over-long to free herself.

The rope resisted her attempts, though. A solitary bead of perspiration strayed down her face, soon followed by another. Nadine wiped the perspiration off on her shoulder with a movement of her head. Her gown soaked the moisture easily.

Suddenly the door cracked open. Nadine froze. She immediately closed her eyes, feigning sleep, praying that Severine would not come too close. Praying that he would not hear the desperate pounding of her heart or her barely controlled ragged breathing.

Naught happened. No footsteps coming her way. No touching hands testing her ties and finding her knife.

Nadine dared one quick glimpse. Severine stood in the doorway for what seemed like an eternity, then turned and closed the door behind him.

Nadine sighed in relief. She listened to Severine settle down on the ground outside her door, where he usually slept. For a while he moved around, then quieted down. She waited a little longer before renewing her efforts.

At last, the ties gave away, and her hands fell free. She flexed her fingers and felt the painful flow of blood through her veins. As soon as the pain was gone she cut the ties that bound her feet and rose from the pallet.

The loud rustling of the straw-stuffed mattress filled the small room. Nadine's heart slammed against her chest. She held her breath, expecting Severine to charge into the hut any moment, but all she heard was silence.

Relieved, Nadine tiptoed to the door and opened it carefully. Stepping over Severine's sleeping form, she found herself outside her prison for the first time in weeks. She breathed in deeply the fresh, cool night air, tucked a stray strand of hair behind her ear, and after a quick glance at Severine, stole away into the woods.

The bright full moon illuminated Nadine's way through the thick foliage and trees of the forest. Though it had been some time since she had been brought to this isolated hovel, she hoped to remember her way back to the beach.

Relying partly on memory and mostly on instinct, Nadine forged her way. Breathless, but exultant, she reached the beach. Her gown clung to her like a second skin, drenched with the sweat of her exertion. As she stopped to catch her breath, the cold night air hit her in full, drawing shivers from her.

Nadine braced herself against the cold. Her eyes roamed up and down the small strip of beach, and then strayed to the Channel. A little far from the shore an anchored ship was clearly visible under the bright moonlight.

Sacré Coeur! Her escape seemed to be blessed by fate.

But how would she reach the ship? She could not possibly swim in the dark. Or could she? She was a deft swimmer. Her papa had made sure of it, after she had almost drowned as a child in the pond near Rosemanor.

Still, deft swimmer or nay, the chilly, dark waters of the Channel would not be an easy conquest. Mayhap, she should wait and see who came ashore. If friends, she would be saved. If foes, she would still have a chance to hide away.

But what if nobody came ashore? What if they were ready to depart? It mattered not the ship's destination. Anywhere 'twould be better than her miserable captivity.

She must reach that ship.

At that moment a shuffling sound in the woods caught her attention. She turned and saw Severine appear amidst the thick foliage. Sighting her he raced forward with murderous intent in his eyes. With nowhere to run or hide, Nadine quickly made her decision. She dashed toward the Channel, hoping Severine knew not how to swim, and thankful he was incapable of speech. He would not be able to warn the ship of her escape.

Without a backward glance she forged ahead in the frigid water, ignoring the immediate numbing effect on her body. Breathing rhythmically, she counted every stroke. One arm after another, one breath after another. Endlessly.

Stealing a glimpse ahead of her, she hoped to see the ship at arm's length, only to discover it loomed seemingly unreachable.

Thoughts of her life in Rouen warmed her heart. Marie-Elise's kind face amidst her beautiful roses, her papa's endearing smile and eternal patience with her. Even Roland, a permanent fixture at Rosemanor, reinforced her determination to survive. She must reach that ship. No matter how far it loomed, she would reach it.

Though her small hands felt like big, awkward paddles breaking through the water, and her legs weighed her down like an anchor, Nadine fought to maintain control over her limbs. Methodically she restarted to count the strokes. One, two, three . . . until she thought she could not go on.

And then she touched wood.

She made it!

With frozen hands Nadine grabbed the rope ladder that dangled from the ship, struggling to hold on to it. Afraid of falling back into the water, she entwined her arms around the ladder and with extreme effort lifted herself to the first rung.

Painfully and slowly she climbed up. Halfway she

stopped and gathered her strength, then she looked up.

And then her world collapsed.

From the top of the rail, Benoit, her captor, stared down at her with blazing eyes. "Damn foolish lady," he cursed.

Crestfallen, exhausted beyond words, Nadine's head fell in defeat. Fighting her desperation, she swallowed down tears of frustration while staring down at the dark water. It offered her an escape. Freedom.

Nadine shook her head. Death was not a choice. She had not come this far only to give up. Alive, she could escape again. Alive, there was hope for her.

"Take my hand," Benoit offered as he bent over the rail and extended himself down the ladder in an attempt to reach her.

Resigned, Nadine disentangled her right arm from the rope ladder. She managed to raise it above her head but could not reach Benoit's outstretched hand.

Fighting the debilitating weakness that threatened to overwhelm her, Nadine stretched her endurance and her body to the limit. Their fingers touched. Benoit caught her slippery hand into his. He held on to her while she tried to disentangle the other arm from the ladder. As she reached up to him, her numb feet slipped out of the rope and her hand out of Benoit's, and then she catapulted back.

The world stopped, and time froze for an endless moment, as Nadine fell toward the water. She thought of Marie-Elise, she thought of her papa. She regretted not having listened to his protests. She should never have insisted on going to that fair in Champagne.

Her impetuosity had caused this predicament. Had she the chance, she would do it differently. If she survived, she would never take unnecessary risks again.

With a splash Nadine hit the water. She sank into the darkness, struggling, uncertain if her efforts were bringing her closer to the surface or propelling her farther down. She held her breath as long as she could, but her lungs threatened to explode. Still, she refused to surrender to death. With the last remnants of her depleted strength Nadine turned to God.

Mon Dieu, she prayed. *Do not let it end this way!*

And then all was darkness.

Chapter 1

"NADINE, LOOK AT this."

Nadine du Monte halted her pleasurable stroll down Rue du Gros-Horloge in the heart of historical Rouen to look at her friend, Denise, pointing to a sign on a darkened window of a small shop.

Know the Future in the Palm of Your Hands? Nadine shook her head and resumed her walk. "I'm not wasting my money on such nonsense."

"Oh, but it'd be so much fun!" Denise cried.

"Your idea of fun and mine are two very different things," Nadine shot over her shoulders.

"What are you afraid of, Nadine?"

Nadine halted. She brushed her fingers through her short hair, tucked a strand neatly behind her left ear, then she turned around slowly. "You know, every time you say that, and I unwisely respond to your teasing, I get into some kind of trouble."

"Oh, please." Denise rolled her eyes. "You've never been in trouble in your entire life."

"No? Well, let me refresh your memory, dear friend. I give you two words: *tattoo* and *Jacques*."

"I take responsibility for the tattoo," Denise conceded, "though I don't understand what you're complaining about. After all, you have this beautiful rose tattoo on your shoulder, whereas I ended up with an unidentifiable symbol that crazy woman forced me into choosing."

Nadine snorted. "Nobody ever forced you to do a thing in your life."

Acknowledging the statement with a little amused smile, Denise continued, "Now, Jacques is another story. Even though I was the one who called your attention to him, I also told you from the beginning he was trouble."

"And you were right. I wish I'd listened to you."

"Don't be so hard on yourself." Denise walked up to Nadine and laid a hand on her shoulder. "How could you've known Jacques was such a conniving liar? A married conniving liar at that?"

"I should've known." Nadine's eyes filled with tears, which she promptly fought back. She'd been so blinded by the possibility of having found the perfect love, like the one her parents shared, that she'd ignored the telltale signs: his secrecy, his unavailability, his smooth talk.

"There's no way you could've known the truth. Not until his wife entered the picture, anyway."

The memory of that humiliating moment made Nadine shudder.

"You should consider yourself lucky," Denise continued, "that she interrupted your *tête-à-tête* before the crucial moment. At least, no great harm was done."

No great harm. How about her broken heart? Her disappointment? Her shame? Her guilt? Of course she was glad they hadn't consummated the act—one less thing to regret—but to have her perfect dream destroyed in such a fashion was hardly easy to forget. Add to that the fact she was still a virgin at twenty years of age . . .

"Besides, that's all in the past." Denise took a step across the sidewalk. "You should concentrate on the future now. Tomorrow you'll return to London to continue your studies of that most unnatural language—English." She paused as if to impart some important news. "Did you know that French was the spoken language throughout Europe in the Middle Ages? If things hadn't change, you wouldn't need to learn English now."

"Denise—" Nadine warned. If she was not careful, Denise would embroil her in inconsequential conversation for the rest of the day, and she still had some shopping to do.

"All right." Denise shrugged, then touched her chin in a thoughtful manner. "Where was I? Oh, now I remember, your plans for the future. It's London, then back home to continue your part-time job with preschool children—though why you'd choose to work with little brats is beyond me. And then the university, where I'll take art classes and you'll delve into the darkness of the human psyche."

Denise's rather critical description of Nadine's carefully planned out life was apparently not over yet. She stepped closer to the window, standing beside the palm reader's sign. "Wouldn't you like to know if there's anything in your future that might've escaped such meticulous planning?"

Nadine knew exactly where Denise was leading. At times she envied her friend's carefree way, so different from her own predictable, structured life, but at others it only served to make her weary. "I'm sure I won't find my future in there."

"God have mercy on the skeptical minds," Denise said. "You're way too serious, my dear friend. There's no harm in having a little fun, is there?"

Nadine sighed. She knew Denise wouldn't relent. Besides, she was right, what harm could it possibly do? "All right, you win. But you, my friend, will pay for this entertainment."

Laughing, Denise turned to the entrance, but before she had a chance to knock, the door swung open, revealing a small, dark woman dressed in the colorful garb of a gypsy. She stepped to the side, allowing Denise to enter. Nadine followed behind.

Candles in various degrees of consumption illuminated the small, stuffy room. The smell of burning wax mixed with a sweet-scented incense nauseated Nadine immediately, and a decidedly uneasy feeling assaulted her as soon as the door slammed shut behind her.

As far back as she could remember, Nadine had avoided dark, confining places. They made her feel trapped, defenseless, though she could not pinpoint the exact reason.

The same way she could not explain her terror of water.

"Nadine, are you all right?"

Denise's voice penetrated Nadine's daze. How could she explain to her friend the irresistible urge to flee that had so suddenly assaulted her? She couldn't. She took a deep breath, then forced herself to smile. "I'm fine."

"Are you sure?"

Nadine nodded, then gently nudged her friend. "You go first."

"All right." Denise walked to the small round table where the gypsy sat, waiting. Nadine stood behind her friend.

The gypsy took Denise's left hand into hers and, following the lines in her palm, whispered her predictions. Nadine relaxed as she heard bits and pieces of the predictable fortune-telling stuff the gypsy fed her friend.

Denise gave her a conspiratorial wink when her reading was over, and Nadine took her turn, feeling silly over her initial uneasiness.

She offered the gypsy her left hand, as she had seen Denise do. The room was warm and Nadine's hands felt clammy, but the woman's touch was as cold as a corpse.

Their eyes met. The gypsy held Nadine in a mesmerizing trance.

"Death is only a transitional time. Who knows what it leads to?" the gypsy whispered.

Death? That was not what Nadine had expected to hear. What about the handsome man, beautiful children, and other nonsense the woman was supposed to be telling her? Why was she talking about death? What could she possibly gain by frightening her so?

Nadine tried to pull her hand away, but the gypsy held her in an iron grip. A suffocating feeling overtook Nadine. A strange buzz filled her ears as the room began to spin.

Sacré Coeur! She was going to faint.

Nadine opened her mouth to cry for help, but the sound never came out. The room spun around her in a crescendo of speed, until she was the only unmoving thing in the surrounding vortex.

Suddenly Nadine felt transported to another realm of reality. She found herself in a dark, dirty little hut, lying on a hard mattress, with her hands tied. With a small knife she desperately cut through the rope. There was an urgency to her actions that Nadine couldn't explain. She was living the experience but somehow felt detached from it. Unbound, she rose from the mattress, and the room began to spin around her again.

Then, in a blink of an eye, she was back at the gypsy's place. The room was still stuffy and suffocating as before, but spun no more. Stunned, Nadine sought her friend. Denise stood behind her, giving her an encouraging look, with no apparent knowledge of the fantastic occurrence.

Nadine shifted her gaze to the gypsy, who concentrated on Nadine's hands and seemed unaware of what had just passed.

Could Nadine have been the only one affected? What had happened here? Was she having hallucinations?

"Listen to your heart and you shall find the answer you seek. You must learn to trust yourself. Remember: We walk by faith, not by sight."

The religious saying threw Nadine off. What a totally strange thing for a gypsy to say. Puzzled, Nadine tried to make some sense of the enigmatic words as she followed the path the gypsy's scarlet fingernail traced in her palm.

"A most handsome man will cross your path to complete what was interrupted. You will be given a second chance. Do not waste it." The gypsy stared at Nadine. "Beware of water. As it can bring you great happiness, so it can take it away."

Foreboding stirred Nadine's blood, and she groaned in dismay. She did not need to be reminded of the dangers of water.

Abruptly the gypsy let go of Nadine's hands. She stood up, and smiled, obviously proclaiming the readings closed.

Confused, Nadine stumbled out of the room like a sleepwalker, leaving Denise behind to pay for the services. Outside, the glare of the afternoon sun blinded her momentarily.

"What happened?" Denise asked when she walked outside and found Nadine standing in the middle of the sidewalk. "You look like you've seen a ghost. I didn't hear everything—what did that woman tell you?"

Nadine breathed deeply, then revealed the gypsy's predictions to Denise, but said nothing about the bizarre vision.

"The woman was teasing you," Denise said. "Don't take her words seriously. She probably saw how uptight you were and decided to have some fun with you."

"Maybe." But why would she mention death, and water? And what did she mean by her cryptic words? *We walk by faith, not by sight?* And what about the strange episode she experienced that nobody else seemed to be aware of? Nadine shivered. Forcing the uneasiness away, she decided to return home. Somehow she didn't feel like shopping anymore.

● ● ●

The next morning found Nadine ensconced in her mother's little garden. The sweet scent of the wisteria surrounded her, and the colorful array of roses reminded her of a Monet painting. Nadine loved this place. It was her refuge, her secret corner, though she knew it was not really hers, but her mother's. Still, she felt entitled to its intimacy, its comfort.

After yesterday's vision at the gypsy's place and last night's nightmare, Nadine was uneasy. Though vivid dreams were not new to her, this one left an indelible mark on her mind. In it she was drowning in the Channel, frantically struggling to surface, but knowing she couldn't save herself. As the waves unmercifully pushed her under, a prayer echoed in the depths of her soul. *Mon Dieu, do not let it end this way!*

The feeling of helplessness held her heart in iron clutches even after the night and the dream were over.

She wished she had never seen that crazy gypsy. The woman and her theatrics gave her the nightmare, no doubt. Never having felt really comfortable around water, she didn't need any further incentive to keep away from it.

Nadine was glad she was flying to London this afternoon, and though she wasn't very keen on the idea of being encased inside a small plane, she would rather that than take the ferry across the Channel, which she had never done in her life. It was a matter of facing the lesser of two evils. Especially now after the gypsy's warnings.

"Whatever's making you frown, I wish it gone this very minute."

"*Maman.*" Nadine accepted the steaming cup of coffee her mother handed her and patted the bench on her side, indicating to her mother she should join her. Elise sat down, placed her arm around Nadine, and brought her closer in a hug. She caressed Nadine's hair as she so often did when they were sitting together like this.

"Last night I had a horrible nightmare," Nadine said. "I've never felt so lonely, so helpless."

"It was only a dream, *ma petite fleur*."

"I know. Still . . ."

"What's really bothering you?"

Nadine took a deep breath, then shifted around, better to face her mother. She lost herself in her mother's calm blue eyes, eyes so unlike her own golden ones, inherited from her father, and for a moment all her troubles disappeared.

She couldn't bring up the subject of death. She didn't want to upset her mother. "I feel I'm on the threshold of something very important, some drastic change. I'm not sure exactly what." Nadine struggled with the right words to explain her feelings.

"You're not a child anymore, Nadine," Elise said. "It's only normal that you feel insecure about your life." She kissed the top of Nadine's head. "Once you finish your studies in London, you have some decisions to make about your future. You have an entire life ahead of you."

"Will I ever have a love like you and papa share?" Nadine asked in a stumble.

"Just because you had one big disappointment, it doesn't mean you'll never meet a man worthy of you." Elise's fingers ran through Nadine's hair in a gentle caress. "Be not afraid to live, *ma petite fleur*. It's not the mistakes you make that help you grow, but the way you react to them."

Reassured, Nadine snuggled closer to her mother. "I'm going to miss you, *Maman*, when I return to London."

"And I'll miss you." Elise held Nadine tighter to her chest, and Nadine abandoned herself to the sweetness of her mother's embrace.

Nadine arrived in London feeling tired and depressed. After spending the weekend home, with her parents, the prospect of an empty flat was not a welcome one. Perhaps her decision to study in London had not been a wise one after all. Yet, something had compelled her to come here, to leave the security of her family and try out the wings of independence, to find out if she could make it without the protective network of family and friends.

Nadine was determined to succeed, yet she felt unsure.

She opened the front door with her own key, hoping Mrs. Keller, the landlady, would have already retired for the night. Nadine wasn't in a mood for idle conversation.

That was not meant to be. As soon as Nadine stepped in, Mrs. Keller—pacing under the arch that divided the living room from the foyer—stopped and rushed to Nadine.

"I'm so glad you're finally here."

"Is something wrong, Mrs. Keller?"

"Oh, dear, I'm afraid so." Mrs. Keller cleared her throat. "We received a phone call for you late this afternoon, but I had no way of contacting you."

"Why? Was the message urgent?"

Mrs. Keller shot Nadine a sympathetic look, and then she did something unusual for the cool English lady. She hugged Nadine.

"Oh, my dear. I'm so very sorry," she whispered.

Confused, Nadine stepped away. "What happened?" Dread insinuated in her heart.

"There's been an accident. A car accident." Mrs. Keller paused. "Your parents . . ."

Maman, Papa. "*Sacré Coeur!* Are they hurt?" Fear swelled inside her heart to the point of explosion.

"I'm so very sorry, my dear. They died on site."

"No!" The scream escaped Nadine. She shook her head in denial as an excruciating pain paralyzed her. Memories of her parents flooded her mind. Their kind faces, their unconditional love for her, the wonderful time they had spent together this weekend. And now they were gone, gone, never to come back.

"But I have just left them," Nadine mumbled, trying to understand the incomprehensible. Tears immediately sprung to her eyes. "This is not possible. You must be mistaken." Bewildered, Nadine stared at her landlady, wanting her to deny the undeniable. But Mrs. Keller's sorrowful eyes only confirmed the horrible truth.

"I'm sorry," Mrs. Keller said over and over.

Numbly, Nadine whirled around. Her hand reached for the doorknob.

"Where are you going?" Mrs. Keller asked.

"I must go back home." She should have never left.

"You must rest first, you've just arrived. It's late. It'll be better to leave tomorrow. Besides, there's nothing you can do now."

"I can be with them," Nadine whispered.

"Let me, at least, make plane reservations for you. You cannot just leave like this." Mrs. Keller took Nadine's arm and gently directed her into the living room.

Nadine stood rigidly with her back against the wall, tears flowing freely down her face, while Mrs. Keller busied herself with the telephone.

"There are no more flights tonight for Paris," Mrs. Keller said. "I booked you on a morning flight. I'll take you to the airport tomorrow."

"How about the Chunnel?"

"The Chunnel is closed, I heard it this afternoon. Some kind of accident damaged the tracks."

"Then I will take the ferry." Nadine pushed herself away from the wall and walked to the door.

"The ferry? But, my dear, you're afraid of water," Mrs. Keller protested as Nadine stepped out of the house and into the night.

Like a zombie, Nadine boarded the ship that would take her to her dead parents. A light drizzle misted the air, and she held her coat tightly closed to ward off the invading chill.

Inside, the air was musty and asphyxiating. She sat on a

corner, avoiding contact with the surrounding people. The smell of food and the buzz of conversation intruded on her thoughts, warping her perception of reality.

Time stood still.

Smothered by so much life, she rose from her seat and fought her way outside. The strong wind almost knocked her backward but saved her from certain suffocation. She rested against the wall to steady her wobbly legs.

The well-illuminated deck shed no warmth to the cool night. Nadine pushed herself away from the wall and walked about aimlessly, wallowing in her unbearable grief. She reached the rail and braced herself against it. Below, the dark, swirling water issued an invitation.

It would be so easy! The thought intruded on her mind as she watched the rough Channel waters hit the ship's hull. So easy to just slip down and sink to eternity . . .

Except, death could not be the answer. Death was the cause of this agonizing and excruciating pain.

Nadine tried to push herself away from the rail, but a sudden dizziness overtook her, robbing her of control. For a moment she thought she was levitating: her body weight-less, her mind blank, her heart empty.

Her head dropped forward, and powerless to prevent it, her body fell into the cold water of the English Channel.

Chapter 2

From atop his destrier, Faulk watched the birthing of a new day over the waters of the English Channel. The beauty of the sun's crimson rays fusing with the silver water of dawn contrasted sharply with the state of disrepair in which he had found Whitecastle upon his arrival yester-morn.

And especially with the great emptiness in his heart at knowing his father was dead.

Unwilling to call his son home, Lord Warren had kept his prolonged illness from Faulk. And he had died waiting for his son's promised return.

Faulk's hands tightened in fists, the leather of his destrier's reins cutting through his bare palms. Had he returned to England soon after the Crusades, as he had promised his father, instead of roaming about the Christendom, then joining King Richard on his war against Philip of France, he would have seen his father alive one more time.

He would have heard his sire's long-sought words of approval. He would have given his father his most cherished wish—an heir to the Brookstone name.

Guilt overshadowed his pain, bringing forth a new resolution. Having failed his father in life, he would not fail him in death.

Upon his arrival, Faulk had sought a missive or a betrothal amongst his father's belongings. He found naught. Yet even if his father had desisted of the matter, Faulk would not. He would seek a befitting wife and thus honor his vow to his father.

Fortunately, King Richard had granted him the choice of wife in recompense for Faulk's having saved his life on the battlefield. However, mingling generosity with cunning, as kings were wont to do, Richard had ordered Faulk to recruit and train able-bodied men to aid his campaign against Philip and defend the English possessions in France.

"A little task for you while you idle away in marital bliss," the king had said.

Faulk only hoped marital bliss would not elude him the same way victory against Philip eluded King Richard.

Elizabeth. The memory of her betrayal still cut his insides, but his second wife would have no such chance. Firstly, he would not give her his heart, as he so foolishly had done with Elizabeth. Secondly, he would make undoubtedly certain the child she carried was his.

As soon as he found the perfect lady, and she carried his heir, he would be able to dedicate himself more thoroughly to the king's task, and to bring Whitecastle to the splendor of earlier times.

He owed his father that much.

Faulk urged his mount through the waves, unsettling the stillness of the dawning day. He inhaled the fresh scent of the sea as he pushed his horse harder and faster, reveling in the freedom the early morning afforded him. Cold water splashed at him, plastering dark strands of hair against his face. After a while he slowed down, content in being the only person around on the deserted beach, when, in the distance, a sight caught his eyes.

A cloak flapped in the wind like a banner in a conquered land. As he approached it, he discovered that the cloak covered the limp form of a human body lying on the beach.

He dismounted and knelt down beside it, immediately turning the body faceup. The sun shone brightly on her unusually short golden hair, and as he gently brushed aside the strands that fell on her face, he uncovered a most angelic visage.

His gaze raked her body, taking in her odd garment, exposed by the open cloak. The soft material clung to her like a second skin, revealing small, round breasts. The costume had curious little decorations—he believed they were called *boutons*—all the way from her neck down to the middle of her thighs, where it lay open, exposing a pair of well-shaped legs. She was barefoot.

Faulk listened to her heart, and the faint signal told him she was still alive but cold and thoroughly soaked. He removed his cloak and covered her frozen body, then carried her to his horse.

After he mounted, he gave a last look around in search of a boat, a ship, anything that might explain her presence. He found naught, and in finding naught, a thought crossed his mind. A memory of a long-ago encounter with a witch.

Her words echoed in his mind. *A golden vision of beauty shall come to you through the water. And when she comes, you shall know 'tis her without a doubt, for she bears the mark of the rose. The brightness of the sun shines on her hair, and her golden eyes shall bewitch your heart.*

God's teeth! Could the prophecy be true?

Whitecastle stood a few miles away from the beach on top of a small hill. Its name derived from the color which it no longer possessed, its walls covered with dirt accumulated throughout time. The keep was an old one, remnant of the

Norman Conquest, though largely altered through the years. Constructed with defense in mind rather than aesthetics, its square towers watched over the lower vale where the small village stood.

As Faulk rapidly approached the keep, he caught sight of the sentries lodged on the parapets. Recognizing their lord, they immediately lifted the portcullis and opened the gate for him.

Robert Baldwin, Faulk's friend from the Crusade, who had also recently arrived at Whitecastle with his wife, came to him as Faulk entered the great hall. "What have you there?"

"We shall talk later." Faulk crossed the hall and reached the stairs. Taking two steps at a time, he arrived at his bedchamber without delay.

Mildred was inside, finishing unpacking his trunk. She moved out of his way as Faulk deposited his charge on the huge bed that dominated the room.

"I found her on the beach," Faulk said.

Eyeing the body with curiosity, Mildred approached the bed.

Mildred had taken care of Faulk's mother when soon after his birth Lady Ann had fallen into a sickness that had killed her six years later. And all this time and beyond she had also taken upon herself the responsibility of caring for Faulk.

Like a mother hen, she smothered him with all her attention and sometimes hung perilously close to insubordination, but Faulk usually tried to avoid the first situation and mostly ignored the latter.

Mildred was also the only person he had ever told about the witch's vision that many years in the past before he had left for the Crusades. Would Mildred remember it?

Faulk decided not to remind her, at least not until he knew more about the mysterious lady. "I trust her into your care," he said before he left the room.

• • •

Mildred quickly pulled the odd garment over the girl's head. Underneath, she found a small, triangular piece of fabric that did not seem to serve any real purpose. She had trouble removing it, for it had no lacing to undo and stretched as she pulled on it. Finally she managed to drag it down the girl's legs.

Could this be a chastity belt? 'Twas not very efficient as such, but what other use could it possibly have?

Well, 'twas not her concern.

Dismissing the thought, Mildred picked up a flask of almond oil Lord Faulk had brought from the Holy Land and warmed it up a bit in the heat of the hearth. She returned to the bedside and massaged the inert body with the fragrant balm.

The stranger's skin was damp and cold but also very soft, with no visible scars to mar her beauty. Her smooth hands had long fingers and clean, well-shaped fingernails. No calluses there, nor on her feet, denoting high upbringing. She was obviously a lady. A beautiful lady. All golden and silky soft.

A sudden thought struck Mildred. Could she be the one foretold to Lord Faulk so many years in the past? After all, he had found her on the beach, and she had golden hair as the witch had prophesied. Would she also have golden eyes? And what about the mark of the rose?

Mildred remembered well how Lord Faulk had regretted telling her about the encounter with the witch and how he had demanded she forget all about it, as he would.

But how could she forget about a prophecy that decided the fate of his line? How could *he* forget about it? Especially now that good Lord Warren was dead? Mildred had a mind to ask Faulk. When she found the right opportunity, of course.

For lack of a lady's garment, Mildred dressed the lady

with one of Lord Faulk's cambric tunics. Surely he would not mind.

But as she lifted her, Mildred let out a small gasp. On the back of the lady's shoulder there lay the most beautiful rose, intricately drawn on the pale skin, just as the prophecy foretold.

Faulk returned to the room in the late forenoon. He had wished to return earlier, but every time he turned around, there seemed to be a body in need of him. Twice he had sent his squire to find out if the lady had come to. He always returned with the same negative answer. Finally Faulk was able to get away. He found Mildred bent over the bed, diligently wiping her charge's face with a damp cloth.

"How does she fare?"

"She is with fever."

"Has she spoken at all?"

"Nay." And then Mildred shot him one of her looks.

"Speak your mind, Mildred."

Mildred took a deep breath. "I thought, mayhap . . . Well, my lord, methinks she is the one," she blurted out.

Though startled by Mildred's blunt assertion, Faulk understood her meaning immediately. So Mildred had not forgotten the witch's predictions.

He strode to the bed and gazed at the immobile figure. Could the prophecy be true? All these years he had tried to bury the memory of the old hag's words, but suddenly he could not dismiss the possibility as easily as he had done in the past. Now, he gazed at the lady in his bed and wondered.

"My lord . . ." Mildred hesitated. "I have seen the sign."

Faulk spun around. "What is your meaning?"

"The rose. She bears the mark of the rose."

"Are you certain?"

Mildred nodded. "On her right shoulder."

Faulk turned to the bed. Gently he pushed the tunic down the mystery lady's shoulder. Lifting her slightly, he stared, stunned, at the exquisite mark.

He had not wanted to believe. But there 'twas, as clear as the sun in the sky. The proof of the old witch's words. The truth he had denied for so long.

Only through his children can a man live forever. His father's words echoed in his mind.

Could this lady be the only one capable of ensuring the continuity of his name as the witch prophesied? As far as he knew, no child was ever born from his loins. And, after Elizabeth's debacle, no other woman had tried to foist a bastard upon him.

If the prediction of the golden beauty's appearance had come true, could the rest of the prophecy also be true?

Uncertain, Faulk stared in shock at the beautiful lady. Would he have children by this woman and no other? Now, more than ever, he needed her to recover from her malady.

Faulk checked on the lady's progress that day and the next. Each time Mildred assured him there was naught else to do but wait and pray.

Thankfully, her fever soon abated, but she did not recover consciousness.

When the long shadows of the second eve fell into the room, Faulk once again returned.

"Still no change, Mildred?"

"Nay, my lord, but she is not uncomfortable. I have fed her some broth from time to time, bathed her, and brushed her hair." She paused. "Why would her hair be so short? 'Tis unseemly in a lady."

Faulk nodded. He had wondered about it himself. "We shall know the answers when the lady awakens."

He approached the bed, irresistibly drawn to this damsel in distress. The flickering flames of the candles and the fire from the hearth shone brightly on her short hair. Its brilliant color framed her face like a wave of sunshine, brightening her countenance. There was an odd quality about her that suggested fragility and strength all at the same time.

Faulk stepped back, annoyed at his whimsical thoughts. He was not a fanciful man, but even a warrior should acknowledge the power of fate. This beautiful lady was delivered to him as prophesied.

Mayhap 'twas destiny after all.

Mildred filled a chalice with wine and gave it to Faulk before leaving the room. He drank the heady wine greedily, then sat on his chair and closed his eyes. His mind filled with convoluted thoughts. Sleep took over him as he pondered over the mystery of fate.

Her touch was as soft and hesitant as a butterfly's wing. But soon the touch became less tentative, bolder. It sensitized the skin of his forearm, making the fine hair rise. Faulk held his breath as his heart pumped briskly. The vision of golden loveliness knelt before him as her honey gaze rested upon him. He wished to ask her the question that had mystified him since the moment he found her on the beach, but as if reading his mind her finger covered his lips to silence him.

"I am the one," she said simply, then smiled, and the room filled with such radiance as if the sun itself had made its appearance.

So 'twas true. She was the one prophesied to be his. Faulk reached for the golden lady, bringing her to his lap, nestling her in his arms. He found her lips and lost himself in their sweetness. Their breaths mingled in the soft caress. His life drained into her mouth, and in the next breath, hers flooded into his. He kissed her passionately, interminably, until all his senses reeled. When he finally came up for breath, he felt totally lost without her. His lips slid down to the hollow between her neck and shoulders and his tongue laved her skin, kissing it, licking it, until it reached her breasts. His lips closed around the turgid nipples, suck-ling, caressing, tasting.

She writhed against his throbbing member, making him shudder. His hand shifted down her body until it reached her center, and its hot moisture seared his fingers. He groaned at the contact. She moaned softly. His thumb found her magical bud, and he teased it expertly. She moaned again, and again, and again. Every sound that escaped her lips was an erotic stimulus to his ears. Slowly he slipped a finger inside her warmth. The tight passage closed around it. She was so deliciously hot and tight, so much softer and sweeter than any other woman on earth.

He straddled her upon his thighs, but the position was not satisfying. He lifted her, brought her to the bed, and settled himself between her thighs. "Open up to me, my fair lady. I must make you mine."

She opened to him like a flower opens to the morning dew, and he could do no more but enter her. She was so tight, but, oh, so wet. He tried to be gentle but his member had a mind of its own and kept on pushing itself deeper and deeper inside her until it could go no farther.

He longed to remain still and savor the heat and tightness of her. He wished to allow her to get used to the fullness of him. He meant to move slowly and tantalizingly, elicit-ing from her the same hunger that assaulted him, but it was all too much. The unbridled throbbing of his drowning manhood drove him to madness, and he plunged into her with a fervor and an urgency he could not control.

What was it about this lady that undid him so?

A powerful emotion overtook him as he was about to spill his seed inside her glorious body. The seed that would fructify her womb and fulfill the prophecy and his vow to his father.

A banging sound suddenly invaded Faulk's thoughts, dis-turbing his actions. He stopped in mid-motion, annoyed to no end, and lifted his face from the crook of his lady's shoulder. Did the sound come from her? Astounded, he watched her disappear. His hands grabbed for her, but the flimsy figure melted away before his very eyes.

The intrusive sound persisted until it tore Faulk completely away from his dream. Unsure of what was happening, he found his mystery lady still abed, though obviously totally unaware of him.

Frustrated, Faulk took a deep breath to control his raging body and darkening mood and rose from the chair. He opened the door in one swing.

"What?" he bellowed to his squire.

The boy stood paralyzed at the door, eyes bulging with apprehension.

"I have brought you some food, my lord," he stammered.

Faulk took the trencher from him, then slammed the door on his face before the boy realized the true cause of his foul mood.

Resting his back against the door, Faulk inspected the huge, painful bulge in his breeches. "Damn," he cursed. " 'Twas only a dream."

Yet, deep inside, he sensed it was much more than that.

Chapter 3

NADINE OPENED HER eyes and tried to focus ambiguous images into recognizable shapes. She almost fainted back into unconsciousness when she discovered, hovering above her, the wrinkled face of an old woman. Her hand instinctively covered her mouth, barely suppressing the scream that rose from her throat. She stared back at the woman in alarm.

The woman touched Nadine's forehead and then, without further ado, disappeared from her scope of vision, leaving Nadine to doubt her own eyes. Feeling like an open drawer with its contents spilling out in a disorganized manner, Nadine painstakingly sorted out her thoughts.

Her first comprehensible notion was that her body ached all over. It seemed someone relentlessly pounded a hammer inside her head. The throbbing resonated throughout her body. With some difficulty, she lifted her head from the pillow. The motion caused a new wave of pain and a bout of nausea that forced her right back down. She closed her eyes for a long moment, taking deep, steadying breaths.

Carefully Nadine pushed herself upright, and, as her eyes focused and her head cleared, she scanned her surroundings. She lay on a huge bed in the center of a strange room immersed in semidarkness. At the foot of the bed she saw the corner of what looked like a leather trunk. To her right, the odd woman stood in front of a rustic-looking table and chair, and above the table, hanging on the wall, a magnificent tapestry depicted a white castle overlooking the ocean.

Forgetting about the woman, Nadine stared at the picture. The building itself was a rather plain and old-fashioned structure with square towers and flipping banners, but the majestic way it loomed above all on top of the hill entranced her.

A crackling sound made Nadine turn her gaze to the gigantic fireplace. In the semidarkness the sparks shot up in the air like fireworks, lending an eerie feeling to the room.

A shiver ran through Nadine.

The woman returned to Nadine's side, holding a metal cup in her hands.

"Where am I?" Nadine asked in her native French, but the words echoed in the stony room, sounding incomprehensible to her own ears.

The blank look in the woman's face confirmed her assessment, and Nadine repeated the question. Yet the words, once again, stumbled out of her mouth incoherently.

"Dear Lord, but the poor lady is addle-witted."

Nadine barely understood the oddly accented French, but there was no mistaking the old woman's thoughts judging by the way she crossed herself and the look of pity she shot Nadine.

Before she could set the woman straight about her wits, the woman thrust a cup into Nadine's hands.

Her parched throat begged for refreshment, and Nadine took a sip from the cup. She was surprised to taste wine, though it was a much-weakened version of the liquor she was accustomed to drinking. And however much she'd have preferred water at this time, the wine served as well to unravel her tongue enough to allow a few intelligible words.

"Where am I?" she repeated, this time clearly enunciating the words.

A look of relief crossed the old woman's face, and she smiled. "In my lord's solar."

Lord's solar? The woman's French was atrocious. "How did I get here?" Nadine asked.

"You were brought here by my lord."

"Lord?" *As in God?* The incomprehensible thought took hold of Nadine. And then, abruptly, a plethora of memories flooded her mind. She recalled her visit with her parents, her return to London. She relived the terrible news of their death, the agonizing trip across the Channel en route to their funeral.

But she had never arrived there. What happened? She remembered her sudden dizziness, the bizarre floating sensation, her fall into the English Channel.

Sacré Coeur, had she died? Had she drowned? But if she were dead, how come she hurt so much, physically and emotionally?

And what was this place? Heaven? If that were true, then she might see her parents again. Hope warmed her insides.

Nadine gazed back at the woman, seeking confirmation. However, for the first time, she noticed the peculiar way the woman was dressed. She looked nothing like an angel.

"What is your name?" Nadine asked.

"Mildred."

At that moment the door opened, interrupting Nadine's tumbling thoughts. The most handsome man she had ever seen crossed the threshold with a sure stride. He brought with him the brightness of the sunshine, the vitality of life.

Her mind played tricks on her.

Nadine stared, mouth agape, at the gorgeous man standing by the foot of her bed. Dark luscious hair framed his face where the brightest, bluest, most incredible eyes shone like beacons for hopelessly lost ships.

He could be an angel. Or the devil himself.

"How fare you, my lady?"

And he, too, spoke an odd French.

Her heart thundered. She couldn't disguise her anxiety. "Am I in Heaven?"

He grinned, and a dimple appeared on his right cheek. Nadine stared at it, mesmerized. "This is Whitecastle," he said.

A castle? Could that be what Mildred meant by lord? Nadine's gaze sought Mildred, but the woman was nowhere to be found. And then Nadine realized how ridiculous the Heaven theory was. Heaven would not be an ancient castle. . . . Comprehension hit her in full—she was alive, alive to face the endless pain of being utterly alone.

"Is this England?" It must be. Their French sounded too odd, almost archaic. Besides, she had been much closer to the English shore when she fell into the water.

"Aye."

And so it was. "How long have I been here?"

"I found you three morns past."

Did he mean she'd been in this place for three full days? The realization made Nadine shudder. If that were true, then by now her parents were probably buried. She knew they had made funeral plans long ago. They told her they wanted to spare her the agony of such arrangements. Everything would be taken care of. Even in death they thought of her.

A heavy weight settled in Nadine's heart. They were gone forever now, and she hadn't had even the chance of saying goodbye.

She stifled a sob but couldn't prevent a lone tear from rolling down her cheek. "Has anybody come looking for me?" Perhaps Denise or Mrs. Keller knew where she was.

"Nay. No one has come for you."

Nadine closed her eyes for a moment. She threaded one hand slowly through her hair, pushed a strand behind one ear, then let her hand fall to her lap. A deep loneliness took hold of her and she could no longer hold the sobs at bay or the tears that flowed freely down her face.

With one fluid movement he moved to her side and sat on the edge of her bed. With his thumb he wiped away her tears.

Surprised, Nadine stared as he took her hand into his huge one and placed her palm against his chest. The intimate gesture puzzled her. The sudden heat of his skin burned her hand, and the strong pulsating of his heart misled the steady melancholic rhythm of hers. Scooping herself against the pillow, Nadine withdrew her hand, fighting the out-of-place, out-of-control feeling.

He allowed her hand to slip free from his, then rose to his feet, standing by her side. "What has befallen you?"

Nadine stammered under his concerned gaze. "I remember little," she said. "I was on the ferry, and I fell into the Channel." She refused to dwell in the strange, levitating feeling. "Were you on the ferry, too? Did you rescue me?"

"Nay. I discovered you half dead on a beach nearby. I brought you here, and Mildred and I nursed you back to life."

She remembered nothing after her fall. In fact, how could she have survived such a fall? She could not even swim. How did she end up on a beach? It made no sense.

"I cannot explain what happened to me, but I thank you for saving my life," she finally said.

"I believe 'twas fate," he said. "Have you any kinship? A father, a brother, a husband mayhap?"

She shook her head. "I am alone."

"You shall never be alone again."

Nadine shifted uncomfortably. How could he assure her that? Her gaze shifted from his handsome face, down his immense chest. He wore a white shirt with embroidery on the collar and cuffs under a royal blue vest that matched his eyes and reached above his knees. His legs were encased in a pair of tight black pants that defined his muscular thighs. A sword hung from a leather belt on his waist.

A sword?

Why on earth would he be carrying such a weapon? Come to think of it, he was as dressed odd as Mildred.

Weird. Her gaze moved upward again. Following the curve of his shoulder, she noted the thickness of his neck, the length of his hair. Hair as black as a moonless night. A thick curl rested on the collar of his tunic in such an endearing way she felt almost compelled to reach for it. She stilled her fingers.

His chin was strong and square, and the blue shadow of a beard gave him an almost ferocious look. His lips looked hard and demanding. He exuded a most powerful maleness.

Nadine's gaze rested on the azure of his eyes, and there she found fire and conceit at her close scrutiny of him. Her cheeks burned.

Flustered at being caught ogling him as if she'd never seen a man before in her life—though she'd never seen one such as he—Nadine avoided his eyes.

"Do you always dress like that or are you part of a play?" She hoped to hide her embarrassment and wipe that satisfied grin off his face.

"Are you displeased?"

On the contrary. "It's odd."

"Odd," he repeated. "In verity not all people dress alike. You favor a style of your own," he said as if she had committed a *faux pas*.

Nadine inspected her own clothing, only now noticing she was not wearing her dress. In fact, what she had on looked like a nondescript hospital gown, except it had no opening on the back. She tried to remember what she was wearing when she left London, and surprisingly, the picture came clearly to her. Perhaps because it had been one of her mother's favorite. A long dress of ecru silk, buttoned down the front. It had long sleeves, fitted tight on the bodice, and flowed below the waist. What did he find wrong with it? she thought and so asked.

"Wrong? Naught was wrong with it. 'Twas an interesting ensemble that I have not seen the likes before."

He paused as if waiting for her to explain, but Nadine had no idea what he meant. As if desisting of the subject, he abruptly asked, "Who is responsible for cropping your beautiful golden hair?"

Unconsciously Nadine treaded her fingers through her short hair, remembering how long it had once been. Denise had nagged her to have it cut. "Time to modernize," she had said. In fact, Nadine liked it short, though she would never forget her father's look of disappointment the first time he'd seen her.

The memory of her father saddened her.

"It matters not," he quickly said. " 'Twill grow back."

Was he trying to pacify her?

"And I shall find suitable clothing for you. For now you rest." He strode to the door, then turned back.

"Fair lady," he called. "How shall I address you?"

"Fair lady" sounds pretty good. "Nadine du Monte is my name. What is yours?"

"Faulk Brookstone," he said and shut the door behind him.

Faulk. The word glided smoothly on her tongue. It sounded so masculine, so strong. Nadine decided it suited him to a tee.

Outside Faulk leaned against the door, trying to put his thoughts in order. Though she declared not her fate as she did in his dream, Nadine must be the one foretold to be his. The mark of the rose, the golden hair and honeyed eyes, the coming from the water, all pointed to that.

'Twas obvious she had been through a terrible ordeal,

yet she was not like any other lady he had ever known. Her dress was indescribable, her manners strange, her speech decidedly odd, even though she spoke the common *langue d'oil.*

Where from did she hail? Normandy, Aquitaine . . . It mattered not, as long as she came from any of Richard's domains and not Philip of France. That would complicate matters considerably.

There were many questions he wished to ask her, but her weary, desolate look convinced him to postpone the inquiry.

A luxury he afforded after learning there was no one to claim her.

"Faulk."

Faulk pushed himself from the door. His friend and knight, Robert Baldwin, stood before him.

"You have avoided me of late," Robert said.

"I have been occupied." Faulk strode to the stairs.

"You have skulked about the castle, more evasive than your usual self since you brought that woman here." Robert followed Faulk down the steps. "Mildred is the only one to reach you, and she has not relayed one single word of what is happening."

Faulk smiled inwardly. 'Twas good to know his trust had not been betrayed. Mildred was very loyal, but she was also a woman, and as such had a loose tongue.

And Robert was his friend. They had relied on each other to watch their backs in the long campaigns they fought together. Faulk admired him, liked him as he would a brother. He deserved an explanation. He had avoided Robert long enough.

"Care to join me for a tankard of ale?" Faulk asked as they entered the great hall.

"With pleasure, my lord."

They settled with their cups. "The castle is buzzing with rumors. Who is the mystery lady?"

"The lady shall be my wife," Faulk announced, surprised at his own decision. He had resisted the prophecy from the onset, yet Nadine's appearance proved the prophecy true, and if the prophecy was true, then he must wed her to secure the continuity of his name.

Shocked, Robert shot up in his chair. "Wife?"

" 'Tis a long tale, Robert. Lady Nadine was foretold to be mine, and I mean to fulfill the prophecy."

"You are wedding a woman based on a prophecy?"

"She is . . . unique," Faulk said.

"She must be," Robert mumbled, eyeing Faulk as if he had gone insane.

And mayhap he had.

Nadine reclined in bed, lost in thought. She felt very weak, which wasn't a surprise considering she'd been unconscious for three full days. Three days of her life she couldn't account for. She had survived a near drowning, been rescued, and been brought to this strange place. Meanwhile, her parents had been buried without her presence.

Nadine was certain the arrangements had been carried out. How she regretted having missed the funeral. Her last chance to see her parents robbed by her unfortunate accident. Deep sadness filled her heart.

Nonetheless, she needed to get out of this bed and return home. Denise must be sick with worry, probably thinking she was dead. She had to let her friend know she was all right. *All right.* Nadine smiled bitterly at the words.

She sought the window, not sure what time it was. The room was dark, badly illuminated by candles and the fireplace. Could there have been a power outage? She finally located the window—or whatever the narrow slit on the wall was called—covered with a leather blind. Little light infiltrated the inadequate cover. It must be very late.

Physically exhausted and emotionally drained, Nadine closed her eyes, willing her mind to go blank. But the image of Faulk invaded the nothingness she sought. What a strange man he was. Stranger still was her reaction to him. In the midst of such emotional turmoil in her life, how could she feel attracted to a total stranger?

Mildred's return interrupted Nadine's musings. She brought with her a bundle of clothing, which she settled on top of the leather trunk. "Lord Faulk sent these garments for you," she said.

"Thank you, Mildred."

"You have been through a terrible ordeal, my lady, but all shall be well now."

Mildred's kindness touched Nadine.

There was a knock on the door. Mildred opened it, and two young men entered the room carrying a huge bathing tub. Surprised, Nadine followed their movements, but they were too intent on their job to pay her any attention. It took them several trips to fill the oversized tub. Once the job was done Mildred shooed them out.

"I have ordered you a bath," she said. "My Lord Faulk seems to think a bath helps purge an illness. Methinks too much water serves only to turn a body into mush." While talking Mildred offered Nadine her hand. "You need not bathe, if you wish not."

Feeling like an invalid, Nadine accepted Mildred's help. "Oh, but I would love a bath." She stood up, then waited for the dizziness to dissipate. Her body ached and her head felt heavy, but what was a little physical discomfort when compared to the emptiness of her heart?

She looked at the huge wooden contraption. What a nuisance it must be to have this thing brought in and out of the room on a regular basis. This must be a very old castle indeed, if they hadn't yet come around to modernizing its bathrooms.

Perhaps Faulk was an impoverished aristocrat, surviving by using his castle as a historical resort. That would explain their odd clothing. Could this be one of those places where reenactments were set out for history buffs' entertainment?

Nadine remembered an article she read about a place in England, she thought it was called Torquay, where they had such a resort. Still, if this place catered to tourists, they'd better modernize real fast.

"Thanks for having a bathtub brought to the room, Mildred, but I could've walked to the bathroom."

Mildred's blank look puzzled Nadine. The woman looked as if she hadn't understood a word Nadine said. Perhaps she had not. Nadine remembered all too well how difficult it was to speak a foreign language. Should she speak English? Nadine decided against it. Her mind was far too taxed at the moment for the added pressure of thinking in a different language. "Could you please show me the way to the bathroom?"

"There is no such chamber," Mildred replied. "Lord Faulk bathes in his solar. This is his bathing tub."

Well, they might not have a *bathing chamber*, as Mildred called, but they surely should have toilet facilities. The idea of using a hole in the ground could not appeal even to the most stalwarts of historians.

"I meant the toilet." Another blank look from Mildred. "I need to use your facilities," Nadine explained. Still nothing. "I need to relieve myself," Nadine finally said, blushing to her roots, embarrassed at the absurd conversation.

"Oh," Mildred uttered, then pointed to an almost ridiculously obvious chamber pot.

Nadine groaned at the obvious implication. Almost as bad as a hole in the ground.

"Thank you, Mildred." She waited for the woman to leave, but Mildred didn't move. "I'd like some privacy." Did she have to spell it out?

"You might need my help," Mildred insisted.

Mildred seemed genuinely concerned. However, helping with such intimate function was way beyond any housemaid's duty.

"I think I can manage it on my own. Thank you."

"Very well." With apparent reluctance, Mildred left the room.

As soon as Mildred was gone, Nadine slowly walked to the door and checked it for a lock. Unfortunately the door lacked the security device.

Making hasty use of the chamber pot, she decided to bathe as well before Mildred returned.

She stepped into the tub and sat down. The water reached the top of her breasts. Warm, soothing water lapped against her skin. Funny how she never felt fear in a bathtub; only large bodies of water seemed to freak her out. She reached over the rim and found a deliciously rose-scented soap, which she eagerly used to wash off a lingering smell of almond from her skin. How did it get there, anyway? She dismissed the thought. It really didn't matter.

After washing her hair, and rinsing it as well as she could, Nadine sank back into the warmth, allowing the tension in her muscles to ease away.

When the water cooled off, she rose from the tub, feeling much better. The dizziness was gone, though her body still ached. She picked up a huge cloth that lay on the bed and dried herself, then turned to the leather trunk to take a look at the clothes Mildred had spread there for her.

There were two pieces of clothing. One was a long-sleeved, soft linen dress, and the other, a long fur-hemmed gown of green silk. There was also an embroidered sash, a pair of soft leather shoes, stockings, and a cloth veil with a circlet, but no underwear.

The costumes were beautiful, but Nadine wasn't in the mood for playacting. All she wanted was a simple, clean dress, so she could get out of this room, make her call and head home, today if possible, tomorrow if necessary.

Home. The word hurt deeply. There was no home as it was before. Nobody there waiting for her. Still, she had to return, she had to find a way to start a new life, though she had not a clue how to go about it.

Choosing the linen dress, Nadine ignored the rest. It felt funny to wear nothing underneath, but she was not about to ask Mildred for underwear.

As if summoned, Mildred entered the room without knocking.

"Allow me to help you dress, my lady."

"I'm finished, thank you," Nadine said as she put on the shoes, which fit her perfectly.

"But—"

"I'm not into this reenactment thing, Mildred. What I have is fine. I just need to make a phone call before I leave."

Looking puzzled, Mildred opened her mouth, then shut it up without pronouncing a word.

Mildred's peculiar behavior worried Nadine. This was getting weirder by the moment. There must be a good explanation for the oddity she had witnessed so far.

"Could I have a mirror and a brush?" Nadine asked.

Mildred pondered about her request for long seconds as if Nadine had asked her for the stars. Finally she moved to the big leather chest and removed from it what Nadine assumed was a mirror wrapped up in soft fabric. She uncovered it and passed the small silver hand mirror to Nadine, almost reverently, as if it was a sacred relic.

Their hands overlapped, but Mildred did not let go of the mirror. Confused, Nadine withdrew her hands. "Would you like to hold it for me?"

Mildred jerked the mirror forward as if it had suddenly burned her, thrusting it into Nadine's hands. "Nay, mistress, 'twill fare better in your delicate hands." And almost as an afterthought, she explained, "Lord Faulk is very protective of it."

Protective of a mirror? The man was certainly handsome; could he also be a narcissist?

Nadine took the intricately carved silver mirror and looked into it, astonished to realize it wasn't at all like any mirror she had ever seen. For one thing, it wasn't made of glass, but rather a highly polished surface. It must be an antique, Nadine realized, and therefore probably very valuable. That would explain Mildred's reluctance in handling the object, and Faulk's protection of it.

The dark reflection that stared back at her from the small mirror astounded Nadine. It was herself, yet it was not. There was something different, alien that she couldn't quite pinpoint. Something wrong, out of place that couldn't be blamed on the poor quality of the mirror.

Uneasy, Nadine set the mirror down on the bed, then picked up the small ivory comb Mildred had produced and pushed it through her straight, short hair. Not daring a second look in the mirror, Nadine turned to Mildred. "Where I can find Lord Faulk?"

"He is in the great hall. I shall send for him."

"It's not necessary, Mildred. Just show me the way, and I'll go to him."

Disapproval was evident in Mildred's eyes, but she obviously decided to keep her opinions to herself.

"As you wish, my lady."

Nadine followed Mildred out of the room and down a long, narrow flight of steps. It seemed to take forever to reach the landing. Finally Mildred moved out of the way, and Nadine stepped into the hall.

What she saw stopped her dead in her tracks.

Chapter 4

LIKE A DEER caught in headlights, Nadine stood paralyzed by the scene before her eyes. Overwhelmed by the mingling smells of charred meat, cheap wine, and overheated bodies, she held her breath in protest.

The *great hall* was nothing like she had expected. It was a huge room, drafty, dark, and densely populated. People dressed in costumes, much like Mildred and Faulk, crowded the long trestle tables flanked by low benches. Coarse laughter and animated conversation permeated the air.

Someone tossed a bone carelessly to the ground. Two overgrown dogs immediately leaped to it, fiercely fighting over the bone.

A sliver of dread ran through Nadine's heart. This was no ordinary castle, she realized. Instinctively she spun around in search of the exit. Instead of the way out she found herself facing a pair of the brightest, bluest eyes that could only belong to one person.

Faulk.

Her insides warmed unexpectedly at his sight.

"What do you do half-dressed in my hall? You should

be in bed, resting." Though not shouting, Faulk's voice resonated strongly above the chaotic background noise, which immediately began to fade into total silence.

Nadine glanced back at the sea of bobbing heads that stared at her curiously, though not openly, then returned her gaze to Faulk. His self-righteous stance, his lips pursed into a thin line, his forbidden expression would have intimidated anyone. Somehow though, despite the obvious power that emanated from him, Nadine didn't feel threatened by his presence.

"I'm not half-dressed and I'm not at death's bed, as you can see." She ignored her wobbling knees. "Nevertheless, I appreciate your concern."

He scowled. "You have been through a terrible ordeal. I only mean to assure your well-being."

Nadine was unsure if Faulk was truly worried or merely annoyed. "I don't mean to sound ungrateful. You've saved my life and I cannot thank you enough, but it's time I returned home."

"You cannot leave," he said.

"What do you mean, I cannot leave?"

"You are destined to be mine," he said matter-of-factly.

Destined to be his? Nadine took a cautious step backward.

"Once again I thank you, but I really must be going." She whirled around and blindly hurried across the hall, stopping only when she reached a great wooden door, which she hoped led to the outside world.

Her fingers reached for the crossbar, but the moment she touched the wood, Faulk's huge, calloused palms covered hers, stilling her movements.

Nadine stood motionless, her heart pumping furiously. Expecting him to yank her back, she was totally dumbfounded when his strong fingers lifted the crossbar effortlessly and opened the door wide for her.

Was he letting her go?

Though surprised, Nadine didn't hesitate. She darted across the threshold without a backward glance, almost falling down a flight of three steep steps.

Pitch blackness greeted her. For a moment, Nadine stood unmoving, trying to accustom her eyes to the darkness. Then, little by little she began to recognize some shapes. She could distinguish the silhouettes of a building or two, and in the distance, seeming to surround the property, a tall, imposing wall loomed forbiddingly.

Nadine took a few steps into the yard. Her feet, encased in the soft leather shoes Mildred had provided her, felt every little bump on the hard ground. The neigh of horses sounded nearby, startling her. A solitary dog howled mournfully in the distance. Or was it a wolf? Suddenly the idea of dashing heedlessly through the darkness lost its appeal.

She lifted her eyes to the sky, and the spectacle that greeted her took her breath away. The moon hung huge, reigning supreme, surrounded by a diamond-sprinkled mantle of millions of shining, blinking stars, twinkling back at her. Nowhere in sight was there any artificial light to mar such exquisite display.

How far from civilization was she? How could she find her way home on her own?

"Nadine."

Nadine spun around. Faulk leaned against the castle's wall, one foot pressing against it, the other firmly planted on the ground. His stance was nonthreatening, almost nonchalant. His features were indistinguishable in the darkness. Yet, she remembered his face. The handsome lines were forever etched in her memory.

Nadine grew warm under his stare. A stare she didn't see but rather felt. Her heart pounded harder. In the silence of the night, she could almost hear its encompassing tempo. She shook her head to dissolve the spell.

Big mistake. Her head now pounded as furiously as her

heart. What was going on with her? One minute she drowned in anguish, in the other, she trembled with desire, and in the next she ran scared. What a roller coaster of emotions!

Not like her at all. *Get a grip!*

"You said I cannot leave. Do you mean to keep me here against my will?" She tried not to, but her voice quivered.

Faulk pushed himself away from the wall and reached her in two steps. His long fingers touched her face in a soft caress. Nadine trembled.

"My fair Nadine. Your coming was prophesied, and so I expect you to stay. Your fate proclaims what I declare."

"What are you talking about?"

"You carry the mark of the rose on your shoulder, do you not?"

What did her tattoo have to do with anything?

"So?" she asked hesitantly.

" 'Tis the proof that you belong to me. That we are destined to be together."

Sacré Coeur, the man was as crazy as he was handsome.

"Listen, Faulk, I don't understand your Shakespearean act, but it really doesn't matter. All I want to do is go home. And that is what I'm going to do." She spun around and stalked off.

Faulk followed her. " 'Tis dark. Where can you go?"

She ignored the amusement in his voice and kept walking.

"Very well, Nadine," he said a moment later. "If you wish to leave, then I shall grant your wish. Gilbert, open the gates."

Surprised, Nadine stopped. She searched for Gilbert and the gate, finding the first guarding the latter where a moment ago she could have sworn there was nothing but darkness.

"At this hour, my lord?" Gilbert asked.

"Do as you are bid."

"Aye, my lord."

Once more Faulk surprised her. One moment he scared her stiff with his demands, in the other, he complied with her wishes. What was his game?

Nadine waited, impatiently, for the huge gate to be opened. It took forever for the portcullis to be pulled up and a drawbridge lowered. *Mon Dieu!* This was indeed a true castle.

Without hesitation Nadine crossed the gates but stopped short of the bridge. She peeked under it, and discovered the moon reflected in the water. Carefully she stepped over the wooden planks until she reached the other side.

At the edge of the descending hill she scanned ahead. In the distance she could see the silhouette of huge trees. Or mountain peaks, she wasn't sure. There were no streetlights in her line of vision. Hell, there weren't even streets in sight. There was nothing out there but more darkness. A multitude of unknown sounds suddenly picked up momentum, dampening Nadine's already waning enthusiasm for running away.

Nadine darted a look over her shoulder to see if Faulk was still there. And there he was. Waiting. It finally dawned on her why he had been so accommodating. He knew she wouldn't go anywhere on her own. It galled her to give in to him, but she had to admit, she wasn't sure which situation scared her the most.

A castle, at best filled with overzealous historians, at worst with lunatics; or getting lost in the dark woods.

"All right, Faulk. You win," she whispered, and then turned back.

He said nothing.

As soon as she reached him, she said, "I will return inside with you, but I insist in using your telephone to call a cab."

"God's teeth, Nadine. You surely have a strange way of

speaking." Faulk left his sentinel position and escorted her back to the castle.

Well, he didn't exactly escort her, for she almost had to run to make up for his large steps.

"You are one to complain about speaking strangely," she said when she finally caught up with him at the entrance of the great hall. "Though I understand French is not your native language, you don't need to use these outdated expressions heard only in historical plays. 'God's teeth,' " she mimicked.

"Do you know King Richard?" Faulk stopped at the bottom of the narrow stairs, then motioned her to move ahead of him.

"Do I know him? You mean, do I know about his life? Not really. I just read somewhere he was fond of that expression."

"He is a great warrior," he said as he followed her inside the great hall.

"You know much about him?" Nadine asked.

"I should, I fought alongside him for many years, until quite recently in sooth."

Nadine stopped abruptly at the center of the great hall, completely ignoring the audience. He did say he fought alongside King Richard, didn't he? "You mean, in a play." It was a statement, not a question. There was no margin for such question.

"God's teeth, Nadine. Once and for all, I am no troubadour. You have hinted at such for the last time. I am Faulk Brookstone. Lord of Whitecastle. Knight of the Crusade and King Richard's loyal vassal."

His words were clipped with outrage. If he wasn't an actor, then what was he? Certainly not the things he said he was. It was impossible. The thought was ridiculous. This playacting was going a little too far.

"May I use your telephone now?" she asked abruptly.

Faulk let out an exasperated groan. "I understand you

not, Nadine. I know not your meaning," he spoke between his teeth.

Great! This must be his convoluted way of saying there was no phone here. Well, it didn't matter. Tomorrow she would get out of this place, even if she had to walk back home. In the light of the day everything would look better.

"Very well, Faulk. Good night, then." She rushed to the stairs that led to the upper level of the castle, holding her dress up so she wouldn't trip on its long hem. She managed to reach the bedroom door, open it, and cross the threshold before Faulk caught up with her.

"I believe we must talk," he said, holding the door open.

Nadine didn't want to talk. She didn't want to hear any more absurdities. "I'm exhausted. Perhaps tomorrow before I leave we could talk again."

"You cannot leave."

"There you go again."

"We must finalize the betrothal, Nadine."

"Betrothal? Like in marriage?" *The man was crazy.*

"Aye. I offer you the fulfillment of your destiny."

Utterly confused, unsure if she had understood him right, Nadine asked, uneasily, "What destiny?"

"To be my wife. You shall bear my heir."

Nadine moaned. She resolved not to fight over something so unreal. "Whatever you say, Faulk."

Apparently taking her words as agreement, he smiled, revealing his little dimple. Nadine stared at it, her breath caught in her throat. The smile softened his face, lending him an almost boyish quality.

"We must seal our agreement with a kiss."

Nadine meant to object. She was neither agreeing to marry him, nor would she allow him to kiss her. She opened her mouth to protest but was effectively silenced.

His mouth descended upon hers in a proprietary way. His lips were soft, nonthreatening, and evoked in her emotions she had no business feeling. She knew she should struggle, but she didn't. He was the one who terminated the too delicious touch.

"I shall call the banns immediately. I cannot wait overlong to make you mine."

The torpor left Nadine instantly. What was the matter with her? She had just lost all that was dear to her. She had no idea where she was and what to do with her life. And here she was, totally taken by a strange man's kisses. A man whom she had met only three days ago—and most of this time she had been unconscious—and who wanted to marry her.

Marry her? "You've just met me—why would you want to marry me?" she asked mystified.

"You are destined to be mine, Nadine. The village seer foretold your coming. The circumstances of your appearance, your golden hair and honeyed eyes, even the unusual rose mark on your shoulder, all are evidence of the truth. There can be no doubt. You are the one to fulfill the prophecy."

Nadine stared at Faulk with growing alarm. *Prophecy? Village seer?* What could he possibly mean? Was he referring to fortune-tellers?

"Were you not told?" he asked.

And then a memory of the gypsy woman and her words came to Nadine. *A most handsome man will cross your path to complete what was interrupted. You will be given a second chance. Do not waste it.*

Could it be possible? Could Faulk have had a similar experience? Could their meeting be predestined?

We walk by faith, not by sight.

Nadine shivered at the remembered words. Still, even if their meeting had been, for some unfathomable reason, marked by fate, to jump from that into marriage was a completely different story. Especially with a man who played with swords for fun.

" 'Tis no use to fight." Faulk reached for her.

Nadine avoided his arms. "Why do you say so? What is this place? What do you want from me? Who are you?" She felt the desperation creeping up her voice.

"I am Faulk Brookstone. Lord of Whitecastle. Knight of the Crusade—"

"Oh, stop," Nadine moaned frustrated. "Stop with this play of words. I don't know what game you're playing, but have no doubt about one thing. I will leave this place tomorrow morning, with or without your permission." She slammed the door on his face.

Faulk stomped down the steps to the great hall, ruminating Nadine's words. The witch had obviously forgotten to warn him that the golden loveliness carried more than the mark of the rose. She also bore a streak of stubbornness very unbecoming in a lady.

He had expected her to be compliant to his proposal, even eager to share her life with him. Instead she was unyielding, almost indifferent.

Nay, that was not true, he thought with a measure of satisfaction, she had not been indifferent when he had kissed her. She had melted in his arms, and he had wanted to deepen the kiss, to bring her soft body against his hard one, to show her the passion he was capable of giving.

Faulk groaned in frustration. How well he remembered his dream. That was the way it should have been. Nadine should have come to him declaring her fate, placing herself into his hands, accepting her role in his life.

Instead, she fought him, denied her destiny, spoke unknown words whose meanings he failed to understand. And most important of all, insisted on leaving Whitecastle.

He scowled. Why would she want to leave? Where would she wish to go?

"Who could have possibly displeased you so?"

Robert Baldwin's voice stole Faulk from his reverie. He spotted his friend sitting alone at the high table and strode to his direction. As soon as he dropped into his chair, a full tankard of ale immediately appeared in front of him, brought by a solicitous serving wench. Faulk took a deep swallow of the drink, ignoring Robert's question.

"Or dare I venture a guess?" Robert persisted, lifting an inquiring eyebrow at Faulk. "The lady seemed less than taken with your charms this eve, Faulk. As incredulous as that might seem." A little grin spread on Robert's face, as if the thought of a woman, any woman, resisting Faulk amused him.

Faulk glared at Robert. He was not amused. He was galled at Nadine's refusal, not only for the incredible honor he felt he was bestowing upon her, but specially for the utter importance of her compliance.

"I trust, Robert, that Nadine shall come to her senses soon enough and realize how utterly ridiculous is her refusal to be my wife."

"She refused to wed you?" Robert's voice rose abruptly.

Faulk glared at him and Robert had the grace to look embarrassed.

"I speak as your friend," Robert said. "You can choose just about any woman in the Christendom. Why would you choose one that is reluctant to wed you?"

"She can give me heirs."

"So can any woman," Robert replied.

"Nay, Robert, you understand me not. She is the *only* woman who can give me heirs."

Robert stared stunned at Faulk. "The prophecy?"

Faulk nodded. "Have you ever wondered why there were never any bastards foisted upon me?"

"I assumed you have been as careful as I have."

"Nay. In sooth, at times, I have been purposefully negligent."

"Why?"

Faulk shrugged. "To prove the prophecy wrong."

"You have bedded many women. How can you be sure none of them carried your seed?"

"You think a woman, lady or nay, would pass up the opportunity to grasp some of my lands and influence for their offspring? I think not," Faulk said.

Robert nodded in agreement.

"But are you certain Lady Nadine is the one? Are you willing to risk the future of your line on a prophecy, knowing that if you are wrong and she does not conceive, your chances for a legitimate heir are practically nil?"

"I must, Robert." Faulk took a long, deep draught from his cup. "Do I defy the prophecy and wed another, and _she_ fails to conceive, I shall have lost my chance with Nadine, forever. I must wed her."

Faulk rose from the table with a plan in his mind. If he could not prevent Nadine from leaving, then he would join her on her journey. 'Twould be a good opportunity to learn more about the future mother of his heir. "Prepare to depart for Londontown on the morrow."

"On the morrow?"

"Lady Nadine wishes to leave. We shall escort her."

"Escort her? But—"

"Cease," Faulk interrupted. "Say no more, Robert, I know you mean well, but I know what I must do. Besides, we must begin recruiting men for Richard, and I know a few noblemen in Londontown who might be of help to us."

"Very well. How many men for the journey?"

"Four will suffice, besides you and me." With most of his men-at-arms still in France with King Richard, Faulk had a reduced retinue. He must not leave the castle unprotected.

"May I suggest we take Eva with us as a companion for Lady Nadine?" Robert offered, and then confessed, " 'Twould do Eva some good, too."

"Aye," Faulk agreed. "A happy newlywed couple might help convince Nadine that marriage is a viable option."

A shadow crossed Robert's face.

Was there trouble in paradise? Faulk had been so preoccupied with the king's affairs, his own, and with Nadine that he had not had a chance to talk to Robert about his recent marriage.

"Robert, if there is—"

"Naught to worry, Faulk," Robert interrupted.

Faulk understood Robert's reluctance. He, himself, would rather take action than discuss the subject of his woes. On the morrow he would depart with Nadine to Londontown, therefore preventing her from fleeing. By taking control of the situation, he prevented her from crossing the Channel. Faulk would not forget the witch's warnings. *As she comes through the water, so can the water take her away.*

Naught would take Nadine away from him. The continuation of his line depended on her.

Chapter 5

A THUNDEROUS ROAR brought Nadine out of her dreams. Alarmed, she jerked to a sitting position, for a moment unaware of where she was. Realization came soon enough, as she recognized the walls of Whitecastle.

The rumble resonated closer now, mingled with shouts and grunts. Fully awake, Nadine walked to the window. She pulled back the heavy fur that covered the opening, discovering the great thickness of the wall.

Through the narrow gap part of the yard and some of the wall that encircled the property were visible. Down in the yard several men dressed in armor and helmets that covered most of their faces fought each other with swords.

No, not fought, but exercised or participated in some sort of rehearsal, Nadine realized when a woman stepped to her line of vision and waited, bucket in hand, on the sideline.

Some of the men walked toward the woman and dipped a big ladle into the bucket, drinking from it thirstily before returning to their positions.

Baffled, Nadine observed the scene that very well could be part of a movie. Yet she saw neither cameras nor regular-dressed people. Maybe they were hidden from her view. There was much unexplained in this place, she mused, but she wouldn't stick around long enough to find out.

She must return home and pick up the threads of her life. Thoughts of her parents filled her then, and an immense sadness choked her. How lonely her life would be without them. A solitary tear escaped her eyes, soon followed by others. She wallowed in grief for a while, but soon wiped her eyes dry. Sadness or not, loneliness or not, she had no alternative but to go on. She owed her parents that much.

If only she could call Denise, but according to Faulk, there was no such thing as a telephone in this place. How was she going to call a cab then? How was she going to leave? Suddenly Nadine remembered she had no money on her, no documents. She would have to go to the French embassy in London to report her missing passport and obtain some kind of identification to be able to enter her own country. Then go to the bank and withdraw money. Notify the school . . .

So many details to take care of. Details she had completely overlooked until now.

But who could blame her? She had lost her parents, almost drowned, been unconscious for three days, woken up in a medieval castle filled with weird people . . .

Hey, what else could possibly happen to her?

Nadine entered the empty great hall intent on leaving the castle. A huge shadow crossed her path. She found herself facing Faulk's overpowering smile and that delicious dimple. It caused her skin to sensitize and her heart to stammer.

" 'Tis late, but you may still break your fast if you so wish," he said.

She did feel weak, though she chose not to dwell upon the cause of her weakness. "I guess I could use some food before I leave for London."

Wordlessly Faulk led her to the main table. Encouraged

he hadn't offered any struggle at her mention of leaving, Nadine sat down. A young woman immediately brought her cheese, bread, and a metal cup.

Nadine nibbled at the hard but tasty cheese, then took a sip from the cup, almost choking on the bitter-tasting beer.

Beer for breakfast?

She set the cup down on the table. "Would you, by any chance, have some coffee?"

"Coffee?" Faulk repeated with a blank look.

Oh, well, she should've known. This was England, and they drank tea. Still, tea was better than beer at this time of the morning.

"Tea would be fine."

"Nadine, you speak words I understand not."

"You know tea, that hot brown drink made by pouring hot water on little crushed leaves? Tea, that you, English, insist on drinking with milk?"

"I know of no such drink."

Nadine shook her head in dismay. She was really not up to this.

"Do you feel well?"

"I feel fine," she said and rose from the bench. She refused to continue this word game with him. "Once again, I thank you for all that you've done for me. There are no words to express my gratitude for your saving my life. Perhaps one day we'll meet again, and I might be able to repay your kindness." She extended her hand in goodbye, expecting him to shake it. Instead, he took her hand and pulled her closer to him as he rose.

With his face inches away from hers, Nadine breathed in his manly scent mixed with pine. His brilliant eyes held her captive as his lips touched hers and desire ran through her body. His tongue grazed her bottom lip, and Nadine trembled in response. Her knees threatened to buckle, and she laid a hand on his chest for support.

"You cannot leave me, my fair lady," Faulk murmured between her lips.

The enchanted moment dissipated. Nadine pushed away from Faulk and sighed. The game had become tiresome.

"*Au revoir*, Faulk." She stepped around the table and him, but before she had a chance to reach the door, it opened with a thud. A giant blond man clad in armor, looking just like a Viking, stood in the doorway.

"Good morrow, my lady." He bowed politely, then looked over her shoulder to address Faulk. "Are you ready, my lord?"

The Viking spoke the same odd French as Faulk and Mildred. It almost sounded medieval—the old *langue d'oil* maybe? That was the language spoken throughout Europe in the time of Richard *Coeur de Lion*. And wasn't that also the time Faulk and his troupe were portraying? Nadine had good ears for languages and some knowledge of the medieval French. She also spoke English fairly well and knew enough of Italian and German to get by. Maybe that was why she could understand them.

Pivoting, Nadine faced Faulk. "Did you press a secret button under the table to summon reinforcements?"

Faulk ignored her comment. "As soon as Lady Nadine and I reach an understanding, we shall depart," he answered over her shoulder.

"What understanding?" she asked after the Viking stepped outside.

"That you make Whitecastle your home." Faulk approached her and swiftly took her into his arms. "That you accept your destiny. I vow to protect you and honor you for the remainder of your days. Cease your struggles. Put yourself in my hands and let me take care of you."

"I can take care of myself, thank you." Nadine struggled to get free from the iron manacles that were his arms. "Let me go."

He remained impassive.

Well, it was obvious she couldn't fight his strength, and so Nadine tried another tactic. "You dress as a knight of the realm, yet you have none of a knight's honor if you insist in keeping me prisoner here."

Faulk dropped his hands immediately. "Never doubt my honor, Lady Nadine."

Seething, he stepped back. God's teeth, but the woman tried his temper. She not only rejected his offer of marriage, his protection, but she also attacked his honor, acting offended when she should have been thankful.

If only he had succeeded in locating the old witch. Mayhap *she* could have convinced this disagreeable woman to fulfill the prophecy. However, the witch was nowhere to be found.

For a moment Faulk wished he could ignore the prophecy, his vow, his duty, and just send Nadine away. He was tired of the game she played. As 'twas, he knew he could not. He had set himself on this path and he would not rest until he had accomplished what he needed. Nadine was indispensable to his future. Without her there would be no more of his line. He would find a way to convince her to comply. He would not fail his father again.

Mayhap he could start by reassuring Nadine he meant her no harm. "I have no intention of keeping you prisoner. In verity, I shall escort you to Londontown."

Faulk ignored the suspicious look Nadine darted him. "Tell Mildred to pack a trunk for you. We shall depart as soon as you are ready."

"I'm ready. I have nothing to pack."

Faulk gave her a pointed look. Nadine still wore the same chemise she had last eve. He could not understand why she insisted on going about half-dressed. He also wanted to ask her to wear a veil and cover her short hair, but decided against it. Obviously, it had not been her choice to have her fine hair chopped, yet she chose not to show embarrassment. Faulk admired her grit. However, he could not allow the future mother of his heir to dress thus.

"Could I prevail upon you to make use of the garments I provided?" He tried not to sound sarcastic, but knew he failed when his words met her silence.

"If you wish to depart soon, I suggest you do not tally about." He stalked from the hall, leaving Nadine behind.

Clouds partially shaded the midmorning sun when Nadine finally walked out onto the courtyard. A cool breeze chilled her, and she was glad she had accepted Mildred's suggestion of wearing a cloak. She also had changed her clothes. She figured it would be better not to antagonize Faulk too much, especially now that she was almost out of here.

Yet she wondered what people would think when they arrived in London dressed like that.

She could not worry about that now. First things first.

In the light of the day Nadine saw buildings she had failed to notice in her night foray, and more people acting out the medieval play.

She searched for Faulk, but he was nowhere to be found in the flurry of people in the yard. Two women, chatting amiably, crossed the yard carrying baskets full of clothing. In front of a small building a man beat incessantly at an anvil, the sound resonating in the open space. Children—the first she had seen in this place—played around noisily, cheerfully.

All so perfectly natural.

And so astonishingly weird.

Uneasiness stabbed her. For a moment she felt like running. She couldn't wait to return to normality. Even her anguish over the loss of her parents seemed to be overshadowed by these inexplicable circumstances.

"Lady Nadine."

It took Nadine a moment to realize she was being addressed. She turned to the direction of the voice and was met by a beautiful young woman who smiled sweetly at her.

"Are you ready to depart?"

Nadine didn't remember seeing her before, which wasn't a surprise, for the faces she'd seen last night were all a blur in her mind. Yet this one looked too young and too pretty to belong in this farce.

"Ah . . . yes," Nadine said as she saw, with the corner of her eyes, a few teenage boys leading horses across the yard.

"I am Eva, Robert Baldwin's wife."

"How do you do?" Nadine said, not having a clue who Eva or Robert was.

"We are accompanying you to Londontown," she explained. " 'Twould not be proper for Lord Faulk to journey with his betrothed without chaperones."

Nadine couldn't believe her ears. Faulk was going around telling people they were to be married? He had no right. She was going to have to talk to the man.

"I hope you are agreeable," the petite beauty said, probably noticing Nadine's darkening expression. "I so long to see Londontown."

"I take it you haven't been there before."

"Nay. I have lived all my life in a small keep with my family until my wedding to Robert and the move to Whitecastle."

So, she was part of the crazy clan.

"Why would you want to live here?" Nadine asked.

Eva shot Nadine a confounded look. "Whitecastle is a wonderful place, much larger than where I come from."

"I see you are ready." Faulk's voice came from behind Nadine.

"I see you finally showed up." Nadine twisted around. "We have a few things to discu—" She forgot what she was going to say.

Faulk, too, had changed his clothes. He now wore armor, like the Viking and the men she had seen through her window. Tiny little metal circlets intertwined in a mesh formed the long-sleeved tunic that reached above his knees. He looked more dangerous than ever. Larger than life. Nadine could not stop staring. He was certainly going out of his way to assure authenticity to this fantasy.

"Are you ready for battle?" she managed to ask, gulping her surprise.

"Always," he said. "We should depart now, the morn grows late."

Nadine suddenly noticed a commotion behind her. Four men dressed in padded tunics and armed with swords and shields walked huge horses in Nadine's direction. The Viking—Robert?—helped Eva atop a mare.

"You shall have no trouble with this mare," Faulk said. "She is docile enough."

They were going to ride horses? She should've known. These people would go to any length to protect their charade. Evidently London must be just around the corner. If only she knew the direction, she could probably walk there.

"If I knew we were going to ride horses, I would have worn pants, or I should say breeches. Or would that offend your medieval mind?"

In light of the look of abject horror Faulk shot her, Nadine realized she failed miserably at her attempt at humor.

"Sweet Lord, give me patience," he whispered. Then, without warning, his huge hands encircled Nadine's waist and propelled her atop of the horse.

If there was someone who needed patience, Nadine thought as she clutched the saddle horn to avoid falling, that someone was she, who had to put up with these people's crazy fantasy. But not for long. Once she reached London, she would run, not walk, away from Faulk and his friends.

Thankful she had some experience with horses and for the fact she wasn't expected to ride sidesaddle, Nadine settled in what she thought would be a short ride. Her wide skirt billowed down her legs, effectively covering every inch of skin. How proper!

Nadine observed Faulk mount a monstrous horse with the barest effort. She had to admire his skill, but uneasiness returned when her eyes strayed from him to the entourage that obviously would accompany them to London.

Two by two, they rode across the courtyard and through the gate. The wooden bridge vibrated with their combined weight. She gripped the pommel for security. Following a well-traveled path down the hill, they skirted the woods and ended up on an unpaved road.

Soon they passed through a small village. Several huts gathered around a wooden church. A field of what looked like wheat grew on the right. And people in medieval garb mingled about.

The scope of the charade had outreached the castle.

After that they rode for what seemed an eternity. The sun broke out of the clouds, and Nadine began to sweat under her coat.

Finally Faulk veered his horse from the path into a barely marked trail in the woods. The entourage followed his lead to a small clearing.

A little stream ran nearby invitingly, beckoning Nadine with its cooling waters. Without waiting for help, she dismounted. As her foot touched the ground her body gave away to her weight, bringing her down to her knees.

Faulk was beside her barely an instant after her collapse. "You should have waited for my help," he chided, lifting her into his arms and taking her to the shade of a huge oak tree that stood majestically beside the stream. He removed her shoes and began massaging her ankles and feet.

The feeling to her legs returned with a vengeance and with it the painful prickly sensations that usually accompanied it.

Nadine moaned.

" 'Twill soon pass," he said gently, intensifying his stroking.

Nadine held her breath for a few seconds and the painful sensations soon began to diminish in intensity, eclipsed by the growing pleasure of Faulk's touch, working its magic through the fabric of her stockings, bringing forth sensations she would soon avoid altogether.

Desire flared in her, isolating her in a chamber of feelings she wasn't ready to accept nor surrender to but could hardly deny.

Yet deny them she would. How could she feel desire and distrust for the same man? She brushed Faulk's hands away. "Thank you, I feel much better."

Visibly annoyed, he stood up and moved to where Robert and the other men unsaddled their horses.

Nadine rested her back against the giant tree trunk and closed her eyes. She couldn't allow her out-of-place attraction for Faulk to cloud her judgment. She should confront him. Extract, once and for all, the truth about this game he played.

Her eyes fluttered open. She watched Faulk unsaddle his horse and walk it to the stream. He crouched down by the water with his back to her. Cupping water with his hands, he splashed his face and head, and raked his fingers through his thick, luscious hair, slicking it back. The rays of the sun, filtered through the canopy of trees, shone brightly on the dark, wet strands.

At that moment he stole a glance at her direction, and the hungry gaze he shot her blazed her insides. All thoughts of confrontation momentarily escaped her mind.

With the passing hours Nadine became more unnerved. What was she thinking, following these people? Where were they leading her? Nowhere had she seen any signs of civilization. *Sacré Coeur*, how far into the country could they be? Nadine knew they couldn't have gone too far on horseback, still she should've seen some sign of modern life. Telephone wires, airplanes, smokestacks, anything.

Though Nadine liked to plan, to know what was going to happen, to be prepared, she had failed to inquire further about their travel plans. She had assumed they would reach London in a matter of an hour or two, yet most of the day had gone by, and London was nowhere in sight.

Nadine drew her mare closer to Faulk's horse. "How far from London are we?"

"At this pace, three or four days I should say."

"Three, four days? On horseback? I thought—"

"Would you rather ride an ox?"

Nadine didn't appreciate Faulk's sarcasm, but having learned he would dismiss any modern concept as unintelligible, as he did when she asked for a telephone, she refrained from reminding him of more modern ways of transportation.

Soon Faulk led his little entourage off the *main* road and into a path.

"We shall procure accommodation here for the night," Faulk announced as a house appeared in sight.

So far Nadine had seen nothing that would reveal their location. There were also no signs of civilization whatsoever. And now they stopped at yet another strange place. She considered racing away from the group, but knew she wouldn't get far. Her poor mare was probably as exhausted as she was. Besides, where would she run to?

But what really kept her put was that no matter how confused, how uncomfortable she was with this charade, a little voice inside her urged her not to run. She decided to rely on her instincts, and prayed she wasn't going insane.

The house was one huge room, sparsely furnished. They were greeted by a couple dressed in the medieval garb. They must've had a sale in some costume shop nearby, Nadine mused, trying to pacify her growing distress at the situation. Faulk's men camped outside, and while Faulk and

Robert sat with their host, the wife took Nadine and Eva to a corner behind curtains where they could freshen up.

Nadine washed the dust of the road from her face. "Eva, how long have you been at Whitecastle?"

"Since my wedding, a few days before your arrival."

"Oh, you're newlywed." Nadine dried her face and turned to Eva with a smile. "Congratulations."

"Thank you." Eva blushed slightly.

"And how long have you been doing this reenactment thing?" Nadine asked trying to sound nonchalant.

"I beg your pardon?"

"You know, this medieval play thing."

"I understand you not," Eva said, visibly confused.

Nadine had hoped Eva could offer her some explanation, but it seemed she and Faulk were in this together. And Robert, too, of course. And the castle people. And the village people. And this couple who offered them accommodations for the night. Why would all of them go to such length for her benefit? Why not admit the ruse, so they could all laugh together. It made no sense.

Unless . . .

Unless they were speaking the truth.

The thought was unthinkable. That would mean time-travel, or a parallel world, or some other sci-fi explanation. Nadine wasn't prepared to even consider such scenario. She must reach London. London would be a place no one could re-create.

Dawn stole Nadine away from a dream of a faraway place she had never seen before. A spacious room filled with the scent and colors of wildflowers where she felt safe and warm. She opened her eyes to find herself sandwiched between Eva and another woman on a hard bed in a strange house.

The weak dawn light infiltrated the small window, falling like a blemish on Nadine's face. She blinked and moved

slightly, awakening her bed partners. The strange woman—
her hostess, Nadine finally remembered—rose swiftly,
prompting Nadine and Eva to remain abed. She disappeared
behind the curtains that separated the sleeping quarters with
the rest of the room.

Soon Nadine heard the sounds of the awakening house-
hold. Banging of pots, splashing of water, a door opening
and closing. She heard male voices, Faulk's voice, as the
hostess returned with water and towels. Nadine followed
Eva out of the bed. They washed and dressed, then joined
the men at the table for breakfast.

The smell of burnt grease nauseated Nadine. After one
quick look, she refused the cup offered to her, longing for
a cup of strong coffee. She took a few bites of the dark,
unappetizing bread, and nibbled on the small portion of
cheese given her, but left the strange-looking meat untouched.

"How do you fare, Nadine?" Faulk asked in his husky
voice.

How did she fare? Should she tell him about the fear that
gripped her heart? Should she hurl accusations at him for
trying to drive her insane with this charade of his? Or
should she just play along until they arrived in London?

"I feel fine, Faulk. Ready to go when you are."

By the fourth day of their journey, Nadine convinced herself the world had gone crazy. After that first night spent
in the medieval house, they had camped out for the second
night of their trip, and last night they had found shelter at
a monastery.

And now they rode again.

"There is much mystery about you." Faulk broke the silence that had been their code of the past days, surprising
Nadine.

"I could say the same about you."

"There is no mystery about me. I am who I am. But

you . . ." he paused. "What do you seek in Londontown?"

The question took Nadine aback. What could she tell him? After all she had witnessed these past days, the historical reenactment theory was getting thin. Then what had happened to her? To the world?

"I seek answers."

"Answers to what?"

"To what happened to me on that boat," she said. "There's much I don't understand. Much I don't remember. Faulk, I should have died. I don't swim, I was far from the shore. How did I end up on a beach nearby your castle?"

"And you think the answers wait for you in Londontown. Do you hail from there?"

"No, I'm from Rouen."

"Then who is in Londontown who shall grant you the answers you seek?"

"No one in particular," she said. The city itself should be her answer.

Evidently realizing she had no intention of extrapolating, Faulk returned to his position as leader of the column. Nadine watched him go, relieved.

The rest of the day dragged on. Wearily Nadine turned her attention to the lowering sun. Though there was still enough light to keep the shadows of the coming night at bay for a while longer, darkness would soon fall upon the earth.

So absorbed was she that she almost collided with Faulk when he suddenly halted in front of her. She maneuvered around him and stopped at his side.

"Londontown," he said.

Nadine followed the direction of his eyes, and for a moment she thought she would faint. *London?* It could not be.

Chapter 6

"LONDON," NADINE WHISPERED, feeling the blood drain from her face.

Of all the incredible things she'd seen in this trip, nothing would ever come close to the surrealistic picture sprouted ahead of her. Nestled in a plateau, surrounded by walls, forests, and cultivated fields, London looked small and primitive.

The unmistakable proof of its identity rose before her eyes. The White Tower—the central building of the Tower of London—built by William the Conqueror when he invaded England in 1066. The massive structure, surrounded by a huge wall and deep moat, stood elegantly across the Thames, leaving no doubt of its authenticity.

Nadine almost choked on her rising fear. Bewildered, she followed Faulk through a small settlement until they reached a bridge—if one could call *that* a bridge. Half wood, half stone, suspended by several pillars and arches, the bridge extended between the two margins of the Thames. On top of it little wooden buildings flanked both sides of the narrow roadway that constituted the crossing. A multitude of people, carts, and animals mingled about the place in a cacophony of sounds and smells that threatened to overwhelm her senses.

"Shall we cross Londontown Bridge?" Faulk invited, after paying the toll.

As his words sank in, Nadine panicked. In the back of her mind, in the little corner of her heart, she had kept the hope that it had all been a grand joke, a hallucination of some sort, a dream.

However, at the face of this very early version of London, which extended across London Bridge, Nadine realized the dream was a reality, the joke was on her. She could no longer deny the undeniable. For some unfathomable reason, she had been dragged centuries back in time. Her life, as she knew it, had ceased to exist; vanquished in a past she knew nothing about.

A bubble of nervous laughter threatened to erupt from her throat, and no amount of power could stop its release. The strange sound exploded uncontrollably, completely out of place or context. For moments it reverberated in the air, then it turned into heart-wrenching sobs, shaking Nadine to her core.

Faulk rushed to her side. "What ails you, Nadine?"

The concern in his voice penetrated Nadine's foggy mind, yet she couldn't drag her eyes from the bridge.

"What frightens you?" he asked, taking her trembling hands into his.

She turned unfocused eyes to him. With his thumb he wiped off the tears streaking down her dusty face. "Is it the water?" he asked. "Is that what frightens you?"

She couldn't answer him, her voice caught in her throat.

"The bridge is quite sturdy," he whispered, squeezing her hands.

Nadine heard Faulk's words, felt his reassuring tug on her hands, but they didn't quite register. Her eyes drifted back to the bridge.

"The bridge shall not fall," he insisted, his voice a bit more urgent.

The bridge shall not fall.

Unexpectedly an old nursery rhyme echoed in her mind. *London Bridge is falling down, falling down, falling down . . .* The absurd thought diverted her, distracting and drawing her away from the edge of insanity.

Taking several steadying breaths, she tried to control her wayward emotions. Stalling for time, she threaded her fingers through her hair, then wiped her eyes dry.

The concern etched on Faulk's face tugged at her heart, and she suddenly realized he had told her the truth about himself. He was what he said he was. He wasn't crazy. He meant her no harm.

She didn't know why, but the thought eased her mind somehow.

Forcing a tentative smile to her lips, she played in his erroneous notion that she feared crossing the bridge because of the danger of falling into the water. Even though the thought was abhorrent to her, it was not what was shaking the life out of her.

"Are you sure it will not fall down?"

He exhaled audibly. "It has never fallen down, my fair lady," he said. "It has been brought down, yet never fallen. You shall be safe."

"Faulk, we are obstructing the way," Robert called.

"Shall we?" Faulk let go of her hand.

Nadine took a deep breath and nodded.

She followed Faulk down the chaotic pathway of London Bridge and through the huge gate that guarded the city of London. The horses' hooves clattered down the main cobbled street, echoing distantly in her ears. They veered into dirt-packed streets with inward drains that smelled of decay, then back to cobbled streets. The wooden buildings slowly gave away to more elegant stone houses bordering the river.

Here and there, the unmistakable sign of a cross identified the many churches scattered about the city. The symbol of God choked Nadine with emotion, and a prayer echoed in the depths of her soul, disconnected of reason or rationale.

Do not let it end this way!

Distracted by a hurrying Faulk, Nadine soon forgot the unexpected thought.

As night fast approached, Faulk led them with the certainty of one who knows where he was going, and Nadine was thankful. If left to her own devices she wouldn't know where to go, overwhelmed as she was with the sights and sounds of a London she knew nothing about.

None of London's most famous landmarks were in sight. Neither Big Ben nor Buckingham Palace. Only the White Tower.

London of her time and London now were two very distinctive places.

Finally they arrived at their destination. Servants scurried from an impressive stone building and helped them dismount. Faulk's men-at-arms took their horses and followed the servants to a side entrance. Nadine pulled Faulk aside.

"What's this place?" she asked.

"This is Lord Heathborne's manor. He is a friend of my family. We shall ask him for accommodations while we remain in Londontown."

"Will he not mind? After all, we arrive unannounced."

He looked surprised by her question. "He shall be no less overjoyed to offer us hospitality than I would be to offer him the same," Faulk said. " 'Tis the way it should be."

"Still, he's your friend, not mine."

"My friends are your friends, Nadine. We shall wed soon, after all."

She must disabuse Faulk of that notion. She might have accepted she'd been transported back in time, but it didn't mean she had any intention of remaining here a minute longer than necessary. There must be a way to return to her own century, and she was determined to find it. Therefore, she couldn't allow Faulk to believe they had a future together.

However, she couldn't tell him the truth, either. Women in this time were burned as witches for much less than claiming time-travel.

Nadine wasn't going to chance it.

"Faulk, we must talk," she started. "I believe it would be better if you mention nothing about our marriage to your friends."

"Whyever not?"

"Because I have yet to agree to marry you."

"God's teeth, Nadine. What must I do to convince you that you belong with me?" he roared, his fists balling up.

Nadine took a cautious step backward. Faulk's belief in the prophecy was undeniable, yet she didn't belong to this place. She didn't belong to this time. And, therefore, she didn't belong with him.

But she couldn't tell him that.

"I told you I came to London . . . er . . . Londontown in search of answers," Nadine said. She had to be more careful with the way she spoke. From now on she would make a concentrated effort to appear to be like everyone else. "I cannot commit myself to you until I find them."

"You have yet to tell me of your quest."

He wasn't going to give up, she realized. She needed time to think. Night had finally fallen, and Robert and Eva waited patiently outside the door for them to finish talking. Nadine felt guilty. They depended on Faulk to arrange accommodations.

"It's late, and I am exhausted. Could we continue this conversation tomorrow?"

Faulk didn't look too agreeable, but he, too, must have noticed Robert and Eva waiting for them.

"Very well. But this matter is far from resolved."

Nadine followed Faulk through a huge oak door and into a great hall of stone floors and tapestry-adorned walls illuminated by several torches and a huge fireplace.

"Welcome to my humble keep." A man, as wide as a wine barrel—Lord Heathborne, Nadine guessed—greeted them as soon as they stepped in. He embraced Faulk affectionately, then stepped back to bring a young woman forward.

"My daughter, Judith," he said.

Faulk bowed. "As beautiful as I remembered."

Judith was a voluptuous redhead, richly dressed and heavily perfumed. Lavender always reminded Nadine of old things. It didn't suit Judith at all.

Or maybe it did.

Judith curtsied. "Your memory deceives you, my lord. Last time you saw me I was but a freckled little girl." She smiled coyly, batting her eyelashes.

"A little girl who blossomed into a great beauty," Faulk said.

Nadine almost gagged at the exchange. Faulk had never said anything remotely flattering to her. With her, he had been all matter-of-fact. *You belong to me. You are destined to be mine. You cannot leave.*

For some reason, Nadine was not amused.

Nadine glanced down at her own body, especially thin after her ordeal and this awful trip, and frowned. Her travel-weary attire—dusty and wrinkled—left much to be desired when compared to Judith's luxurious garments, but at least she was dressed properly to this century's standards. It would raise fewer questions.

"Allow me to introduce my friends," Faulk said. "Sir Robert Baldwin and his wife, Lady Eva." Robert bowed his head respectfully and Eva curtsied.

Faulk touched Nadine's elbow and brought her forward. "Lady Nadine du Monte . . ."

Would Faulk introduce her as his betrothed?

"Lady Nadine is under my protection," Faulk explained.

So, he finally decided to do as she asked. Why wasn't she pleased?

Judith looked pleased, though. Like a cat trapping a mouse.

"You and your friends are welcome to remain here as long as you wish," Lord Heathborne said.

"We appreciate your generosity, my lord," Faulk said.

"Judith," Lord Heathborne called. "Take our guests to their bedchambers so they can freshen up before supper."

Nadine's room was small but pleasant. A hot bath was brought to her almost immediately. Judith appeared to see if she needed anything else.

"Thank you," Nadine said. "I have all I need."

"Very well. I shall leave Harriet to help you with your bath."

Nadine was about to decline the offer, but Judith didn't wait for her answer.

"I must go and personally supervise Lord Faulk's bath," she said and left the room.

Nadine was struck mute. *Help Faulk with his bath?* What did she mean? Did she mean help with the preparations, or was she talking about hands-on help? Oh, she'd better not . . .

Nadine caught herself in time. Why should it matter to her if Judith bathed with Faulk in the same tub? The man didn't belong to her. She had no rights over him. Why should she care?

But she realized she did. And it scared her.

Feeling refreshed by a hot bath and a change of clothes, Nadine returned to the great hall. Faulk, Sir Robert, and Lord Heathborne stood by the huge fireplace drinking from metal goblets. Judith and Eva conversed a few feet away from the men.

Nadine stared at Faulk. His dark, wet hair curled slightly at his shoulders. His face was clean-shaven, in contrast with the other men, who were bearded. His profile denoted strength; his patrician nose, nobility; his square chin, stubbornness. He had removed his armor, or hauberk, as it was called, and donned a dark blue tunic. With a golden cup in his hand, he stood tall and magnificent. His broad physique overwhelmed the more wiry Robert and the definitely rounded Lord Heathborne.

The sound of his husky laughter filled the hall, resonating in Nadine's heart. He was so strikingly handsome. So dark, and powerful. And he had been very patient with her, she knew now, especially when he believed she belonged to him. He had brought her to London as she requested, instead of forcing her into marriage, as she knew a man of his time and position could've done. Even in the few intimate moments they shared, he had stepped back immediately when she hesitated. Many a modern man wouldn't have been so accommodating.

The thought of never seeing him again was suddenly very disagreeable.

"Finally, you arrive." Judith's irritated whisper penetrated Nadine's thoughts. She glanced at Judith in time to see her malevolent smile turn sweet before she pivoted and strolled to the men. "We may now begin our supper."

Eva shot Nadine a questioning look, evidently noticing Judith's veiled animosity. Nadine shrugged. She could guess Judith's reasons.

The seating accommodations left Nadine somewhat isolated at the end of the table, which was unusually covered by a spotless ivory linen cloth. The meal was an elaborate affair. The endless parade of food served on golden plates, not the concave piece of bread she'd grown accustomed to these past few days on the road, surprised Nadine. The

Heathbornes obviously wanted to make an impression. Nadine didn't have to wonder on whom.

With the eating knife Mildred had packed for her—Nadine had learned during this trip that everybody carried their own eating knife—Nadine ate sparingly of the greasy food, washing her meal down with the good wine served.

The cadence of the voices combined with the wine she drank lulled Nadine into a sense of peaceful well-being. However, she knew it was false. Nothing was really well. She must plan. Somehow she must find a way out of this bizarre situation.

But she couldn't concentrate. Faulk kept sending burning looks her way, sometimes with desire, sometimes with exasperation. The poor man didn't know what to make of her, and she couldn't blame him one bit. She herself wasn't sure.

There was one person in this room, though, who knew exactly what she wanted. Judith. She hung at Faulk's every word, oohing and aahing at every story he told, no matter whether a gut-wrenching war tale or a hilarious court anecdote. She used every opportunity to touch him, to smile at him, and to show off her more than voluptuous figure, in the most blatant flirting Nadine had ever witnessed.

Weren't medieval damsels supposed to be demure?

Judith's antics would have been mildly amusing if not directed at Faulk. As it was, Nadine was taken by surprise with the prick of the green-eyed monster's bite. Jealousy was an emotion she had little experience with in her life.

An only child, Nadine had never had to compete for attention or love. Both had been bestowed on her in endless supply. Even with Jacques, the only man she had been emotionally involved with, she had never experienced the feeling. She suffered rage and pain at his betrayal. She endured sorrow and guilt at her unwilling participation in his deceit, but never jealousy.

Yet, suddenly, she was overwhelmed by this irrational

need to rise from the table, yank Judith's hands from Faulk's arms and shake the woman until her teeth rattled.

Nadine struggled to get a hold on her emotions. The past few days she had experienced such an array of strong feelings, she feared she would go insane.

Faulk had just finished telling an obviously funny story, for they all laughed, when Judith suddenly raised her voice. "Oh, Lord Faulk," she said shooting Nadine a commiserating look. "Mayhap you should not tell such tales in Lady Nadine's presence."

Faulk looked puzzled at Judith, then turned a speculative gaze to Nadine. "Have I offended you, my lady?"

"No, of course not." As a matter of fact she hadn't heard a word of the tale.

"No need to be vexed," Judith said. " 'Tis obvious you are intended for the monastic life—"

Faulk gasped, almost dropping his cup on the table. Eva choked on her drink, and Robert lifted her arms until she caught her breath. In the silence that issued, the burning wood in the fireplace snapped like firecrackers.

"What makes you think so?" Nadine asked.

"Well . . ." Judith shrugged. "I just assumed . . . Your short hair and your garments denote a vow of humility suitable to a religious life."

Nadine realized her clothes were not as luxurious as Judith's or as well fitting as Eva's, but they were clean and seemingly proper. Poor Mildred must've altered some old gowns for her in a hurry. She certainly wouldn't have had time to sew Nadine new clothes, nor could she have gone to the nearest store to purchase new outfits.

Besides, if appearances betrayed one's inclination, Nadine could very well make a guess of her own concerning *Lady*, and she used the term loosely, Judith's main goal in life.

"Well, you are mistaken," Nadine said. "Have *you* ever considered joining a religious order, Lady Judith?"

"Me?" she cried, as if the mere thought was preposterous.

Which it was.

Lord Heathborne suddenly laughed, breaking the tension. "My beautiful daughter is more suitable to the court and the marriage mart than to a monastery. Though she sings like an angel," he added.

An angel with horns, Nadine thought.

Chapter 7

"WHILE YOU ESCORT Judith to the market," Faulk told Robert, "I shall visit a couple of landowners to begin our recruitment for Richard."

Robert grunted, visibly annoyed at the task left to him.

Faulk could not blame his friend. What warrior wished to spend his day escorting a lady to the market? Especially one he had no interest in. Yet Faulk knew Richard would soon be breathing down his neck. He needed to begin the gathering of men for the king as soon as possible.

Besides, 'twould be best if Robert escorted Judith. Faulk could hardly stand the woman's drooling all over him. 'Twas more than a mere nuisance, considering she was the daughter of a good friend he wished not to offend. Judith's unwanted attention also provided added conflict betwixt him and Nadine.

And that he could not afford.

Nadine's panic-stricken face when they arrived in Londontown burned in Faulk's mind. He had assumed her panic was caused by fear of water. After all, she had almost died of drowning. Yet could there be another reason for her fright? Could it be related to the answers she sought in

Londontown? What did she seek? Nadine had yet to explain her quest to him.

Faulk disliked secrets. He had made it clear to Nadine that he believed she was the one destined to be his, and that she would bear his heir. Nadine, on the other hand, veiled herself in mystery. Consequence of her ordeal, mayhap. Or lack of trust on her part. Whatever 'twas, though, it did not explain her odd ways. Ways that fortunately she had begun to amend.

During their journey, and especially in the short time they had been in Londontown, Nadine's speech and manners had changed somehow. She had even ceased speaking those odd words that held no meaning to him.

Still there were many unanswered questions about Nadine, and he intended to seek the truth.

Faulk spun around ready to leave when his gaze fell upon Nadine. Stuck to the floor he watched her sashay into the hall. 'Twas like the sun filtering through a window.

Nadine sighted him, smiled, and then sauntered to his side. He could not leave now, not before speaking with her.

"You look beautiful, my lady," he said.

Nadine blushed. Enjoying the effect his attention produced on her, Faulk toyed with the idea of seducing Nadine. Once he made her his, she would have no choice but to wed him. What was the point of using logic with a woman, anyway? So far, it had worked to naught.

"Good morrow, my lord," Nadine said and curtsied.

Pleased at Nadine's courtly behavior, Faulk smiled at her. His pleasure was short lived though, for in that instance, Judith burst into the room in a cloud of lavender, ignoring everyone's presence and prancing to his side.

Not now! Faulk almost groaned.

With no escape, he turned to Judith and bowed courteously, swallowing his discontentment.

"I hope you have not waited overlong, my lord." Judith straightened her shoulders, bringing her more than generous bosom to his view. Faulk swiftly averted his gaze back to Nadine.

"A wait worth every moment," he said, looking at Nadine.

As if suddenly noticing Nadine, Judith turned to her. "You look unwell. Should you not return to your bed for more rest?"

Tucking a strand of hair behind her ear, Nadine shot Judith an amused glance. "On the contrary, I feel wonderful. So much so I shall go exploring this morn."

Judith shrugged, dismissing Nadine. "Do not lose you way about town." She sounded as if she wished Nadine would do just that.

"Good morrow." Eva joined the little group, stopping beside Robert, who barely nodded to his wife.

'Twas obvious something was amiss, Faulk thought. He must speak with Robert. As an example of marital bliss, Robert and Eva were failing miserably.

"Shall we go?" Judith asked, taking Faulk's arm in a very proprietary way.

Trapped, Faulk was about to pawn Judith to Robert when a thought crossed his mind. He turned to Nadine. "Where do you go exploring, my lady?"

Looking surprised by his question, Nadine hesitated. "I heard the mention of a market fair not far from here. I thought a good idea to visit it."

"Indeed?" Faulk grinned. A seed of an idea grew in his mind. The more time he spent with Nadine, the better his chances to find out what she sought, and to put into action his plan of seduction. The king would have to wait a little while longer. Faulk had a lady to woo into marriage. "Then you must accompany Lady Judith and me. That is where we intend to go."

"But, Faulk—" Robert began.

"You may wish to visit Southwark," Faulk interrupted Robert, shooting him a warning glance. "I am certain you shall find there free men willing to fight for the king's cause."

Ignoring Robert's amused grin, Faulk returned his gaze to Nadine. He would halt at naught to fulfill his vow to his father.

"I believe Lady Nadine might benefit from a longer rest," Judith insisted, hanging on to Faulk's arm.

"Your concern is heartwarming," Nadine said. "I assure you I feel fine and would be delighted to accept Lord Faulk's escort." She turned to Eva. "You will be coming too, of course."

This time Robert interrupted. "I believe my wife is rather fatigued. 'Twould be best if she remained behind."

Faulk watched Eva steal a weary glance at her husband, but she did not contradict Robert. And neither would Faulk. 'Twas a matter betwixt them, and he would not interfere.

Nadine thought otherwise. She stepped toward Eva. "Do you feel well? Would you like me to remain with you?"

" 'Tis a grand idea," Judith offered. "You both look like you need a rest."

Faulk admired zeal in a woman, but Judith had just crossed the line.

"There is no need," Eva told Nadine. "I shall be fine."

"Are you sure?" Nadine insisted.

Eva nodded.

Apparently reassured, Nadine turned to Faulk, ignoring Judith. "Shall we go?"

Flanked by Judith and Nadine, Faulk left the hall. Mayhap Judith's attention would serve him well, after all.

As they rode away from the manor, Nadine mentally kicked herself for having forgotten her plan to sneak away to the market on her own. It was too late for regrets now; she had already accepted Faulk and Judith's company, but their presence would be an impediment to her plans.

However, the look of total chagrin on Judith's face ameliorated Nadine's regret. What an infuriating creature the woman was.

Nadine shook her head. She had more important things to think about than Judith. The image of the White Tower filled her mind. How could such an incredible thing like time-travel have happened to her?

Faulk's reasoning she was destined to be his was just too simple. She couldn't even be sure she was indeed the woman of the prophecy. Besides, why her? Why not someone from his own time? Someone with an identity here, with history, family, roots.

She had none of those. She didn't belong to this time. What she had to do was find a way to return to her own time, even though the thought of leaving Faulk weighed on her heart.

That was why she had opted to go to the market. There, Nadine hoped to find someone who could help her understand what had happened. This whole mess had started with a gypsy in Rouen. Maybe a medieval gypsy could end it for her.

And the market fair would be the logical place to find one.

Soon Nadine found herself following Faulk, Judith, and her man-at-arm into a clearing behind a church. They left their horses there in the care of several boys, then walked to the square in front of the church.

It was midmorning and the place was packed. Richly gowned ladies and lords, knights and servants—recognizable by their less than luxurious garments—strolled about the square. Tables of various sizes were set up with merchandise ranging from tools to fabrics to food. Scents of spicy food, strong perfume, and unwashed bodies mingled in the air, and Nadine was thankful the market was held in an open area.

Judith stopped at one of the tables littered with small containers of perfumes. She chose a flask, unstoppered it, and a powerful lavender scent wafted through the air. She picked up several of the same flask, paid for them, then stuffed them inside a small satchel she carried with her.

No doubt, stocking lavender for life.

Faulk and the man-at-arm strayed to a stand nearby where they inspected a leather saddle, and Nadine took the opportunity to blend with the throng of people mingling about. She might have a chance to search for a gypsy and be back by Faulk's side before he noticed her absence.

A group of men watched a play of dice, and from a short distance Nadine looked on. A running dog swerved to avoid a boy and hit a small stand instead, almost collapsing the flimsy structure. The vendor caught his end of the table in time to avoid the spreading of his precious merchandise on the dirty floor. He cursed fluently.

Nadine laughed but soon sobered. If not for their medieval clothing, she could almost believe she was in one of those little country fairs. But this was the real thing. For a moment the absurdity of it all almost overwhelmed her.

If she was to find a solution, she must keep her wits about her.

Determined, she walked on. The smell of freshly baked bread and pies drew Nadine to a vendor. Her mouth watered at the sight and aroma of the goodies. She'd left the house without breakfast, and her stomach complained audibly.

As she stepped up, Nadine noticed a dark woman sitting on a stool behind the pie stand. The woman, who had the dark looks of a gypsy, locked eyes with Nadine, beckoning her to come closer. With her heart thundering, Nadine trekked to the woman.

"For a small price, I can tell your future," the gypsy offered.

Nadine hid her excitement. "I have no coin."

The gypsy eyed Nadine from head to toe, then pointed to her middle. "I take your girdle."

Her belt? Without hesitation Nadine unhooked the golden-linked belt that hung just below her waist, and handed it to the woman. She stuck the belt behind her back and took Nadine's hand into hers.

"I see a handsome man—"

"Skip the man," Nadine interrupted, looking around. She wasn't sure how much time she had before Faulk came searching for her. Now was her chance to find out how to return to the future, and she wouldn't waste it in small talk. "Do you know much about travel?"

"You shall visit foreign lands—"

"No," Nadine interrupted again. She would have to be a little more specific. "I mean another kind of travel, like in through time?"

The gypsy gave her a blank look, but before Nadine had a chance to explain, a woman yelled from behind Nadine, "You lying witch."

Nadine turned and saw a small, rounded woman advance to her direction with a big stick in her hands.

For a moment Nadine feared the woman meant to attack her, then realized she had her eyes set on the gypsy. "You took my coin and told me I had a baby in my belly," she said, advancing menacingly. " 'Twas all a lie. There is no baby. I want my coin back, or by God's wounds I will bash your head in."

At the sight of the stick-brandishing woman, the gypsy dropped Nadine's hand and fled, carrying Nadine's girdle with her.

The accusing woman gave chase, cursing the gypsy's parentage. More people joined in the pursuit, but Nadine wasn't sure if they all had a grievance of their own, or if they just decided to join the melee.

The gypsy was evidently a fake. What would she do now? Where could she go for answers?

Disappointed, Nadine stepped back, away from the angry crowd, and into the wall of a human chest.

She pivoted to find Faulk frowning at her. Judith stood by his side, and her man-at-arm stood sentinel behind her.

"I told you she was here somewhere. You had no cause for alarm." Judith glared at Nadine.

"Were you looking for me?"

"I feared for your safety. You must not wander away, my lady."

The scowl on his face told Nadine of his exasperation, but the stiltedness of his words revealed his worry.

"I am sorry," Nadine said. "I must have wandered off without noticing."

He didn't seem mollified by her explanation, but said no more.

In silence they returned to their strolling, wandering about the several stands, until a colorful display of ribbons flying in the morning breeze caught Nadine's attention. She stopped to look at them and wistfully entwined the rainbow of strands between her fingers. She had always loved ribbons, preferring them to elastic bands for her hair, but with her hair so short she hadn't used them at all. And it would take a long time for her hair to grow long again.

Sacré Coeur! That was the least of her problems.

With a humph Nadine set the ribbons down and was about to walk away when Faulk stepped to her side. He scooped a handful of ribbons and perused them attentively.

"These would look beautiful on you." He chose a couple of wide bands of a rich emerald color and draped them over her head. He flipped a coin to the vendor. "It complements its golden hue."

Nadine's heart skipped a beat at his fluttering touch. His kind gesture rescued her from her sinking mood. Faulk was not at all what she expected a medieval man to be. He was big and strong, yet he moved with a lithesome gait; he was powerful and commanding yet gentle in his treatment of her; and though he pursued her relentlessly, he also proved to be more than patient with her strange ways. And how strange she must look to him.

She gazed at him and the intensity in his azure eyes left no doubt of his feelings. Faulk desired her. If truth be told, she couldn't say she was immune to his charms. Was she really destined to be his, as he believed?

Holding the ribbons to her heart, Nadine smiled uncertainly. Time would tell. Only she wasn't sure how much time she had.

Roland du Monte, head high, chest puffed, promenaded into the market square of Londontown. 'Twas good to be able to purchase whatever he fancied. To finally be looked upon with respect. To be eyed favorably by ladies who weeks ago would consider him below the salt.

An array of pungent smelling jars caught his attention. The vendor, eager to dispense with his ware, shoved a small jar under his nose. " 'Tis said to make hair grow thicker, my lord."

Roland laughed and pushed the jar away. "I have no need for such embellishments, old man." Secure in his fair looks, Roland considered himself quite handsome, especially now that he was also wealthy, or would be once the king sanctioned his claim.

The new lord of Rosemanor of Rouen! Not bad for a bastard kin of the powerful Roger du Monte. Pride and resentment mingled in his gut.

In verity, throughout his life he had lacked neither food nor shelter at Rosemanor, yet his humiliating position as a charity case and the servants' constant sneers behind his back had always eaten at him.

Well, no more. No one would ever look at him again with disdain or pity. He had paid his dues.

He had managed Rosemanor's ledgers and the farming tenants for many years for his benefactor. A position he had obtained thanks to Roger's despair at making a knight out of him—a despair Roland had encouraged, for he had no intention of becoming any lord's fighting beast.

Roland dreamed of being his own lord. And with that in mind he had withdrawn small pittances from the du Montes' fortune along the years. Mere crumbs that meant naught to Roger and his daughter—the fair Nadine—yet could make the difference betwixt life and death in Roland's old age.

Obviously Roger had thought otherwise. His suspicions had forced Roland into action. To cover his pilfering, Roland had Nadine abducted. However, even distressed at his only daughter's disappearance, Roger had not relented on his inquisition, forcing Roland to act again and dispose of his once benefactor.

Killing Roger had been unavoidable.

Still, Roland had meant Nadine no harm. He had watched her grow from a pretty child into a beautiful lady, and he had lusted after her as he had for no other. Nadine possessed all he wished in a woman. Wit. Beauty. Wealth.

But she had always been unattainable. That is, until her father's death. A fortnight after the burial, Roland had sent word to Benoit, his subaltern, to return Nadine to the bosom of her family. He had planned to console the grieving daughter, then finally entice her into marriage.

Unfortunately, that stupid Benoit had butchered even that simple task. Roland had been furious when he learned of Nadine's death. Even though he had inherited her fortune by default, he had wanted it all. Wealth and Nadine.

Oh, well, one out of two was better than naught. There were no ties to connect him to either deaths—he had made sure of that—therefore, he was a free man, wealthy and—

Roland stopped dead in his track, feeling like someone had just punched him in the stomach.

'Twas impossible!

The blood drained from his face as he stared in disbelief at a beautiful lady who resembled his Nadine. She wore no headdress and her short golden hair framed a face Roland could never forget. He remembered instructing Benoit to send a lock of Nadine's hair to her father as proof he held her captive, but never would he have allowed Benoit to chop her glorious tresses to no more than a page's length. Oh, he should have killed the bastard when he had the chance, instead of only maiming him.

Unconsciously Roland stepped closer and watched, befuddled, the lady survey a colorful array of ribbons spread on a stand. He remembered well how Nadine loved ribbons. Unable to believe his own eyes, he almost surrendered to the irresistible urge to approach and confront her. He hesitated, though. She was not alone. A giant of a man stood by her side. Deciding upon caution, Roland stepped back, but his eyes never left her.

She lifted her face to the giant, and the unusual honey color of her eyes beamed at him like the sun in a summer sky. His heart skipped a beat. *Mon Dieu*, she must be his Nadine. Hope and apprehension unfurled in his heart.

What would she be doing in Londontown? Why had she not returned home? Was she gathering aid to take by force what was rightfully hers? If 'twas thus, then she must have learned of his involvement in her kidnapping. Benoit had sworn she knew naught, yet obviously the man had lied to him about her death. Would he not also have lied about what he had told her?

Roland's mind spun around like a whirlwind. He must approach her. He must know with certainty if she was indeed his Nadine, but first he must get rid of the giant.

He retraced his steps to the back of the church, where the horses were kept. A few boys, heedless of their chore, kicked a small ball fashioned from a piece of cloth filled with straws. Each time the small ball flew into the air, it grew smaller as the straw escaped through the holes pierced by their little feet.

While they were distracted, Roland inspected the horses,

then chose a destrier. Untying it from the line, he was about to walk away with it when one of the boys left the game and rushed to him. Roland tossed a gold coin into the air. All the boys scampered to catch it. As the dust swirled up in the air, Roland led the warhorse away undisturbed, forming his plan.

The man would surely seize the chance to flaunt his strength to the lady, trying to stop the wayward horse. As he stepped away, Roland would approach her and ascertain once and for all her true identity.

When he determined he was close enough, Roland took a thorn he had picked up from a bush and mercilessly thrust it into the horse's rump. The pricked animal stampeded out of control and into the square, kicking and stomping everything in sight.

As the destrier flailed through the throng, people flew out of its way screaming and cursing. A few men half-heartedly attempted to stop the beast, but only one brave soul managed to grip the horse's mane for a moment before the mighty beast dislodged him.

The man's attempt and the increasingly confining area of the square slowed the warhorse, and it swirled around on its hind legs, neighing furiously and striking out with its powerful hooves.

Nadine's terrified scream alerted Roland that his diverting plan had turned awry. And the giant was too far to save her.

Chapter 8

A KNIGHT'S WARHORSE was as much a weapon in battle as was his sword, and the destrier rearing for attack was in a fighting mode. Horrified, Faulk watched as it raised its powerful forelegs, capable of destroying anything in their path and crush down with a terrorizing neigh.

Nadine, trapped against the ribbon stand, tried to inch away from the beast's hooves, dangerously close to becoming its victim.

Faulk had stepped away from her for a moment at Judith's urging. Now he dropped the box he carried for Judith and dashed to Nadine.

There was no time for warnings. Faulk lunged, flying through the air and landing hard on Nadine. Gripping her in his arms, he rolled over several times on the dusty ground, away from the beast's reach. He kept her pinned beneath his body, protecting her with it, until with the corner of his eyes, he saw the destrier stomp over the stand and dash away from the square.

With a fluid movement Faulk half rose to a kneeling position, bringing Nadine up with him. While she gasped for air, he frantically patted her head and arms in search of broken bones. Relieved she had suffered naught more damaging than a few bruises, Faulk pulled her tightly into his embrace, oblivious to the curious eyes gathering around them.

God's teeth, he had been scared! He inhaled the fresh, clean scent of Nadine's hair. Had he taken a moment longer to reach her, she could have been trampled to death. He waved away visions of a broken Nadine splattered on the ground.

Suddenly realizing he held her a little too tight, and embarrassed at his show of emotion, Faulk released her abruptly. When she almost toppled back, he held on to her shoulders, steadying her.

"Are you hurt?" he asked.

"Do you plan to make a career out of saving my life?" Her voice shook.

She was breathless and trembling, yet she jested! Faulk chuckled, his tension easing a little.

"I vowed to protect you, my lady, and protect you I shall."

He glanced back at where Nadine had been a moment ago and shuddered. The stand—now reduced to splintered wood—and the colorful ribbons Nadine had so admired littered the ground.

"Thank you for saving my life, again," Nadine said.

Resisting the urge to kiss her, he rose, then helped her up.

"Ouch," she cried.

"You are hurt," he said, looking her over. Dust clung to her torn gown, and her girdle had disappeared, yet he saw no signs of blood or any serious injury.

"I think I twisted my ankle." Nadine clung to his arm for support as she lifted her gown to examine her foot. She had lost one shoe, and her stockings were torn.

Faulk kneeled down and checked her foot. 'Twas not

swollen, but at his touch, Nadine winced. Wordlessly he stood up and lifted her into his arms.

"It is not that bad, I can walk—"

"Hush, Nadine," he said, carrying her away from the chaotic square. "Would it be too much to ask that you allow me to carry you?"

He did not want to put her down. He did not want to lose her. He told himself 'twas because she was so important to the future of his line. Without her there would be no more of his family. And that was why he shook inwardly.

That and naught more.

With a mix of relief and annoyance Roland witnessed the giant's rescue of Nadine. Instead of getting rid of the man, Roland had given him the means for his heroic stunt.

Irked to his bones, Roland followed the couple. Keeping a safe distance and his eyes on the pair, Roland collided with a wench. He immediately steadied her and apologized, yet he had no intention of offering her further aid. However, in those precious moments he also lost sight of Nadine.

"Damnation," he cursed.

"I beg your pardon," the wench replied, all ruffled up.

After a cursory glance, Roland realized the wench was a lady. Now he would have to redouble his apologies, losing precious time. "I beg your pardon, my lady," he said gently, though inwardly he felt like snapping her little neck.

"And so you should. Has chivalry died without my knowledge?" she asked rhetorically as she continued on her tirade. "First, my escort is so absorbed in saving the Lady Nadine he leaves me behind unattended but for one man-at-arm. Then I find myself subject to your foul language. There seems to be no safe place for a highborn lady anymore." She glared indignantly at him.

Roland cared naught for her feelings, or her situation, for

that matter, especially at this moment when he shook inwardly with the confirmation of Nadine's name. *His Nadine.*

"I beg your pardon again, my lady. Mayhap I could offer reparation?" He laced his voice with as much contrition as he could muster.

"Mayhap you could," she snapped.

"I am Roland du. . . . Chasse." He decided, at the last moment, to lie about his name. Evidently the lady knew Nadine, and Roland could not be certain of how much Nadine knew nor how much she had confided in others. "Those are my knights," he pointed to two men who stood a few feet away from him. "If the lady allows me, I shall be honored to escort you home."

She inspected his knights from a distance, then turned her gaze to him, evidently deciding whether he was wealthy enough, and therefore honorable enough, for such exalted duty. The bitch! Roland thought, but kept his semblance calm and obsequious.

"I am Lady Judith Heathborne," she finally said. "And I accept your offer." She turned to her man-at-arm. "Bring my packages."

Around them the melee slowly died down. The warhorse had finally been caught and taken away. A few splintered stands were removed, and the merchants collected their dispersed ware. The onlookers returned to their browsing, and Roland escorted Lady Judith across the square. He was not in a hurry anymore.

"Who was the man who saved the lady . . . what was her name again?"

"Nadine du Monte," Judith answered.

The air sucked out of his lungs. There was no doubt now.

"And her savior is Lord Faulk Brookstone, of Whitecastle."

"Friends?"

"Guests. Lord Faulk I know for many a year, but Lady

Nadine I have just met and know little about," Judith supplied.

"I see," Roland said. As 'twas, Nadine might not have confided in Lady Judith, yet Lord Faulk was another matter. If Nadine had any knowledge of Roland's involvement in her kidnapping, she might have sought a champion to avenge her. Yet, what would she be doing in Londontown instead of Rouen, especially if she had Lord Faulk's protection? He must proceed with caution until he knew for certain.

Nadine's heart thundered as Faulk carried her to his horse—he wouldn't even allow her to ride on her own. She had thought to protest, but shaken as she was she didn't mind one bit being in his strong arms.

Obviously it was a major point of honor for medieval men to be the protector. She wouldn't begrudge Faulk that. After all, he had saved her life twice and deserved a little leeway.

Besides, since this whole nightmare had started, beginning with the death of her parents, Nadine hadn't felt safe. But now, as she settled against Faulk's massive chest, a feeling of safety, of belonging, seeped through her, muddling her determination not to get involved with him.

If only she could confide in Faulk. Tell him of her time-travel. He was a man of faith, a man who believed in prophecies, maybe . . .

No, what was she thinking? Faulk was a medieval man, with medieval superstitions. He would be horrified, think her crazy. Probably turn his back on her. She couldn't chance that. Without him she would have nowhere to go. She needed him.

For the time being Nadine would have to make up a convincing story to keep him from digging deeper. But would that be enough to handle his expectation of marriage to her? An expectation she couldn't possibly fulfill?

Nadine moaned in frustration.

"Are you in pain?" Faulk immediately asked.

"It was too scary out there."

"That 'twas. For a moment I feared I would not reach you in time."

"A man like you feeling fear?" she jested. Faulk was such a giant of a man, so sure of himself. He couldn't possibly be frightened. Or so she thought.

Faulk gave a brittle laugh. "These days I seem to be fearful of many things."

"Such as?" She knew she pried, but she couldn't help.

There was silence for the longest moment. "Unfulfilled duties, broken vows—" The whisper stopped abruptly, as if Faulk had revealed more than he wanted to. "You must not fret," he amended. "The danger has passed."

Had it really?

They fell into silence after that, and in a few more minutes they arrived at the house.

"I shall take you up to your bedchamber," Faulk said.

"No, I am fine, please put me down."

He hesitantly complied.

Nadine took a couple of steps. Her ankle was sore but didn't hurt as much. "See, it is much better. It is not even swollen." She smiled to pacify him. "I was told there is a nice garden in the back of the manor. I think I will just go there and rest awhile."

Limping slightly, Nadine strolled out of the hall.

A few oak trees lined the property around the small garden, and its center was filled with flowering shrubs and plants. The heady scent of the roses that bloomed profusely reminded Nadine of her mother and their little garden in Rouen.

Even though it had been only days since she had lost her parents, so much had happened that it felt like an eternity had passed. Yet, never in her life had Nadine felt so lonely, so adrift. Sadness filled her heart.

"Oh, *Maman*," she cried. "I wish you were here with me."

A soft breeze touched Nadine's hair, and the scent of roses wafted up to her. Nadine closed her eyes. She felt her mother's presence. She saw her gentle face with the eyes of her mind.

"We must talk." Faulk's voice jerked her out of her reverie.

Nadine sighed. She knew what he wished to talk about, yet she had no notion of what to tell him.

Still, she couldn't just ignore him. She spun around and faced Faulk.

He pointed to a small wooden bench. They walked to it and sat side by side.

"What happened in the square reminded me we might not possess the luxury of time," Faulk said.

Time. What irony!

"I must wed and beget heirs, Nadine. 'Tis my duty and responsibility as I am the last of my family. Long ago a prophecy foretold your coming and your place in my life. Yet, you refuse me."

"I have no choice." *Mon Dieu!* In any other time or circumstances, she would be overjoyed to hear such words, but not now. Not here.

Faulk's face grew taut with frustration and suspicion. "Whyever not? Have you given your heart into a man's safekeeping?"

Nadine thought of Jacques, and promptly realized she had never really loved him. She had been in love with the idea of being in love, eager to emulate her parents' incredible relationship.

"No," she said truthfully. "But that is not the problem." She averted her gaze from him.

That simple action was not lost in Faulk. God's teeth! What was Nadine hiding from him?

"I have not told you the whole truth about myself," she said.

Faulk stiffened. He should have known. Nadine had lied to him. Stoically, he waited for the truth that could destroy all his plans.

"I have not told you the truth," she repeated, "because I do not know it myself."

"I understand you not."

"It is difficult to explain." She threaded a hand through her fine hair, tucked a strand behind one ear, then she rose and walked to the rosebush she had been staring at. Her fingers touched the delicate rose petals in a soft caress.

She pivoted to face him. "Since my accident in the Channel, I have only sparse memories of my life—the few details that I have already revealed to you. The rest is all a blur. My past, my life . . . There is this immense blank in my mind that I cannot fill."

Nadine had lost her memory? He had heard of such malady only once, years ago, in a soldier with a head wound—the man had no recollection of who he was. Could that have happened to Nadine? Yet Nadine had *some* memories.

Frustrated with this new complication, Faulk rose and joined Nadine. Her beautiful golden eyes shone with unshed tears, and in their depth there was pain. Her obvious despair touched him, and a fierce need to protect her overtook him, doubling his frustration. He could only shield Nadine from the dangers from without. The dangers from within, from the unknown, were beyond his reach.

"Is that what you expected to find in Londontown? Memories?"

She nodded.

Then why did she not go to Rouen, her hometown?

The question bothered Faulk, but he had no intention of asking Nadine that. Not now, anyway. Had she wished to return to Rouen, he would not have allowed her to go anyway, resolved that he was to heed the witch's warning about the water taking her away from him.

Besides, she could not have been eager to cross the Channel so soon after almost drowning in it.

"Has any memory brightened the darkness of your past?" Was that what upset her when they had first arrived here? Some frightening memory?

"No," she whispered. "And that is what upsets me."

Faulk knew Nadine was a highborn lady, despite her, now improved, odd manners and speech. Nevertheless, that was not a factor in his decision to wed her. That she brought naught to their union but herself mattered not. Her value hailed not from properties and wealth she might possess, but from the immeasurable gift only she could bestow upon him—his heir.

And for that Faulk would overlook all else.

However, how could he trust her affirmation that her heart was free? How could she know that when she claimed she remembered little of her past? What if the lady had a husband for whom she held no esteem? Would it not be logical for her to forget about him? Could she have been fleeing from him when she fell into the Channel?

Faulk shook his head, swiftly rejecting the notion. The prophecy would not fail him thus. 'Twould not promise him a lady who could not be his.

Having accepted the prophecy as the ultimate truth and the solution to his plight, Faulk could not even fathom the consequences were he wrong in his belief.

"Is that why you refuse me? Because of your lack of memories?"

"How can I commit myself to you when I have so many unanswered questions about myself? How can you wish to marry me under these circumstances?"

Faulk took Nadine's hands into his. "There is only one answer I seek, Nadine."

He could speak to Nadine of his faith in the prophecy.

He could praise her beautiful golden eyes and sunlit hair. He could explain again her importance in his life, but he thought it wise to bring her flush to his body instead, and show her how well they fit into each other's arms. Man to woman, hardness to softness, strength to gentleness.

"The past matters not," he said. "The future matters all. Will you fulfill the prophecy, Nadine? Will you wed me?"

She stared wide-eyed at him.

To drive his point home, Faulk kissed her. His lips slanted over her soft ones, his tongue delved deep into the warm recesses of her mouth. His blood flowed heavier, hotter in his veins, filling him against Nadine.

She moaned and laced her arms around his neck, surrendering to his kiss.

God's teeth, but Nadine knew how to kiss. Her soft lips and wicked tongue fueled his hunger for her, driving him to such heights of desire, of need, he spun out of control. He wanted her. He must have her.

He could not take her in the garden of a friend's manor, like any wench. Nadine would be his wife, the mother of his sons. She deserved his respect.

Gently, but firmly, Faulk pushed Nadine away from him. His member throbbed painfully, and it took him a great effort not to pull her back into his embrace.

Damn his chivalry!

But 'twas how it should be. He desired Nadine, hungered for her, but would not allow his need to overpower him.

"Pardon me, my lord."

Relieved and exasperated at Robert's sudden interruption, Faulk stepped away from Nadine and pivoted to face his friend. "I thought you in Southwark, Robert."

"A message from the king has been forwarded from Whitecastle. It arrived here soon after you left."

What could the king wish with him? Surely he could not possibly expect results in such a short time? Faulk groaned.

He had to resolve this impasse with Nadine. 'Twas taking too much of his thoughts and time.

He turned to Nadine. "I shall expect your answer soon, my lady." Then he bowed and left the garden in the company of Robert.

"I need you to battle for me," Judith said as soon as she returned from the market fair.

Lord Heathborne stood up abruptly. "Has any one offended you?"

"Nay, Father, 'tis not that." She dismissed his concern. "Remember when I agreed to wed old Lord Brentford you promised me I would have my choice of husband if I ever remarried?"

"Aye. You were very clever in extracting that vow from me, knowing old Lord Brentford could not possibly live long."

Judith smiled knowingly. "He lived longer than I wished. But that is of no consequence. I have decided to remarry."

"Lord Faulk, perchance?"

"You are very observant, Father."

"Good Lord, the way you have carried on about the man since his arrival, only a blind man would not see it."

Judith shrugged. "He is a difficult man to entice."

"Mayhap his interest lies elsewhere."

"Not that freak of a lady he is escorting." She snickered.

"She has some appeal," Lord Heathborne said.

"To boys-oriented men, mayhap. Surely not to a virile, masculine, handsome man such as Faulk. She is too skinny, too flat, and that horrible short hair. Sweet Lord, what was she thinking?"

Judith perched on the edge of the table facing her father. "It matters not," she continued. "I want you to negotiate an alliance betwixt our families. Make it worth his while, Father. I want Faulk." She shot her father a determined look. She would not be dissuaded.

"I shall speak with him, but I promise naught," he said.

"Very well. And I shall make sure he finds me more than desirable."

Chapter 9

THE KING'S MISSIVE had been emphatic, he had lost too many men and needed more. He even hinted at the possibility of Faulk's return to the battlefield.

Damn his kingly soul, Faulk cursed inwardly as he hurled the missive to the table and pushed to his feet. His monarch was depleting him of men. Faulk had already given him more than his alloted share, yet the king wanted more.

The king's allusion of wanting his return was only a threat. Richard needed him in England, recruiting for him, not in the battlefield. At least, not now.

"As soon as we return to Whitecastle, I shall send five of my own men to the king," Faulk told Robert.

"Allow me to lead the men to the king," Robert said.

Surprised, Faulk glanced at his friend. "You know I need you at Whitecastle. There is much to be done."

Frustration etched Robert's face.

Robert was not himself. The man was tauter than the string of a crossbow. Could this be related to the tension he sensed earlier this morn betwixt Robert and his wife?

"I would have thought you the last person to wish to

return to France, Robert. Is there any matter you wish to discuss?"

Robert muttered something underneath his breath, then pressed his lips together grimly.

Faulk was befuddled. As the youngest son of a minor baron, Robert would inherit naught from his father. That had been the reason he had joined the Crusades—in search of riches of his own. As a landless knight, Robert had returned to England willing and eager to provide him service. Besides, Faulk had discussed with Robert the possibility of setting him up in a small holding, sometime in the future.

"I would offer advice, but first I must know what is the matter."

Robert let out an exasperated breath. "Frankly, Faulk, as long as I live I shall never understand the female mind."

'Twas as he thought. Robert was having troubles with his wife. Faulk grunted agreement, then returned to his chair.

"They use their wiles to entrap you, then they turn cold and distant like a snowy mountain," Robert said, warming up to the subject.

A distant memory flashed in Faulk's mind. Elizabeth. He had lusted after her, and she had known. She had teased him, and played coy, until she had finally allowed him to take her. As inexperienced as he had been, Faulk had gloried in the privilege. He still remembered the profusion of blood she had shed in that first breaching.

Since then he had learned much. No woman would ever deceive him again.

Faulk scattered away the memories. Elizabeth had paid dearly for her treachery with her life and that of her child. But Faulk's gullibility would haunt him forever. He vowed never again be overcome by lust or heart.

And this time he would know with certainty if he had planted his seed in a chaste womb.

" 'Twas so much easier before, when we sampled them, then left them behind," Robert grumbled.

What could he tell his friend? Faulk faced an even worse predicament with Nadine. At least, Eva was Robert's wife, under his power. Nadine was beyond him. That is, for the time being.

"Eva is your wife. Surely there are ways you can guide her to her duty."

Robert was about to extrapolate on the matter when Judith rushed into the bedchamber.

"Oh, pardon me, I thought you alone, Faulk."

"I was about to take my leave," Robert said. "I speak with you later," he told Faulk, then left the bedchamber.

As Judith strolled in, Faulk made sure the door remained wide open. He spun around to find Judith sitting on his bed. From where he stood he enjoyed an unimpeded view of her more than generous breasts. Faulk moved to the table and slumped on the chair.

He was no slave to lust, but he had been without a wench for quite some time now, and his brushes with Nadine added to Judith's unsubtle pursuit compounded his frustration.

"I believe you owe me an apology, my lord," Judith said. "For abandoning me alone at the market fair."

Conveniently ignoring the fact that Faulk had left her with her own man-at-arm, Judith pouted. Faulk resisted the urge to remind her of that fact.

"I beg your pardon. I hope you understand the mitigating circumstances."

Judith sighed. "I might be persuaded to forgive you. For a boon." She patted the bed in a blatant invitation.

Faulk fidgeted on his chair. Though he had no intention of succumbing to Judith's wiles, how would he get her out of his bedchamber without offending her and possibly her father?

Judith grinned, well aware of his predicament. "Would you brush my hair?" she asked innocently.

Faulk exhaled, relieved. That he could do. He strode to the bed, took the brush from her hands, and sat a safe distance away.

Turning her back to him, Judith sat on her haunches so he could reach the entire length of her long, flaming hair that fell below her derrière.

As he stroked Judith's hair, Faulk's thoughts veered to the past, to his deceased mother. He remembered he had brushed his mother's beautiful raven hair only days before she had died.

For a long time after that Faulk had felt responsible for her death, for she had sickened with his birth.

His father had exonerated him. "Giving birth is a miracle God bestows upon women," Lord Warren had said. "All a man can do is plant his seed and pray."

And that he would do. He would plant his seed in Nadine's womb and pray 'twas fertile, for the continuation of his name depended on that.

Unconsciously he brought a handful of hair to his nostrils, but the strong lavender scent brought him abruptly out of his reverie. He was shocked to see entwined in his hand Judith's flaming mane instead of the golden luxury of Nadine's.

He let his hand fall brusquely and jumped to his feet.

"Oh," Judith moaned. "Do not stop, my lord, I beseech you."

"I believe 'tis time you left," Faulk said, walking to the door. God's teeth, he should have never let Judith enter his bedchamber in the first place.

Judith did not seem put off. On the contrary, the corners of her mouth curled upward in a pleased smile. She picked up the brush, rose from the bed, then strolled past him. Before she left, she spun around. "I almost forgot. Father wishes to speak with you before supper."

• • •

The encounter with Faulk in the garden shook Nadine more than her brush with death earlier at the marketplace. Faulk's single-mindedness in wanting to marry her coupled with the impossibility of her compliance threw them at a standstill.

And the undeniable attraction between them didn't help matters.

How she hated deceits. Yet that was all she'd given Faulk. All she could give him.

Nadine slumped down on the bench in the garden. How long would she keep him at bay with her lies? How long could she avoid getting emotionally involved with him when his kisses awakened a hunger in her she didn't know existed?

The longer she remained in this century, the more devastating her departure would be to both of them. She must find out what caused her catapult in time and what would take her back to the future. Could she be whisked forward anytime without warning? Was there some kind of time limit connected to this experience? Some guiding principle behind it? Was she to remain here for the remainder of her life?

Those questions must be answered.

And Whitecastle, where it had all begun, seemed to be her only option. Maybe a visit to the beach where she was found could yield some clue to her jolt through time. She could also try to find the witch who had foretold her coming. *She* should have some answers.

Making plans kept Nadine focused, preventing her from dwelling too much on her turbulent feelings for Faulk and his demand of marriage. She must take one day at a time. One problem at a time.

If only she had her mother with her. Nadine felt so bereft without her guidance. Even Denise, her dearest friend, could offer her some comfort and support.

But Nadine was alone, and she must learn to rely only on herself.

The immense burden weighed her down, and Nadine trudged out of the garden and into the manor.

Evening came almost as a surprise. Nadine rolled off the bed where she'd spent the whole afternoon and dressed in a hurry. Through the window she could see it was dark outside, though she couldn't say what time it was.

She rushed out of her room. Supper should be served by now, and she was starving. Her ankle bothered her some, but in the scheme of things it was the least of her problems.

As she began to descend the torch-lit stairs Nadine noticed Robert and Eva were just ahead of her. She was about to call to them when Robert's growl reached her.

"I warn you, Eva. My patience is at the end."

"I am sorry," Eva whispered.

"By all that is sacred," he spat. "Do you continue to deny me I shall find myself a leman."

"Nay." Eva touched Robert's arm for a fleeting moment, then lowered her head as if in resignation.

"You leave me no choice," Robert mumbled.

Nadine stepped back and waited a few moments until the sound of their footsteps echoed away. Then she took to the stairs again.

What was Robert talking about? He seemed terribly upset with Eva. A lover's spat soon to be resolved, no doubt. And yet Nadine sensed it was more serious than that.

Nadine shook her head. It was none of her business. No one had asked her opinion, and she was not about to interfere in a married couple's problems. She had her own matters to resolve.

Moments later Nadine entered the great hall. Eva, catching sight of her, left Robert's side to join Nadine. Robert continued to the table where Faulk and Lord Heathborne were already seated, sharing an intimate conversation over their metal goblets.

Eva's smile didn't reach her eyes, and Nadine was aware of the reason. Unsure if she should ignore Eva's distress or say something comforting, Nadine hesitated as she smiled back. Judith strolled to their side making any further conversation impossible.

"Lady Nadine, can you guess the content of their conversation?" Judith pointed to her father and Faulk.

The hair on the back of Nadine's neck prickled. What was Judith up to? "The king's message?" Nadine suggested.

"Well, the king must have come up in the conversation, but nay. 'Twas much more personal."

Nadine waited in silence. She had no doubt Judith didn't need to be prodded.

"They talk about a betrothal agreement," Judith elucidated, barely concealing her delight.

Nadine's heart skipped a beat. Why would Faulk discuss their betrothal with Lord Heathborne? And why would Judith be pleased with the news?

"Whose betrothal?" Eva asked.

Judith spared Eva a quick glance, then returned her attention to Nadine. "Why, mine and Lord Faulk's, of course." Judith positively glowed.

Sacré Coeur!

"That is not possible," Eva said, clearly shocked. "Lord Faulk is—"

Nadine squeezed Eva's hand in warning. Surely Judith was just baiting her, as she'd done since Nadine's arrival at her house.

"I foresee no difficulty in obtaining the king's approval."

Judith spoke as if the king's approval were a mere formality. Had Faulk already agreed to this? But how could he when hours ago he had asked *her* to marry him?

Could he be that desperate for an heir that he would consider this wasp for a wife? Nadine just couldn't believe it. What about all that talk of prophecy and destiny? It made no sense.

Either Judith had gone insane, or Nadine had been totally wrong about Faulk.

Nadine would rather believe the first.

Yet what if Faulk had decided to accept what was so blatantly offered to him? Could she condemn him? Faulk had repeatedly asked Nadine to marry him, and she had not only refused him, but had never given him any hope she might change her mind.

Didn't Faulk have a right to live his life? Wasn't she planning to leave this century, and therefore him, anyway?

"I believe someone shall be very disappointed this eve," Judith said, pivoting and sauntering to the table.

Unable to move, Nadine took great pains to hide her qualms. Try as she might, though, she couldn't quite master the fake smile plastered on her face, nor swallow down the bitter taste of doubt. She told herself that if Faulk had decided to marry Judith, it would be for the best, for the thought of leaving him had weighed on her. This way she would be free to return to her own time without regrets.

But if she truly felt this way, why did her heart ache so?

"Worry not, Nadine," Eva said. "Lady Judith is a witch. Lord Faulk would never act so dishonorable toward you."

The petite blonde looked up at Nadine and reassuringly squeezed her hand. Her show of friendship moved Nadine. "Thank you for your support, Eva, but Lord Faulk has every right to—"

"Nadine."

Her heart thumped uncontrollably. Faulk's voice had this ability of shaking her.

"Please join us," he said, escorting her to the table. As they sat, he whispered, "Do not contradict what I say, I beseech you."

Unsure of what Faulk wanted of her, Nadine kept her silence. She stole a glance at Judith, who didn't look nearly as smug as before as her father whispered in her ear.

Lord Heathborne turned his attention on Faulk. "I am saddened to learn you must depart on the morrow."

They were leaving? A sliver of hope unfurled in Nadine's heart.

"One must not make the king wait overlong," Faulk answered.

Nadine relaxed. She had been right. The conversation had been about the king's missive.

Lord Heathborne nodded. "Kings are not known for their patience."

Knowing a little about the history of kings, Nadine thought it an understatement.

"I thank you for your hospitality," Faulk said, "and for your aid in gathering the neighboring lords this forenoon."

Lord Heathborne accepted Faulk's thanks with a small nod. "Lords are notorious for not wanting to part with their men, seasoned knights or nay. Yet the king needs our support. Besides, our families have been friends for generations. I could not deny a friend's request."

"I am in your debt."

Lord Heathborne looked pleased. "I wish you good fortune in your endeavor. And on your wedding."

Mon Dieu! Nadine's heart constricted. She had been wrong. It was about a wedding. Hers or Judith's?

Faulk took Nadine's hands into his. "Lady Nadine must continue on her quest. As soon as we find her family, we shall solemnize our betrothal."

Nadine gasped. Faulk squeezed her hand gently, and when she turned to him, he smiled at her, dimple and all, but his somber eyes warned her to be quiet.

Nadine glanced back at Judith—who had turned the color of her hair—and she felt sorry for her. Did Judith love Faulk?

"You shall be hard-pressed to obtain the king's permission to wed a *lady* without family or connection," Judith spat. Derision dripped from the word *lady,* leaving no doubt of her opinion of Nadine, erasing Nadine's commiserating feelings toward her.

"After all," Judith continued, "you are hardly a landless knight. The king has a vested interest in you."

"Verily," Faulk replied calmly. "Yet knowing I am one of his most loyal vassals in England, the king saw fit to grant me the right to choose my own wife. And I choose Nadine."

"May good fortune be on your side," Lord Heathborne said, visibly pinching his daughter to silence.

And I choose Nadine.

Nadine basked in the joy of such words, yet the realization of what those words meant sent her into a new spiral of worry.

Faulk meant to marry her as soon as he located her family. What he didn't know was that there was no family to be found, and that finding her family was not the real reason behind her refusal to marry him.

"I have never been so humiliated in my entire life," Judith raged. With her guests abed—they would depart early on the morrow—Judith, exploding with anger, hurled through the air whatever objects had the misfortune to be in her path, mindless of the ruckus she caused.

"How could you not convince Lord Faulk to wed me instead of that bag of bones he calls Nadine?" Judith demanded of her father. "A woman without a family, property?"

Ducking from a heavy leather-bound ledger that barely missed his left ear, Lord Heathborne tried to calm his wayward daughter. "What would you have me do? Throw him in a dungeon until he agreed to wed you? The man had his mind made up. Besides, he is too powerful a lord to be antagonized."

"Antagonize? You should have killed the bastard for refusing your daughter."

"You speak nonsense, Judith. Lord Faulk refused the union betwixt the two of you with the utmost respect, and assured me his aid, in case of need. Besides, he is in my debt now. Even you can understand what that means."

Frustrated, Judith sat back down a heavily ornate carving of a dragon she had intended to cast at the wall. "Aye, Father, I understand. Lord Faulk is indeed a precious ally, but not so the bag of bones."

"Judith," Lord Heathborne warned. "I forbid you even to consider doing harm to the lady. 'Twould surely bring Lord Faulk's wrath upon our heads."

"What am I supposed to do, then? Meekly accept this ignominy?"

Lord Heathborne walked to his daughter's side and embraced her. "We shall find you another suitable husband," he soothed. "Lord Faulk is not the only worthy man in Christendom."

Judith seethed. She wanted no other man. If her father would do naught for fear of jeopardizing his friendship with Faulk, then 'twas up to her to find a way to get what she wanted. And she *would* get what she wanted.

Chapter 10

ROLAND DU MONTE sat atop his horse a safe distance away from the Heathborne's manor. He had set spies to watch the manor all night long, but when dawn arrived, he could not stay abed and wait for tidings. His Nadine was alive, and the very thought he could see her again thrilled him to action.

He debated how best to proceed, and decided to try and learn more from Lady Judith. If, perchance, he saw Nadine there, he would pretend surprise. He would explain he thought her dead, and be overjoyed by her fortuitous return.

Nadine would, no doubt, be overjoyed to see him, too, her only family kin. That is, if she knew naught of his involvement in her abduction. But surely, she did not, otherwise she would have already returned home and displaced him. Especially if she had the help of a Faulk Brookstone. He was a complication Roland was not sure how to deal with.

What he had learned in his inquiry about the man had utterly displeased him. A seasoned warrior, a wealthy landlord, and a loyal vassal to the king, one specially liked by Richard.

All brawn and no brain, that was his kind. Surely Nadine would not choose Faulk over him. Doubt nagged at Roland. Nadine had been less than overtaken by his charms before her kidnapping. Would she change her mind now?

He must chance it.

As Roland rode closer to the manor, a caravan of mounted, armed men left through the side gate and marched into the street. Roland slowed his horse down, pretending to be just a passerby. Soon he spied Nadine leaving the manor along with another lady, followed by Lord Faulk and a knight. Their mounts were ready, waiting for them.

Roland continued on, passing the manor, intentionally indifferent to the commotion, until he reached the corner of the street. There he turned, hiding behind a small wooden area. He watched the cortege pass by, counting four men-at-arms, the ladies, Lord Faulk, and one knight. Not too impressive of an escort, though all were big men, armed to their teeth.

A physical confrontation was not in Roland's mind. He was not a fighting man. Cunning was his weapon. He observed the entourage disappear out of his line of vision, then turned around and headed for Judith's manor.

"I hope you will forgive my calling on you so early in the morn," Roland said as he sat before Judith in front of the hearth, "but I was restless to assure myself you have recovered from your ordeal."

" 'Tis kind of you to care," Judith said as Roland accepted a tankard of ale from a servant. "I cringe to think what could have happened had you not come to my rescue at the market fair."

Roland had a feeling Lady Judith knew exactly how to take care of herself, but he would not dispute her words. "I pray you are well."

"Indeed." The corner of her mouth twitched bitterly.

"I trust your guests are equally well." He was eager to find out more about Nadine's destination.

"My guests have departed." Judith smoothed an invisible crease on her skirts. "Lord Faulk had matters to resolve with the king, and a quest to undertake for the Lady Nadine."

"A quest?" Roland sat up in attention.

"Aye. A quest to locate the little twit's family." Judith dropped all pretense. Her chair screeched in protest as she rose. Unable to contain her rage Judith paced in circles. "I cannot comprehend how a man like Faulk can possibly be interested in such an insipid creature. She cannot even remember her family. Ha!"

" 'Tis odd, indeed," Roland agreed. "The lady remembers not her family?"

"That is what she claims. As if a little accident could erase a person's memory." Judith sneered in contempt. "Nonsense. I say the woman is lying through her teeth. She more than likely knows she is a nobody, and has created this delusion to sway Lord Faulk into wedding her. Once the deed is done, he is too much of an honorable man to set her aside. The witch! She should be burned at the stake for her evil ways."

Roland listened to Judith's tirade with feigned sympathy. He could not believe his good fortune. Heaven smiled upon him. Even if Nadine had learned of his involvement in her kidnapping, she would probably never remember much. After such an ordeal, her mind should be empty and pliable. A plan formed on his mind.

"I concur. Such terrible deeds should not go unpunished," he said.

Judith stopped her jittery pacing and eyed Roland intently. An evil light shone in the woman's light blue eyes. She walked slowly back to his side and sat at the chair before him. "Do you believe the lady could be proven false?"

" 'Twould be a difficult task to undertake."

"Lady Nadine has played me for a fool and I shall demand reparation. 'Tis a matter of justice."

"Justice comes in different measures." Roland paused. " 'Tis a treacherous time we live now. Outlaws scamper about making the roads such a perilous place to be . . ."

Bending forward, Judith exhibited her more than generous breasts to his review. "Mayhap fate could be aided by an avenging angel." She reached deep into her bosom and withdrew a huge ruby attached to a long, thin, silver cord and dangled it before him.

Roland waited in silence for a long moment, as if pondering on the wisdom of her request. Then, taking Judith's hand, along with the jewel, within his, he brought them down on his knees.

"Mayhap I could be persuaded to be the instrument of your justice, my lady." Oh, he was so clever! Roland beamed inside.

Judith smiled wickedly. She ran her hand up his thigh and touched him where he wanted. "And I shall use you accordingly."

Nadine teetered on the brink of despair.

When she'd found out she'd traveled back in time, her first reaction, besides the obvious panic, had been to immediately find a way to return home.

However, each minute spent in this century made home a very indistinct place. Where was home? In the future where she had come from, where her detailed planned life remained unfulfilled, waiting for her? Or here, in this medieval setting, where she couldn't see herself fit in any particular scheme but Faulk's arms?

Faulk. The sight of him, the smell of him, the thought of him embedded her thoughts. He was dependable, honorable, and truthful. All she wished in a man.

Why couldn't she have met him in the future? Why

wasn't she born in this century? It would all be so simple then.

In this state of mind Nadine welcomed Faulk's silence. Perhaps he, too, was caught in conflicting emotions. Nadine was certain he must have his doubts about her. She knew she didn't behave as a normal medieval damsel. If only she could tell him the truth. That was another weight on her mind. She hated lies. Yet, sometimes the truth could hurt more than a white lie. For now she needed to stick with her amnesia story.

Nadine lifted her eyes to the cloudy sky. It would soon rain. They'd left London behind two days ago and now they were in the middle of nowhere, with no shelter from the coming rain but the canopy of trees in the surrounding forest. The wind picked up momentum, flapping her uncovered hair to her face. Brushing the strands away from her eyes, Nadine saw Faulk rushing suddenly to her side. She thought he wished for her to seek shelter, but soon realized the urgency on his face had nothing to do with the coming rain.

Before she had a chance to understand what was happening, she found herself, along with Eva, rounded up inside a protective circle formed by Faulk and his men, all still mounted. Comprehension finally hit her when a band of men, brandishing swords in the air, hastened toward the circle.

Some days ago, in a chance conversation with Eva, Nadine had inquired about the need of an escort for their trip. Misunderstanding her, Eva had proceeded to defend Faulk and her husband, explaining that seasoned men-at-arms, chosen for their strength and bravery, composed their small escort.

At the time Nadine had decided not to correct Eva of her erroneous notion, accepting her reassurance, when she really had thought the protection unnecessary.

Now she hoped Faulk hadn't been too conservative as the outlaws visibly outnumbered them.

Taking her cues from Eva, who stoically sat on her mare, Nadine held to the horse's reins for dear life. Eva swirled her mount to the back, leaving Nadine to face the opposite side. This way they could watch each other's back. There were no need for words between them, and Nadine was glad Eva had not started crying in panic, for if she had, Nadine was sure she couldn't have contained her own gripping fear.

In the inner safety of the circle, Nadine watched horrified the melee around her. Each man had at least two attackers to contend with, but Faulk seemed to have been singled out. Maybe they thought if they disabled the obvious leader, then the rest would flee or surrender.

As the seconds slowly trickled by, the fight became fiercer. The protective circle decreased and increased, forcing Nadine to struggle to control her distraught mare. The whinny of the horses commingled with the grunts and cries of the fighting men in a disharmony of sounds.

Faulk, Robert, and the men-at-arms wielded their mighty swords in all directions, their blades cutting through flesh like sharp knives through cheese. The assailants fell like swatted pesky mosquitoes, but still their numbers were overpowering, and as many would fall, others would take their places. The metallic smell of blood, clinging sweat, and scared horses permeated the heavy, humid air. Grunts of exertion blended with moans of pain and the sound of swords clashing.

One of Faulk's men suffered a mortal hit and fell to the ground. His horse, after trampling the poor man, stampeded to the nearby woods, leaving a gap in the safety circle. However, instead of venturing inside, the attacking men ignored the opportunity and piled up against Faulk.

In that moment Nadine realized this was more than a random attack, a robbery attempt. In the pit of her stomach she felt Faulk was the intended victim. And she would be damned if she would stand idle and allow these demons to harm him.

But what could she do? Her hands sought the eating knife inside the pouch on her saddle. Her fingers gripped the handle of the small weapon. Instinctively she pitched it through the air and into the attacking man's neck with unerring precision.

Incredulity at what she had done paralyzed Nadine with shock. Hazily she witnessed the attacker fall gurgling to the ground, bringing with him the sword he had pointed at Faulk's uncovered head.

Faulk dispatched two more of his attackers. And as their numbers dwindled, the remaining assailants, obviously aware of the losing battle, chose to flee into the woods instead of fighting to their deaths. Robert and one man-at-arm promptly chased them.

The sky chose that moment to tear apart and deluge the ground with its cleansing rain. Thick, cold drops fell down over the scattered bloodied corpses.

Shaking, Nadine fought the bile that rose to her throat. *Mon Dieu,* she had just killed a man. She, who couldn't kill a fly without feeling guilty, had just killed a man.

Nadine closed her eyes to erase the image in front of her.

As her tears mingled with the blunt drops of the rain, the full realization of what had just happened hit her. Faulk could have died! She could have died!

Life was just like the engorged drops of water falling from the sky. Unpredictable. Unstable. Unreliable.

Nadine felt strong hands pull her off her horse. She opened her eyes, and in a daze she fell into the safety of Faulk's arms. Smashed against his armor, Nadine let out her fear and sorrow and heartrending sobs.

" 'Tis over now," he whispered. "You handled yourself well, my fair lady."

She clung to him in desperation, abandoning herself to

his embrace as if there wouldn't be another. He'd saved her life twice, and she'd just saved his. A deep bond formed between them, binding her to him as surely as he must now be bound to her.

After what seemed an endless time, Faulk pushed her gently away. "There is much to be done," he said, turning his back to her and examining his surroundings.

"Edgard," he called to one of his men-at-arms. "Remove Simon to the shelter of the trees, so he can be better tended." Pivoting, he addressed Nadine. "You, too, should seek shelter from the rain." The words were barely out of his mouth when he wavered unsteadily on his feet.

Nadine spotted his sway at the same time she saw blood trickling down his face. She stepped up to him, her hands reaching for him. A huge bump rose above his left eye like a volcano about to erupt. She had been so preoccupied with herself, she hadn't even noticed Faulk was wounded.

"Sacré Coeur! You are hurt!" she cried. Her hands flattened against his chest as he swayed forward. He tried to compensate, moving backward, only to end up collapsing on his back. Nadine held on to him, but it was like holding on to a plane crashing. She fell with him, on top of him, and the impact on his armor-covered chest stole her breath away.

Faulk woke up with a thundering headache. He tried to rise, but the pain exploded in his head, bringing him down with a moan. Confused, he closed his eyes and reached up with his hand to the offending forehead. His fingers touched a minuscule bandage over his left eye, yet above it a huge lump rose unbidden.

"Do not move," a sweet voice told him.

His eyes flared open, and he lost himself in the golden pond of Nadine's eyes. She bent over him, her expression a curious mix of worry and relief. He meant to smile at her but managed only a grimace. And then, in a flash, he knew what had happened.

"My men?" he asked.

"Simon is doing well, and the other men had only minor wounds." She paused. "Remy . . . Well, Remy was buried in the forest."

Faulk's shoulders slumped at the loss of one of his men. He had lost many in battle, but to lose one's man-at-arms in a senseless ambush was much worse.

"Oh, Faulk, we were all so worried about you. After you fainted—"

"I fainted?"

"Well, it was not a surprise considering the hit you received in your head. You were fortunate that the blunt side of the blade hit you instead of the cutting edge. You would probably be dead now, if that had happened."

God's teeth, he had fainted! In all his years of battle not once had he been overtaken by an injury, though his body bore the marks of his many wounds. Yet a mere bump on the head had befallen him, and in front of Nadine, of all people.

"I am happy to see a little color coming to your cheeks," she said, smiling. "You were so pale, I feared the worse."

Faulk groaned.

"Is he awake?"

Faulk turned his head to the sound of Robert's voice. A cool breeze entered through the open flap of the tent. The rain had stopped, and the day outside was bright.

"He just came to," Nadine said.

Did Faulk hear joy in her voice? Determined not to show any more weakness to Nadine, Faulk half-rose in the cot, ignoring the splitting of his skull. "I am awake," he thundered, or at least he tried to, though his voice sounded disgustingly feeble in his ears. "Did you apprehend any of the attackers?"

"Killed two; one coward made his escape."

"Thus we are none the wiser of their intentions," Faulk muttered, the tent spinning around him. "Sit down, Robert. I fear breaking my neck looking up at you."

Robert complied. There were no chairs in the crumpled space; therefore he sat on the edge of the cot. " 'Twas obvious they intended to kill you, Faulk. This was no robbery, nor random attack. They wanted you dead."

"Aye, I assumed so."

"Why would anyone wish to kill you?" Nadine asked Faulk.

Faulk shrugged. "We all have enemies."

"Mayhap 'tis someone you have yet to meet," Robert said.

"Why would a person who Faulk does not even know wish him dead?" Nadine shook her head. "It makes no sense."

"Mayhap 'tis someone who believes Faulk has something of his." Robert stole a glance at Nadine. "A husband seeking his stray wife."

Faulk understood Robert's innuendo immediately, and he did not like it. "You reach for straws, Robert. We must find our nemesis elsewhere."

Nadine must have also picked up on the clue, for she rose to her feet in one long graceful leap. "What are you trying to say, Sir Robert?" Her voice was cool and defiant.

Robert also rose to his feet, forcing Faulk to bend his neck to look at both of them. Accursed weakness! He grabbed the sides of the cot for balance.

"Mayhap there is someone in your past, my lady, who would feel justified in killing Faulk to recover you," Robert said, crowding over Nadine.

She blanched. "I have no husband."

"But, my lady, I understood you remember naught of your past," Robert said.

Nadine went from pallid to crimson. Did she remember

more than she told him? Faulk wondered. But even if she did, 'twould be his affair, not Robert's.

"Enough, Robert," Faulk bellowed.

"I am just pointing out the facts—"

"Cease! You speculate, naught more. I shall have no one, not even you, casting shadows at Nadine. The lady has saved my life, forget it not. I expect an apology."

Robert snapped his lips together for a moment, then relented. "I meant no disrespect, my lord."

"Not to me, to Lady Nadine," Faulk grunted.

"I beg your pardon, my lady. I spoke out of turn."

Looking stricken, Nadine nodded. "I am sure you spoke with Faulk's best interest in mind, but let me assure you," and then she turned pleading eyes to Faulk, "and you that I could never wish you harm." She left the tent swiftly.

Faulk turned his attention to Robert. "What is the matter with you?"

"I could ask you the same. Forgive my impetuous tongue, Faulk, but as your friend, and your knight, I feel I must point out to you how incongruous your behavior has been since you met the Lady Nadine."

"You speak nonsense."

"I speak the truth." Robert stepped closer to Faulk. "You have let your barriers down, my friend. You have lived and breathed every moment since you found Lady Nadine with the sole purpose of making her your wife, based upon an unverifiable prophecy, I might add. You have neglected your task for the king, forgotten your castle, your people, to roam about the kingdom in a bogus quest at the bequest of a lady who either has no memories of her life or wants you to believe it thus."

Faulk's head swirled with Robert's damning accusations. He could not deny the verity of his friend's words, yet only he could fathom the utter importance of Nadine's role in his life. Only through Nadine could Faulk honor his vow to his father and carry on his line. He had failed once. He would not fail again.

And Nadine had saved his life. When he had held her shaking body after the attackers disbanded, Faulk had felt the connection betwixt them strengthened. The prophecy might not be a substantiated document, but Faulk had no doubt of its authenticity.

"She is not my enemy, Robert. She is the answer to my prayers."

"Then bed her, Faulk. Fill her womb with your seed before you make her your wife. Waste not your chance in a flimsy prophecy."

"Do not mistake the easiness with which I treat Nadine as weakness. Think you I know not what I must do? Nadine is of the utmost importance to my plans, and she shall be mine and shall bear my heirs. Worry not about me, Robert. You have your own duties to fulfill." There was a ruthlessness in his tone of voice that brook no doubt of his intentions.

Chagrined, Robert said, "As you wish, my lord." Then he changed subjects. "As soon as you feel well enough, we should raise camp. I like not our present position, and, moreover, we are still a good two days ride from White-castle."

"I am well enough," Faulk said and waited for his head to stop pounding. It did not. Ignoring the throbbing, he swung his legs to the side, and the shock of his bare feet hitting the floor traveled up his leg and body, shaking up his brain. He groaned. Undaunted, he rose to his feet, and as the floor refused to remain still, he feared he would faint again. God forbid! He fought the draining feeling with all his strength until he had it under his control.

"We can move forward as I am eager to reach White-castle. I believe 'tis time for the fulfillment of the prophecy."

Chapter 11

THE SIGHT OF Whitecastle's walls illuminated by a crimson sunset brought an inexplicable surge of happiness to Nadine. A distant feeling echoed in her heart—home. She dismissed the thought; any place would feel like home after so many days on the road. And on a horse's back, for that matter.

Fixing her eyes on the approaching castle, Nadine turned her thoughts to Robert's accusations. His distrust grated on her, and though she couldn't, in good conscience, blame him, she had since avoided any contact with the man.

Faulk had been silent, too. Did he harbor Robert's doubts about her?

The fact that she had escaped death on three separate occasions in the span of just a few days since arriving in this century added extra weight on her mind.

Had she catapulted centuries through time just to die in a freak accident, or was she sent to save Faulk's life as she had done? Was she destined to be his, as he believed? Was Faulk the man the gypsy of the future had told her about?

Nadine was certain that somehow her return in time was connected to Faulk. Now she needed to know how and why.

They finally reached Whitecastle and entered the stronghold. Mildred waited for them in the courtyard. As Nadine was helped off her mare by an eager stable boy, she caught Mildred's look of relief at the sight of her. Then Mildred turned her attention to Faulk, fussing over him like a mother over a baby in the cradle. Again, Nadine felt keenly her own loneliness. A deep longing to be once again part of a loving family washed over her.

Distressed, Nadine followed the others into the great hall. Mildred shouted orders to the serving wenches to make haste and bring food and drink to all, then she ushered Faulk through a side door.

Grabbing an offered chalice, Nadine gratefully gulped the wine down her parched throat, then sat down at the main table. Eva joined her. She set the knife that had saved Faulk's life on the table before Nadine.

Nadine shivered at the sight. She couldn't touch it. "I hope never to use it again." Not in a hundred years would she forget that knife had taken the life of a human being.

"I have never seen a lady wield a knife like you," Eva said.

Neither had she, Nadine thought, still stunned at having accomplished the deed. "Dire actions to dire situations, I guess."

"Would you teach me?"

"I think your husband is better suited to give you such lessons."

Eva shook her head. "Robert is . . . unhappy with me."

Since Nadine overheard Robert and Eva's conversation that last night in London, she noticed Robert was on edge. Could that be the reason he was so distrustful of her?

"Married people sometimes fight," Nadine offered, not knowing what to say. She knew very little about these people and their lives. She hadn't wanted to know, to care. Her passage in this time could prove to be temporary, and Nadine wanted to be prepared to leave without much thought.

"I hope 'twill be different for you, once you wed Lord Faulk, though I cannot see how 'twould. 'Tis a woman's lot in life to endure the bedding. A jest of nature, no doubt."

Bedding? Nadine followed the resigned look Eva darted at Robert. He stared back at her, a huge scowl plastered on his face, his eyes a flaming determination. The undercurrent between those two traveled across the table like an electric charge.

Was that the reason for Robert's foul mood? "Are you telling me that the intimacy between a man and his wife is not something to look forward to?"

" 'Tis a thing to dread, to endure." Eva's hand reached for Nadine's knife, her fingers tightening around the handle. She caught herself, and relaxed her grip, allowing the knife to rest on the table again.

Nadine remembered Faulk's kisses, his caresses, the heat that emanated from his powerful body, and she could not fathom making love with him being anything but wonderful.

She turned her attention back to Robert. He was a handsome man, but maybe he was an inept lover, a medieval man without knowledge of foreplay. But who was she to judge him? She knew something about the mechanics of making love, but she was, technically, only a virgin. A knowledgeable one, but a virgin nonetheless. Could sex be such a disappointment, as Eva evidently felt it was?

"I think you should talk to each other about this," Nadine suggested. "Maybe you can find out what both of you like—"

Eva shot Nadine a horrified look. "I should not like any of it. 'Tis disgusting, demeaning, and only necessary in the breeding of children."

Nadine was the one horrified now. There must be a way she could help Eva get over her inadequate ideas about making love. If only she had more experience.

"I have not thanked you properly for saving my life." Faulk abruptly appeared by her side.

Surprised, Nadine glanced up at him. He wore a bandage over the bump.

"Mildred lanced it for me," he explained. "She assured me I shall survive."

Forgetting about Eva, Nadine watched Faulk sit by her side.

"Who taught you to wield a knife with such skill, my fair lady?"

Didn't anyone realize it had been pure luck she'd hit the man? She couldn't even explain how she'd done it, she had just reacted. *Sacré Coeur*, she could have hit Faulk instead. She could have killed him.

Nadine took a good swallow of wine from the forgotten chalice in her hand. She was remorseful of killing a man, even in self-defense; how much worse would she feel if she had killed Faulk by mistake?

"Lucky shot," she said.

He chuckled. "Not with such steady hands." He took her hands into his, turned them palm up, and then kissed their hollow center. First one, then the other. Soft, fluttering, barely there kisses. His warm breath fanned her skin, giving rise to an electric charge that traveled up her arms and exploded in her breasts, swelling them with need. Her nipples distended against the fabric of her gown, begging for his touch.

Nadine's mouth went completely dry as his raven head lifted from her hands and stopped inches away from her face. The azure of his eyes shone upon her like the brightest star.

"I shall be forever grateful." He smiled, flashing his adorable dimple. Nadine swallowed hard, watching that beautiful face. At this moment all she wanted was for him to kiss her. To envelop her in the cocoon of his powerful arms. To make her his in the most primitive way.

Slowly he rested her hand on the table. " 'Twas a long journey. We should eat, then seek our rest. On the morrow I shall take you to the beach where I first found you, as you requested."

Eat? How could she eat when her stomach somersaulted into knots? The best she could do was to drain her goblet of the last drops of wine hoping to douse the burning unfulfillment of his tantalizing touch. And for the first time Nadine felt a certain kinship with Sir Robert Baldwin.

The sun had just appeared on the horizon bathing the land with its flaming rays when Nadine followed Faulk into the bailey of Whitecastle. Today she could find the answer she sought. Today she could be making the decision to return to her own time and leave Faulk and this century behind.

Though the future didn't hold any expectation of happiness, it was where she belonged, where she was from, and to where she should return.

Then why did she feel as if invisible threads were silently and efficiently binding her to this time? This century's customs and primitive ways no longer shocked her. At breakfast, this morning, she clearly recognized the drink she was served—mead—though she'd never tasted it before. Even their archaic French sounded more and more clear to her ears.

It tore at Nadine to be pulled in two different directions. And her own ambiguity disturbed her. One minute she yielded to the call of the future, and in the next she succumbed to the draw the present exerted on her.

Maybe once she'd seen the place where she'd first appeared, she would know what to do.

However, no matter what she decided, the ramifications would spread out in many different directions, like the woven web of a spider.

"I dispatched two men to Rouen to inquire about your family," Faulk said as he helped her onto her mount.

Nadine sighed. Faulk was going through so much trouble for nothing. First that useless trip to London—well, not exactly useless, for it had revealed her time-travel—and now he wasted his manpower in a fruitless pursuit.

"We shall find them." He patted her hand in reassurance, obviously mistaking her forlorn expression.

"If there is anyone to be found, I have no doubt you will find them, Faulk."

He grinned, evidently pleased with her trust in him.

After leaving the castle they veered into the forest. Nadine inhaled deeply the pure, clean air of the dew-covered grass in early morning. The chirping of the birds followed them like a chime in the morning breeze, yet suddenly Nadine felt chilled to the bone.

It was as if someone was watching her. She stole a quick glance around her but found no one. Urging her mount forward, Nadine followed Faulk in a well-worn path through the thick foliage. It took them a while to reach the beach.

Nadine approached the strip of sand with trepidation. Here was where she'd been washed ashore. Here was where it had all begun. Yet she had no recollection of any of it.

They dismounted. Faulk walked to an unmarked spot. "I found you here."

Nadine moved cautiously to his side, staring numbly at the sand. She circled around slowly. Sand in front and behind of her, the thick forest on her left, the mighty Channel on her right. Nadine felt a stab of uneasiness at the sight of so much water.

She turned her face to the forest, and a sudden dizziness took hold of her. Her head began to buzz and Nadine fell down on her knees, closing her eyes. When she flared them open, all was different. Daylight was gone; night now reigned and a cool breeze whispered through her hair. From the forest emerged a perfect image of her. It was she, yet it was not. She—the image—walked down an unfamiliar stretch of beach illuminated by a full moon.

She scanned the place for a escape. Yes, the certainty came sharply to Nadine, she was escaping. In the Channel a ship wafted, and its sight meant freedom. Nadine felt the exhilaration, then the sudden fear when a thin, small man appeared on the edge of the forest—her pursuer, no doubt.

As she dashed to the Channel, Nadine felt the cold water sting her skin. But the fear of water was not there, only determination and desire to escape as she numbly stroked toward the ship. Feelings of love and home bombarded her, driving her farther and farther into the Channel.

In the distance Nadine heard her name. It took her a moment to recognize Faulk's voice. And then the vision was gone. Out of her mind like a popped balloon in a child's hands.

Nadine struggled to dissipate the feeling of numbness still possessing her limbs. She took a deep breath, willing her heart to slow its maddening pace.

Slowly, painfully, Nadine regained control of her body. She turned her head to the Channel, and the invisible hand of panic once again grabbed her heart at the sight of so much water. Yet a minute ago she had braved it without hesitation.

A sudden conviction broke through the barriers of her consciousness. A resolution to live that echoed in the depths of her soul.

"Nadine, what happened?" Faulk's anxious voice settled her. His strong hands lifted her from the ground.

Nadine shook her head. "I was escaping. I was kept prisoner, and I escaped." What was she saying? She was never anyone's prisoner, the first time she had even considered the thought was when she met Faulk. And he was *not* the weak man who pursued her in her vision.

"Nadine, you have started to remember," he said in wonder.

Baffled, Nadine stared at Faulk. How could she explain to him that the vision could not possibly be a memory, for she'd never faced such a situation? Then she remembered another vision, at the gypsy's place in Rouen, where she'd seen herself tied down on a bed. Could these two visions be somehow connected? Nadine couldn't explain why she had the strange feeling she had lived both situations. How was it possible?

Oh, she couldn't face any of it right now. She wanted to get away from the Channel, from this beach, from the vision.

"Please, take me away from here," she begged Faulk.

Nadine paced her bedroom like a caged animal. Once more, what she'd hoped would yield answers had only succeeded at bringing more questions. What was happening to her?

Feeling suffocated by the walls of her room, Nadine dashed out to the bailey. The sun was high in the sky, and for a moment, she stood disoriented. Then she saw Faulk. She strode closer and admired him while he demonstrated sword-fighting techniques to a dozen men. The sword in his hand appeared weightless as he brandished it through the air in intricately practiced movements. Perspiration shone on his naked back. The droplets slithered from his neck, down his back, disappearing on the waist of his pants. The muscles on his shoulders and back rippled with the movements, showing off their strength.

Desire flowed through Nadine obliterating her thoughts, her plans, and her fears. She was drawn to Faulk like a bee is drawn to the flower. And she knew she could love him. He could be her soul mate. Together they could have what her parents once shared. What she had always wished for. A perfect love.

But what if she was snatched back to the future without warning? Could she survive the loss if she allowed herself to love Faulk and then lost him?

Her heart squeezed at the thought. Turning her back to Faulk, Nadine marched to the gate. Treading cautiously over the weathered boards of the bridge, she reached the other side, then rushed to the forest. She wouldn't go far, she didn't want to get lost. All she needed was the calming effect of the forest around her.

Under the canopy of giant, ancient trees, Nadine sat down and breathed the clean, fresh air. A butterfly hovered over a wild yellow flower, fluttering majestic wings in the air. Its beauty, its delicacy, its place in time stole Nadine's breath. Captivated, she followed its antics. A hazy image of her beloved parents pulled at her heartstrings, stretching them yet not lacerating as before. Nadine's heart sank heavy with longing but not with the usual despair at their deaths.

Suddenly she felt watched as closely and as attentively as she had watched the butterfly. Snapping her head up she saw, standing not two feet away, a woman of unidentifiable age. At first glance she looked young with her long, flowing, dark hair, but a second look revealed a wrinkled face that attested her longevity.

Her benign demeanor prevented Nadine from scampering to her feet and running, as had been her first impulse.

"You are troubled," the woman said. "You need not be. 'Tis as it should be. You belong with him, there is no denying."

By *him* Nadine intuitively understood Faulk. Could this woman be the witch? "Are you the one who told Faulk about the prophecy?"

The witch nodded.

Nadine jumped to her feet. Maybe now she would have some answers. "Then you would know if I am the woman of the prophecy."

"You are the one."

She was the one!

The implication of such confirmation alarmed Nadine.

Her coming was foretold, predestined. How about her staying in this century? Would fate rob Nadine of her free will to choose whether to stay or depart?

"Against fate there is no choice, and I must have a choice."

"Destiny weaves infinite paths for our lives." The witch shrugged. " 'Tis always our choice which ones we take."

If that were true, then it was her choice to return or not to the future. Assuming the witch knew about her predicament—after all, she had foretold Nadine's coming—she would also know what would take her back to her own time. "How can I return home?"

The witch hesitated for a moment, then stared at Nadine with those fathomless eyes of hers. "The water has brought you here, the water can take you away."

Sacré Coeur! Nadine's hand involuntarily covered her mouth. So, it was as she suspected. The Channel was her ticket out. Not such a simple task for someone so afraid of the water.

"You were given a second chance," the witch continued. "Do not waste it."

Those were the same words the gypsy of the future had told Nadine. "A second chance at what?"

"What have you always sought?"

Love? the thought intruded. "I do not belong here." Nadine grasped for some logical thread.

"But you do, my lady, you do."

There was such certainty in the witch's voice that Nadine almost believed her.

"Listen to your heart," she continued. "And 'twill tell you what to do."

Mon Dieu! Was the witch telling Nadine to surrender her heart to Faulk? Could she trust fate not to separate them as it had separated her from her parents?

Indecisiveness cut through Nadine. She shook her head,

unable to wave away the thought of having her heart shattered again by a twist of fate.

"Do you wish to turn your back on your destiny, do so now my lady," the witch warned, "before you take what fate offers you. Do you take what fate offers you, you shall not leave until the time of new birth, and by then, you shall have to fight to remain here."

The wind whistled loudly through the trees, carrying the witch's words in the sudden chilled air. A bird flew near Nadine's head startling her. She swayed to avoid it, and when she next returned her gaze to the spot where the witch had stood, she was no longer there.

After a split moment of hesitation, Nadine dashed into the woods, in pursuit of the witch, but soon realized the woman was gone and she would probably get herself lost if she insisted in braving any deeper into the forest.

Disappointed, Nadine turned around.

Now what? Should she heed the witch's warnings and follow her heart?

Would she have the courage to do so?

The hall was empty but for a few servants arranging the tables for the midday meal when Nadine took the stairs to her bedroom. As she passed Eva's room, she heard sobs.

For a moment she hesitated. Should she interfere? She had her own problems to deal with, yet she couldn't just ignore another person's pain. Nadine knew all too well what it was to be lonely and filled with problems.

She knocked on the door. "Eva, it is Nadine. May I come in?"

A moment later the door opened. Eva's eyes were red and swollen. She motioned Nadine to enter.

"I do not mean to pry, but is there anything I can do?"

Two fat tears rolled down Eva's face as she shook her head. " 'Tis all lost. I have failed in my wifely duties to Robert."

Was Eva referring to the problem they briefly discussed yesterday? The bedding? "I am sure all will be well soon."

"You cannot possibly understand, Nadine. You are still a maiden." Eva slumped down on her bed.

"Yes, but I am not totally unlearned in these matters." Nadine followed Eva. As inexperienced as she was, thanks to a modern education, she probably knew more about sex than Eva would ever learn.

Eva shot Nadine a baffled look. "You are not?"

"Well, theoretically speaking."

"Knowing about it is vastly different from experiencing it."

"Maybe, still I can listen, if you wish to talk."

Eva hesitated. "I do not wish to offend you, but if you are willing, I would wish to speak of it."

"You will not offend me." Nadine patted Eva's hand in reassurance.

"Very well." Eva took a deep breath. "On my wedding eve I dutifully endured my husband's attention. Robert was gentle, but I was so scared and it hurt. . . ." She stole an embarrassed glance at Nadine. "I knew naught about the bedding, and since then I have not been able to accept what I have learned. Thus far, Robert has been patient with me, but lately he has threatened to take a leman, or worse, to set me aside if I do not fulfill my duty to him. I love Robert, Nadine, and I do not wish to lose him, but I know not what to do."

What Robert and Eva needed was a marital counselor or a sex therapist as it was obvious that due in part to a wedding night gone awry and a lifetime of noninformation, Eva was petrified of intimacy. But in this century where could they go for help?

Nadine racked her brain to remember something valuable from the few psychology classes she'd taken, but she was nowhere near qualified to play the counselor. Besides, she lacked the factual experience.

However, she did remember an article she once read about a sex therapy for couples. Nadine couldn't remember all the details but it revolved around getting to know each other intimately, finding pleasure in each other's touches without the added pressure of intercourse, until both of them were ready for it.

"I once read in a magazine—"

"What?" Eva asked, totally confused.

Startled, Nadine realized she had slipped in her conscientious effort not to use modern expressions. With a sudden flash of ingenuity, she amended, "I once heard a tale spun that related to a problem similar to yours."

"Indeed?"

Nadine nodded, relieved Eva hadn't questioned her slip. "This lady loved her husband very much, yet she could not make him happy in the marital bed."

Eva blushed.

"You see, she was afraid of her own feelings about it."

"She knew she would never enjoy it," Eva said.

"She *thought* she would never enjoy it," Nadine corrected. "But she wanted to make her husband happy, and she wanted children," Nadine added for good measure.

"Aye." Eva's eyes watered again. "Was there an answer?"

"A simple one, indeed. She consulted a witch—a good witch—who gave her a wise counsel. A few easy steps to follow and all would be well. But the husband and the wife must be willing to trust each other."

Doubt shadowed Eva's face. "What exactly must be done?"

"Well, the couple should touch each other intimately—"

Eva's eyes widened in terror.

"—as long as it is pleasurable. But no penetration is allowed until they are ready for it."

Eva's face turned crimson. No doubt a reflection of her

own face, Nadine thought as the thought of playing such a game with Faulk warmed her insides.

Eva looked skeptical. "I know not if I can address such matters with Robert."

"Do not let fear blind you." Nadine noticed Eva didn't seem unwilling, only frightened. And that she could understand. "The future of your marriage is in your hands. Fight for it or give it up. It is your choice."

Suddenly stunned at the parallel between her situation and Eva's, Nadine wondered if she would have the courage to trust her heart as she had just demanded of Eva.

Chapter 12

A STRONG SMELL of pine invaded Faulk's nostrils as he soaped and scrubbed his body with glee. Scum from the filth of the road and the sweat of exertion gathered in the water around him. He had meant to bathe last eve, after supper, before pursuing his seduction of the fair Nadine, however, his splitting head convinced him to give himself, and her, a night's respite.

This morn he had forgone the bath in lieu of more pressing matters, yet when this eve arrived, he postponed no more. Having noticed Nadine's penchant for baths, Faulk washed himself with deliberate attention. He was all for cleanliness, prescribing weekly baths to himself and all in Whitecastle, though he knew few followed his advice. Yet, Nadine took it a step further. She intended to bathe daily, according to Mildred, who complained to him that Nadine would surely sicken with so much washing.

For a lady who had almost drowned, 'twas peculiar she so enjoyed bathing. Faulk was baffled but not displeased. In sooth, he delighted in the fresh, clean smell of her skin, and the rose fragrance of the soap she used, which lingered on her even when they had been on the road.

Faulk closed his eyes for a moment and the memory of her scent engulfed him. He hardened in anticipation.

Nadine was an unusual lady, he thought as he glided out of the bathing tub and dried himself. She was secretive, almost solemn at times, she was stubborn, yet she was also witty and sweet. On occasion she had looked utterly out of place, but there were times when she fit perfectly. Her speech, though improved, still retained that hint of oddity he could not quite place, yet her poise declared her high-born status. A walking contradiction Nadine was, and Faulk knew he should look closer into her past. He, of all people, should know how treacherous a woman could be.

And this particular woman was far too important to his line.

Yet whoever Nadine was had no bearing in the prophecy, and thus he cared not. The puzzle of her past would eventually fall in place. In sooth, the first piece had already been revealed this morn, on the beach, when Nadine suddenly remembered being kept prisoner before they met, confirming his earlier suspicions of foul play.

He rolled the drying cloth into a ball and cast it to the floor. Whoever meant harm against Nadine would pay dearly for their perfidy. Meanwhile, though, 'twas time to make Nadine undeniably his. Once impregnated with his seed she would have no choice but to accept her role in his life.

Faulk felt so strongly about the prophecy that he dismissed his nagging doubts about Nadine's availability. Nadine was destined to be his, and she could belong to no other.

He remembered her knowing kisses. That she had been kissed before was a fact. How much more did the lady know? In his youth Elizabeth had duped him, but since then he had learned much. If Nadine possessed her maidenhead intact, he would know. He wished not to dwell on the possibility that she did not.

Aye, seducing her would be a pleasurable task, no doubt, for the lady was beautiful. Nevertheless, Faulk reminded himself, were the lady as ugly as a spitting-fire dragon, he would still bed her, still wed her, still make her his.

In sudden haste Faulk finished dressing and went in search of Nadine.

There was no sign of her at the hall, which surprised him not, for Nadine had a penchant for arriving late for the meals.

"Where is Lady Nadine?" he asked Mildred, who hurried by him carrying a flask of wine and goblets.

"Humph." Mildred halted. "She bathes again. Lord Faulk, you must speak with her—"

"Worry not, Mildred." Faulk took the flask and two goblets from Mildred's hands. "I shall do just that." He spun around and headed back to the stairs, taking two steps at a time.

Outside Nadine's bedchamber he stopped. He pushed the door slightly ajar and was about to enter when he heard her sweet voice singing a love melody.

The melodious sound aroused his senses. His heart thudded in his chest, his shaft lengthened in agony. He pushed the door open and the vision of pure loveliness that greeted him took his breath away.

Nadine stood with her smooth back, perfect buttocks, and shapely legs bared to him. The sight jarred his insides.

"God's teeth! You are the fairest of them all."

Nadine almost shrieked at hearing Faulk's husky voice behind her, yet, somehow, she controlled herself and swallowed down the last verses of Charles Aznavour's love song. She straightened her back and spun around, allowing the towel she was using to dry her hair to fall and partially cover the front of her naked body. She would show no fear. She was not a wimpy medieval virgin. Well, she was a virgin, and she did feel like a wimp sometimes, but she was *not* medieval.

With one hand Nadine held the towel in place, and with the other she ran her fingers through her tangled hair. She had wanted this to happen. However, to think about it, to fantasize about being with Faulk was one thing, to have his powerful presence in her room while she stood half naked, dripping water on the cold stone floor was another.

"You are the fairest of them all, Nadine," he whispered again, and his eyes devoured every uncovered inch of her.

Nadine's heart thumped desperately in her chest and her blood hummed loudly in her ears. What on earth was she supposed to do now? She surely didn't want to send him away. After all that talk with Eva about facing one's own fears, she couldn't back out now.

"At least shut the door," she said, before she lost the little courage she possessed. "There is no sense in exposing myself to the entire castle."

He cocked his head in surprise, then grinned, showing that wicked dimple, making her heart pump impossibly faster. With the back of his booted foot he shut the door, then walked to the table, where he set down the flask and two chalices he had been carrying.

While Faulk poured the wine—the gurgling sound reached her clearly in the silence of the room—Nadine composed herself, hastily wrapping the towel around her body and knotting it above her breasts, thankful for the semidarkness of the room which would undoubtedly mask her flaming cheeks.

She watched as Faulk strolled lazily to her and offered her a chalice of wine. She took a good swallow.

She could do this.

"You know why I am here?" he asked.

She nodded.

"Do you send me away?"

She shook her head.

He grinned, then reached for her and pulled back a strand of wet hair that had fallen on her face. His huge hands burrowed in her hair, cupping her nape and tilting her head up. His sparkling blue eyes darkened a shade, or maybe it was the darkness of the room that made them look so intense, so dangerous. He brought his head down and closer to her face, looming above her for a moment. Nadine closed her eyes and inhaled the pine scent from his skin. His lips brushed hers. The noninvasive touch surprised her, but with each new nibble he reached deeper, explored further, demanded more.

Nadine's senses reeled, her stomach clenched, her head spun dizzily. He pulled her closer to his powerful body, molding her to his hardness, letting her know without a doubt the extent of his desire.

She could do no less.

The chalice fell from her hand to the floor with a clank as Nadine encircled Faulk's waist and pulled him to her. He growled savagely, lifted her up and pulled her legs around his hips, then carried her with him to the bed.

He fell on top of her. Thankfully, he had the presence of mind to brace one arm against the mattress, thus avoiding crushing her under his great weight. The towel hiked up her legs, exposing her to him, reminding her he was still fully clothed.

How unfair, Nadine thought, but when his tongue invaded and possessed and conquered her mouth once more, all her thoughts turned to smoke. He rocked against her, eliciting sensations she'd only dreamed of. A desire to reach . . . somewhere, something . . . grew in her with agonizing relentless. A frustrating and at the same time exhilarating feeling.

Nadine moaned in anticipation.

And Faulk rolled off of her.

"Oh, do not go," Nadine cried, surprised at her own audacity.

"Ah, my fair lady. I go nowhere but back to you."

He got rid of his clothes with swift, economic movements, presenting himself to her in all his naked glory. His massive frame of rippling muscles looked leaner than the Mister Universe's pictures she'd seen, yet Faulk was still tremendously powerful.

His washboard stomach—had she ever seen anything like it?—tapered down to a mass of dark curly hair. Nadine's gaze lowered, then she swallowed hard.

Now, she should scream.

"I vow to be gentle with you," he said as he knelt down by her side on the bed.

Nadine scooped herself up, unraveling the knot of the towel. It opened invitingly. What did he mean by that? Was he always gentle, or was he going to make an effort to be gentle with her? Nadine hoped Faulk had total control of his impressive physique.

Eva's forlorn words chose the wrong moment to invade her thoughts. *The bedding is a thing to dread, to endure.* Could it be true?

Doubt washed over her. "Faulk . . ."

With a soft touch of his finger to her lips he hushed her. " 'Tis as it should be." He stretched alongside of her and introduced one leg between hers as his hand crept up her side. Trailing kisses down her nose and lips and throat, he reached her breasts. He devoted an inordinate time worshipping them. Nadine never guessed how sensitive they could be. Liquid fire scalded her insides.

His finger probed her moist core, testing its depth, his palm cupped her, rubbing against her sensitive skin. Nadine's eyelids fell closed, and she surrendered to the sensations Faulk's mouth and hand elicited from her. Sensations no human could be expected to endure without dying of pleasure. She writhed against him, wanting to escape from his touch and at the same time knowing that she would die if he moved away.

Nestling himself between her thighs, he withdrew his hand and positioned his steeled member at her entrance.

"Look at me, Nadine." His voice was husky, restrained.

She flared her eyes open.

" 'Tis I who takes you. Faulk Brookstone who lays rights upon you."

She opened her mouth to dispute his pretentious words, but at that moment he entered her in one sweeping thrust.

This time, Nadine screamed.

Faulk could not hold back the roar of satisfaction that escaped his throat as he tore through Nadine's maidenhead. She had been untouched. She was now undeniably his. The prophecy had not failed him.

The triumphant emotion was almost his undoing. Fighting the escalating explosion, he held himself completely still, controlling his mind, willing his body not to give in too soon. He had planned a long seduction of his fair Nadine. He had expected the need for it, yet as always, Nadine surprised him, surrendering as she did. And he had pressed on, as any warrior worth his salt would have, for complete victory.

God's teeth, but she was tight. And hot. And wet. And if she did not stop wriggling under him, 'twould soon be all over.

"Cease your struggles, my fair lady. The pain shall soon pass."

"Easy for you to say," she said, but heeded his warning.

He almost chuckled, but the sight of her pained expression disquieted him. Mayhap he had been too forceful. Yet, had he given her time to think, Nadine would have denied him again. 'Twas her way. And that he could not have chanced. The pain he caused her was inevitable, yet fleeting; 'twas now his task to guide her to pleasure.

His lips touched hers tenderly, but at the first taste of her he became restless again. His tongue found refuge in her welcoming mouth, and as he plunged into her soft depths the irresistible urge to thrust into her tight sheath almost overwhelmed him.

Drawing from a depleted pool of willpower, Faulk resisted the calling. Lifting his face from hers he drew in a deep breath. "Easy," he whispered, not sure if to himself or to Nadine. "Are you still in pain, my fair lady?"

She bit her bottom lip, then whispered, "No."

With their gazes locked, Faulk pulled back, almost entirely withdrawing from her. He heard her intake of breath. Saw the emotions cross her expressive face—anticipation mingled with apprehension.

" 'Twill feel good," he promised, wishing to see pleasure stamped on her face. He understood not why 'twas so important to him, yet he longed for her total capitulation, for his mastery over his fair Nadine.

Holding himself above her, he deliberately raked his hand down her body to where they were still joined. Burrowing his finger in her golden curls, he found her pleasure spot hid within. With the pad of his thumb he circled it until her eyes grew wide, and continued the caress until he was rewarded with her moans.

In an offering he could hardly refuse, Nadine arched to him. As he slowly sunk into paradise, Nadine remained with him. With each new deep thrust in the old cadence of love, Nadine followed him. And when he drowned in the pool of pleasure that was her, her passionate cries mingled with his shout of release as his seed found shelter in her womb.

God's teeth, Faulk thought as he rode into oblivion, but the lady unmanned him.

A slit of weak sunlight filtered through the window, awakening Nadine. She promptly closed her eyes again and stretched lazily. For the first time in weeks she had slept like a stone, even though she had only fallen asleep at the onset of dawn. She tossed to the side and opened her eyes to an empty pillow beside her. Faulk was gone.

Memories of the night came rushing to her along with Faulk's pine scent in the pillow she embraced. Never in her predictable, organized, simple life could she have dreamed that making love could be so . . . The words failed her. So incredible, so overwhelming, so powerful.

For a moment last night she had actually doubted her wisdom in allowing Faulk to remain in her room. Of course, the fact that the discomfort she had expected to feel at the first penetration turned out to be a lacerating pain had something to do with it.

The memory of the earsplitting scream she had let out brought heat to her cheeks. She wasn't the screaming kind. Yet last night she had cried out more than once. She giggled. If she'd known then that the pain would so soon disappear, obliterated by such pleasure she never even dreamed existed, she'd have saved Faulk's eardrums from that first scream.

However, she wouldn't withdraw any of her cries of pleasure every time they made love during that long, incredible night, when she doubted it could get any better, then discovered that indeed it could.

Making love with Faulk had sealed her fate. Now that she had allowed him into the recesses of her body and soul, she knew it would devastate her if she lost him, like she had lost her parents. She hoped that the prophecy would hold true, that she, in fact, belonged with Faulk, for all time.

An overwhelming need to see him took hold of her, but before she had a chance to rise from the bed, Mildred entered the room. She took in the disarray of the bed, the wet towel on the floor, the still full bathtub on the corner of the room in silence, then walked straight to the table and set down a food tray.

Mortified to think Mildred had guessed what happened

in this room last night, Nadine was thankful Faulk had left earlier.

Blushing furiously, Nadine wrapped herself in the bed-sheet, before she tossed the coverlet aside. As soon as she rose she noticed the bloodstain—the proof of her compromising—glaring from the white sheet. Catching Mildred's knowing eyes, Nadine realized it would be useless to try to hide the evidence. She swallowed down an embarrassed groan.

"Here, my lady," Mildred offered. "Allow me to help you." Taking Nadine's arm, Mildred guided her to the chair with the utmost care, then she turned and busied herself making the bed.

Nadine glanced at the tray, but suddenly her appetite was gone. She closed her eyes for a moment. When she opened them, Mildred was at her side.

"Be not vexed, my lady. Lord Faulk has announced your coming wedding to all who cared to hear."

Sacré Coeur! Did the whole castle know what happened in this room last night?

The idea of walking into a great hall filled with people who would stare at her knowing she had made love with Faulk dismayed Nadine. She hadn't counted on her love life becoming public domain. Yet she should've known that gossip would sparkle instantly the moment it was discovered that Faulk had spent the night in her room.

The knock on the door made her jump. Mildred never knocked before entering, Nadine thought, and the notion probably never crossed Faulk's mind.

Eva peeked from behind the door. "May I come in?"

"Please do." She might as well start facing them, one by one.

Eva pushed the door open all the way, then glanced inside, as if assuring herself Nadine was alone. She looked like the messenger of bad news.

"Is something wrong?" Nadine asked.

"I heard your scream last eve." The words rushed out of Eva's mouth. "I wished to come to your rescue, but Robert ordered me not to interfere. I am sorry." She was downcast.

Speechless, Nadine felt the heat rising to her face again. How many times would she have to blush this day?

"We were passing outside your door. We could not help hearing," Eva explained.

"I see," Nadine managed to say. At least her indiscretion had not carried over to the hall. At least she hoped it had not.

"How do you fare?"

Considering Eva's feelings on the subject, she probably expected torn limbs and bloody walls. Nadine smiled reassuringly. "I am fine."

Assessing the truthfulness in her words, Eva was apparently satisfied Nadine would survive. She merely nodded and handed over a flask she held in her hands. " 'Tis a salve. 'Twill make you feel better."

Nadine was indeed sore, yet knowing now what she knew about making love she would risk serious pain for the incredible pleasure she had experienced.

"I appreciate your concern, but I am really fine." Nadine took the flask from Eva's hand, ignoring her mystifying look.

"Lord Faulk seems inordinately pleased with himself." Eva scowled, then padded Nadine's hand in doubtful reassurance. "Fear not for your reputation. Lord Faulk has announced your coming wedding. Besides,"—she smiled in womanly camaraderie—"I understand you had no choice last eve."

Nadine bristled. "I most certainly had a choice. Faulk did not force himself on me, Eva. He gifted me with the most glorious experience of my life."

"You need not lie to me." Clearly Eva didn't believe her.

"I speak the truth," Nadine insisted. She wouldn't allow

Faulk to be perceived as a violator of women. He'd never forced himself on her on the many occasions he had the opportunity, even though she knew he believed he had the right to. For a medieval lord with power of life and death over the people under him, he'd behaved in a exceedingly honorable manner with her, and for that she would always respect him.

Besides, she had to let Eva know how wonderful making love could be.

"Then you must jest. By now you know there is no pleasure in the bedding. You need not try to convince me otherwise." Turning her back to Nadine, Eva walked to the hearth.

Nadine followed her. "There is pleasure and happiness in the bedding when two people care for each other. And if you love Robert, Eva, you better heed my words."

Thank God the hall was empty!

Nadine crossed the hall rapidly and stepped into the bailey. The sun was past its zenith, and a cool breeze whispered in the air. Nadine shivered. How was Faulk going to treat her today? Last night he'd been loving, attentive, demanding, too, and she'd been ready to respond to him, to give him what he wanted, and to extract from him what she needed. Today, however, everything could be changed, and Nadine feared the awkward moment of the day after.

As she scanned the bailey, her eyes unerringly rested on him. Faulk was just finishing an archery practice with his men. Their target, a scarecrow of sorts, pierced by arrows in every possible part of his straw body, dangled from a tall spike.

As she approached him from behind, Faulk whirled around, crossbow in hand. A dark morning shadow adorned his unshaved face, lending him a menacing look. At the sight of her he grinned. The smile flashed sinful sensuality on his dangerous visage.

Dazzled, Nadine's thoughts mumbled. "What possible harm could this poor creature have caused your men to deserve such a treatment?" She pointed to the punctured scarecrow.

"That is what my enemies need expect from my men," he said, his eyes devouring her. "God's teeth, Nadine." He groaned. "Do not stand there looking so adorable. You wish I forget my place and ravish you here, in my bailey, in front of my men?"

"The thought has not crossed my mind," she lied, breathless.

He stepped closer. His overpowering presence shadowing her. "But it has crossed mine."

Nadine inhaled audibly. The faint smell of pine mingled with his manly smell pleased her. "Faulk . . . About last night."

"Worry not, my fair lady." He touched her face. "I shall do right by you. Mildred is already at work on your wedding garment, and I have spoken with Father Anselm. At the end of this week I shall make you my wife, as the prophecy foretold, as your destiny anticipated, as my honor demands."

Though Faulk's promise agreed with Nadine's wishes, the haste with which everything was happening frightened her. For the first time since arriving in this century, Nadine had dared to hope her loneliness would end, that her innermost wishes would come true. A family, an everlasting love, a place and people to belong to. Would what had started as a nightmare turn into a blissful reality? A chill of unwelcome foreboding ran down her spine.

A strident horn blow pierced the air, jolting Nadine from her thoughts. She whirled around and saw a young boy running to them.

"Visitors approach, my lord," the boy said as soon as he reached Faulk. "And the men you sent to Rouen return with them."

Faulk nodded and the boy dashed back to his lookout position.

"My fair lady," Faulk said, facing the big wooden gate. "Your past draws near."

Curious, Nadine turned to the same direction. How could a past that never existed ever catch up with her?

Chapter 13

THE STRANGER LEAPED from his horse and dropped to his knees at Nadine's feet. "I had doubted the wonderful tidings true, yet my eyes now confirm what my heart had feared to believe."

His hazel, worshipping eyes impaled Nadine as he rose to his feet. "The sight of you fills my heart with joy," he said, then kissed her hand.

In stunned silence Nadine endured the stranger's attention. She chanced a glance at Faulk, and though he masked his surprise well, she knew he couldn't be pleased with the man's familiarity with her.

"My dearest, sweetest Nadine," the stranger continued, oblivious to her silence. "I have finally found you."

Nadine? How could the man know her name? Uneasy, Nadine took a step back, freeing her hand from his. She looked him over. He wore no knight's armor but expensive-looking clothing. A trimmed, dark blond beard covered his face, and his long hair, a lighter shade, fell on his shoulders with casual elegance. Appearing to be a few years older than Faulk and quite a few inches shorter, he lacked Faulk's massive, authoritative presence. Nevertheless, he exuded self-confidence.

For a moment Nadine had a fleeting sensation of recognition, but that was impossible, she'd never seen the man before. Maybe he reminded her of someone from the future, though for the life of her, she couldn't think of who that might be. He upheld her scrutiny with a benevolent smile, yet, for some reason, Nadine sensed chaos underneath the well-groomed, unruffled appearance.

One of Faulk's men, who had gone to Rouen in search of her family and who had returned with the stranger, stepped up, diverting her attention.

"My lord," he said, bowing to Faulk. "This is Monsieur Roland du Monte, Lady Nadine's kin, whom we met on our way to Rouen."

Roland turned to Faulk and bowed respectfully. "My lord, I shall be forever indebted to you for rescuing my beloved betrothed."

Nadine gasped audibly as her heart lurched. *Betrothed?*

The words of denial stuck in her throat. She shot Roland a horrified look. Did he say he was a *du Monte*, like herself? A kin, Faulk's man had said, a relation. Yet he claimed they were betrothed, and he called her by her name.

A ghastly thought flashed in her mind. Could there be another Nadine in this century? An ancestor of hers, maybe? But would an ancestor bear such likeness that Nadine would be taken for her? And with the very same name? How could it be possible?

Utterly confused, Nadine shook her head. Once again her world had turned upside down. She needed to know more about this medieval Nadine, but how could she query Roland without sounding like a lunatic?

"Monsieur du Monte." Nadine forced the tremor out of her voice. "Have you any proof of your claims?"

" 'Tis true then," he said, turning a worried expression to her. "I was told you remember naught of your past. Oh, my sweetest, fear not, all shall be well as soon as we return home to Rouen."

Home? Rouen? *Sacré Coeur!*

Nadine wavered unsteadily on her feet. Faulk and Roland reached for her at the same time, but Faulk got to her first, circling his arm around her waist and pulling her to his side.

"Whosoever you are," Faulk's voice thundered, "I suggest you do as the lady says and show proof of your words or return to wherever you came from."

Undaunted, Roland swirled on his feet and strolled back to his horse, returning with a leather bag strapped to his shoulder. He reached inside and handed Faulk a rolled-up parchment, then turned to Nadine and gave her a raggedy doll.

"Marie-Elise sent you this," he said. "She has suffered much with your disappearance, my sweetest, and so have I."

Nadine blanched at the sight of the doll. A buzz filled her head, her eyes glazed over, and she found herself transported to a beautiful garden, a much bigger and elaborate garden than her little place in Rouen. On a fragrant bed of grass sat a child of five or six years of age. She held in her arms a brand-new doll—undeniably the same raggedy doll Roland had just given Nadine—while a young woman combed the child's long, golden hair.

"*Ma petite fleur*," the woman said.

At the sight of the woman's face, Nadine cried out, "*Maman.*"

The vision disappeared and Nadine was once again back at the Whitecastle's bailey.

Shaking with the intensity of her feelings, hugging the doll to her heart, Nadine leaned against Faulk. She was certain her trembling legs would buckle at any moment.

Faulk tightened his arms around her, supporting her. "Nadine?"

Roland also stepped closer, watching her intently.

Nadine gazed from one man to the other, but said nothing. What could she say? That she was plagued by visions that looked and felt so real, but that she couldn't explain? Who were the medieval child and woman? In the depths of her soul Nadine knew they were herself and her mother. But how could they be?

Though Nadine had never seen her mother as a young woman—when Nadine's mother gave birth to Nadine, she was already over forty—she had no doubt the way the woman in her vision looked would be the way her mother would have looked at the same age. She didn't know how she knew this, yet she had no doubt about it.

Were the woman and child of the vision ancestors of her own mother and herself? Roland seemed to have no doubt she was his betrothed.

Drawing from strength she didn't know she possessed, Nadine straightened herself up. "I am just a little dizzy." She clutched the doll with her trembling fingers.

" 'Tis best we go within," Faulk said, half-dragging her with him.

Overtaken by mystifying feelings, Nadine struggled to keep up with Faulk's long strides. Last night she'd believed she'd found a new beginning for her, with Faulk. Today her life was once again in total chaos. Faulk's doomful words were proving to be true. Her past had indeed come. And there was more to it than she could ever have dreamed.

Now, more than ever, she must unravel the true reason for her catapult through time.

Roland du Monte sat across the table from his Nadine. *Mon Dieu*, how beautiful she was! Even more so than he remembered, though he truly disliked her short hair. Mayhap he could find a potion to make it grow faster. He would also feed her better, for she was painfully thin, and he liked soft flesh around a woman's bones. She looked slightly older, nay, not older, but more mature, infinitely more enticing, with a glow about her that had not been there before.

If only that detestable giant did not sit by her side. Hiding his contempt, Roland glanced inconspicuously at the obnoxious Lord Faulk, who, tight-jawed, examined the parchment closely. With the forged betrothal document, Nadine's blessed loss of memory, and Faulk's misguided sense of honor, Roland would finally possess all he deserved.

Roland shifted on his chair. 'Twould have been so much simpler, though, had those stupid brigands he hired done their job. By their sheer number they should have overcome Faulk's small group on the road from Londontown. Incompetent bunch! He was surrounded by the likes of them. That was why he had decided to come himself after Nadine. This time his plans would not be thwarted by witlessness.

After taking a sip from the tankard in front of him, Roland grimaced with distaste—weak ale. Immediately he set it down. Wine was so much better. He could not wait to depart from this decrepit castle.

Hurling the document across the table to Nadine, Faulk glared at Roland. In response Roland barely managed to subdue a derisive laughter. He grinned instead.

"As you can see," Roland said, "this document proves Nadine is my betrothed; therefore I claim my rights over the lady and announce our departure as soon as she can gather her belongings."

Nadine's face paled at his words, but Roland paid her no attention. His battle was with Faulk at this moment; Nadine would have to wait her turn.

"And what say you to that, my lady?" Faulk asked Nadine, his voice deceptively amiable.

Nadine perused the document for a moment, then stared at Faulk with a mix of bewilderment and apprehension.

"Lord Faulk," Roland interrupted with a dash of impatience. " 'Tis already proved the lady has lost memory of her past. We cannot rely on her testimony to uncover the truth."

"How convenient," Faulk said.

Roland shrugged. *Indeed!* "I understand you might feel entitled to compensation for your troubles. I am a generous man. Ask your price, lord rescuer, and I shall reward you."

Faulk's mouth twisted in a dangerous snarl. His hand closed up in a fist. No doubt wishing he could smash his face, Roland thought amused. The highborn lords of the kingdom, bound by honor with their likes, totally despicable with their underlings. Fortunately, Roland was one of the lords now, and Faulk could do no less by him. Oh, he so enjoyed besting the man with his wits.

"Monsieur," Nadine called.

Mindful Nadine had been unusually quiet thus far, Roland turned his attention to her. The lady he knew would not have endured such discussions without venturing her opinion—her father's fault, for having overindulged the chit. Mayhap, her exile had influenced her manners. A subdued Nadine? What a thoroughly delightful thought.

"We share a family name," she said. "I believe you said we are kin?"

Was she trying to wiggle herself out of marrying him? Not bloody likely. Not even the laws of consanguinity could touch them. They were too far related, though it had served him well when he had claimed Nadine's fortune.

"We are a very distant kin," Roland said, hoping she would leave it at that.

Nadine's distrust was something he had been prepared to deal with. However, much as he was overjoyed by her lack of memories, he must ascertain she trusted him enough to take his word as the truth.

"What can you tell me about . . . myself?" she asked.

Roland reveled in the opportunity. "I have known you since your birth," he began. "Your father raised me, and with the passing of the years I became his most trusted man. In recent times he saw fit to reward my loyalty by betrothing you to me. We were about to announce our wedding when you were abducted." He hoped she would not contradict him. She did not. He went on, "We moved heaven and earth seeking you, but to no avail. . . ." He paused, showing hesitation. "I am saddened to be the bearer of bad tidings, Nadine, but your dearest father perished in the search."

Nadine's already pale face lost the little color it held. The pain on her face was evident. Her eyes seemed to glaze over like earlier on in the bailey. Roland thought she would swoon, but she just sat there, staring through him. Had her ordeal caused more extensive damage than a mere loss of memory? He wished not an addle-witted wife. Though it could suit his purposes.

Roland watched Faulk reach for Nadine over the table and rest his hand on top of hers. His touch seemed to have a calming effect on her. She swallowed hard, shook her head, then turned a tentative smile at Faulk.

So the chit had feelings for the obnoxious giant. Well, as soon as he had her under his control, Roland vowed, he would obliterate any and every feeling Nadine might have that related to anyone but him.

Pursing his lips, Roland waited until Nadine turned her attention back to him.

" 'Twas the greatest loss," he said. "He was like a father to me, and as thus I loved him. I was only glad he did not suffer the terrible news of your death, which reached us after his demise. As for me"—Roland lowered his head as if the mere thought was too much to bear—" 'twas the last blow to my already broken heart."

He darted a surreptitious glance at Nadine, expecting to see a flash of understanding in her face, mayhap a sliver of compassion, but she stared at him with blank eyes.

"I have loved you all my life," he said, watching her openly now, and that much was true. He had loved her hopelessly, now 'twas his chance to have her. "And you loved me, too. How can you not remember?" Nadine shot him a confused look. Good. His little speech was having some effect on her. And also on Faulk, whose mask of control looked about to fall.

"How can you be certain this lady is the one you seek?" Faulk asked. "You have just revealed you believed her dead."

"I was told that Nadine drowned somewhere in the English Channel not far from here while attempting to escape her captors, yet her body was never found."

"And how did you learn of her fate?"

"I apprehended one of her captors and *persuaded* him to confess, but by then 'twas too late, Nadine was already believed dead. I had no inkling she was still alive until a few days ago when someone spotted her in Londontown and sent me the wonderful tidings. I was also informed of your rescue of the lady, thus I immediately came to claim my betrothed. I met with your men on the way, and they confirmed the tidings. Thus, here I am."

A long moment of silence fell in the hall. Certain Faulk could do naught but deliver Nadine to him, Roland smiled agreeably.

"Under the circumstances," Faulk said, straightening up in his chair, "my honor demands I bring forward tidings of my own that might upturn this matter."

Roland's blood congealed in his veins. What treachery was Faulk up to?

"Lady Nadine could be carrying my heir," Faulk said.

The words, spoken in such a cold and calm fashion, took a long moment to sink in. It floated in the air with unpredictable consequences, then crashed down with the weight of its importance.

Neither Roland's bewildered glare nor Nadine's stupefying stare disturbed Faulk's outward placidity, yet his inwards were being eaten alive with fury.

Not even when he had learned of Elizabeth's deceit had he been this livid. He had been deeply hurt, as only a young lad can be hurt. He had been bewildered. He had been ashamed. Yet never had he felt such indisputable, wide-spread rage.

"I beg your pardon," Roland no more than whispered.

With wrath threatening to overpower him, Faulk directed his frigid glare at the dumbstruck Roland. The look of stunned shock on Roland's face gave Faulk some measure of satisfaction. If the man thought he could ride into his castle and take Nadine away without so much as a by-your-leave, he was sorely mistaken. Faulk had detested Roland at first glance, and even though the betrothal agreement he produced looked sufficiently legitimate, Faulk could not shake his distrust. Roland's kinship with Nadine needed to be looked upon with the utmost care.

Since Faulk's first glimpse of that beautiful rose on Nadine's shoulder, he had believed in the prophetic reason of their encounter. *Nadine* would bear his heir and no other. All his actions had geared to assure this outcome. His blind belief in the prophecy, his ardent wish to fulfill his vow to his father, his certainty Nadine was the one, had brought him thus far.

When Nadine surrendered to him and he sank into the paradise of her body, he had thought he had accomplished the deed. He had believed the prophecy fulfilled. He had reveled in the glory of being justified in his pursuit of her.

Until he knew for certain his seed had not taken fruition in Nadine's womb, she would go nowhere. And no little weasel would take her away from him.

Faulk's hand tightened around the handle of his sword, the only outward emotion he would allow. Would the prophecy fail him now? Did Nadine carry the seed that would ensure the continuity of his line?

"You heard me well," Faulk said. There was no need to repeat what could not be ignored.

"You vermin," Roland spat, lurching at Faulk with a dagger in his hand. In a flash Faulk swung his sword upward, easily dislodging the weapon from Roland's hand. The dagger flew in the air and fell down silently on the rushes as Faulk forced Roland down on the bench with the tip of his sword.

Both ignored Nadine's distressed cry.

"How could you dishonor a damsel in distress?" Roland demanded in disbelief, his body bent backward in an attempt to avert the sharp weapon pointed at his chest. "Nadine is a highborn lady, not one of your serving wenches." His voice trembled with outrage.

"I dishonored no one," Faulk spat, wishing to pierce Roland through with his blade and be done with it. Instead, he slowly sat down, keeping the sword on the table between them, the tip still pointed at Roland.

"The lady shall be my wife," Faulk announced. He had enjoyed Nadine's body, he had even allowed himself to care for her—inasmuch as he would for the mother of his heir. He vowed to treat her with respect, to provide for her, to protect her with his life. All for the sake of the immeasurable gift she would grant him. There was no dishonor in that.

"Over my dead body!" Roland attempted to rise, but Faulk prevented it easily.

"That can be arranged."

Roland eyed Faulk and his blade with rage, then suddenly relaxed, looking like a hawk that had sighted his defenseless prey.

The hair on Faulk's nape spiked in sudden awareness.

"You have already dishonored Lady Nadine and me," Roland said. "Would you go insofar as murder me to steal my betrothed?"

God's teeth, but the man dared much!

"An unarmed man?" Roland continued, raising his hands to prove his point.

Roland carried no sword, only his dagger—a coward's weapon for certain—which now lay on the rushes. Damn

Roland for his games. He was toying with him, Faulk knew, toying with his sense of honor. Roland knew he would not kill a weaponless man.

"Nadine is my betrothed," Roland continued. "And I shall not set her aside."

"Surely you see 'tis in the best interest of the lady to wed me," Faulk said in the coldest of voices. "Now, be wise and accept the fact that I have taken the lady to my bed, have robbed her of her maidenhead, verily might have planted my seed in her womb." With every word Faulk rose a little, and by the time he finished he was on his feet, facing Roland down.

"I understand you might feel entitled to compensation for your troubles," he mocked Roland's earlier words. "I am a generous man. Ask your price, and I shall reward you."

"You could not possibly afford what Nadine is worth," Roland spat. "I shall wed her, Faulk, and you shall never know whose child she carries." A victorious little smile twitched on Roland's lips as he also rose to his feet. "And there is naught you can do to prevent it."

Turning to the forgotten Nadine, who silently witnessed the men's exchange, Roland said, "Worry not, my sweetest. I shall make you forget the horrors you experienced in this pit of iniquity."

"The lady goes nowhere," Faulk said, stepping to Nadine's side.

Roland circled the table, standing opposite Faulk on Nadine's other side. " 'Twould be unwise to disregard my rights upon the lady."

" 'Twould be equally unwise to disdain *my* rights upon the lady and her child," Faulk retorted.

"Enough!" Nadine cried suddenly, rising between the men. "Both of you have forgotten one tiny detail."

They turned a surprised gaze at her.

" 'Tis my life, and I shall decide what to do with it."

Chapter 14

FAULK AND ROLAND stared at Nadine as if she'd grown two heads. " 'Tis not your decision to make," they spoke in unison.

"It most certainly is," Nadine said.

They fought over her the way little boys fight over a toy they both felt entitled to own. Only she wasn't a toy. And she would not stand for it.

"I have made my decision," she announced. "I go to Rouen in search of my home." Speaking the words out loud made them seem real, plausible, almost attainable.

Roland grinned, obviously pleased with her decision. Faulk, on the other hand, shot her a withering glare. "Home is where your loyalties lie. You carry my heir in your womb, Nadine. Whitecastle is your home."

Faulk's single-mindedness didn't surprise Nadine. In fact, she had grown accustomed to this trait of him, expected it, even admired it. It comforted her, the predictability of his behavior. Nevertheless, his stubbornness could also be very dangerous.

She knew he couldn't possibly understand her turmoil. He had no inkling of her fantastic trip across time nor of

the strange visions that assaulted her. When those visions
had first happened, Nadine thought them mere hallucinations, but now, especially after learning of the existence of
a medieval Nadine who looked just like her, Nadine realized they held meaning. Like a child's picture book where
the combined pictures told a story.

Once the story of her look-alike ancestor unfolded, the
meaning would become clear and Nadine would know
without a doubt her fate in this century. Only then could
she belong unconditionally to Faulk. Only then could she
build a life with him. Only then could she marry him.

Her coming through time had not been a fluke; she had
not stepped out and fallen in a black hole by chance. There
was meaning to this madness, and it was more than just
belonging to Faulk.

"Though you would like to ignore it, Faulk," Roland
said, bringing Nadine out of her musings, "Nadine's loyalties lie with me—her deceased father's choice for husband—and with the people of Rosemanor who anxiously
await her return."

That was not what she meant. She was going to Rouen
to learn about herself, not to marry Roland. Even though
Roland had no qualms in swearing his love for her, Nadine
had no way of gauging his sincerity. Besides, his claim that
he would marry her and no one would be the wiser of who
was the father of her child had come across not like an act
of love but of control. There was no way Nadine would
ever marry Roland.

She was about to disabuse Roland of the notion when
Faulk pointed out, "Nadine's prior commitment cannot possibly overrule the fact she carries my heir."

"That is not a fact, Faulk," Nadine felt compelled to say.
She couldn't even conceive the implications of being pregnant in such uncertain circumstances. At this point she
didn't even want to think about it.

"Have you not humiliated Nadine enough?" Roland said.

"Must you keep reminding the lady of her one moment of insanity?"

"One?" Faulk grinned and pushed Roland back none too gently.

Nadine sighed in frustration. They were talking about her as if she weren't even present. "Must you both be so mule-headed and ignore my feelings in this?"

"I beg your pardon, my fair Nadine—"

Nadine didn't like Faulk's mocking tone, but before she had a chance to remark on it, Roland interrupted Faulk.

"You should beg *my* pardon—"

Roland's indignation was cut short by Faulk's menacing growl.

Nadine sighed. They didn't get it. They would never get it. "This is not about you"—she pushed her finger against Faulk's chest—"nor you"—she did the same to Roland. "This is about me, my life, my future." She tromped away, angry at their shortsightedness, frightened of the implications of her decision to go to Rouen.

She parked herself in front of the hearth, with her back to the men, staring at the flickering flames, but the burning logs failed to warm her sinking heart.

Numerous questions plagued her mind. Did the medieval Nadine die when she fell into the Channel? If not, could they both coexist in the same time? Or would the presence of one disavow the other? Could they have traded places? Had the medieval Nadine catapulted into the future while Nadine time-traveled to this century?

Should Nadine take over the medieval lady's life? If she did, according to medieval laws who would she be expected to marry? Faulk, with whom she had shared her body and heart? Or Roland, who held legal claims on her? And how was she going to avoid a war between the men? Warrior that he was, Faulk would not hesitate to engage Roland in battle, and for all that he tried to appear disinclined to fight, Roland was obviously a man of some importance and power. Nadine believed he would retaliate or even amass an offensive of his own.

How could she dismiss the validity of Roland's claims? And how could she deny her feelings for Faulk? Not to mention that she might indeed be pregnant. No, she didn't want to go there. It was too early, too complicated, too scary a thought.

Nadine had no choice. She must go to Rouen. She must meet Marie-Elise. She must find the threads of a past that seemed intricately interwoven with her own life.

However, to return to Rouen meant crossing the Channel. The familiar tightening of her throat came swiftly at the thought.

As she comes through the water, so can the water take her away. The witch's words buzzed in her ears. She didn't take them lightly, but there must be more than one answer to this puzzle. Maybe crossing the Channel wouldn't necessarily mean being transported back to the future, or, God forbid, facing death by drowning.

Besides, the witch had told Nadine if she took what fate offered—and Nadine assumed that meant Faulk's love— then she would have until the time of new birth to return home. *Time of new birth. Spring?* She'd given her body and heart to Faulk; surely the water would not take her away now.

Mon Dieu! Do not let it end this way. The prayer echoed once again in her mind.

Feeling trapped and overwhelmed, Nadine almost rushed from the hall, but Faulk and Roland's bewildered expression at her explosion halted her escape. She couldn't hide from them for long, besides she must face what was ahead of her. No one could do it for her.

Nadine took a deep, cleansing breath. There were explanations and reassurances she must offer to Faulk and some points she must make abundantly clear to Roland.

Faulk was the first to recover and march toward her. His

bright blue eyes were shadowed with impotent fury on the verge of exploding. "I give you not leave to depart, my fair Nadine." He growled out the endearment.

"But you must," Nadine said, eyeing Faulk with a calm she was far from feeling. "Only when I know who I really am, only when I am a complete person, can I be yours. I must go, Faulk."

If only he understood the importance of her decision to both of them. But how could he, when she gave him only excuses?

"All I know, Nadine, is that you might be carrying my heir, and therefore you already know who you are. You shall be my lady wife and the mother of my son."

"Is that all I am to you, a vessel to carry your offspring to life?" *Mon Dieu!* She wanted to be more than that to him.

" 'Tis your most sacred task," he whispered, balling up his fists alongside his powerful thighs.

Nadine understood the longing in his soft whisper. She heard the pain of unfulfilled wishes in his words. She saw how difficult it was for him to accept her decision by the rigidity of his posture. Faulk was a medieval man with medieval expectations, yet more than once he had behaved toward her in a way outside the constrictions of his own time. He had given her every opportunity to come to him willingly, instead of forcing her. To let her go, to be denied what he deemed her destiny, would eat at him. Would he do it? Could he let her go?

"That it is, my lord," Nadine said, touching his stubborn chin, running her fingers across the dark shadowed stubble on his handsome face. "Once you told me I was destined to be yours," she whispered. "God willing, I shall return to you, Faulk."

His hand slowly lifted to her face. His thumb lingered over her cheeks, her lips, her throat in a barely there caress.

Nadine's heart felt like exploding. How could a man who

lived by his strength be capable of such gentle touch? Love filled her up to overflowing, making her decision to leave weigh more heavily in her heart. By returning to Rouen she risked the only chance she might ever have at true love. All her life she had longed for a love like her parents had shared. With Faulk she had that chance. Yet he deserved more than she could give him right now. He deserved her body, her heart, her soul, and only when she possessed all could she give all to him.

To have him, she must go.

To have her, he must let her go.

"Is there anything I can do or say to convince you to stay?"

She shook her head.

"Very well." He dropped her hand. "Gather your belongings," he said, then whirled around and marched out of the hall.

He was letting her go! Relief washed over Nadine, then a shadow caught her eye—Roland. She had forgotten about him. And by the look on his face he was not pleased with the scene he had just witnessed.

Nadine felt a sudden dislike for the man and was immediately ashamed of her emotions. Roland had every right to be angry; after all, he, too, believed he had rights. She must tread with care and find a way to extricate herself from his legal clutches. For there was absolutely no way she would ever wed Roland du Monte.

"An interesting scene," he said. "Utterly inappropriate, of course."

"I am sorry, Roland, but you must know I return to Rouen to uncover my past, not to marry you."

"I shall repeat myself, Nadine, 'tis not your choice to make. You belong to me, and neither Lord Faulk's ravishing of you nor your wishes change that." And he, too, walked out of the room.

Shocked by the vehemence in Roland's words, Nadine

stared at his retreating back. Roland would be a problem, she realized, yet she had faced much in these past days, and one more problem would not stop her.

"Well, Monsieur Roland," Nadine whispered to the empty hall. "That remains to be seen."

"Where did these come from?" Nadine asked Mildred as the woman packed new garments in a small leather trunk.

"While you were away in Londontown, I mended some of Lady Ann's old gowns for you. 'Tis a shame Lord Faulk got rid of Lady Elizabeth's belongings. They would suit you much better."

Lady Ann? Lady Elizabeth?

"Thank you, Mildred." Nadine avoided Mildred's eyes as she touched one garment, feeling the softness of velvet underneath her fingers. "Who are those ladies you just mentioned?"

"Lady Ann was Lord Faulk's mother," Mildred said, continuing her packing. "A sweet lady she was, loved her boy so much. Pity she lived not long enough to see how strong and handsome he turned out to be."

Faulk was motherless like her. "Lady Elizabeth was his wife, and died in childbirth."

Faulk had been married? The disagreeable news took hold of Nadine. Not that it should matter. After all, the woman was dead. Unless he started comparing her to Elizabeth, but no, he hadn't even mentioned her. Why wouldn't he mention her?

Mildred stopped her packing and turned to Nadine. "My lady. Will you return to Lord Faulk?"

If she survived the Channel crossing, nothing would keep her away from Faulk. "If I can, I shall return."

"With the babe? Lord Faulk's heir?"

Everybody had always taken for granted Nadine would marry Faulk, and now it seemed, they did the same with her pregnancy. "*If* there is a baby, it shall return with me."

"Lord Faulk must produce an heir. With his father's death 'tis expected of him, especially after Lady Elizabeth." Mildred turned back to her packing as the last words left her mouth.

An heir. How much of Faulk's wish to marry her was tied to the need to produce an heir? Surely the prophecy had merely served the purpose of getting them together. Faulk must have deeper feelings for her; otherwise he would not pursue this marriage between them with such insistence.

They had much in common. Both had suffered their share of losses. Faulk was alone in the world, and so was she. Maybe together they could fill the void in each other's lives. If only fate cooperated.

"Monsieur Roland's claim on you is not easily undone," Mildred said. "I fear he shall not allow you to return, my lady."

Nadine shivered. "It is not impossible, is it, to undo such claim?"

Mildred avoided Nadine's eyes. "Worry not, my lady, Lord Faulk shall find a way."

Mildred's words had the opposite effect they were surely intended. Wouldn't it be a terrible irony if Nadine ended up stuck with Roland in this century? But no, that wouldn't happen. She wouldn't allow it to happen. Yet suddenly it dawned on her things might not turn out the way she hoped.

Eva appeared at the open door. "I see you are ready to depart."

Nodding, Nadine waved her in.

"It must be truly horrible to discover you belong to another man," Eva said, "after what happened last eve. . . ."

Nadine had already surmised the betrothal was a legal bidding contract in this time and age, but surely there was some legal loophole. She would have to discover it.

"I am sure the betrothal can be annulled," Nadine said, not sure at all.

"Oh, certainly." Eva exchanged a dismayed look with Mildred.

"Lord Faulk shall find a way," Mildred repeated.

A heavy silence fell in the room. Nadine felt not at all encouraged by the women's assurances.

"I wish I could go with you," Eva said, changing subjects, "but Lord Faulk ordered Robert to remain behind, and therefore, so shall I."

"Is Faulk sending an escort with me?"

"He is escorting you, himself," Eva revealed.

"Oh," Nadine whispered. She should've known Faulk wouldn't allow her to handle this without interference. Though his presence might make things more difficult with Roland, considering the latent animosity between them, Nadine was glad she wouldn't be alone.

" 'Tis surprising, you allowing Lady Nadine to go," Robert said.

Faulk, standing by the window, peeked through the small aperture into the bailey where men and horses gathered for departure. " 'Tis not as though she departs on her own."

He moved away from the window and perched himself on the edge of a small table in the bedchamber he occupied since Nadine's arrival. "Nadine's quest for answers is a valid reason for her to wish to go to Rouen, and I must seek King Richard in France to petition for the dissolution of her betrothal to Roland; thus I accompany her."

"Still, you could force her to remain at Whitecastle while you seek the king."

Faulk tipped a tankard to his lips, taking a good swallow of the soothing drink. *To keep her you must find love in your heart, for love is the uniting thread betwixt you.* Faulk intently overlooked that part of the prophecy, for he had no intention of giving his heart to Nadine or any other woman, yet neither could he chance chasing Nadine away. If he tried to keep her at Whitecastle against her will, that was what would happen. Besides, by accompanying her he would have a chance to learn more about her and also Roland. However, Faulk felt no need to share these thoughts with Robert. "I could, but I shall not," he simply said.

Robert did not insist. "Do you believe the king shall grant your petition?"

"Once he learns Nadine carries my heir." Faulk smiled, unconcerned, refusing to allow anybody, not even his friend, a glimpse of his turbulent soul.

"Roland du Monte seems determined to keep her."

" 'Twill do him no good."

"Still, he worries me," Robert continued. "Any man in his position would have either challenged you to battle over his honor or accepted compensation for his loss. Yet, he did neither. 'Tis odd."

Faulk had also wondered about Roland's motives, immediately dismissing the man's claims of undying love. If that were true Roland would not have hesitated to fight him. Instead he chose to take Nadine back, even knowing she might be carrying his child. Odd, indeed! There was more to this man than he had let on, and Faulk intended to find out. The first rule of battle was to know your enemy well, his strengths, his weaknesses. Roland possessed many visible flaws, but the ones he hid were the ones that interested Faulk.

"I shall deal with Roland at the appropriate time," Faulk said, striding to the door. "Meanwhile, I trust you to safeguard Whitecastle in my absence, continue the recruiting until my return, and begin implementing the improvements we talked about. I shall be away no longer than necessary."

Outside, the early afternoon sun peeked through the dark clouds. A cool breeze chilled the air. Spring was not living up to its potential, Faulk thought as he stepped down to the bailey. Just as well, for his mood was as dark as the day was threatening to be. This morn he had awakened with

the satisfaction of having accomplished his duty. This forenoon had him once again in battle with fate.

The sight of Roland du Monte atop a beautiful gelding
annoyed him further. Too much horse for the likes of him;
an ox would suit the man better.

Faulk perused the ten men-at-arms he carefully chose to
accompany him. He intended to leave most of them with
Nadine, once he left Rouen in search of the king.

He glanced back at Roland, and the man's scowl helped
ameliorate his deteriorating mood.

"Who invited you to accompany us?" Roland asked.

"I escort Lady Nadine."

"I have enough men to escort her."

"I escort her from you and your men," Faulk retorted.

"My betrothed's safety is well-assured in my hands."

Dropping the reins of his destrier on the stable boy
hands, Faulk sauntered to Roland's side. He grabbed Roland's tunic by the neck and dragged the man's face down
to the same level of his horse's head. "Just one warning,
Roland: Touch one strand of Nadine's golden hair, and you
shall wish you were dead. Betrothal or nay, Nadine belongs
to me and to me she shall return."

Roland wheezed with the pressure on his throat. "You
can delude yourself with words of bravado, my dear Lord
Faulk, but Nadine returns with me to Rouen, and with me
she shall remain."

Faulk's temper suddenly snapped. He shook Roland so
forcibly that the man's teeth rattled.

"Faulk," Nadine called, penetrating the fog of rage that
was his mind.

Twice this day Faulk considered ending Roland's miserable life, and twice he decided against it. More was the
pity. Regretfully Faulk let him go, and Roland sprang back
in the horse's seat like a rock from a catapult. Faulk turned
to Nadine as if naught had happened.

Nadine stared at him in alarm. Faulk walked away from

a gasping Roland, closing the gap to her. His eyes moved from her full lips to her golden eyes, and their intensity pierced through his rage. And then, unexpectedly, she stood on her tiptoes and kissed him in the mouth. There, in the bailey, in front of all the men, in Roland's presence. 'Twas a soft kiss that barely allowed him the sweet taste of her.

Disregarding the pleasure her open demonstration filled him, Faulk steeled his heart. She would not pacify him with so little. Her defying ways put him through enough trouble. She deserved a thrashing for it. He knew what was best for her. Could she not, for once, trust in his decision?

She stepped back, disappointment in her eyes. Faulk ignored the contrition in his heart and the desire to take her into his arms and smother her with kisses, and stood his ground.

She sighed and looked over his shoulder. He knew what she was seeing, his men-at-arms, ready to depart, and his own destrier awaiting nearby.

"So you accompany us," she said, glancing back at him.

He nodded, waiting for her recriminating words.

She grinned instead. "Well, shall we go?"

Hiding his astonishment at Nadine's ready acceptance of his presence on this journey, Faulk passed her in two strides and helped her swing atop her mare. He mounted his destrier, purposefully ignoring the glaring Roland, then gave the signal for departure. He immediately positioned himself beside Nadine, escorting her out of the bailey and into the drawbridge. Roland caught up with them, stationing himself on Nadine's other side.

'Twould be a long journey, Faulk thought as they trotted along the wooden planks.

Chapter 15

THE SIGHT OF the mighty English Channel bathed by the silver rays of the dawn churned Nadine's stomach. Inhaling deeply, she tried to ignore her fear and anxiety and stepped forward. Faulk and Roland immediately flanked her. Together, they drifted toward the water amidst men-at-arms and fishermen in the small fishing village where they'd spent the night.

"I must caution you anew, Nadine," Faulk said in lieu of "good morning." "You still may change your mind and return to Whitecastle."

"We have already discussed that." *Dieu*, but the man was single-minded!

"Let us not forget," Roland joined in. "Nadine is my betrothed, thus 'tis her duty to return home with me."

Nadine sighed. "We have also discussed that, Roland." Obviously her conversation with Roland where she asserted her intention of not marrying him had fallen on deaf ears.

" 'Tis not your decision to make," Roland retorted like a broken record.

" 'Tis true," Faulk interceded. " 'Tis the king's will. And he shall award Nadine to me."

"In the king's eyes Nadine's fate lies in the hands of her family and betrothed. And I am both."

With a growl Faulk advanced toward Roland. Nadine stepped between the two men. "I will be forced to marry no one," she said. Not even at gun's point, or, more appropriately, at sword's point, would she be coerced. "Now, could we please try to behave in a civilized manner?"

They considered her words for a long moment, eyeing each other like fighting cocks, then both took a step backward.

They had been at it throughout the journey. Quarreling and vying for her attention. It was annoying and dangerous, and she didn't know how much longer she'd be able to keep them from tearing each other's throat.

As if that was her only concern, Nadine thought as they resumed their trek to the Channel. Amidst the small fishing boats setting out for their day of labor, the big ship stood out with its row of oars and triangular sails rigged on their masts. Nadine eyed the ship critically, wondering if they would all fit inside. Faulk's men-at-arms added to Roland's equated almost thirty, and their horses would be boarded as well.

" 'Tis my ship," Roland said. "You may procure your own, for I shall not leave any of my men behind."

"Very well," Faulk said, stepping between Nadine and Roland. "You may depart with your men. I shall escort Nadine to Rouen as soon as I procure another ship."

"You shall go nowhere with my betrothed."

Nadine sighed. "How about if both of you stay and I go by myself?" She stomped away.

At the water edge, though, Nadine halted. Hypnotized, she watched the waves hit the shore. The cool morning breeze blowing from the water penetrated the thick wool of her coat. Nadine shivered.

Sacré Coeur! What made her think she could do this? Memories of her last trip across the Channel filled her with dread. What if the witch was wrong? What if Nadine had misunderstood the woman's cryptic words? What if she returned to the future now? Or died as she crossed the Channel?

Shuddering, Nadine stepped back. Maybe she should return with Faulk to Whitecastle. After all, she did love him, and she may even be carrying his child at this moment. What more did she need to know?

Nadine glanced over her shoulder and saw Faulk marching toward her, followed closely by Roland. As much as she wanted, she couldn't give up her search now. Before she committed to Faulk, she needed to assure herself she belonged with him in this century, and that she would not be torn again from a beloved.

She must find her connection with her medieval ancestor. In the depth of her soul Nadine felt that need. And Rouen held the answers. Therefore, albeit the risks and her fears, she would cross the Channel, for the alternative would be to never know, never be secure, never be certain.

And Nadine couldn't live with uncertainty. She needed to belong. She needed to find her place. That was why she needed to go to Rouen, not only for the sake of her relationship with Faulk, but also for her own sake, her own peace of mind.

Besides, now that Roland believed he had found his betrothed, he would not sit idle and allow her to choose Faulk over him without a struggle. Nadine realized she was subject to the medieval laws and customs, but she vowed to find a legal way to extricate herself from Roland's clutches.

"Are you considering swimming across the Channel?" Roland's voice startled Nadine almost into the water. She took another step back, swirling around.

"Not anytime soon, if I can help."

"I should think not. 'Tis certain after your near-drowning you would shy away from old habits."

Old habits? "You mean, I can swim?"

Roland shot her a confounded look. "You, my sweetest, swim like a mermaid. Was it not how you survived the mighty Channel?"

How uncanny that she and her ancestor had faced a similar accident in the Channel, and even more so that she, who didn't know how to swim, had survived.

"Your tendency for unladylike pursuits always worried me," Roland continued, drawing Nadine out of her thoughts. "Thus 'tis pleased that I am with your change of heart. Mayhap 'tis too much to hope that you have also desisted of throwing knives like a man?" Roland's lips twisted in obvious displeasure. " 'Tis a dangerous practice. You almost made me a target once, when I unwisely crossed your path while you practiced with your father."

Faulk stepped up, pulling Nadine to his side, never missing an opportunity to touch her, to show Roland to whom she belonged. "I am most grateful for Nadine's abilities. She saved my life, and as far as I am concerned, she can practice her skills any time she wishes." He grinned, obviously pleased with the thought of Roland as her practice target.

Nadine, on the other hand, was not grinning. She was stunned. On that fateful day on the road from London she had believed she'd saved Faulk's life by mere luck. Faulk and Eva had remarked on her skill then, but Nadine had dismissed their comments without a thought, until now.

Reliving the incident in her mind, she remembered how she'd reached for the knife and thrown it with unerring precision. The medieval Nadine possessed such skill but not her.

Sacré Coeur! Could she be the medieval Nadine's reincarnation? That would explain the uncanny resemblance between them, the remembered skills with the knife, the fact she hadn't drowned when she fell into the Channel. Did she swim to that beach near Faulk's castle? Oh, how she wished she could remember.

You will be given a second chance, do not waste it. The gypsy's words of the future returned to Nadine. Was that what this was all about? A second chance to live her life over? That would explain her travel through time.

Still, the medieval Nadine seemed to have been a daring woman. She swam—Nadine was petrified of the water. She threw knives skillfully—just the memory of killing Faulk's assailant made Nadine shiver with dread. If she was the reincarnation of the medieval Nadine, how come she had become so tentative, so timid in her future life?

Consequence of what happened to her in this century, maybe?

There was no going back now. She must reach Rouen at all costs. Nadine steeled herself for what was yet to come.

Somehow, it was agreed they would all travel together. In a manner of speaking. Faulk's men and their horses took to one side of the deck, while Roland's took to the other, separated by an invisible, yet very real wall of hostility. Faulk and Roland unceremoniously ushered Nadine to a small cabin. Actually, to call it a cabin was a gross exaggeration, for it was but a big square box fastened to the wooden planks in such a careless way that she wondered if it hadn't been put there solely for her benefit.

She half crawled through the small opening and wished she hadn't. The inside didn't look any more promising. The only furniture were a small table with a bowl on top of it, flanked by an uncomfortable-looking cot. And the confining walls were not a welcome sight, either. Yet the alternative would be to face the Channel directly, and she wasn't ready for that.

Nadine disliked confining places, but she dreaded the open water.

At least the small entrance held no door, affording a little light and air to filter through the two pairs of legs that guarded it, making the place less suffocating. Therefore, inside she would stay.

The boat rocked suddenly. They must be on their way. Queasiness overtook her and Nadine trudged to the little cot, slumping down on it. Taking deep breaths, she waited until the bile slithered down her throat, and prayed this wasn't an indication she was about to be whisked through time.

Yet the levitating feeling never came, neither the dizziness that preceded it, only a mild queasiness that she could attribute to her empty stomach, or her undeniable phobia of water.

Nadine closed her eyes, forcing her thoughts to go blank and her body slack, trying to control the *mal de mer* and the sweeping emotions of dread. After she tossed and turned endlessly on the cot, the blessed slumber finally took over her.

An abrupt motion of the ship pitched Nadine out of her soothing dreams and almost off the cot. She hung on for balance. Stealing a peek through the door, she saw that the day had turned dark. The ship lurched again, toppling the bowl on top of the small table into Nadine's lap. Water splashed on her face, stealing her breath away. An overpowering feeling of dread overtook Nadine as she was swept away by another vision.

Frigid waves rippled over her head as Nadine sank into the dark water, struggling to break the surface. Yet her efforts pushed her farther down into the darkness and coldness of the Channel. She fought bravely, but with her lungs about to explode, Nadine turned the remnant of her depleted strength into a prayer, *"Mon Dieu, do not let it end this way!"*

The cry leaped from the vision into reality. Nadine pressed her back against the flimsy wall of the cabin and fought to chase away the vision, while her prayer echoed in her mind. Did she cry it out loud?

"Nadine," Faulk called, rushing to her side. She clung to him in desperation. Dread from past and present mingled in her gut, constricting her throat. She didn't want to die. She refused to die.

Faulk rubbed her trembling limbs. "Fear not, my fair lady," he said. "I shall protect you."

Could Faulk protect her against fate? The water had taken her away once, she couldn't allow it to happen again. A sudden understanding came to Nadine. She had once died in this same Channel, hence her phobia of water. Well, she was going to win the battle this time. She was going to survive and live her life through.

A courage she never knew she possessed was born in her heart. She lifted her face to Faulk. Lost herself in the brilliant indigo of his eyes. She was thankful for his presence, his strength. Even though Faulk had never declared his love for her, his actions spoke volumes of his feelings. He'd dropped everything just to escort her. Sensing her need, he rushed to her side and offered his support.

Faulk's warm lips grazed her own, breathing life into her frozen heart. Nadine slanted her face to deepen the kiss when Roland's voice broke through the idyllic moment.

"So here you are."

Nadine cursed inwardly. Faulk grunted.

"I grow tired of your liberties with my betrothed," Roland said.

Hand on the hilt of his sword, Faulk rose and faced Roland. "If it pleases you, I am most willing to settle this matter hither and now."

The invitation was unmistakable. Nadine didn't want them to fight. Even though she believed Faulk would be the victorious one, she couldn't risk the chance he could be hurt or even killed in such a confrontation.

She positioned herself between the two seething men. "I am sure we can resolve this by peaceful means."

Roland ignored her, addressing Faulk instead. "Are you

also willing to risk Nadine's safety just to soothe your pride?"

Nadine frowned. How would her safety be compromised if they fought? Could she be caught in the confrontation? Or did Roland mean to harm her?

Whatever it was, Faulk was obviously not willing to risk her being harmed. His hands dropped from his sword and balled up alongside his powerful thighs in an obvious sign of frustration.

"I thought not." Roland smirked. "You are a wise man, my Lord Faulk. Now, be wiser and realize that not even by the force of your sword shall you take Nadine away from me."

Faulk stepped in front of Nadine and faced Roland. "By God and King alike Nadine belongs to me. Yet, if I must"—his hand caressed the hilt of his sword—"I am prepared and willing to defend what is mine. Make no mistake about it."

After the interminable Channel crossing and the endless hours on the river Seine, they reached Rouen. It was still dark when they disembarked, but morning dawned as they left the docks and veered into the countryside, bypassing the town.

Nadine absorbed the beautiful scenery, inhaling deeply the fresh air. She listened to the birds chirping and tried to calm her racing pulse as emotion gripped her. She was coming home. She wished she'd seen her hometown, even as different as it might look in this century, but to reach the medieval Nadine's home was more important at this time.

There, just around these trees, home awaited. The thought came out of nowhere, startling Nadine.

"We are almost home," Roland said, pulling to her side, confirming what she shouldn't have known, but did. Faulk immediately took her other side.

And then, there it was. *Rosemanor. Home.*

Nadine's heart stampeded as she rode through the iron-fortified wooden gate and into a bailey overpopulated with huts, people, and animals. They crossed a second gate into a smaller bailey and into the great stone keep.

Once inside, Nadine's attention darted from the colorful tapestries and banners on the walls of the great hall, to the stone floors—surprisingly, sans rushes—and to the raised dais.

Drawn in by an invisible thread, Nadine silently distanced herself from her escorts and wandered to the dais. There she caressed the intricately carved back of the lord's chair as if it was a person.

The visions returned then. They came swiftly, over-whelmingly. Scenes of happiness, of joy, in this very hall, with herself as protagonist. Scenes that flashed so rapidly they looked like slides in motion, confounding her with their colorful memories.

"I am home," Nadine whispered. Her words reverberated in the silent hall, finding echo in her heart. Faulk stared at her with wonder; Roland's eyes gleamed with an unidentifiable emotion.

"Ma petite fleur."

Nadine turned, uncertain if she was seeing another vision. She stared at the woman dashing at her with open arms and tear-filled eyes. Reality only sank in when Nadine found herself plastered against the woman's soft body in an embrace not likely to end anytime soon.

"You are alive," the woman cried harder, caressing Nadine's hair.

Two thoughts collided in Nadine's mind. *Marie-Elise. Maman.* Past and future, meshed in jumbled images and emotions, overloaded her senses. Without a sound, Nadine collapsed to the floor.

●　　●　　●

The heady aroma of roses eased Nadine out of her unconsciousness. Slowly she opened her eyes, and through a diaphanous veil, she saw a bowl filled with a rainbow of roses across the room. She stared at it for a moment, and incomprehensibly, she knew where she was. She recognized the room, the furnishing, the wider-than-normal windows.

She was in her bedchamber.

Nadine sprung up in the four-poster bed. This was not a vision. She knew she was in her bedroom, as she'd known Rosemanor lay beyond the trees before Roland's announcement. Somehow she was beginning to remember her past life, not in out-of-body visions, but in memories that came in a haphazard manner.

"Ma petite fleur, how do you fare?"

Nadine's heart lurched when the woman she'd seen earlier at the hall poked her face between the bed curtains. *Maman?* Nadine almost fainted again as she stared at a younger version of her mother. *Mon Dieu*, if she was the reincarnation of a medieval Nadine, would this woman be the early incarnation of her own mother?

Emotion constricted Nadine's throat. Fighting the tears, she trembling reached for the woman's face. *"Maman."* The whisper had barely escaped her lips when her fingers touched her mother's face.

"Ma petite fleur."

They fell into each other's embrace. When Nadine felt her mother gently caressing her hair, as she had always done, Nadine's control snapped. Tears sprung forth in a convulsion of sobs.

"There, there," her *maman* soothed, herself crying softly. "Worry not. You are safe now. You are home."

With her heart about to explode with joy, Nadine gently pushed her mother away from her. Still holding her, Nadine stared at her *maman*, marveling at having been given such wondrous gift—her mother. It was more than she could have ever wished for.

Marie-Elise, the name suddenly flashed in Nadine's mind as memories came to her. Scenes of motherly concern and love filled her mind and heart, and Nadine realized Marie-Elise was not the medieval Nadine's mother, but her nurse.

How could Marie-Elise be anything but her mother?

"You are not my mother," Nadine whispered, shocked at the revelation.

Marie-Elise's face blanched. "I love you like a daughter."

Oh, she had not meant to hurt Marie-Elise. "Forgive me," Nadine said. "I meant no disrespect. I . . ." Nadine lowered her eyes. *Mon Dieu*, how was she going to look at Marie-Elise without wishing she was her mother? And how was she going to control her emotions every time she faced that beloved countenance? "I am a little confused. My memories are mixed up. Please, forgive me."

Marie-Elise took Nadine's hands into hers. Her pained expression was gone. Concern etched her face. " 'Twas a great ordeal you have been through, but 'tis over now. You are home."

Home. It was her home, yet it was not. Marie-Elise was her mother, yet she was not. She was the medieval Nadine, yet she was not. So much to absorb, to understand, to accept.

Nadine rose from the bed and strode to the nearby table. She poured water from the carafe into the bowl with the ease of an often-repeated action, and splashed her face with the cool water.

As she spun around, Marie-Elise waited with a cloth. "Your captors sent your father a strand of your hair as proof they kept you, but I never thought they would do such a dreadful thing to your beautiful hair."

Avoiding Marie-Elise's sorrowful gaze, Nadine took the towel from her hands and dried her face. "It does not matter." She tried to sound nonchalant. If her short hair elicited such reaction, how would she explain her tattoo to Marie-Elise?

That was a subject she'd rather not discuss right now.

She folded the towel and set it on the back of the chair. "I must go down to the hall. I do not trust Faulk alone with Roland. I hope they have not killed each other by now."

"Is Faulk the handsome man with the brilliant blue eyes?"

Nadine grinned. "Lord Faulk Brookstone in the flesh."

"He seemed very protective of you. When you swooned, he shot through the hall like a straight arrow to you."

"That is Faulk." Nadine chuckled. "I love him." The confession escaped her lips, stunning Nadine. Why would she feel compelled to share her innermost feelings with Marie-Elise? Maybe because she would have done so with her mother. Maybe because she instinctively trusted in Marie-Elise. Yet having gone this far Nadine chose not to stop there. "And I shall marry him as soon as the king agrees to annul my betrothal to Roland."

"Your betrothal to Roland?"

The shock stamped on Marie-Elise's face alerted Nadine. "Were you not aware of that?"

"Nay," Marie-Elise vehemently denied.

"Roland has a betrothal document, signed by my father."

Marie-Elise shook her head. " 'Tis impossible. I am certain, as I am that your father lies in his grave in Rose-manor's graveyard, that he would not betroth you to Roland."

"How can you be so sure?"

"Before your abduction, your father spoke of betrothing you to the son of an Englishman, a friend of his, but with your disappearance I forgot all about it and we never spoke of it again."

"Maybe the betrothal was never finalized and my father decided to give me to Roland?"

"I cannot fathom your father delivering you to a such a maladroit man. Roland's inability to become a knight was a great disappointment to him."

"If my father had such a low opinion of Roland, how

come he kept him at Rosemanor?" Nadine searched her
mind for memories of Roland, but the man was like a house
fixture, something you knew was there, yet paid no attention to it.

"Your father was honor bound to give Roland a chance
in life." Marie-Elise sighed. "In his fostering years, your
father met a distant cousin with whom he formed a close
friendship over the years. On the eve they were knighted
there was a huge feast. All within the castle drank themselves into a stupor in joyful merriment, but before that eve
was over tragedy struck.

"Your father got involved in a fight. In the melee that
issued, with his wits mellowed by ale, your father almost
got himself killed. His distant cousin saved your father's
life, and in doing so he was mortally wounded. At death's
door he begged your father to take care of his bastard son—
Roland, who was a babe at the time. Roland's mother—a
village wench of low birth—gladly delivered him into your
father's hands. And that was how Roland came to be here."

Her father was an honorable man, and he could have
done no less by Roland, but would that include betrothing
his only daughter to him? "Would *Papa*—" Nadine stopped
abruptly, suddenly realizing she remembered the medieval
Nadine's father as her own. More and more Nadine understood the riddle of her return in time. What she couldn't
understand was why her mother of the future was not also
her mother in this time.

Nadine glanced at Marie-Elise, who stared at her, waiting
for her to finish her question. "Would *Papa* betroth me to
Roland as part of his debt to the cousin who saved his life?"

"I believe not. You were your father's greatest treasure,
ma petite fleur. He loved you with all his heart. He wished
much more for you than Roland."

Maybe. Maybe not.

"Is Roland aware of his circumstances?"

"Aye, your father told him as soon as Roland was old

enough to understand what that meant. However, even after your birth, I believe Roland secretly fancied himself your father's heir."

She was her father's heir. Would Roland fake a betrothal agreement to possess her and therefore Rosemanor? Or was she deluding herself instead of facing the unfathomable reality of having to marry a man she didn't love? And what about the Englishman? No, she would not even consider him. There was no indication of the existence of any other agreement but the one Roland had produced.

And one unwanted betrothal was enough.

Chapter 16

STILL MULLING OVER her conversation with Marie-Elise, Nadine returned to the great hall. Her gaze instantly fell on Faulk. The sight of him sent electrical waves throughout her body. Responding to the irresistible urge to be by his side, Nadine smiled and sauntered to him.

As if sensing her presence, Faulk turned to her and stood up. So did Roland.

Nadine's smile disappeared. The sight of Roland at the lord's chair—her father's chair—filled her with such intense anger, she overlooked Faulk and dashed blindly the few feet that separated her from Roland's side. At the same time she reached for her girdle, but the absence of the expected dagger jolted her.

She stopped abruptly, staring at her empty hand.

Realizing what she'd been about to do, Nadine fought for control over the foreign emotions. Each added memory pertaining to a past life she couldn't completely understand—yet could hardly deny—added a new dimension to her. They transformed her, completed her, changed her into the new person she was rapidly becoming, or the old person she used to be.

And it scared her out of her wits.

Nadine's glance shifted from her empty hands back to Roland, and her anger stirred anew. "Why do you sit in my father's chair?"

She resisted the urge to forcibly yank Roland out of that chair, realizing it would be to her advantage, at this point, to curb her confrontational instincts. At least, until she knew for sure what game he played.

Shooting Nadine an outraged look, as if she had no right to question him, Roland stiffened his stance. " 'Tis my place as you betrothed."

His response confirmed Nadine's nagging doubts about Roland's motives to wish to marry her. They had nothing to do with his professed love for her—a love he insisted she shared but of which she had no recollection—and everything to do with the fact Roland aspired to be the lord of Rosemanor, the successor of her father.

"We are not wedded yet, Roland. You dishonor my father's memory by usurping his place."

Roland's face turned crimson.

"May I be of assistance, Nadine?" Faulk asked.

Nadine knew Faulk was itching to fight Roland, but she also knew that wouldn't be wise. Roland was too much of an unknown, his rights over her not completely delineated yet. Caution was the best avenue for now. "I am sure Roland understands my feelings about this." She glared at Roland until he hesitantly moved to another chair.

Relieved, Nadine sought her place at the table, expecting to find Marie-Elise by her side, but Marie-Elise sat at a trestle table below the dais, surrounded by Roland's knights and two of Faulk's men. The remainder of Faulk's men-at-arms would be at the garrison's quarters, Nadine knew, not even questioning anymore the source of her knowledge.

Without hesitation, Nadine strode down to Marie-Elise's side. "Come sit by me," she asked.

Marie-Elise darted a glance at Roland. "He shall not be pleased."

"But it shall please me." The fact that Marie-Elise was not her mother didn't diminish her importance in Nadine's life, both past and future. And for that alone she would respect her. Besides, she knew Marie-Elise had always sat at the main table, by her side.

Beaming, Marie-Elise followed Nadine. As soon as they reached the lord's table, Roland presented his objections. " 'Tis not proper for servants to sit at the lord's table, Nadine. No matter how dear they are to us."

"Marie-Elise is not a servant." Ignoring Roland, Nadine gently sat Marie-Elise down on the bench beside her, before sitting herself. "She has always sat by me, and she shall continue to do so."

Nadine wouldn't allow Roland to ride roughshod over her and the people she loved. Especially Marie-Elise. Such assertiveness surprised and delighted Nadine. She had always wanted to be less timid toward life. Maybe her wish had finally come true.

Roland scowled. "I see you are more and more yourself."

It was obvious Roland's comment was not meant as a compliment, yet Nadine decided to take it as such. The bombardment of information, emotions, and memories she sustained, though overwhelming, could only unite her own differences, completing her as nothing else could. "Thank you for your concern. It has indeed been a trying time for me."

" 'Tis pleasing to see you begin to unveil the darkness of your past," Faulk spoke again. "And take your rightful place as 'twas intended."

Nadine fixed her gaze on Faulk's stirring blue eyes. He grinned, and the little dimple on his cheek made an appearance. Faulk hadn't smiled much of lately, but now he seemed pleased. No doubt because she followed his example and clashed with Roland.

How much more pleased—or annoyed—would he be if he knew Roland's plight? She had to talk to Faulk alone. Tell him what she had learned and surmised. Hear his reassuring thoughts.

Touch him . . . kiss that incredible mouth of his . . . lose herself in his powerful embrace . . .

Nadine needed Faulk in the most primal way. He was the link to her present life. Not to her medieval life, which she remembered, but couldn't quite surrender to; not to her life in the future, which she couldn't forget, yet didn't quite matter at this point; but to the present, to the new life, to the life not lived yet that waited for both of them.

After the incredible night of passion they had shared, they hadn't spent a moment together, and Nadine needed to be with him again. To renew, to strengthen, to consolidate the ties between them.

As soon as this blasted supper was over, Nadine decided, she would find a way to drag Faulk somewhere private. The thought of dragging Faulk anywhere was ludicrous, of course, and amusing. A smile blossomed on her lips.

"As soon as supper is ended, I wish a word with you, Nadine."

Faulk's sudden request—or demand?—anticipated her wishes. Maybe *she* would be the one dragged to somewhere private, and the thought was equally pleasurable. "As you wish, my lord."

Both ignored Roland's disagreeable mutter.

Her fantasies were not to be fulfilled, Nadine realized as soon as the hall emptied of everyone except herself, Faulk, Roland, and Marie-Elise.

"I have been overly accommodating of your improper behavior," Roland said. "But I shall not condone such behavior under this roof."

"Marie-Elise will chaperone us, so you need not be worried about improprieties," Nadine said, wishing for the very improprieties she was forced to deny.

"Whatsoever you must say to Lord Faulk, you may say it in my presence." Roland's eyes narrowed. "Or are you planning to flee with him as I turn my back? I warn you, Nadine, I shall follow you to the ends of the earth."

"I have no need to steal Nadine away," Faulk interrupted, standing up and looking down on Roland. "Whatever rights you may think you have over Nadine shall soon be dismissed."

Roland yawned. "I grow tired of this duel of words betwixt us, Lord Faulk. As much as you would wish otherwise, you and I both know to whom Nadine belongs."

He turned to Nadine. "Say what you must to Lord Faulk, for he must depart soon on his futile quest to seek the king, and I wish to retire for the eve." He yawned again.

In a move so fast, Nadine could only gasp in astonishment, Faulk reached across the table and grabbed Roland by the lap of his tunic, pulling him up from his sitting position. The bored expression on Roland's face swiftly disappeared. "Until the king avows the betrothal betwixt you and Nadine, what you have is a useless parchment that gives you no right over her."

Nadine nodded agreement. Roland had no right to tell her what to do.

"Our union is approved by Nadine's father," Roland said. "Which is much more than you can say about yourself."

Nadine's heart constricted. Could her father have really wished for her to marry Roland?

"Or so you profess," Faulk said.

Obviously Faulk had the same doubts she had. Were they deluding themselves?

Faulk continued to hold Roland in the air. "I wish to speak with Nadine in private. Since I am an honorable man, I shall allow Marie-Elise to remain with us. But you, Roland, I want out of this hall, now." Faulk clearly enunciated the words, then abruptly dropped Roland to his feet.

Seething, Roland held on to the chair for balance. He rearranged his clothing, then turned to Marie-Elise. " 'Tis your duty to safeguard your lady's honor, as despoiled as 'tis." Then, he slowly made his way out of the hall.

Roland's outrage could be construed as a just reaction from a thwarted man. Still, something didn't quite ring true to Nadine. She searched the recesses of her mind for some memory of Roland that could elucidate the puzzle.

As children, growing up at Rosemanor, Nadine and Roland had led very separate lives, for the simple fact he was male and she female, which determined the activities in which they participated.

As adults they met at mealtimes, or when he came into the hall and solar seeking her father, or on the occasions Nadine ventured into the bailey. Sometimes they rode together with her father, their conversations polite and ordinary.

Then why did she feel uneasy about him?

"He is gone," Faulk said. "We may speak now. Have you found what you sought, Nadine?"

Faulk's question shook Nadine. She wasn't even sure anymore what she sought. What started as a search for an answer to her return in time had turned into a quest for an identity.

There was a time in the future when Nadine thought she had it all—a wonderful family, even love. However, what she believed was love turned out to be betrayal, and her family—the only thing that really mattered—lost in a freak accident.

That was when she'd been whisked back to this century, where her life began anew. Nadine caught sight of Marie-Elise smiling at her, and her heart filled with love for the woman.

Fate took away her *Maman,* yet now it gifted her with Marie-Elise.

Nadine's glance swept the great hall of Rosemanor, and she felt strangely at home. Her memories of this past life were easing her into this century, into this life, into this manor.

Fate took her away from the future, from where she thought she belonged, yet it gave her back this medieval identity in this medieval time.

And then there was Faulk. The handsome, stubborn, medieval lord, whose smile brightened her day, whose strength kept her going, whose faith never failed her.

Family. Home. Love. All within her reach. Her choice.

Second chance. Both the gypsy and the witch had warned Nadine she'd been given a second chance to complete what was interrupted.

Would she take the chance? Was she brave enough to bridge the gap between the two emotional beings warring inside of her? One part of her wanted to bury her head in the sand and wait to see what would survive after the tornado had passed. The other urged her to forge on, to live life to the fullest, to not waste the second chance fate was giving her.

Faulk had indeed asked the most relevant of questions. Had she found what she sought? She lifted her gaze to him. His jaw clenched, waiting for her answer.

"I am Nadine du Monte, of Rosemanor of Rouen. I have found what I sought." A warm sense of peace filled her heart.

He gave her a little smile, a quick glimpse of the dimple on his face, then peered wearily at her. "Do you remember the betrothal?"

Nadine shook her head. "I have no recollection of a betrothal." Yet, according to Roland, she should. Could it be that she couldn't remember or was there nothing to remember?

"However," she continued, "I have learned some interesting facts."

Faulk's eyebrows rose in attention. "Indeed?"

Nadine related what Marie-Elise had told her about Roland, but said nothing about the Englishman. She didn't think Faulk would appreciate yet another man's possible claim on her. "There is a possibility," she said, "that Roland might be lying about the betrothal."

"The thought has crossed my mind. Unfortunately, we need more than suspicion to prove Roland false. After all, he possesses a tangible document that we lack."

Nadine nodded. "You told me the final decision lies with the king."

"Verily."

"And you know where to find him?"

"I shall head to his last encampment—a three day's ride from Rouen. If he has moved, he is not far from there. Richard fights Philip over his English possessions, and he would be near his domain."

Nadine nodded. "Good. Then I shall go with you." That way she would be with Faulk and away from Roland. Could they take Marie-Elise with them? Nadine would certainly not leave her behind.

"Absolutely not."

Faulk's refusal slowly penetrated Nadine's brain. "What do you mean, absolutely not?"

"You shall go nowhere. 'Tis my duty to petition the king. Besides, I cannot afford to be slowed down by you."

"So you rather I stayed at Roland's mercy? Such protection you offer me."

Faulk groaned, frustrated. Would Nadine ever not gainsay him? Would she ever trust him to know what was best for her? She had once doubted his honor, now she doubted his ability to protect her. "I have made arrangements for you safety, Nadine. I would not leave you unprotected. It behooves you to trust me."

"What arrangements?"

"Do you recall Sir Reggie? A stocky man with arms as thick as tree trunks and hair as red as fire?"

Nadine took a moment to answer, then she nodded.

"I met him on the Crusades years ago and was pleased to see he is a knight at Rosemanor. He and your father's men-at-arms swore to protect you in my absence."

"I was under the impression that my father's men-at-arms answered to Roland," Nadine said.

"In a manner of speaking. At least, until the betrothal is proved false—"

Nadine rolled her eyes.

"However," Faulk continued, "the men are loyal to you, Nadine. You are the lady of Rosemanor, and they shall not forget it. I made sure of that."

Looking unconvinced, Nadine exhaled audibly, making no effort to hide her doubts, yet she said naught more.

She should know he would weigh the risks before deciding she should remain at Rosemanor. 'Twould be so good to have Nadine trust him and abide by his wishes without gainsaying him at every turn. Mayhap once they were wedded, she would be more biddable.

Faulk snorted at the thought. The only time Nadine had been biddable was when she had surrendered her body to him. That was how he wished her to be, totally under his control.

Yet even then, Faulk was forced to admit to himself, she had wrestled the control from him when she straddled and rode him like a mighty destrier. When she touched him in ways that reduced him to moans of pleasure. When he exploded, like an alchemist's mixture, when he sank into the paradise of her body.

Faulk shot his fingers through his hair, shaking off the erotic memories. God's teeth, but the lady had bewitched him. He shifted uncomfortably on his feet and cleared his throat. "I depart at dawn, and shall be no longer than I must." His voice sounded raspy to his own ears.

Nadine said naught.

Annoyed, Faulk pivoted and stepped outside the hall, running into Roland. "Be forewarned," Faulk said. "I shall skin you alive do you harm Nadine in any way while I am gone."

"Come on, Marie-Elise," Nadine urged as she scurried the corridors of Rosemanor in the darkness of predawn. In one hand she held her gown up so she would not trip on the long hem, and in the other a foul-smelling torch that sputtered more smoke than light. "I cannot allow him to depart without seeing him again."

"Nadine, you are heels over head in love with this man. You saw him at supper!" Marie-Elise grunted, hurrying to catch up with Nadine.

Heels over head? Wasn't it head over heels? Nadine smiled at Marie-Elise's grumpiness, knowing she was really worried about being discovered sneaking about the manor at this hour of the night, not about Nadine's obvious feelings for Faulk.

Yet it was those feelings that made her want to see Faulk again. The way they parted last night had not been the way Nadine had planned. She didn't want him to leave unhappy with her. She should've just trusted his judgment, after all he had her best interest at heart. It was not like her at all to be that confrontational.

Or maybe it was.

Since discovering her past life in this medieval time, Nadine saw her rather timid nature run over by the more flamboyant medieval Nadine. It was almost as if she had a split personality. She did and said things that were at the same time natural and unexpected to her. Her behavior astounded and pleased her. Maybe with time she would be able to blend flamboyance and caution to a perfect fit.

Meanwhile, she planned to use the time Faulk was away to discover more about herself and with a little luck uncover the truth about this betrothal to Roland. She couldn't put all her hopes on the king's decision. What if he decided against her? No, she would conduct her own investigations.

They reached the great hall, and though it was folly to try and cross it—she would be too visible—she had no alternative. Oh—the thought suddenly flashed in her mind halting her steps—she should've gone through the chapel and into the garden. Nadine pivoted, intending to retrace her steps, when she heard footsteps coming her way.

Now she really had no alternative. Nadine flew down the stone steps, followed closely by Marie-Elise. The great hall appeared empty. The trestle tables still reclined against the walls, but the pallets the servants slept on were already removed in preparation for the morning meal. The great hearth gave away enough light, so Nadine discarded her torch.

She tiptoed to the front door, which lay half-open. Carefully she peeked through the gap. Dark clouds partially covered the moon, yet dawn was not far behind. The darkness prevented Nadine from seeing much, but darkness would also serve as a cover to her.

"Go, Marie-Elise. Send Faulk to me in the garden," Nadine whispered.

"Are you certain this is wise? If Roland learns of this mischief—"

"He shall never learn of it if we do not tell him. Please, Marie-Elise, I must see Faulk before he departs."

Marie-Elise sighed. "Very well."

Relying on instincts and touch to guide her, Nadine scurried along the manor's wall, toward the back and the garden, while Marie-Elise went the opposite direction.

The heady fragrance of roses filled Nadine's nostrils, and her feet softly crushed the dew-covered leaves on the ground of Rosemanor's garden. She'd been here many times and would have found it even with her eyes closed, Nadine knew. Unerringly she hastened to a secluded spot where a stone bench stood. The vines and bushes surrounding the place provided her with a most private spot.

Nadine smiled, pleased with her boldness.

Damn Roland to hell! Faulk cursed as he prepared to leave Rosemanor. If Roland had not appeared at Whitecastle when he did, Faulk would now be wedded to the fair Nadine and his seed would have undoubtedly taken root in her womb.

Instead, here he was, once more traipsing about the kingdom seeking ways to assure his right to the continuity of his line. Faulk detested the idea of having to rely on the king's whims for such an important task, but there was no other honorable way.

Many a time he wished he had skewed Roland through with his sword and ended, once and for all, his claims over Nadine. Yet, as much as the idea pleased him, Faulk knew he could not do away with Roland in a disreputable fight. And the little vermin avoided any fair confrontation with him.

The earlier he left Rosemanor, the better. Faulk hoped to find the king, obtain what he wished, and return no later than a sennight. Meanwhile, his men's presence, and Nadine's own men-at-arms, led by Sir Reggie, assured him that she would be safe.

A whistle distracted Faulk from his thoughts. Suspicious, he sought the source. A shadow warned him of a presence half-hidden behind a post. With sword in hand Faulk moved stealthily to the spot.

"Speak," Faulk hissed, pressing his sword against the person's heart.

"Oh, please, do not harm me." The cloak hood fell to reveal the face of Marie-Elise. Surprised, Faulk withdrew his weapon, then he stiffened. "Is something amiss with Nadine?"

"Nadine is well, my lord. She wishes to speak with you in the garden."

What did Nadine want with him? Faulk followed Marie-Elise into the darkness of the garden. He found Nadine sitting on a stone bench. She rose immediately at the sight of him.

"I could not let you go without saying farewell," she said.

"We have said our farewells." Was she planning to trick him into taking her with him, even after he had made it abundantly clear he would not?

"But not in a satisfying manner." She took a step toward him, then stood on her tiptoes and kissed him lightly on the lips.

Faulk gaped at her. Did she mean to soften him first, then demand to accompany him? If that was her intention she would be sorely disappointed.

A cool breeze whispered through the leaves then. The dark clouds dissipated in the sky, and the moon shone silver sparkles on Nadine's golden hair. Her cloak, gathered at her throat, flared open in the front, revealing the thin chemise she wore. Her nipples distended against the fine fabric. Faulk almost fell to his knees.

He shook his head. "What do you seek, Nadine?" He would not allow her to control him.

"I ask you to be very persuasive when you speak with the king. I have no intention to be tied forever to Roland."

"And so you risk his wrath to meet with me alone, in the garden, at dawn?"

Her long fingers caressed his shoulder. "I could not allow you to leave without an incentive to return." Her golden eyes settled on him, and she gave him the most brilliant smile a woman had the right to give.

He was but a man, and a bewitched one at that. Faulk excused himself as he pulled Nadine flat against him, making no attempt to hide his growing desire for her. He wished to fuse his body to hers until they formed only one body, one breathing life. His lips took total possession of her mouth, and his tongue delved deep into her soft recesses.

God's teeth! But she made it difficult to leave her.

He was growing too attached to Nadine. Too hungry for her favors. Too pleased with her touch. No woman should have such power over a man. But what would it matter? He would have Nadine under his control. Soon she would be large with his child, and the prophecy would be fulfilled. His vow would be completed. His life would return to normal.

Meanwhile he would brand her once again as his. As often as he could. As deep as he would.

He imprisoned Nadine against a trellis covering the stone bench, and in response she lifted one leg and embraced his hip. Nadine's wild nature excited him. That she desired him pacified his own overwhelming feelings for her. He pushed her chemise up her thighs and touched her wonderful secret spot. So moist, so ready for him.

He undid his ties and his breeches fell. He lifted Nadine and brought her down on him, pushing himself into her. The world swirled around him as he thrust inside her glorious body until they both exploded.

'Twas over too soon, he regretted, holding on to her until their breathing returned to normal. He brought her down to her feet and kissed her luscious lips tenderly, caressing her soft hair. "Nadine," he whispered, wishing he were back home at Whitecastle with her, instead of traipsing around to assure she belonged to him.

He took a step back and rearranged his clothing. A hustling noise behind him warned of another presence. He spun around, hiding Nadine with his body. Marie-Elise's worried face appeared betwixt the foliage.

Somehow the day had dawned without his knowledge.

Faulk took a deep breath, exhaling slowly, then pivoted

to face Nadine again. His gaze fell on her swollen lips and he cursed the need to depart. Yet he must depart, so he could return soon. Nadine belonged to him in more ways than one, and he would not let her go.

He kissed her once again. "Farewell, my fair Nadine. Be true to me while I am gone."

Standing on her tiptoes, she kissed him back. "Farewell, my lord. Be swift in your return."

Hiding in the bushes, Roland seethed with anger at the scene before him. *Lord Faulk Brookstone shall never reach the king*, he vowed. Indeed, the thought of Faulk lying on a pool of his own damnable blood pleased Roland immensely. Mayhap he should have ordered his minions to return Faulk's head to him. Nay, not even dead he wished to see the likes of Faulk again.

He would have to content himself with possessing Nadine. To enjoy the pleasures her sweet body would yield, the favors she had so freely bestowed on Faulk. Then, and only then, would Roland decide her fate.

Chapter 17

MARIE-ELISE JOINED NADINE in the garden after Faulk had left. They sat side by side on the stone bench, watching the morning grow late.

"I could stay in this spot forever," Nadine said.

"You always loved it here. As a child, many a time you hid yourself behind these bushes, and I went insane seeking you."

Nadine touched Marie-Elises's hands. "You have always been so good to me. Like a mother."

A shadow crossed Marie-Elise's face.

"What is the matter?"

Marie-Elise rose and offered her hand to Nadine. "Come with me, *ma petite fleur.*"

Without questioning, Nadine followed Marie-Elise across the garden, over the stone path, and into the far back of the manor.

At the sight of Rosemanor's graveyard, Nadine halted. Heart pounding violently in her chest, Nadine glanced back at Marie-Elise, who nodded encouragement at her, then back at the series of dirt mounds covered by wildflowers. She stepped carefully between the old graves marked with wooden crosses—her family's graves—then stopped at a particularly well-kept sepulture.

There were no markings indicating a date, just a name on the wooden cross—*Celeste. Her mother's grave.* Nadine felt nothing. Shouldn't she feel some modicum of sadness? Even if she had never met this medieval mother who died giving birth to her?

The mere thought of losing her mother in the future weighted Nadine's heart with sadness. Why didn't she feel the same about her medieval mother?

Nadine said a brief prayer, then moved to the next, more recently dug grave. Immediately her heart bled. *Her father's grave.* Memories of her father in the future mingled with the memories of her medieval father, choking her with such intense grief Nadine cried bitter tears for her double loss.

Feeling a comforting hand on her shoulder, Nadine lifted her gaze to Marie-Elise and found in her presence the strength to let it go. She rested her hand on top of Marie-Elise's. "I am so glad I have you, *Ma*—" Nadine stopped short of calling Marie-Elise *Maman.* The urge was so intense she bit her lips.

"Oh, *ma petite fleur!*" Marie-Elise cried out. "There is so much I must tell you. So much I must beg forgiveness."

"Forgiveness?" Nadine rose and embraced Marie-Elise. She smelled of roses, like her mother, and she was slightly shorter than Nadine, like her mother.

Marie-Elise pushed Nadine gently away. Her trembling hands swiped away a runaway tear. "Long ago," she began with a tremulous voice, "when I was a young maid, I visited a spring fair nearby the castle I lived. There I met a most handsome knight with whom I fell instantly in love."

Marie-Elise shot Nadine a nervous look. Was Marie-Elise going to tell Nadine her life story? Nadine searched her memory but found no recollection of how Marie-Elise came to be at Rosemanor. She had just always been there, and Nadine had never questioned her presence.

"Go on," Nadine prodded when Marie-Elise hesitated. There could be nothing in this sweet woman's past that could make her look so uncertain.

"He—this knight—seemed to be taken with me also." She smiled sadly. "We spent that day together, and before we parted our ways, we kissed, and I knew then that I would love no other."

Again Marie-Elise paused.

"Did he ever return?" Nadine asked, knowing the answer, for Marie-Elise had never married.

"Aye, but not for me." Marie-Elise looked Nadine straight in the eye. "He returned to wed the Lady Celeste. The knight I fell in love with was your father."

Shocked, Nadine took a step toward Marie-Elise. "My father deceived you?" The thought was incomprehensible. Her father was the most honorable man she'd ever known. He wouldn't have done such a thing to Marie-Elise.

" 'Twas not his fault. When we met I thought him a mere knight, not the son of a baron, the du Monte heir. His betrothed had been chosen for him years before without even his knowledge. I was but the daughter of a knight, a companion to Lady Celeste, a position my father obtained in reward for his many years of service to Celeste's father."

"I cannot believe it," Nadine whispered.

"I swear 'tis the truth."

"Oh, I believe you, Marie-Elise," Nadine hastened to say. "What I cannot believe is that my father wronged you so. I am so sorry."

" 'Twas not meant to be." Marie-Elise waved her hand in dismissal. "A highborn lord shall not wed the daughter of a landless knight. He loved me, he told me so, yet he could not go against his father's wishes."

Nadine was suddenly aware of how much circumstances ruled the lives of people throughout the ages. And how lucky she was to be in the same class as Faulk, though he had wanted to marry her even before he knew who she was. The thought warmed her insides and made Nadine love Faulk all the more. She was just so disappointed that her own father had failed his heart so.

"Why did you come to live here? It cannot have been easy for you all these years."

" 'Twas beyond my control. After the wedding ceremony, Lady Celeste insisted I accompany her to her new home."

"Did she ever know?"

Marie-Elise shook her head. She took a deep breath as if to brace herself for the rest of the story. Nadine waited.

"Your father and I avoided each other as much as possible, yet there were occasions . . . 'Twas difficult, for both of us. One eve we found ourselves alone together." Marie-Elise's face grew crimson. "It happened only once, and never again."

"What happened?" Nadine asked, but Marie-Elise's guilty expression revealed the truth to her. *Sacré Coeur!* They had made love. Her father and Marie-Elise had made love. Nadine didn't know what to make of the revelation, or even the reason Marie-Elise would tell her this story now. What purpose would serve to let Nadine know her father had not only wronged Marie-Elise, but had also been unfaithful to her mother?

Marie-Elise broke down in tears.

Still not understanding her reasons, Nadine tried to calm her down. "You must forgive him, Marie-Elise," Nadine whispered. "*Mon Dieu*, you must have loved him so to remain at Rosemanor, to care for his daughter like a mother would. I cannot thank you enough for your sacrifice."

"Oh, *ma petite fleur*, 'twas no sacrifice. You have been a wonderful daughter to me."

Nadine shook her head ready to contradict Marie-Elise and beg her forgiveness for all the mischievous little things she had done as a child, when she was suddenly struck by the revealing truth in Marie-Elise's words.

There could be only one reason it was so important for Marie-Elise to tell her this story.

"You are my *Maman*," Nadine said. *Mon Dieu!* Marie-Elise was her mother, as she had wished, as it was supposed to be, as she would be again in the future when she would finally be reunited with Nadine's father and be happy together for so many years. That was why she felt toward Marie-Elise the way she felt. That was why she had felt nothing at Celeste's grave. Marie-Elise was her mother. She had gotten her mother back.

That very same day, fortified by the wondrous news of finding her mother alive, Nadine began her journey into the medieval life. More and more memories came to her filling the blanks of her past, easing her into a way of life that had, days ago, been totally unknown to her.

At first she craved her daily cup of strong coffee and missed the constant companion of radio music, but soon Nadine relegated those memories to a forgotten corner of her mind. The future no longer mattered. She had her mother, she was rediscovering herself in a past life, and she had Faulk. Or would have if she ever got rid of Roland.

She spent the next days searching the manor for an answer. And yet she found nothing.

That is, until three nights after Faulk had left.

That night Nadine woke up with the odd sensation of being watched. She jerked up in bed and glanced at her mother sleeping peacefully in a makeshift bed at the foot of the fireplace. Through the open window moonlight and a soft breeze infiltrated the room. Her gaze traveled the darkened corners finding nothing but shadows.

It must be her nerves, Nadine thought, lying back down. She closed her eyes, willing herself back to sleep when the odd sensation returned. Her body filled with tremors, and instantly alert, Nadine sat up in bed, eyes flared open.

She immediately recognized the figure standing at the foot of her bed. *"Papa!"* she cried. *Mon Dieu!* Was she dreaming?

Unable to believe her eyes, Nadine rubbed them. Yet, when she looked at her father again, there he stood, smiling at her.

Throwing the covers to the side, Nadine jumped to her feet, but before she could take a step toward him, her father's expression changed from peaceful to anguished. His gaze urged Nadine to look at the floor.

There was a box there. A beautifully carved wooden box in which her father used to keep his valuables. What was he trying to tell her? Confused, Nadine gazed back at him, but he continued to point at the box until his image became hazy and disappeared in the darkness.

Sacré Coeur! What was her father trying to tell her? What was in that box?

"It must be here somewhere," Nadine muttered with her face buried inside the huge wooden trunk that had been her father's. It could not have disappeared without a trace. Frustrated, she sat on the floor. "Where could it be, *Maman*?"

"It used to sit right there on his table," Marie-Elise said, looking under the bed. "But since your father's death and Roland's appropriation of this bedchamber, I have not seen it. Mayhap Roland got rid of it."

Nadine began refilling the trunk she had just emptied. "My father kept his signet ring, jewelry, important parchments, even gold in that box. Roland would not get rid of it."

"He would if it implicated him in any way," Marie-Elise pointed out. "Besides, how could its content possibly help you?"

Nadine shook her head. "*Papa* came to me in a dream. Surely it means something."

Marie-Elise sighed. "We have searched hither and thither and found naught. The only places we have yet to search are the stables and the garrison's quarters."

Finishing her task, Nadine walked to the bed and sat down. Marie-Elise sat by her side. "The stables should not pose too big of a problem, but the garrison's quarters . . ."

"Especially now that Roland sleeps there," Marie-Elise added.

"I have an idea." Nadine jumped. "How about a military inspection?"

"A what?"

"*Papa* used to inspect his men-at-arms' quarters all the time."

"You are not your *papa*, Nadine. You know naught about training and men-at-arms and weapons. What could you possibly inspect?"

"I am my father's heir. Can I not show interest in the state of my own manor and its defense?"

"Would you seek the box under the men-at-arms' derrière?"

Nadine smiled at her mother's sense of humor. "That shall be your task, *Maman*. I shall keep them occupied."

" 'Tis a bold idea."

"Indeed. Yet it might work."

Her bold idea amounted to nothing. That same day, taking advantage of Roland's temporary absence from Rosemanor, Nadine succeeded in entering the garrison's quarters, thanks to Sir Reggie's help. While she distracted the men, Marie-Elise searched the area Roland had set for his private quarters. Unfortunately she found nothing.

The stables yielded similar results. Where on heavens was that box? Did Roland hide it? Nadine couldn't shake the feeling that its content could be her salvation.

Back at her own room, Nadine rid herself of her clothing and stepped into the tub prepared for her bath. Her mother went about the bedchamber tidying the place up.

Nadine wished Faulk hurried back. Not only because she hoped he would bring her freedom from Roland, but because she missed him. Life seemed fuller, rosier when he was present.

Thankfully, Roland had kept his distance these past days, imposing his presence on her only at suppertime, and even at those times he had been eerily polite. He had also acquiesced to her request to move into the garrison's quarters until Faulk returned and the matter of their betrothal resolved. Yet he had yet to relinquish his control over the ruling of the manor. It was obvious Roland still expected to become the lord of Rosemanor.

That was why Nadine was so confounded at his accommodating ways. Was he so confident Faulk would fail in his mission with the king that he felt no need to do anything but wait? Could their betrothal be real?

Mon Dieu, would she be condemned to a life of misery with Roland? Nadine shuddered at the thought.

"Let me wash your back," her mother offered.

Nadine leaned forward and the warm, aromatic water combined with her *maman*'s soft touch soothed her fears.

"I always loved your birthmark," Marie-Elise whispered, tracing the rose on Nadine's shoulders with her fingers.

Nadine stiffened. She didn't know the medieval Nadine had a birthmark. Faulk was the only one who ever mentioned her rose tattoo. Would wonders never cease?

"For some reason it looks different, though. The colors are brighter, the lines stronger. 'Tis odd I never noticed before!"

Nadine swallowed hard. Her mind spinning desperately in search of an explanation.

"I heard that salt water and scalding sun brighten your skin," Nadine offered, praying her impromptu explanation would not sound even odder to Marie-Elise than the changes in her birthmark. "And I had my share of both during my captivity."

"I meant not to vex you with my thoughtless words," Marie-Elise hurriedly said, obviously more concerned with Nadine's emotions than her rationalization.

"It matters not, *Maman*. 'Tis all behind me now." She patted her mother's hand in reassurance.

Pacified, Marie-Elise resumed her rubbing of Nadine's back with a soapy cloth. "I mentioned your birthmark because it reminds me of your father."

"Papa?"

"From the day I told him I was with child, he began a ritual of depositing a rose on my bed pillow. And every eve henceforth I fell asleep staring at it. 'Twas as though he were there with me."

Nadine peered over her shoulder to her mother's dreamlike expression and realized Marie-Elise no longer thought about the changes she had noticed.

"It surprised me not that when you were born, *ma petite fleur*, you carried the mark of the rose on you. The sign of our love."

Joy and sorrow mingled in Nadine's heart. Joy for having her mother with her and sorrow for her mother's loss. She had to remind herself that one day her mother and her father would be happy together, that their love would triumph.

But the future seemed such a distant dream. Burrowed into her past Nadine felt less connected to it. In fact, the few times she had thought about it now, the memories had come to her in a distant, almost dreamlike manner.

With so much to think and do, Nadine could not dwell on a dream. The future was no more. Her present was threatened. To save it she had a box to find, a secret to uncover, a life to live.

• • •

Roland knocked the chalice of wine off the table with one swift backhand. "Bring me good wine, not this horse piss," he hollered to the poor page who scampered away in terror.

Four days. Four damning long days had gone by and still no tidings. By now his bitter enemy should have become food for the vultures.

Then why had he not heard a word?

The boy returned with a new carafe and fearfully poured another goblet, before setting it on the table. Roland took a swallow. The liquid warmed his entrails yet failed to ameliorate his mood.

Not only had he spent four useless days waiting, he had also done so in the cramped quarters of his men-at-arms, while Nadine and that bird-brain, Marie-Elise, pranced about the manor laughing, whispering, and sharing their stupid female secrets.

Roland had moved his belongings to the garrison's quarters as soon as Faulk had left Rosemanor. He had done so, not to abide by Nadine's wishes or in response to Faulk's threats, but to avoid endangering his own position at Rosemanor. He was aware of the growing disquiet amongst the men-at-arms. With Nadine's return, and the whole matter of their betrothal unresolved, their loyalty to him could not be assured.

For this reason, Roland had been introducing new men into the garrison. Men, whose loyalty to him he had no doubt. Still, he needed Sir Reggie and his men as well.

However, Faulk was Roland's biggest obstacle. Without Faulk, Nadine would surely turn to him. She needed him to run Rosemanor, and Roland would be willing to pretend to forgive her trespasses for the sake of becoming Rosemanor's lord.

Yet, once she became his wife, he would make her pay for the pain she had inflicted on him. Roland closed his eyes, trying to chase away the memory of her wanton behavior in the garden with that damnable Faulk. Roland's blood boiled, and he took another gulp of the wine. The image would not leave his mind.

"My lord?"

Roland lifted his gaze to the door, allowing himself a measure of satisfaction at being called lord. He so enjoyed the word. Two of his chosen men-at-arms flanked a bedraggled, wounded creature.

Ah! Finally, tidings were forthcoming.

Roland rose. "Is my enemy dead?"

Unable to stand on his own, the man fell to his knees as soon as the men-at-arms let go of him. His dirty face hit the equally dirty floor. Roland felt no compassion. Ignoring the man's pain, he stepped to him and grabbed him by the lap of his tunic. "Speak," he commanded.

"We failed, my lord." The tremulous words were barely out of his mouth when Roland hurled him into the wall.

"Damnation!" Roland turned his ire to his men. "What have you to say?"

"We found the ground littered with bodies, and this pitiful creature wandering about."

"And my enemy?"

"Not amongst the dead."

"Incompetent imbeciles," Roland cursed.

Rolling into a ball against the wall, the man braced himself for the inevitable blow as Roland advanced toward him.

"What happened?"

"He had unexpected help!" the man cried.

"Help? From whom?"

"I know not, my lord. We were about to overwhelm our victim when a troop of armed men galloped in our direction. I was the only one to escape alive to what amounted to a massacre."

"What good is your miserable life to me?"

"Please, my lord. Be merciful."

"Take this idiot away," Roland bellowed, ignoring the man's pleas for clemency.

Seething, Roland paced the room like a caged animal. *Mon Dieu!* Would he have to take personal care of every little matter? Could he not trust even the simplest of tasks to the bunch of idiots he hired?

Faulk was surely on his way to meet the king, if not by his side already, promising whatever he could to get his hands on Nadine and all her wealth. Aye, the man was no lackwit. In the short time he stayed at Rosemanor, he took stock of its value. The land, the property, the number of knights and men-at-arms. If Faulk was reticent to let Nadine go before, now he would hold on to her like a dog to a bone.

But Roland was persistent, too. Faulk might have reached the king, yet he still had to return alive to claim his prize. Meanwhile, Roland had plans concerning his Nadine.

Aye, 'twould be very enjoyable taming the little bitch. Pity Faulk had already sucked the first honey from her sweet pot. 'Twas of no import, there was still plenty of sweetness to be harvested, for sure. And he would drain her of every drop of it.

Chapter 18

"WHAT IS THIS tale I heard of an ambush?" King Richard demanded.

"Brigands, my liege, naught more," Faulk said.

"Indeed?" The king's eyebrows rose. " 'Tis fortunate then that a company of soldiers arrived just in time to come to your aid."

Faulk nodded agreement. Providential, indeed. Without their help, he would have fallen victim to a band of outlaws and would never have reached the king's camp.

As a warrior Faulk thought naught of fighting enemies in battle. Yet sneaky attacks by nameless opponents rattled him. It happened on the road from Londontown as he escorted Nadine back to Whitecastle, and now as he sought the king.

Were the incidents connected? Faulk had the distinctive impression that on both occasions his head was the prize. The cut on his chin throbbed. He touched it and winced.

Who would want to kill him? Roland came immediately to mind. Had he underestimated his enemy and put Nadine in danger?

God's teeth! He must return to Rosemanor at once.

"And what, pray, brings you back? I see no retinue of men ready to serve me."

Instantly alert, Faulk refocused his attention back on Richard. He had come to the king empty-handed and in a position of beggar. God's teeth, but he hated this. Why had the prophecy chosen such a complicated wench for him?

Suppressing a frustrating groan, Faulk decided to do a little appeasing before he made his request. "At this moment Robert Baldwin is at Whitecastle training the initial group we have assembled. A group I intend to supplement as soon as the matter of my betrothal is resolved."

"You already have my permission to wed whomever you wish. What else is needed?"

"My liege's generosity has overly outdone my humble deeds," Faulk said. "Yet there are complications. This matter is the utmost importance to me, thus I beg my liege's understanding."

King Richard sat straight on his chair. Faulk could almost see his mind working.

"Speak your piece," Richard said after a long, heavy silence.

Faulk inhaled deeply. "There is a lady whom I have . . . compromised."

Richard's eyes narrowed shrewdly. "You wish to set the lady aside?"

"I wish to wed the lady," Faulk promptly responded.

Richard shrugged. "Then wed her. I see no difficulty."

Faulk groaned inwardly. Up to this moment everything had been rather simple in his mind. Nadine was prophesied to be his. She would bear his heir. Therefore she belonged to him. The fact Roland had a previous claim to her had seemed only a nuisance. Had he been overly confident?

"The lady is betrothed to another man." There was no easier way to disclose such fact.

Richard pointed an admonishing finger at Faulk. "I gave you leave to wed any available lady of your choice. I cannot condone your stealing another man's betrothed."

"There were mitigating circumstances." Faulk hated to explain himself, yet he best make it plainly clear all was done honorably. He cleared his throat. "When we met, Nadine had suffered a terrible ordeal and remembered naught of her past. Unaware of a previous commitment on her part, we . . . Well, I had every intention of making the lady my wife. That is when we learned of her true identity and this supposed betrothal."

"Who is she?" the king asked, seeming to enjoy Faulk's discomfort.

"The daughter of Roger du Monte of Rosemanor of Rouen."

"Ah, you chose well, Faulk. The du Monte's wealth is well known in Rouen. An heiress like her could provide a king with much leverage. And you have snatched her from under my nose."

Unhappy, Faulk shifted on his feet. He had already realized Nadine's family was wealthy, yet he had failed to consider what her wealth would mean to the king. God's teeth!

King Richard pondered over the matter for a moment. "I seem to remember a petition of betrothal concerning the du Monte's maiden."

Faulk felt the weight of failure in the pit of his stomach. If King Richard had sanctioned the union betwixt Nadine and Roland, there would be little hope to convince the king to change his mind.

The constriction in his heart told Faulk of how much he cared for Nadine, and the realization shocked him.

To keep her you must find love in your heart, for love is the uniting thread betwixt you.

Faulk rebelled against the witch's warning. He would not allow the quest to fulfill a vow, to prove a prophecy true, to evolve into matters of the heart. He had tried love with Elizabeth and her betrayal had almost destroyed him. He would never give such power to another woman again.

"—Yet at the time I was rather occupied." Richard's voice reached Faulk. "I know not of what became of the document. And I would remember had I set my seal to it. I must set my clerks to unveil the mystery." Waving the matter aside, the king asked, "What says her father?"

"Roger du Monte is dead."

Richard scratched his beard. "Recently, I suppose, since I have not learned of it before."

Faulk nodded.

"And the lady's betrothed?"

"Roland du Monte—a distant kin, I believe."

"A kin has rights," the king said pensively. "If not the lady, at least the lands."

King Richard would surely wish reparation in return for giving Nadine to him, but Faulk could not begrudge his liege-lord. The king would do what he must, and so would Faulk. "I care naught for the lands, my liege. I wish Nadine for a wife."

Richard eyed Faulk intently. "Is she with child?"

Faulk nodded, refusing to consider Nadine might not be enceinte. He hoped his faith in the prophecy would not be his downfall.

"Yours, I assume."

"Aye."

"If she carries your heir, she is yours. The matter of the lands, however, I must consider later."

There were new faces in Rosemanor, Nadine realized. A whole retinue of hard-looking men. Tension was in the air. She could feel it.

Roland had been in a foul mood lately. Last eve, at supper, he kept glaring at her with a blend of desire and hatred. Nadine did not like it one bit.

She should try and send a message to Faulk. At least find out what was keeping him. Almost a sennight had gone by, and he still had not returned. What if he did not return? What if the king refused his petition and he decided to go back to England?

"What is the matter, Nadine? You are restless."

Nadine stopped her pacing. "I like not the changes in Rosemanor, *Maman*. Have you noticed all the new faces?"

Marie-Elise nodded grimly.

"Roland is up to no good. I must find out what he plans." And she could not do it locked in her chamber. She rose and walked to the door.

"Where do you go?"

"I go to the garden. I must think of what to do."

Nadine descended a small circular staircase at the end of the corridor. Booted footsteps behind her warned her she was being followed. She stole a glimpse over her shoulder but couldn't identify the man. He was not one of her father's men or Faulk's. Therefore he must be Roland's.

She would have to speak with Sir Reggie about this. She did not like to be watched. Fortunately, the man stopped outside the door when Nadine entered the chapel. Obviously he knew there was no escaping, for even though she could reach the garden through the chapel, an immense wall surrounded the property, making scaling it a difficult, if not impossible task.

Nadine pulled on the door latch that led to the garden, but the door remained securely fast. Roland must have locked it. Was there another key?

Frustrated, Nadine swirled around and walked back to the two chairs that furnished the small chapel. She had just knelt down on the kneeling pillow on the floor when the corridor door opened and the guard pointed his head inside.

"May I have some privacy to say my prayers?" Nadine demanded. Roland was going too far.

The guard swept the chapel with a suspicious glance but, finding nothing amiss, closed the door without a word.

Nadine joined her hands together in prayer. She recited

the *Paternoster*, then meditated, asking for guidance. She thought of her father and wondered where his box was hidden, and whether there was anything inside that could help her. Her gaze fell on the pristine white cloth that covered the small altar, the gold chalice above it, and on the beautifully carved wooden cross—Christ's symbol of pain and redemption.

A crinkle on the altar cloth caught her eye. Instinctively she stretched her hand to straighten it out, but her fingers touched a hard object. Curious, Nadine scooted closer and lifted the cloth.

Hiding behind it and under the altar she found her father's box.

Her heart skipped a beat, then stampeded out of control. With tremulous hands Nadine pulled the box to her and opened it. Inside, the precious mementos of her father's life spread before her eyes. She touched his signet ring, and tears spilled down her face blurring her vision. Nadine wiped them with her hands. No time for that. She searched the box further, and a small rolled parchment called her attention. It was not sealed, merely tied with a blue ribbon. She untied it. It was a betrothal agreement drawn in a flourishing script identical to the one Roland had produced. Yet this one depicted the union between the only daughter of Roger du Monte and the only son of Warren Brookstone.

Nadine and Faulk's betrothal! The Englishman was Faulk! *Mon Dieu,* it was too good to be true!

In shock, Nadine crushed the parchment against her heart. The box had presented her with her deliverance. She had belonged with Faulk all along. As he had believed.

Surely Roland had never set eyes on this box, for if he had he would have destroyed such damnable evidence. Her *papa* had done it. He had saved her. Nadine lifted her eyes upward and thanked him silently.

Now that she had evidence of Roland's wrongdoing, Nadine had to get this information to Faulk before the king ruled on the matter of her betrothal.

Nadine took the parchment and hid it in the folds of her clothing, then replaced the rest of the contents back in the box and the box to its hiding place.

Nadine related her wondrous discovery to her mother, then sent for Sir Reggie. With his help they would send a message to Faulk and overthrow Roland. The young serving wench returned with the news that Sir Reggie was unavailable and disappeared before Nadine had a chance to inquire further.

Unavailable? What could that mean?

Accompanied by Marie-Elise, Nadine left her bedchamber. Maybe Sir Reggie would be at the hall for supper, or even one of Faulk's men. She had to get a message to Faulk as soon as possible.

Roland was already at the table when Nadine and Marie-Elise entered the great hall. His fingers gripped a goblet of wine, and he sloshed some on the table when he lifted it in salute to Nadine. "My lady." His speech was slightly slurred.

Nadine ignored him, taking her seat. With trepidation, she realized not only was Sir Reggie not at the hall, but none of Faulk's men were there, either.

"What is the matter, my sweetest?" Roland asked.

Nadine winced, then steeled her features. Better not to let Roland guess the reason of her disquiet.

"Feeling a little lonely?" he teased, laughing a humorless laugh.

Nadine shot Roland an annoyed glance and was shocked to see his bloodshot eyes, and his hair—normally neatly combed—hanging in disarray over his face and shoulders. Roland was usually so careful with his appearance. What was eating at him?

Could he have found out about her betrothal to Faulk?

But how could he? Unless he knew about it beforehand. Uneasy, Nadine decided to say or do naught until she had her men about her. She watched as Roland pushed the untouched trencher of food away from him and signaled the page to refill his goblet. Roland had the appetite of a bear and usually devoured twice the amount of food displayed in front of him. However, in the past two nights he had not eaten much but drunk enough to drown a bigger man.

Nadine ate in silence, avoiding eye contact and conversation with the moody Roland. Where the hell were her father's men?

Halfway through supper Roland received a message relayed in a whisper by one of his guards. Without a word he rose and crossed the hall.

At the door he turned and stared at Nadine, then he smiled. A frigid, contemptible smile. A chill of foreboding ran down her spine. *Sacré Coeur!* What was Roland up to?

"Maman," Nadine whispered behind the chalice of wine she brought to her lips. "Is there another key to the garden door?"

If surprised by her question, Marie-Elise's expression revealed naught. "Aye."

Nadine pretended to drink the wine. "Take it and wait for me in the chapel." She set the chalice down on the table, then spoke loud enough for all to hear. "Go and prepare my bedchamber, Marie-Elise. I shall meet you shortly."

Marie-Elise nodded and left. Nadine hastily finished her meal, then left the hall herself. She was immediately followed, as she had expected it. In her bedchamber she donned a light cloak before proceeding to the chapel.

Refusing to acknowledge her keeper's presence, Nadine sped down the circular staircase. At the chapel's door she turned to the guard. "I am sure your duties do not include watching me pray."

He merely nodded.

Nadine closed the door on his face. In the corner Marie-

Elise tried to hide, but if the guard had entered the chapel with Nadine, she would have been easily spotted.

With her finger on her lips in a sign of silence, Nadine took her cloak off and draped it on her mother's shoulder. The hood covered her face slightly. Marie-Elise knelt down and bowed her head in prayer. In that position, she would be mistaken for Nadine if the guard decided to steal a peek inside.

Nadine left the chapel through the garden door and carefully found her way amidst the thick foliage. As she approached the edge of the garden, she heard a muffled voice carried from afar. An angry voice. Roland's voice, Nadine realized.

With her hands she separated the tall vines and spied through it. She saw nothing. She had come this far, she would not stop now. Leaving her secluded spot, Nadine followed the wall into the inner bailey. The closer she got, the clearer she heard Roland. Hiding in the shadows, Nadine spotted Roland arguing with a man. In fact, there was no argument, but Roland waving his finger at the man's face, spitting out expletives and threats.

"If you fail me this time, I shall cut you in pieces and throw your remains to the dogs," Roland spat before he spun around and stalked from the bailey with an uncertain gait.

Nadine watched Roland's retreat until he disappeared inside the manor. Her gaze returned to the man's back. He had surely displeased Roland in some matter. Mayhap she could enlist his aid with the promise of protection from Roland.

Approaching this unknown man would be risky, but Nadine felt she had no recourse. Roland seemed to be losing control. She had never seen him so angry. Besides she had no idea where Sir Reggie was.

She had to chance it.

Disregarding her own safety, Nadine walked out from

her hiding place. The man didn't see her until he spun around.

He jumped back as if seeing a ghost. Nadine jumped in response. A sudden flash of memory came to her. Benoit, the man who had kidnapped her, stood before her eyes.

"My lady," Benoit called as she pivoted, speeding away from him. He gave her chase and caught up with her at the edge of the garden.

"My Lady Nadine!" Benoit could not hide his wonder.

Nadine struggled to free herself. Would her nightmare begin all over again? She had escaped once from Benoit's clutches, and now had fallen into his hands again. *Sacré Coeur!*

"You are alive," he said in wonder.

"Not thanks to you."

"I meant you no harm."

"No harm? What do you call abducting and keeping a lady captive against her will?"

"I thought you dead," he mumbled, ignoring her accusations.

"But I am not." She yanked her arm from his hold. He allowed her free.

"Did you come to finish me off?" she asked. What would she do now?

"I never meant you harm," Benoit repeated.

He looked so apologetic, so nonthreatening, that Nadine forced her racing heart to slow its maddening beat. Benoit had not been cruel to her while he held her captive. At times, in fact, he had acted almost as if he cared. He kept her fed and warm, and tied her up only when he needed to go on one of his nighttime excursions. And he had never made any untoward advances at her.

What was she thinking? Nadine belittled herself for her naiveté. The man had abducted her, kept her prisoner in a little hovel, and watched her drown in the Channel.

"Forgive me if I am not moved by your words."

" 'Tis true, my lady." Benoit stole a glance back at the manor. "Master Roland knows you are alive?"

The way he asked the question made Nadine swallow her ready retort. Roland's parting words to Benoit came back to her. *If you fail me again, I shall cut you in little pieces. . . .*

"If not to finish me off, then why are you here? For another ransom payment?"

Bitter anger filled Benoit's expression. He lifted his hand. "This was my payment."

A hook stood in the place of Benoit's right hand. Nadine took a second look at him. His clothes were bedraggled, dirty. He had lost weight, and his eyes haunted his thin face.

Nadine refused to feel sorry for him. "A just reward for sure."

Benoit stole another glance behind him. "Please, my lady, go away from this place. 'Tis not safe for you."

" 'Tis ironic that you, of all people, should worry about my safety."

Benoit ignored her sarcasm. "Master Roland is a dangerous man. Trust him not."

Nadine needed not to be warned about Roland. She knew firsthand what the man was capable of. "Who should I trust, you? Despite your claims of wishing me no harm, you had me abducted."

Benoit shifted uneasy on his feet. "Master Roland hired me to abduct you at the fair in Champagne."

Floored, Nadine staggered on her feet.

"He never explained his reasons, only paid well for my services," he continued. "I was starved and needed to care for my brother, Severine, thus I accepted this ignominious task. I beg your pardon, my lady, but I never meant you harm. I would have jumped into the Channel after you, had I known how to swim."

Mon Dieu! She should have guessed. It had been Roland

all along. He had her abducted, almost killed, then when she miraculously returned from the dead, faked the betrothal agreement. All with the intention of taking over Rosemanor.

"What does Roland wish from you now?" Was his intention to kill her?

"He wishes to rid himself of a certain man."

Not kill her, but Faulk. "Faulk Brookstone."

Benoit shot her a surprised look. "Aye."

Nadine's mind swirled like a windmill. *Damn Roland to hell!* "What can I offer you to fail this task?"

"Roland shall certainly kill me, and I still have Severine to care for."

"I shall assure your safety and Severine's if you do as I ask."

For the first time Benoit smiled. "My lady, if I can offer you assistance and rid myself of Master Roland, you have my oath of fealty."

She might be crazy for trusting Benoit. Yet it was not as if she had many options. If Benoit could relay her message to Faulk, then she might have a chance to escape the fate Roland planned for her. And she would rather die than wed the vermin.

"Very well, Benoit. This is your chance for redemption."

Chapter 19

NADINE RETURNED TO her bedchamber followed by the ever-present guard. She felt his eyes on her back as she closed the door in his face. Her mother would return later, with the pretext she had left the bedchamber to fetch something for her. Fortunately they were not watching her mother, only her.

Shaking, Nadine rested her back against the door. What she had learned from Benoit this eve changed everything. That Roland had been responsible for her abduction proved he was beyond redemption. Faking a betrothal agreement was despicable enough, but in his uncontrollable ambition to own Rosemanor he had her abducted, separated from her family, and almost cost her her life.

In fact, he had cost her a life, her medieval life. Though relegated to a forgotten corner of her mind, the future was very much present inside Nadine, as was the knowledge she had traveled through time to continue this interrupted life. A life that until recently she had struggled to adjust to.

Now that her medieval life had taken center stage, she would not permit Roland's evil deeds to go unpunished. He had caused her enough grief to last an eternity.

Moreover, even her father's death could be laid at Roland's feet. After all, her father had perished while searching for her. In truth, her father would probably still be alive had it not been for Roland.

And for her, too, Nadine had to admit. Guilt filled her as old memories flooded her. If she had not whined until her father had agreed to take her with him to that fateful fair in Champagne.

If she had not eluded the two-man escort her father had insisted accompany her every step, and disappeared amidst the crowd, she would not have fallen into Roland's trap.

How dearly she had paid for her impetuosity. The short-lived thrill of her sudden freedom had not been worth the pain she had suffered and caused.

Overwhelmed, Nadine pushed herself from the door and threw her cloak on top of the trunk at the foot of her bed. She was not the same spoiled and impetuous girl. The future had taught her caution, prudence, control. She would not fall into Roland's hands again. With swift movements she stripped herself naked, then walked to the table and poured cold water in a bowl. She washed her face with tremulous hands, then picked up a drying cloth.

The door opened with a sudden thud. Startled, Nadine spun around. Roland stood at the threshold. Using the cloth on her hand Nadine inadequately covered her naked body from Roland's view.

"Out of my bedchamber!" she cried. "You have no right to be here."

Wordlessly Roland marched toward her. He hauled her flat against his body. The evidence of his twisted desire rested on Nadine's stomach. She could smell the stench of wine on his breath, and bile rose in her throat.

She struggled to free herself from the manacle of his arms. "Let go of me, you bastard!" she shouted. *Mon Dieu*, if she had her dagger she would kill the man without a second thought.

"That was not how you greeted your lover in the garden, my sweetest," Roland slurred. "Do I not deserve similar response as your betrothed?"

"You are naught to me, and you very well know it."

Roland yanked her head back and pushed his tongue inside her mouth, gagging her. Revolted, Nadine kicked and punched him, yet Roland, though obviously inebriated, had strength enough to subdue her and drag her to the bed, where he fell on top of her.

The air swished out of Nadine's lungs. He shoved his legs between hers, forcing them open, and pressed her hands over her head, against the mattress.

The more Nadine wrestled under him, the more she got caught in the web of his limbs. His mouth slithered down her throat. "Get off of me!" Nadine screamed, fighting tears of frustration and fear.

She buckled under him, trying to throw him off, but Roland continued his assault, running his hand and mouth all over her. She turned her face to the side, avoiding his kiss, but then with a sudden grunt he lifted his weight slightly off her. Taking a deep breath, Nadine swiftly heaved one knee into Roland's groin.

Hollering he rolled off of her. Nadine sprang out of the bed and leaped to the table, grabbing an eating knife. She turned to Roland in time to see him cast Marie-Elise against the wall.

Nadine hastened to her mother's side, realizing her mother had attacked Roland, affording her the precious chance to escape and fight. While helping a disoriented Marie-Elise to her feet, Nadine kept an eye and her knife pointed at Roland.

Crouching on his knees, his hands covering his jewels, Roland shot Nadine a glare full of hatred.

"Out of my bedchamber!" Nadine shouted. "If you ever touch me again, I swear, Roland, I shall castrate you like the animal you are." And for good measure she waved the knife at him.

"There is no fleeing from your destiny, Nadine." Roland held on to her bedpost to rouse himself. "I vow, next time I touch you, you best respond like a woman in love, or you, and yours"—he glanced at Marie-Elise—"shall pay the price for my displeasure."

Roland half-crawled out of the room.

As soon as he crossed the threshold, Nadine slammed the door on his back.

"Mon Dieu, Maman!"

Nadine's hand flew to cover her mouth as she dashed to the chamber pot and retched miserably. Even after she had emptied the contents of her stomach, she continued to heave. Finally her stomach calmed down, and she sank down into a chair.

Marie-Elise wiped Nadine's face with a damp cloth. " 'Tis over, *ma petite fleur*. He is gone."

"I cannot even fathom what might have happened had you not come to my rescue, *Maman*."

" 'Twas fortunate that there were none of his guards outside your door," Marie-Elise said while pouring a chalice of wine. She handed it to Nadine. "Roland must have sent them away when he came to you."

Trembling, Nadine used both hands to hold the chalice. "Fortunate, indeed." She took a good swallow. The spicy liquid cleansed her throat, settling heavily on her empty stomach.

Now that Roland had resorted to rape, what would prevent him from returning and finishing what he had started? What other evil plans did he harbor for her?

Horrified by the depths Roland had descended, Nadine and Marie-Elise barricaded themselves inside Nadine's bedchamber.

Unable to sleep, Nadine tossed and turned on her bed

until dawn, when she resolutely jumped to her feet. Her mother was by her side in an instant.

"*Maman*, we must leave Rosemanor."

"I am sure the guards are back outside, Nadine. And the great hall must be filled with Roland's men. Even if we succeeded in reaching the inner bailey unnoticed, which I am certain we shall not, how are we to reach the outer walls?"

"I had another route in mind." Encouraged by the success of last eve's endeavor to the chapel and garden, Nadine decided there was a good chance they could escape by the same path. Massive wall notwithstanding.

"You cannot be thinking to climb a ten-foot wall, then slide down a twenty-foot decline," Marie-Elise said, guessing Nadine's plans. " 'Tis just not possible, Nadine. Nay, we best wait for Faulk's return. I say we confine ourselves to this bedchamber and await rescue. We have enough food to last us for a while."

"We cannot afford to wait for rescue, *Maman*. A door shall not keep Roland away."

"But escaping is such an impossible task."

"Do not speak of impossible tasks." Nadine stared at her mother. "I have survived certain death in the waters of the Channel. I have returned to Rosemanor, to your arms—my mother's arms. I recognize not the word *impossible*. Besides, I have a plan." Ignoring her mother's silence, Nadine continued, "We can assemble a rope with strips of bedding, we surely have enough cloth for that, then we can tie one end to a heavy rock and throw it over the wall. This way we can—"

"And how are we to lift a rock heavy enough to hold our weight?"

"*Maman*, please." Why was her mother being so difficult?

Marie-Elise sighed. " 'Tis not as simple as you make it. I fear for you life."

Nadine would not be discouraged. "I shall not be in any more danger than I already am."

Marie-Elise's tortured face told Nadine of how much she cared. Finally, with a sigh, her mother agreed with her. "Very well, Nadine. I shall do anything to keep you safe. I can tie the rope to a boulder or a tree, and, provided you are able to climb the steep inner wall, you can use the rope to slide down the decline on the outer wall."

" 'Tis perfect," Nadine agreed, excited. "Once I am on the outer side, I can hold on to my end of the rope, and using it you may be able to climb up the wall and join me on the other side."

Nadine noticed her mother shifting her gaze from her, and guessed her mother would be hesitant to climb a wall. "*Maman*, you must try. I shall not leave you behind."

Marie-Elise answered her with a question. "How are we to carry our burden throughout the manor and out of doors without being seen?"

"Mayhap if we carry a little at a time, and hide it in the garden," Nadine offered. " 'Twill take longer than I wished, yet 'tis better than to sit here like a piglet waiting to be slaughtered."

Nadine would not give Roland the satisfaction of her surrender. She would never forgive him the depths he had sunk to to take possession of her rightful inheritance.

Frustration turned into anger, and anger into determination. Roland would pay for his crimes. She would make sure of it, but first, she had to flee from his clutches.

Nadine and Marie-Elise labored all day tearing apart every cloth they could lay hands on. They ended up with a pile as high as Nadine's bed. They wrapped the strips around their midriffs and legs, then concealed them with their gowns. Without a girdle and with their cloaks on, their enlarged forms would not be too noticeable to the guards. Or so they hoped.

'Twas early eve when they finished. Perfect, Roland would be occupied with his supper. Nadine and Marie-Elise opened the bedchamber door. Outside, the expected men stood guard. Ignoring them, Nadine crossed the threshold followed by Marie-Elise.

Immediately the guards stepped in Nadine's way. "Where do you go?" one of them asked.

Nadine shot a haughty look at the unfamiliar faces.

Marie-Elise stepped forward. "How dare you question the Lady of Rosemanor?"

The man looked Marie-Elise over, then dismissed her promptly. He returned his attention to Nadine. "The Lord of Rosemanor ordered us to keep you within the manor's walls."

"The Lord of Rosemanor, *my father*, is dead," Nadine said. "However, when Lord Faulk Brookstone returns to claim Rosemanor, he shall rid the likes of you, not only from this manor, but also from the face of the Christendom as effortlessly as fire exterminates pesky fleas." Nadine smiled, enjoying the glimpse of doubt that crossed their faces.

"And if you possess any sense at all, you would leave this manor as hastily as possible," Marie-Elise added.

"Now, step aside," Nadine commanded, not really expecting them to drop their swords and run, but mayhap in deference to her station they would allow her to pass.

Impervious to her command, the guard insisted, "I ask again, where do you go?" Then he added with just a semblance of respect, "my lady?"

Nadine sighed. Their skulls were obviously too thick for a subtle approach. "If you must know, I go to the chapel." She added with an acerbic grin, "To pray for your poor souls." Following their doubtful glance at her attire, she explained, "I suffer from cold spells, which you would know had you served me before."

"To the chapel, you say. Mayhap you shall not mind if we escort you there."

They grinned at her like the idiots they were, and Nadine fought the urge to reach for the knife she now carried on her person since Roland's attack and cut out their useless tongues. Mayhap then their idiotic smiles would disappear from their ugly faces. However, if she reached for her weapon, they would surely discover her disguise, and her plans would go down the fosse.

"Going somewhere my dearest?"

Nadine pivoted, her heart racing at the sight of Roland's smug face.

"You look beautiful, as always." He stepped closer. "Oh, my, have you overindulged yourself with food? You look round and lush."

Nadine trembled. Roland knew how she looked, he had seen her naked last eve.

" 'Tis pleased I am. I so loathe a bony wench."

Nadine shot him a suspicious glance. All traces of drunkenness had disappeared. He was once more well dressed, his hair carefully coifed. He looked in control again. And that fact did not assuage her fears in the least.

"As I told your thugs, I go to the chapel. Shall I add your name to the list of lost souls for whom I must pray?"

Roland laughed. A derisive, raspy, tasteless laugh that grated Nadine's nerves. He placed his hand on the small of her back, urging her on. "I shall accompany you, my lady, for I have a prayer I wish to say myself."

With trepidation Nadine descended the narrow staircase that led to the chapel. Had Roland realized she had found her father's box and in it the real betrothal document? Was that why he was escorting her to the chapel? To unmask her? Surely he jested when he said he wished to pray. Roland had never been particularly religious. It had been a bone of contention betwixt him and her father all his life.

Without glancing over her shoulder, Nadine knew Roland followed her closely. She could hear him breathing down her neck. 'Twas a creeping feeling she liked not. Treading carefully not to trip on her gown, Nadine followed her mother and the guard in front of her to the entrance of the chapel.

As she stepped from the dark corridor into the chapel, the sudden luminosity of dozens of candles burning alongside the chapel walls greeted Nadine and cast shadows on her and the room.

Like a ghost, a person emerged from behind the altar. Stunned and relieved, Nadine realized it was a priest. Surely in the presence of a priest Roland would not dare harm her or her mother.

More confidently, Nadine stepped up to the priest. Coming from behind, Roland flanked her. "This is Father Honoré," he said.

Nadine genuflected respectfully, then rose and kissed the priest's crucifix. "Welcome, Father. We are most pleased to have you. Rosemanor shall benefit greatly with your spiritual advice." She glared pointedly at Roland, then smiled back at the priest. " 'Tis long we have waited for a replacement to our dear Father Eugene."

"Father Honoré shall remain at Rosemanor only for a short period of time," Roland said. "He has a very special duty to perform—"

Nadine tried to calm the alarm bells that chimed in her mind at Roland's words.

"Our wedding solemnity."

The bells pealed frantically. Instinctively Nadine stepped back and stared at the grinning Roland. Surely his confidence was due to his belief that Faulk would not return alive to Rosemanor. But she knew better. Or, at least, she hoped so.

"I am not amused, Roland." Nadine spun around, seeking her mother. "Come, Marie-Elise, we shall return later for

our prayers. The chapel is unusually crowded this eve."
Nadine found her mother unable to move, flattened between
two guards.

Nadine's glance swept the chapel. Aside from the two
guards holding her mother, there was a third one guarding
the chapel door, and yet another standing in front of the
garden door on the opposite wall. Roland's intentions could
not be clearer.

With her heart thudding, Nadine refused to accept such
fate. "If your guards are not here to pray, I suggest they
step outside."

"They must stay, my sweetest." Roland took her arm and
twisted her around, pulling her to his side. "I wish them to
witness this momentous occasion."

Sacré Coeur! " 'Tis indeed a momentous occasion when
you enter a chapel, Roland. You best beg God forgiveness
for your trespasses." She tried to free her arm.

"Your words wound me." Roland forced Nadine down
to her knees with him. "Mayhap our bedding this eve shall
sweeten your tongue." He then turned to the priest. "Carry
on, Father. I am most anxious to wed my beloved betrothed."

Nadine felt the blood drain from her face. She lifted her
gaze to Father Honoré. A drop of sweat skittered down his
chubby face, and he shifted nervously on his feet. His obvious uneasiness gave Nadine hope. She pleaded with him.
"I am not willing to wed this man, Father. You must stop
this insanity."

"Hush, my lady," the priest said. "In your predicament I
should think you grateful to this honorable man for wedding you and saving your reputation and your soul from
the fires of hell."

"What?" Nadine stared uncomprehending at the priest.

"No need to be vexed, my sweetest. God is witness to
my good intentions of saving our child from the stigma of
bastardy and you from ostracism. I am certain you shall

repay my generosity by honoring your wifely duties."

Nadine was speechless. This could not be happening to her. After all she had been through to end up with this conniving, unscrupulous, poorest excuse for a man, was beyond contemplation. She could scream with frustration. What could she do? There were four heavily armed men in the chapel.

"You are insane," she spat, then addressed the priest. "I carry not this man's child. I would not lie with him were he the last man in the whole Christendom."

"Such language does not befit a lady," Roland taunted.

Ignoring his sarcasm, Nadine went on, "He is not even my real betrothed. I possess proof of that." Mayhap if she showed the priest the real document . . . She struggled to rise.

Roland's grip on her tightened. "Very clever, my sweetest." The venom in his voice belied the endearing term. " 'Tis yet another of your ploys that shall fail. Father Honoré, carry on."

Visibly shaking, the priest started saying the words that would unite Nadine and Roland forever. With no possibility of escaping such dreadful fate, Nadine considered the only other alternative left to her.

Her left hand crept down her gown. If she could reach the knife underneath it, Roland would be as good as dead. And if she failed, she would kill herself. For she would rather die than spend the rest of her life with Roland.

Chapter 20

BLUNTLY ROLAND YANKED Nadine to his side. There would be no escaping for her. Nadine and Rosemanor would finally be his to hold and behold forever.

With Faulk out of the way and Nadine wedded to him by God's law, the king would no doubt ratify their joining. Even if she carried Faulk's bastard, as Faulk had so adamantly claimed, Roland would find a solution. Children were such fragile creatures. Who could say if Nadine's child would survive the difficult tender years?

He still had time to think about that possibility, and he would not wait to see if Nadine was indeed *enceinte* before he made her irrevocably his. He would do it now and worry about the little bastard later.

Pity he had been too drunk to subdue Nadine last eve. It mattered not, by the end of this eve all would know Nadine belonged to him. Mayhap he would have witnesses to the bedding. Aye, what a jolly idea! The mere thought hardened him immediately.

Shifting on his knees, Roland brought Nadine closer. Father Honoré was taking an awful long time to reach the "until death do thee part."

"Father," Roland hissed. "Get on with it."

Roland knew Father Honoré would not dare gainsay him. He had been dearly paid for his compliance and silence. 'Twas rather simple. All the priest had to do was utter the binding words that would unite Nadine to Roland for all time.

Visibly uneasy, Father Honoré began to do just that when a horrendous thud echoed on the chapel's stony walls, cutting off his words. The garden door crashed down on Roland's guard as Faulk Brookstone and two of his men-at-arms lunged inside.

Furious, Roland dragged Nadine up with him as he sought his safety against the chapel's wall. Father Honoré cried out in fear and rushed to hide in a corner. Marie-Elise was thrown against the wall, falling down on the floor. Roland's men, swords drawn, fought for their lives.

He had to flee, Roland thought, creeping to the gaping whole in the wall, fighting a battle of his own with Nadine. His arms immobilized her in a manacle-like grip, but her legs flailed wildly at him.

"Damn you, Nadine. Cease your struggles." If Nadine escaped him, he would be as good as dead. Roland reached for his dagger. "Cease, or I shall slit your pretty throat." Nadine stilled herself. She might be stubborn, Roland thought, but Nadine was not dim-witted.

Slowly Roland crept to the door, but Faulk cut his retreat.

"Let go of her," Faulk ordered.

"So you can run me through with you sword? I should think not."

" 'Twill be less painful than what I shall do with you, do you harm Nadine."

"I should worry about my own fate were I you," Roland said. "There are scores of men in Rosemanor, all sworn allegiance to me." If he could reach the bailey, there would be help waiting for him there.

The chapel door plastered open. Sir Reggie, followed by

four men-at-arms, rushed in. "Rosemanor is secure, my lord. I wait your orders."

Damn Faulk to hell! Unwilling to surrender, Roland spat, "If you wish Nadine alive, you best let me go."

"Nay." Marie-Elise lunged at Roland.

Faulk held her back. "Let go of Nadine, Roland," he said. "You cannot go far with her, for I shall hunt you down as I would an animal and kill you with less mercy I would show a prey."

"Do you place such a low value on Nadine's life?" Roland said, sliding the dagger under Nadine's chin. A drop of her blood fell on Roland's arm.

Faulk paled.

"I thought not." Roland snickered. "If I escape, Nadine shall live. Do you try to follow me or hinder my escape, I shall slit her throat as I would a pig. Now, give your men the orders to allow me safe passage, and provide me with a horse outside Rosemanor's gates."

Roland saw the battle Faulk warred with himself at this moment, and he gambled his life on the assumption Faulk cared enough for Nadine—especially if she truly carried his heir.

"Do not harm her!" Marie-Elise cried. "Take me instead."

Roland snorted at the suggestion. "Command your men to step aside, Faulk."

Clenching his fists in a clear sign of frustration, Faulk nodded to his men.

The dark, moonless night had surely worked to Roland's benefit, Nadine thought. That must have been why the archers did not attempt to kill him—in the darkness they probably feared killing her instead. Using Nadine as a shield, and creeping alongside the walls, Roland managed to reach the outer wall and the horse that waited for them there.

As soon as they entered the forest, Roland set his dagger

aside—better to grip her arms, no doubt—and immediately Nadine began her struggles again. With a curse Roland choked her with his arm. "Cease, Nadine, or I shall break your little neck and throw you aside like a lump of hay."

Nadine ceased her struggles. She had no intention of perishing. She had survived too much already; she would come through this, too. A more propitious opportunity would appear. Surely Roland would tire and slack his hold of her. She might reach her knife then, putting her on a more equal footing with him.

As the forest thickened, Roland slowed his horse. The dark woods looked frightening and impenetrable. A tree's low branch hit Nadine's hand. The sting made her cry out. Impervious to her pain, Roland continued on the barely marked trail.

Would Faulk be able to find her at all? And what would happen if he did not? Did Roland plan to kill her or keep her prisoner? Nadine knew not which prospect frightened her most.

"I would have been a good husband to you, Nadine," Roland whined. "And a good lord to Rosemanor."

"Rosemanor and I deserve better, and I would rather die than wed you," Nadine blurted out, unable to disguise her contempt.

"Your wish shall be granted, my sweetest," he spat, tightening his hold of her.

Nadine trembled. Her impetuosity would be her death. Could she not keep her mouth shut? What good would it do to antagonize Roland? She must escape the fate he had planned for her, not surrender herself to it. "We grew up together, Roland. We were friends once. How can you do this to me?" Did Roland have any sense of decency left?

"Nay, Nadine. We were never friends. You were the lady of the manor, and I was but a poor bastard kin living under your family's charity."

The bitterness on Roland's voice shook Nadine. "My father took you in when no one else would," she reminded him. "He gave you every opportunity. You chose to take the wrong path, Roland."

"And 'tis all your fault. I could have had it all. Rose-manor . . . you . . ." His hand slithered up her body, over her breast—he gave it a short squeeze—then moved up her neck, her face. His finger traced her lips. Bile rose on Nadine's throat. "I could have made you love me," he continued. "I would have treated you with care."

As Roland spoke, his grip of Nadine relaxed.

Soon, Nadine thought. Soon he would relax enough that she could attempt her escape.

As they left the trail and veered into the thickening woods, Roland was forced to slow his horse even more. Nadine leaned to the side while her hand crept slowly toward her knife.

Hiking up her skirts, Roland eased a hand underneath it. His fingers touched the many layers of cloth she had wrapped around her thighs.

"What the hell—" he cursed.

Nadine took advantage of his confusion and her exposed legs, and grabbed her knife. She sank it down on his thigh with one fluid movement.

Roland jumped in surprise and pain, involuntarily pushing her away from him. Nadine moved with the momentum and cast herself off the horse.

She hit the ground hard. Roland's grunts and curses reached her through her momentary disorientation. Swiftly Nadine rolled over in time to avoid the horse's hooves coming down on her. Swallowing her fear, she scampered to her feet and dashed into the dark woods.

Refusing to glance over her shoulders to see if Roland gave her chase, Nadine rushed blindly into a thicket. That would prevent Roland from following her on horseback, and on foot his injury might slow him down.

Protecting her face with her arms, Nadine rushed through

the darkness, knowing that if Roland caught up with her, she would be as good as dead.

Her heart thrummed in her ears with fear and exertion, drowning out any other sounds. Her labored breathing dried her mouth and throat. The strips of cloth underneath her gown unraveled, and she tripped on them. Nadine pulled at the cloth, leaving behind a trail of white strips.

As she dashed madly away, Nadine jumped over fallen trunks, stepped over small rocks and twigs. Along the way she lost her shoes and shredded her gown, leaving her feet and legs exposed to scratches and cuts.

But Nadine did not slow her run.

Her cloak caught on a tree limb, yanking her backward, almost choking her. Startled, she cried out. With trembling hands she tore the brooch that held it together and threw it down on the floor.

The stitch in her side threatened to burst, the sensitive skin of her bare feet stung terribly, yet Nadine ignored the pain.

She could not stop. The devil himself gave chase to her.

Suddenly Nadine felt the pounding of hooves hitting the ground. Terrified, she lunged forward, stepping on a sharp rock. Pain shot up her leg and instinctively Nadine jumped, losing her balance and falling down a descent she had failed to notice.

Every branch, rock, and pebble down the slide castigated her body, until she finally crashed at the bottom of the descent.

Disoriented, gasping for breath, hurting, Nadine tried to rise. A pair of strong hands grabbed her. *Sacré Coeur!* Roland had caught up with her. She closed her eyes in defeat.

"Nadine?"

The frantic call reached Nadine, and she lifted her gaze to Faulk's distressed face. Relief washed over her as she clung to him. Pressed against Faulk's chest, with his heartbeat echoing in her ears, life filled Nadine again.

"Are you hurt?" he whispered.

Nadine shook her head, unable to utter a word.

Urging his heartbeat to slow its maddening pace, Faulk held tight to Nadine. God's teeth! She could have died. Had he listened to his gut feeling and returned to Rosemanor immediately after the attack on him, none of this would have happened. His mistake could have cost Nadine her life. Guilt filled him.

Gently Faulk lowered Nadine to the ground and knelt beside her. After patting her body for broken bones, he was satisfied she had suffered only minor bruises and superficial cuts. He refused to think their child might have been injured in her fall.

"Did he harm you?" he asked as he busied himself wrapping a strip of cloth around her bleeding foot. If Roland had ravished Nadine, he would never forgive himself. He should have killed the bastard when he had the chance.

"Nay, but I sank my knife in him."

Surprised, Faulk glanced at her. She grinned, obviously pleased with herself. God's teeth, but Nadine had spirit. If their son inherited his strength and Nadine's boldness, he would be a fearless man.

Yet Nadine's boldness could be her downfall. Would she ever do what was expected of her? "You should have waited for me," he admonished.

"If I had I would be dead by now. What took you so long anyway?"

The reprimand stung. She had every right to be angry with him, though. He had failed his duty to protect her.

Even though he had been rushing back to Rosemanor when Benoit intercepted him, his presence had not prevented Roland from taking Nadine with him. Yet had he tried to stop them, Roland would have surely killed her. To allow Roland to take Nadine had been the hardest thing Faulk had ever had to do, and every moment he pursued them after that, he had prayed he would be in time to save her.

Chagrined and frustrated, Faulk rebutted, "Forgive me, my fair lady. Betwixt dodging headhunters and our king's demands, 'tis fortunate that I made it back at all."

She shot him a surprised look. "Benoit attempted on your life?"

"Benoit? Nay. Not only did he tell me about Roland's treachery, but he was also invaluable help in freeing my men and Sir Reggie. Nay, my fair lady. I was attacked on my way to the king."

"*Mon Dieu!* Roland?"

"I assume so."

Finishing wrapping her foot, Faulk took Nadine into his arms and lifted her. Nadine's hands laced around his neck. He shuddered at her touch and at the thought of almost having lost her. Again.

God's teeth! Was this how his life with Nadine would be? Chasing after her endlessly? Worrying some harm would befall her every time he turned his back? Obviously he cared for Nadine much more than he wished.

'Twas because of his heir, Faulk reassured himself, once again purposefully ignoring the witch's prophetic words of love as the thread betwixt him and Nadine. His heir would be all that would unite him to a woman.

To care was to empower. And naught good would come from a woman with power. Elizabeth had proved this to him.

" 'Tis glad I am you are back and unharmed," Nadine whispered. Her breath fanning his neck.

Ah, but her words pleased him. Faulk suppressed a grin. Nadine had a way of easing his mood.

Or sinking him into total despair.

There was naught simple about his fair lady.

" 'Tis time you resign to the fact you belong to me, my fair Nadine. I shall always be at your side."

• • •

Nadine's body ached and her heart constricted with worry as she waited for Faulk's return. He had sent her back to Rosemanor last eve, before he dashed after Roland.

A new day filtered through her window as Nadine paced restlessly. Marie-Elise entered the bedchamber carrying a trencher of food. "What do you do on your feet, Nadine? You should be resting."

"I cannot sleep, *Maman*." Nadine limped to a chair and sank down while her mother arranged the trencher on the table. "I worry about Faulk."

"Lord Faulk can take care of himself, *ma petite fleur*. He is a warrior. He needs not your counsel in such matters."

"I know that," Nadine said irritably. "Yet I also know Roland well. The depths that man can sink is incomprehensible. What manners of treachery lie in wait for Faulk?"

"Whatever 'tis meant to be, shall be."

Nadine had rebelled against fate more than once, and she was not prepared to yield to it just as yet. Her mother poured her a goblet of sweet mead. Nadine took a good swallow of it.

"You must occupy your mind," Marie-Elise said. "Have you decided what you will take with you when you return to England?"

Nadine shook her head. She had not thought about it at all.

"Mayhap you should. 'Tis certain Lord Faulk shall wish to return home as soon as possible."

"Rosemanor is my home." Here Nadine had found her medieval roots, her memories. Would she be able to begin anew at Whitecastle?

"Home is where your heart is, and your heart is with Faulk. You must go where he goes."

She did love Faulk, and with him she would raise a family, grow new roots. What mattered where they lived? She would make Whitecastle her new home. Besides, she could see her beloved Rosemanor again any time she wanted.

"With your help, *Maman*, we shall set Whitecastle aright."

"You wish me to go with you?"

Nadine shot her mother a startled look. "Of course you shall come with me. I shall never be separated from you again."

"Lord Faulk might have a different opinion."

"He would never separate us, *Maman*."

"Do not fight him over me, *ma petite fleur*. You know not how fortunate you are to wed the man you love."

Nadine was fortunate, indeed. She shuddered at the thought of being irreversibly tied to the despicable Roland. Even her mother had never wedded the man she loved. Why did her father not marry Marie-Elise after Celeste had died? It bothered Nadine so much she decided to ask her mother.

"*Maman*, if you wish not to discuss this, I understand." Nadine paused. "Why did *Papa* not wed you after Celeste died?"

Marie-Elise's stricken look was a slap on Nadine's face. She immediately regretted her question. What an insensitive clod she was to bring up such a hurtful subject. "Oh, please forgive me. I meant not—"

"Nay." Marie-Elise waved Nadine's apology away. " 'Tis your right to know. You father wished to wed me, but I refused him."

"You what?"

After a long moment of silence Marie-Elise whispered, "I refused him to protect you."

Nadine was aghast.

"I suppose I should explain it from the beginning." Marie-Elise sank down on a chair beside Nadine. "Celeste and I were *enceinte* at the same time. For obvious reasons I never revealed who fathered my child, yet out of concern for my plight Celeste was kind enough to allow me to remain at Rosemanor. When the time arrived, our babies were born hours apart, but Celeste's baby was stillborn, and I had you." Marie-Elise smiled, glancing with pride at Nadine.

"Your father concocted the idea of switching the babies so he could raise you as his daughter. I knew it meant you would not know me as your mother, but I could not deny you your birthright."

Nadine's heart filled with love for her mother. The sacrifices she had made for her. Still, she could not understand what that had to do with her mother's refusal to wed her father.

"The midwives who attended both births were handsomely paid for their silence and sent on their way. Naturally, we thought no one else knew of the arrangement. Yet, there was someone who knew about it. Your grandfather."

An image of a tall, fierce-looking man came to Nadine. As far as she could remember, her grandfather had avoided her, never acknowledging her existence. An unsmiling, contrary man, Nadine had not been sad when he passed away.

"When Celeste died a few days later, your grandfather, probably fearing your father would offer for me, demanded I leave Rosemanor at once, pointing out how my lowly birth would besmirch you. I was devastated, for I had hoped that I would finally have a family with your father. 'Twas a dream never to come true."

"What happened?"

"I could not bear to part with you, so I bargained with your grandfather. In exchange for my silence and my refusal to wed your father, I was allowed to remain at Rosemanor."

"Why did you not tell *Papa* about the bargain?"

"We were very young, Nadine. Your grandfather had the reins of Rosemanor. Had I told Roger about it, he would have rebelled against your grandfather, losing his title and lands. I could not do that to him or you. Thus, I convinced Roger I had made a vow of chastity as reparation for my sin of conceiving you out of wedlock. He was so furious he threatened to banish me to a convent, but I pleaded and begged, and he finally allowed me to stay and care for you. I believe he never forgave me, though."

"Yet he never wedded another."

Marie-Elise smiled sadly. "Nay."

Deep sadness filled Nadine at the thought of her parents loving each other so much and yet unable to be together.

"After Grandfather died, three winters ago, did you tell *Papa* the truth?"

Marie-Elise shook her head. "And then he was gone, and 'twas too late." Tears filled her eyes.

"Oh, *Maman*." Nadine's heart bled for her mother, her father, for their lost love. "A love this great shall never die," she comforted her mother, but when she tried to remember her parents of the future, the memory came to her in a hazy thought.

Sacré Coeur! Would she forget the future? And if she did, would it matter?

Chapter 21

THE LATE MORNING sun shone hotly on Faulk's head as he entered Rosemanor's gates. Rivulets of sweat skittered down his face and neck disappearing inside the wool shirt he wore under his hauberk. With an impatient gesture he wiped his face dry.

Before his destrier came to a complete halt, Faulk swung to the ground, landing heavily on two feet. He was tired and frustrated. Once again Roland had eluded his grasp. Damn his evil soul. How could he rest knowing Roland lurked somewhere, waiting for the opportunity to strike back? What would he tell Nadine?

Faulk hated loose ends. They tended to unravel at the most inappropriate of times.

He entrusted his destrier to a stable boy and trudged to the great hall.

"Welcome back, my lord." Marie-Elise strolled to him. "Shall I order a bath for you?"

Faulk nodded. A bath would be good. The many days on the road had covered him with dirt and sweat. Yet he should seek Nadine before he saw to his needs. "Where is Nadine? Is she well?"

"She is well my lord. She rests, not having slept at all worrying about you."

He would let her rest; later he would speak with her. As soon as he sat down, food and ale were served. Faulk took a good swallow from the tankard. The cool liquid soothed his parched throat.

"Is he dead?" Marie-Elise abruptly asked.

Faulk shook his head.

"He shall return for her, then."

Marie-Elise was right. Roland would come, but he would not find Nadine here. They must return to England at once. 'Twould be easier to protect Nadine at Whitecastle than at the sprawling Rosemanor. "Begin preparations for departure, Marie-Elise. I wish to return to England at dawn."

"My lady cannot be ready so soon."

"Then 'tis your responsibility to have her ready."

Faulk shot Marie-Elise an ask-no-question-do-your-duty look, yet instead of running to do his bidding, Marie-Elise stared back at him, scrutinizing his thoughts.

He intensely disliked the feeling.

"If you forgive my bluntness, my lord," Marie-Elise began.

Now what?

"Why do you wish to wed my Nadine?"

Faulk was surprised. He had expected Marie-Elise to whine about their departure, even chide him for Roland's escape, but not to ask about his intentions toward Nadine. "Besides the obvious reasons?" He decided to jest.

Marie-Elise did not laugh. "Nadine has suffered much. I wish not to see her suffer anymore."

Faulk was offended. "Do you believe I would cause her harm?"

"I know you for an honorable man, my lord; therefore I have no doubt you shall protect Nadine from harm. My concern is whether you shall also love her as she needs and wants to be loved."

Faulk took another swallow of ale. "That is beyond your right to ask." He did not even wish to think about love, let alone discuss it. Tension gathered at his shoulders. What was so important about love that women had to speak of it constantly? Fortunately, thus far, Nadine had refrained from broaching the matter.

"She carries your child, you know?"

Faulk choked, then stared wildly at Marie-Elise. Realizing he still held the tankard of ale in midair, he slowly set it down on the table. "I see she has confided in you." He tried to sound nonchalant but felt like shouting with joy. He had always trusted the prophecy would be proven true, but having it confirmed was truly gratifying.

Marie-Elise shook her head. "She has told me naught. I believe she has yet to realize it." She paused. "Is that why you want her? For her child?"

"My heir," Faulk corrected. *My heir*! The prophecy had not failed him.

Nadine tiptoed into the solar where Faulk sat in the bathtub with his back to the door. A strong scent of pine wafted in the air, and she inhaled deeply. The fragrance brought her back to Whitecastle, to the eve she and Faulk had first made love. An eve that was indelibly marked on her mind. Faulk had made her blood boil, had unleashed emotions in her she had never even dreamed existed, prompting her to surrender her maidenhead to him in reckless abandon.

Yet, from the beginning—without as much as a flicker of doubt—Faulk had pronounced her destined to be his. And now, all fell into place. Nadine had the betrothal agreement that united her to Faulk, and Roland was ousted from Rosemanor.

Naught and nobody would interfere with their love.

Nadine vowed not to have her dream of perfect love destroyed like her mother's. Fate had given her a second chance, and this time she would not waste it.

Silently she strolled to Faulk and knelt down behind his bathtub. She stared at his glistening back for a moment, tension gathering in her stomach, then she stretched her hand and touched his raven hair. Her fingers sprawled through the soft, wet strands, raking his scalp with her fingernails.

Faulk reacted to her touch with a shudder, but he did not turn around. She drew her face nearer and blew on his ear. Goose bumps spread on his neck. Yet he said naught.

Ah! He wished to play. She was all for it.

She nipped at his ear, then his neck, grating her teeth over the sensitive spot of his nape. The muscles on his shoulders tensed. Enjoying the game, Nadine alternated bites with licks, covering the whole extent of his wide shoulders. For a moment she thought she heard him sigh, but that must have been she, for men did not sigh. They groaned, they moaned—on certain occasions—but they did not sigh, especially a warrior like Faulk.

Whatever 'twas, though, it marked the end of Faulk's passivity, for in a sudden move, he hauled her over his side and into the tub with him, sloshing water on the floor. His wet hands closed on both sides of her face, bringing her to him as he covered her mouth with his lips. His tongue teased inside, dueling with hers, stealing the very breath out of her.

"What took you so long?" he asked, an eternity later. His brilliant eyes sparkling with fire and amusement.

Nadine felt the water seeping into her gown, but she did not care. Legs dangling out of the tub rim, buttocks firmly encased betwixt Faulk's hard thighs, she could not think of a better place to be. "Betwixt dodging fortune-hunters and waiting for rescue, 'tis fortunate I have made it to you at all," she jested.

Faulk's laughter resonated on the bedchamber's walls. "Comely and witty. What a dangerous combination for a lady." He licked a drop of water skimming down her face, following its trajectory straight into her lips.

Witty and clever, Nadine thought. What would Faulk say when he learned the incredible tidings she had unearthed?

Cradling Nadine in his arms, Faulk drank deeply from the nectar of her lips. Knowing she was *enceinte* with his child had made even the frustration of Roland's escape diminish in importance.

"You were right all along, Faulk," Nadine whispered, betwixt kisses. "We were destined to be together."

Had he heard her right? Had Nadine just agreed with him? God's teeth, 'twas too good to be true. Bewildered, he held Nadine away from him.

"I see I surprised you," Nadine said, grinning widely. "'Tis wonderful tidings I have for you."

Then he understood. Nadine spoke of their child. "'Tis indeed wonderful tidings, my fair Nadine."

"Do you already know of it?"

"Marie-Elise told me."

"Oh!" Nadine was crestfallen.

Faulk could have kicked himself. He should have kept his mouth shut and allowed Nadine to tell him. 'Twas obvious she wished to do so. "Be not vexed with Marie-Elise. She thought you knew not."

"How could I not know when I was the one who found the box?"

"Box? What box?" Totally dumbfounded, Faulk rose and, carrying Nadine with him, stepped out of the bathtub. He set her down on her feet. Her sodden clothing clung to her, delineating her fine form. For a moment Faulk forgot what they talked about.

Then he heard Nadine say, "The box that contained our betrothal. What did Marie-Elise tell you?"

Their betrothal? Faulk averted his eyes from Nadine's delightful body. What did she mean? Sidestepping her, he picked up a couple of drying cloths. He draped one around her shoulders and wrapped the other around his hips. He must get to the bottom of this.

"Begin from the beginning, Nadine."

"*Mon Dieu!* You know naught about that, do you?"

Annoyed, Faulk waited, urging Nadine on with an arched eyebrow.

Nadine took her time explaining about her dream, her search for the box, how she had found it, and its wondrous contents.

"We have been betrothed all along," she said.

God's teeth, Nadine had always belonged to him, as he had believed, as the prophecy decreed, as his father wished. In his infinite wisdom Lord Warren had chosen Nadine for him, and Faulk could now honor his wish. He let out a roar of satisfaction.

Naught would separate them now. He reached for Nadine and touched the cloth he had just wrapped around her shoulder. With a flick of his fingers he tossed it to the floor.

Nadine took a step backward. "Now, you tell me what Marie-Elise told you. What she thinks I do not know."

"Later," Faulk said, stepping up to Nadine.

Again she back stepped. "Now, Faulk."

Faulk stopped. "You should tell *me*."

Nadine looked at him as if he had gone insane.

Faulk grinned. Mayhap he should give her a clue. "Just answer one question," he said. "Have you had your monthly flux?"

Nadine blushed to her roots. "*Mon Dieu*, is that what you and Marie-Elise discussed?"

"Well? Have you?"

"Nay, but—" She stopped abruptly.

Faulk watched as the truth finally dawned on her. Her golden eyes grew huge, and her mouth slacked open. "How could Marie-Elise know what I, myself, am not certain of?" She spun around and paced the room. "Even though 'tis true that my—" She dashed him a sidelong glance, then resumed her pacing. " 'Tis too early. I feel no different. Should I not be throwing up or something?" She did not wait for his answer but continued to prattle. "I have been so occupied. . . . How could I not know . . . ?"

"Nadine!" Faulk called, amused at her reaction.

She ignored him. "So many things have happened. There is Marie-Elise. She is my mother, you know. I must tell you this story—"

"Nadine," Faulk called again, marching to her and pulling her into his arms. "Shush . . ."

Nadine silenced. Her face burrowed on his chest. Faulk caressed her hair, held her tight, and waited for her to accept the truth.

" 'Tis true, is it not?" she whispered against his chest. "I am with child."

"Aye." Faulk placed his fingers under Nadine's chin and lifted her face to him. " 'Tis proud and thankful that I am, my fair lady." Two engorged tears glided down from her beautiful golden eyes. "Are you unhappy?" he asked as his thumb cleared the drops away. She could not be unhappy. Surely she wished to bear his child. The thought she might not, never occurred to him.

" 'Tis pleased that I am, my lord. Pleased that I am."

Relieved, Faulk lowered his face to hers, and his lips brushed hers slightly. He returned for another kiss, then another, and another. All had finally fallen into place. He had Nadine, he would have his heir, and he would fulfill his vow to his father. He was about to carry Nadine to his bed, when Marie-Elise interrupted them.

She stood at the threshold, glaring at him. "Not until the vows are spoken."

Two days later they left Rosemanor for England. Behind them followed a caravan of mules and carts overloaded with clothing, jewelry, golden plates and chalices, furniture, and everything Nadine thought she could use at Whitecastle. There was also a trunk filled with seedlings of plants and roses she intended to transplant to English soil.

Nadine stole a glance backward, and for a moment a deep sadness filled her heart. 'Twas as if she would never see Rosemanor again. That was impossible, she told herself. Rosemanor would go nowhere, and she would come back to visit many a time, she was sure.

For a moment the fear of crossing the Channel haunted her. Nonsense, she had already survived the crossing once. Obviously the water would not carry her away as the witch had warned.

"Had I given you one more day, I am certain you would have dismantled Rosemanor stone by stone and carried it to England," Faulk said, distracting her from her fears.

Nadine smiled. "Do you tell me you wish to postpone our journey?"

He shook his head. "We have dallied here long enough. Unless you feel unwell."

"I have never felt better." And that was the truth. She had never felt so empowered or so vibrant since she discovered she carried Faulk's child in her womb.

Faulk looked relieved, as if he had not asked her the same question a thousand times these past two days, and she had not given him the same answer.

"Still no word from the search party?" Nadine asked, knowing Faulk had fortified Rosemanor before they left, expecting Roland to reappear.

Faulk shook his head.

"Roland must be gone for good by now," Nadine said. "He is destitute, possibly even dead."

Faulk glanced askance at her. "I doubt the wound you caused him was mortal, Nadine. As for destitute, he might be far from it. Roland has been robbing your family for years. Cunning as he is, he has surely stashed away some of his ill-gained earnings."

"Roland robbed us?" Why should this surprise her? What

was thievery to a man who committed worse crimes?

"I have gone through Rosemanor's ledgers these past days, and there is clear indication of that. Who else, but Roland?"

"Miserable little vermin," Nadine spat.

"Worry not, Nadine. The vermin shall be squashed sooner or later. We have more pressing matters to consider."

"Could you be speaking of a certain wedding?" She had certainly thought about it quite a lot lately.

"Indeed." Faulk shot Marie-Elise a sidelong glance. "With your *maman* watching over you like a hawk, this wedding cannot happen soon enough for me."

Nadine laughed, knowing Faulk referred to the fact that her mother had not only interrupted their tête-à-tête of a few days ago but had kept guard on her virtue as if her maidenhead was still intact. Nadine did not begrudge her mother's maternal instincts, yet Faulk was understandably not as tolerant.

Mayhap 'twould be good to make him wait. She should have a very eager bridegroom.

The journey across the Channel was uneventful but for a brief moment of panic on Nadine's part. Even knowing she had conquered the Channel before did not completely eradicate her alarm. Yet, strengthened by her recovered identity and the presence of her mother and Faulk, Nadine found the resolve to challenge her fears.

Streaks of orange permeated the sky as the sun lowered on the horizon when they arrived at Whitecastle. Eva was the first to welcome her, embracing Nadine as soon as she dismounted.

" 'Tis a great joy to see you again, Nadine."

"I am happy to see you, too."

"Welcome back, my lady," Mildred said. "I knew my Lord Faulk would bring you back."

"So you had assured me, Mildred. And you were right." Mildred glowed.

Robert stepped forward and bowed to Nadine. "Welcome back, my lady." He smiled. A genuine welcome smile.

Nadine could not believe it. Was this the same Robert who hated her guts? Glancing at Eva, Nadine noticed the glow of pure joy on Eva's face. Surely not only for her return? Had Eva and Robert patched their differences? The thought pleased Nadine immensely. She wanted everybody to be as happy as she was.

"Thank you, Robert. I am glad to be back." Nadine stepped to the side and brought Marie-Elise forward. "This is Marie-Elise . . . my mother. She shall be living with us at Whitecastle."

Bewildered, Marie-Elise stared at Nadine. Nadine smiled at her *maman*. She had spoken with Faulk at Rosemanor about Marie-Elise, and her desire not only to have her mother with her at Whitecastle, but also to have her honored as her mother. Faulk had been supportive of her decision.

And she had loved him the most that very moment. Faulk really cared about her happiness. Another, in his place, would not have been so forgiving of her mother's past.

Faulk's generosity was sure proof they shared a very special bond. A bond that translated into the love she had always wished for. A perfect love!

While servants unpacked the carts and mules, the weary travelers adjourned to the great hall. Nadine was pleased to see Whitecastle in a much better shape than she remembered. The hall was clean and filled with fresh rushes. She could smell the scent of rosemary. Nadine complimented Eva.

" 'Tis all in preparation for your wedding, Nadine. The guests shall begin arriving very soon."

Faulk had taken command of sending notices to friends about the wedding while they were still at Rosemanor. Nadine had no idea how many people would attend. "How many guests?" she asked.

"Ten families, no more," Faulk answered as they sat at the table.

"Do we have enough room to accommodate them?" Nadine asked.

"Most of them will camp outside Whitecastle's walls," Robert said. "Only a few shall be offered accommodations at the castle."

"That should be a challenge in itself." Nadine sighed.

"I heard the king shall make an appearance," Eva said.

Faulk snorted. "I very much doubt that. The king is very much occupied with his war; he shall not take time out to come to a wedding. Besides, he rarely comes to England. Nay, expect not the king and you shall not be disappointed."

Nadine cared not one way or another. All she cared about was that by the end of that week, she would become Faulk's wife.

Two days later, as Nadine descended the stairs that led to the great hall, a whiff of lavender reached her nostrils. *No, it cannot be!* Nadine's first impulse was to turn around and return to her bedchamber. However, as undesirable as the encounter might be, as the lady of the castle, Nadine's duties included welcoming her guests. *All* her guests.

The circumstances had changed since their last encounter. Nadine knew who she was and her worth. She was at home and she would allow no one to intimidate her.

Nadine straightened her shoulders, smoothed a strand of hair neatly behind one ear, then stepped into the great hall. Lord Heathborne and his daughter Judith sat at the lord's table with Faulk. Nadine ambled toward the table.

Faulk and Lord Heathborne instantly rose. Judith took her own sweet time.

Nadine curtsied. "Lord Heathborne, what a pleasure to

see you again." She then turned her gaze to Judith. "Welcome to Whitecastle."

Lord Heathborne smiled. Relieved? Nadine thought. Had he expected Nadine to tear his daughter's eyes out? Or yank every flaming strand off her head? Or even tear apart those expensive garments she wore? Mayhap even squash . . . It took Nadine a moment to remember the name of the fruit that described Judith's bosom. The word finally came to her. . . . Or squash those watermelons flat?

Lord Heathborne should give her some credit.

"We meet again," Judith said.

" 'Tis glad I am you came to witness my wedding."

Judith cringed. Nadine's smile broadened.

"We are honored to be invited," Lord Heathborne said.

After the initial greetings, they all sat at the table, goblets of wine and tankards of ale in hand. "We heard the tales of your ordeal, Lady Nadine," Lord Heathborne said. " 'Tis relieved we are that you have escaped unscathed."

Nadine noticed Judith did not seem to share her father's feelings. "I have Lord Faulk to thank for my rescue."

Faulk snorted, but his smile told her he was pleased with her words.

" 'Tis fortunate you wed Lord Faulk then," Lord Heathborne said. "You shall have perpetual protection now."

"Indeed." Nadine smiled as she wondered about Judith. If the lady thought to cause her any trouble, she best think again. Having survived Roland, a much more conniving creature than Judith could ever aspire to be, Nadine felt prepared to handle the likes of her.

Chapter 22

NADINE AWOKE TO Marie-Elise and Mildred's hushed voices whispering little tidbits about her life and Faulk's. Two mother hens talking about their chicks. Lulled by the soft sound, she closed her eyes again.

"Nadine shall make a beautiful bride."

The words penetrated Nadine's sluggish brain. *Sacré Coeur!* Nadine opened her eyes and sprang up in bed. Today was her wedding day! More than a sennight had passed since Nadine's arrival at Whitecastle, and she had anxiously awaited for this day. And now 'twas finally here.

"The sleeping beauty awakens," Marie-Elise said, sprinkling perfumed oil into a filled-to-the-brim bathtub. "Time to rise and prepare for your wedding, *ma petite fleur*. The morn grows late."

Excitement thrummed through Nadine as she threw the coverlet aside and rose from the bed. Led by the scent of roses beckoning from the bathtub, she sprang to the water.

Marie-Elise washed Nadine's hair twice over, then scrubbed her body until it gleamed, all the while whispering sweet platitudes in her ears.

No doubt to calm her down.

Meanwhile, Mildred straightened out the bed, then lay the wedding garments on it. Nadine caught a glimpse of the beautiful cloth. What would her gown look like?

As Nadine stepped out of the bathtub, Mildred enclosed her body in a huge drying cloth. After being toweled dry, Marie-Elise and Mildred helped Nadine into a fine, soft linen shift. Over it came a pristine white chemise with long, tight sleeves. Dressed thus, Nadine put on her soft leather shoes.

"I always believed Lord Faulk would bring you back, my lady," Mildred said. "Thus, from the day you left for Rouen, I have been sewing this for you." She held the gown up in the air for Nadine's inspection.

The words stuck in Nadine's throat.

" 'Tis baldekin," Marie-Elise offered.

Nadine recognized the expensive silk woven with gold threads. Its bell-shaped sleeves were intricately embroidered in patterns of flowers, with pearls decorating the borders, the collar and the hem. A gown worthy of a queen.

" 'Tis exquisite," Nadine said. "Thank you so much, Mildred."

Mildred glowed. " 'Tis glad that I am you like it. It complements your beauty, my lady."

"Lord Faulk shall be very pleased, indeed," Marie-Elise said, helping Nadine into the gown. A jeweled girdle complemented the ensemble.

They stepped back to look at Nadine. "The circlet," Mildred recalled, picking it up from the bed. They placed the gold circlet decorated with flowers and ribbons of white and gold on Nadine's head.

"Now," Marie-Elise said, eyes moistened with emotion. "You are beautiful, *ma petite fleur*."

"Aye, my lady. Beautiful."

Nadine smiled. What would Faulk say?

• • •

At the sound of bells tolling, Nadine—whose mare was richly adorned with ribbons and flowers—followed the jongleurs who led the wedding procession down the hill to the village's church, where the ceremony would take place.

As her only kin, Marie-Elise rode immediately behind Nadine, followed by Sir Robert and Eva, then the guests, and finally Whitecastle's and Rosemanor's knights.

The beautiful summer morning was balmy, and a little breeze whispered through the trees. The scent of earth wafted up from the crushed leaves beneath the horses' hooves, and Nadine inhaled deeply. Birds sang a beautiful symphony to life.

Along the way a multitude of people flanked the road. They cheered and tossed flower petals at Nadine in good merriment. Children jumped and danced in wild excitement, then hurled themselves to the dirty ground fighting over the coins the wedding cortege threw at them.

In the distance Nadine beheld the church's square tower where the bell tolled, beckoning her. As she approached it, a crowd blocked her view of the front of the church, yet as she neared it, they parted to her as the Red Sea had parted for Moses, revealing Faulk. A knot formed on Nadine's throat at the sight of him.

He stood, ramrod straight, clad in a royal blue tunic and black breeches. His hair was slicked back, as 'twas his way, in defiance to the fashion of short bangs. His handsome face was clean shaved. The incredible blue of his eyes sparkled like the summer sky.

There was so much about Faulk that filled Nadine's heart with love. His gentleness, his faith, his honor. He was the consistency, the pillar of strength, she could rely upon.

And this day, under the blue sky and God's eyes, she would unite her soul and body to Faulk Brookstone. She would not cry, she had promised herself, yet a solitary tear strayed down her face.

And then Faulk smiled, and the adorable dimple flashed

at her as he strolled to her side and set his hands around her waist. The world around Nadine slowed down, the cheers and shouts of good wishes faded away. With their gazes interlocked, Faulk slowly brought her down from her mare to the ground beside him.

"Your loveliness surpasses all, my fair lady."

Nadine smiled, thankful Faulk's hands lingered on her waist until her trembling legs firmed up. Then he took her hand and placed it over his folded arm. Together they took the few steps that separated them from Father Anselm, who stood at the church's door.

The ceremony would be performed outside for all to witness, then the bride, the groom, and the noble guests would enter the church for the mass.

In a daze Nadine answered Father Anselm's questions of being of age, of banns being posted, of their free consent to the union. Her heart thrummed so loudly in her ears, Nadine feared she would go deaf.

She turned to Faulk as he took her hand into his. They faced each other, lost in each other's gaze. His touch calmed Nadine's racing heart, his smile soothed her nerves.

Faulk took in Nadine's loveliness. She looked like an angel. All golden, and sunshine, and freshness, and sweetness. His heart stumbled into a reckless beating he feared all would hear. Without vacillation, he held the ring to Nadine.

"With this ring I thee wed; with my body I thee worship; and with my worldly goods I thee endow."

He steeled his trembling hands as he placed the ring on Nadine's thumb. "In the name of the Father," he said, then moved the ring to the second finger, "and of the Son," and on to the third finger, "and the Holy Ghost." On the fourth finger of Nadine's left hand, Faulk left the ring, saying, "Amen."

Father Anselm placed his hand over Faulk and Nadine's

joined hands and spoke the final, biding words, *"Quod Deus conjunxit homo non separet!"*

A deafening roar rose from the crowd, finding echo in Faulk's heart.

What God has united, no man shall separate! Nadine was now irrevocably his.

All were invited to celebrate the lord's wedding within the castle's walls. The village people gathered in the bailey, where pigs and boars roasted whole on open pits, sending tantalizing aromas in the morning air.

Before entering the hall, where the noble guests would be entertained, Faulk halted, and grabbing a chalice of wine, addressed the crowd. "Hail to the new lady of Whitecastle. The fair Nadine."

A thunderous cheer followed them into the great hall.

Nadine and Faulk sat alone at the lord's table facing their guests, who settled themselves on trestle tables forming an open square.

Food was immediately served, an endless procession of dishes that delighted the ravenous crowd. Robert's toast to Faulk and Nadine was the first of many to come. And the more wine and ale consumed, the lengthier and less meaningful the toasts became.

Then the entertainment began.

The jongleurs' balancing acts and acrobatics made Nadine laugh, and the troubadour's praise of her beauty and wit embarrassed her. Then the troubadour turned his attention to Faulk and sang of the lord's prowess in the battlefields.

Nadine's gaze drifted over the guests and settled on Judith, who stared at Faulk with lust in her eyes.

Annoyance surged through Nadine. She told herself Judith was no threat to her. After all, Nadine had just wedded Faulk. She was now his wife. Judith's presence was only tolerated because of her father's friendship with Faulk. Nadine hoped they would have the good sense not to linger about after the wedding festivities were over.

Shifting her attention to Faulk, Nadine found her husband staring at her with fire in his brilliant eyes. Her body immediately warmed under the glow of his stare, and she forgot about Judith.

"Nadine, Nadine," he whispered.

Faulk's husky murmur stirred Nadine's blood. How much longer were they expected to remain in the presence of their guests? Emboldened, she touched his thigh, and the steel warmth underneath her fingers burned her.

He lifted her hand, palm up, to his lips, then kissed the hollow center. "Soon," he said, reading her mind. "Very soon."

Yet the feast went on for interminable hours. The more everyone ate and drank in merriment, the more debauched they became. Even the troubadour's songs deteriorated from stories of love and war to ribaldry.

Suddenly Faulk rose, pulling her up with him. He kissed her hand, then shot her a smothering look. "Leave, now. I shall come to you shortly."

Desire filled Nadine, weakening her limbs, and she swallowed hard. The crowd, noticing they had risen, cheered wildly.

"Do you need any aid with the bedding, Lord Faulk?" a drunken man shouted. "You may call upon me."

Another interjected, "Judging by the bulge on his breeches, our Lord Faulk neither needs nor wishes our help."

Laughter filled the hall.

Nadine's face burned. Would Faulk follow the custom of a public bedding? She would die of shame if he did.

"Faulk—" she began.

"Worry not, Nadine. Just leave, now."

His voice sounded urgent. Unsure, Nadine sought her mother in the crowd. She found Marie-Elise and Mildred standing at the foot of the stairs. Her *maman* nodded to her.

Nadine glanced once again at Faulk. He had never failed her before. He would not fail her now. He best not fail her.

Robert and some of the male guests carried a half-undressed Faulk inside the bedchamber. A few female guests followed them.

Lying naked on the bed, covered by only a thin sheet of cloth, Nadine rebelled against the barbaric ritual. Though her mother had tried to convince her she had no choice, Nadine knew that if Faulk wished he could bypass such custom. And if he did not, she would.

She would allow no one to gawk at her naked body.

With trepidation she watched as the men lowered Faulk to the floor and summarily stripped him of the rest of his garments. Faulk's reassuring smile did naught to assuage Nadine's anxiety. She glared at him.

Apparently undaunted, Faulk continued to smile as he nodded to Robert.

" 'Tis time we leave," Robert said, turning his back to the bed and nudging the crowd toward the door. "Our presence is not required."

Some grudgingly accepted the order, others complained audibly. " 'Tis no fair," one man said. "We have yet to see the bride."

Faulk pivoted to face the crowd. "You shall see no more than you already have."

An old woman pretended to swoon at the sight of him. The other women gawked at him in admiration, while the men sneered with envy, demanding a glimpse of Nadine's body.

Judith took a step toward Faulk. Nadine immediately sat up in bed. If Judith took another step, Nadine swore to herself, she would forever regret it.

A couple of men-of-arms entered the bedchamber, at Faulk's previous orders, and helped Robert dispatch the rowdy crowd. Judith was the last to leave. As she crossed the threshold, she glanced backward. She shot Faulk a look of pure lust, and Nadine one of pure hate. And then they were gone. The door slammed shut on their backs.

Lazily Faulk strolled back to Nadine.

" 'Tis only us now."

Nadine decided to take Judith out of her mind. She would not allow her to spoil this eve. "Thank you," she said. As always, Faulk had not failed her. He was the epitome of a chivalrous knight, ever considerate of her feelings.

"No one shall see what is meant for my eyes only."

She could dispute Faulk's very male point of view, but truth be told, she wished no one, but him, to look at her.

"Uncover yourself to me, my fair lady."

Faulk's words thrilled her. She had already learned the incredible sensations he could elicit from her, and she had craved him these past days. And now he was here, with her. Her husband, her lover, her mate for life.

Nay, she would not hide herself from his eyes.

Nadine left her sitting position to kneel down on the bed. Slowly she slid the cloth down her body, revealing the top of her breasts, then her nipples, then her stomach, and then the rest of her.

She knew she blushed furiously, but the look of total awe on Faulk's eyes—as if he had never seen her naked before—was so empowering, Nadine did not avert her gaze from him.

He did naught to disguise his desire for her. His nostrils flared, his breathing quickened, his manhood reached for her. Aye, Faulk desired her, and his arousal inflamed her.

Nadine felt her breasts grow heavier, the nipples tauter. Hunger filled her veins, inundating her innermost part with liquid heat.

Faulk climbed into the bed and knelt in front of her. "Fairest of them all," he whispered, then he took her breasts into his hands. He weighed them, molded them, caressed them with the palm of his hands, and then finally he took them, one at a time, into his mouth.

Nadine bent backward, allowing him free access to her. His arms encircled her waist, holding her in place as he worshipped her breasts.

As his lips moved up her neck, his hands advanced up her back, until his fingers interlaced through her hair, the thumbs sprawled under her chin. He bit her lower lip, teasing her until she moaned in frustration, then he took total possession of her mouth.

He pulled her flat against him and Nadine clung to his neck, raking her hands into his soft hair, brushing her swollen breasts against his chest. Faulk's hand slid down Nadine's back, burrowed into the cleft of her buttocks and opened her from behind.

Nadine shuddered at his touch, then began convulsing as he thrust a finger inside of her. The world disappeared as she climbed to heaven in the swirling emotions that overtook her, until she exploded with the intensity of a thousand stars.

Nadine slumped against Faulk, trying to catch her breath, to find words to describe such exquisite, almost painful, sensation.

He seemed to understand, for he held her for a long moment, before he lifted her face to him again. He kissed her lips at first with gentleness, then urgency, and finally with barely suppressed hunger. His arousal throbbed against Nadine's belly, reminding her of what was yet to come. And the thought flared anew her passion.

Faulk sensed Nadine's arousal. Her hands roamed his shoulders, her tongue teased his ear, until he could wait no longer. He was about to lay Nadine flat on her back when her hand slid down his stomach and her fingers closed around his shaft.

'Twas like being hit by a thunderbolt. He stilled himself as Nadine caressed the length of him, but he could not hold back the groan of pleasure that escaped his lips. God's teeth, Nadine's touch would be his undoing.

His hand rested on top of hers, stilling her movements. "Nay, Nadine, no more." Mayhap later after he had spent himself inside her a few times, he would be able to withstand such exquisite torture.

"I want to be inside you when I spill my seed," he said.

"I want you inside of me," she whispered.

Groaning, Faulk spanned his hand over the width of her waist and pulled her to him, lifting her, then lowering her down into his shaft in one swift movement, until her buttocks touched his thighs.

She gasped, and he held her still for a moment, then he directed her in a slow rhythm of lifting and sliding down. Nadine caught on, and was soon rising and falling on her own.

Gratified at her response, Faulk allowed her some control, until a mindless mass of sensations overtook him. The need to thrust into her overwhelmed him.

He could take just so much of this passive position.

Without withdrawing, he pressed Nadine's back against the mattress, and began his thrusting. As he increased the rhythm and the sensations accelerated, 'twas almost as if the sun was falling down on him, blinding him to the world, warming him with its powerful rays, separating him from all.

He felt Nadine peaking under him, and he rode her cresting waves, glorying at every shudder coming from her, until his world hung askew, and he exploded inside of her.

Burrowing his face on Nadine's shoulders, Faulk came down from the floating sensation. He withdrew from her and rolled to the side, bringing her with him.

"You take my breath away, my fair Nadine."

With her face against his chest, Nadine responded, "I love you, Faulk."

Immediately Faulk tensed. Why did she have to say that?

Did she think he wished to hear it? Did she really love him?

Women were wont to praise men's strength, the size of their shafts, the width of their shoulders. Some even thought if they swore fidelity or love, they could gain power over a man.

Elizabeth had been one of those. She had spoken of her love for him time and time again, only to betray him in the most vile way.

Betwixt him and Nadine there would be respect—he deserved that much. There would be lust—it seemed he was fortunate in that. There would be loyalty—he would accept no less. However, there was no need for love. Love was what the troubadours sang about. Unreal. Unnecessary. A myth.

Faulk wanted not Nadine's love.

"What is the matter?" she asked.

"There is something I must do." He gently rolled from under her.

Faulk picked up his dagger and cut a small slit in his thigh.

"What are you doing?" Nadine asked.

"I shall have no one doubting my lady wife's virtue." His blood dripped into the pristine sheets.

"I thought everyone at Whitecastle knew what happened here weeks ago."

"I trust them to keep their mouths shut, yet our guests need a little reassurance." Satisfied there was enough blood, he tore a strip of cloth and wrapped it around the incision, then he pulled on the sheets and hurled them to the floor.

When the morn came, he would display the bloodied cloth on the window, as 'twas the custom, and everyone would know he had taken Nadine's maidenhead, and consummated the marriage.

Nadine scooped down on her knees and kissed the bandage that covered the wound on his thigh. She lifted teasing golden eyes to him. "Is there anywhere else that hurts?"

Faulk groaned and pulled her to him.

Judith awoke with her body thrumming with lust. She had spent half the night obsessing with the thought of Faulk and that insipid Nadine together. That bag of bones could not possibly fulfill the desires of a man such as Faulk.

Judith was best suited to satisfy him. She knew firsthand how to please a man, having experienced many since her wedding night. Her old, decrepit husband had taken her maidenhead, but as soon as he ineptly relieved her of that impediment, Judith had taken lovers.

Yet seeking young, virile, available men had become tiring. She wished to wed and have an eager man constantly in her bed. And she had wished Faulk above all others.

Groaning with frustration, Judith yanked the covers aside and rose. As her maid helped her dress, Judith bemoaned that there was not even a decent man at Whitecastle that she could make use to assuage her frustration.

A good gallop would help, she thought. Riding had some similarities with bedding a man. One kept one's leg firmly encased over a firm body, while the steed moved, bringing one to satisfaction. A poor substitute, she knew, yet better than the alternative.

Judith met her father in the bailey. She wanted no company for this ride but could not dismiss him easily. As they walked to the stables, Judith lifted her gaze to the window of Faulk and Nadine's bedchamber.

As 'twas expected, the blood banner flew proudly, proof of Nadine's lost virtue.

"That bloodstain is as much mine as 'tis Nadine's," Judith spat.

"Forget about Faulk Brookstone," her father said, "and especially forget about Lady Nadine. It matters not whether 'tis her blood or not. The marriage is consummated."

Judith seethed in silence.

"I warn you," her father continued, "do naught to jeopardize my relationship with him. Through Faulk I have a chance to get into the king's grace, and I shall not allow any interference. Not even from my daughter."

Judith shot her father an innocent look. "I have no intention of interfering in your affairs, Father."

Weeks ago Judith had trusted Roland du Chasse—who, she had learned recently, was in fact Nadine's cousin, Roland du Monte—to rid Nadine from the face of the earth. Obviously Roland had never intended to do so. If he had confided in Judith, she would have helped him gain Nadine. His distrust had caused him and Judith a bitter defeat.

'Twas rumored he had perished. Judith wished that was true. If Faulk got wind of what they had planned, he would surely seek revenge against her.

As Judith crossed the castle gates, she glanced back at the window. She had lost Faulk, and for that Nadine would pay.

Chapter 23

Eyes closed, Nadine stretched lazily, trying to wake up. She reached across the bed, expecting to find Faulk. When her hand touched empty space, she opened her eyes and saw he was not by her side.

In his place, on the pillow, Nadine found an object—a dagger. Intrigued, she sat and picked the dagger up. Her fingers caressed the cool, ivory handle, and she smiled at the sight of a perfect rose painted on it. A ruby nested on its hilt. The scabbard in which the dagger was sheathed was made of fine leather dyed gold.

Sliding the dagger out of its scabbard, Nadine felt its weight on the palm of her hand and tested its sharpness with her thumb. 'Twas a fine blade, even finer than the one her father had given, and that she had lost in the struggle in Champagne.

"I hope it pleases you."

Faulk's voice reached Nadine in a husky whisper. She found him sitting at a chair, watching her.

"It pleases me. Thank you." Faulk, like her father, accepted her as she was, unlike most men who would complain of her unladylike pursuits.

He rose and strolled to the bed, towering above her. " 'Tis better than using eating knives on your unsuspected attackers, though I hope you shall never need use it to defend yourself again."

Faulk's words reminded Nadine of how she had almost perished at Roland's hand. Not wanting to dwell upon that, she set the dagger on her pillow, then rolled off the bed.

"I, too, have a gift for you."

"Indeed?" he said, eyeing her naked body.

Nadine blushed. "Another gift." She retrieved it from the leather trunk at the foot of her bed, then returned with it to stand in front of Faulk. She watched as he unfolded the cloth.

"A banner," he said.

She had worked feverishly to complete it in time for their wedding. "I took the liberty of adding Rosemanor's symbol—the volant golden hawk with a rose on its beak—to the Whitecastle's rampant red lion." The lion now appeared to look up at the hawk. 'Twas a pleasant imagery to Nadine. She hoped Faulk would feel the same.

Faulk draped the cloth over his corded arms and inspected it with minute attention. " 'Tis befitting to our union," he finally said. "I am pleased."

Nadine beamed.

As he folded the banner neatly and set it down on the table, Nadine noticed Faulk wore his breeches. 'Twas the morn after their wedding. Surely he did not think to leave her alone. Should they not stay abed all day?

He must have read her thoughts. "I have many duties—"

Surely none as important as the one she had in mind. "I am well aware of that." She touched his chest, running her fingertips across its incredible breadth.

His breathing quickened at her touch. The muscles on his chest tightened. He seemed to grow bigger before her very eyes.

Nadine marveled at Faulk's strength, and admired his

control over it. He could crush her with his bare hands, yet he had never used his force to subdue her will. Not even in moments of great frustration—and there had been many during their courtship.

With infinite gentleness he reached for her, and his huge hands cradled her head. "I think my lady wife has a particular duty in mind." He teased her lips with his, his tongue sliding into the seam. Goose bumps sensitized her skin.

Such gentleness in a giant of a man would seem incongruous, but not to Nadine. She had never feared Faulk's strength. She had always trusted him. She loved him.

And she believed he loved her.

This was the culmination of her dream. She could not have chosen a more deserving man. Faulk was honorable, he was truthful, and he loved her.

Then why had he reacted as if she had hit him with a brick when she spoke of love last eve?

Mayhap 'twas only a male reaction. Like most men, Faulk must see love as a female emotion, translating into need and weakness. Faulk was a knight, a warrior, and a lord of the realm. Mayhap he felt uncomfortable with expressing his feelings for her.

She should not dwell on that. Faulk loved her, of that she was certain. 'Twould be only a matter of time before he declared himself.

Meanwhile there was plenty he was ready to give her. "I have a particularly enjoyable duty in mind that you must not neglect, my lord."

She ran her fingertips down his stomach to the waist of his breeches. Faulk drew in his breath as his hand covered hers. He guided her hand downward, over the ridge of his desire.

Thrilled, Nadine squeezed it.

He moaned. "I would not dream to fail my duty to my fair lady." Then he tore the ties of his breeches with one swift move.

• • •

Nadine spent the next days playing hostess to her guests, and the nights making love with Faulk. Once more she had spoken of love to him, but Faulk had, yet again, balked at her declaration.

Doubt grew in her mind, and she vowed never to speak the words again until Faulk spoke them himself. Yet every time they made love and lay entwined on their bed afterward, Nadine felt the need not only to speak the words but to hear them, too.

It gnawed at her.

Her logical side told her she should not make a mountain out of a molehill. They were only words, and Faulk had surely proved his love for her by his actions. He had wished to wed her before he even knew who she really was; had believed she belonged to him long before he knew they were indeed promised to each other; had followed her and fought for her and wedded her.

What more did she need?

Mayhap, she needed Faulk's reassurance he would have chosen her in spite of the prophecy, and his declaration of love would do wonders to assuage her doubts.

She spoke with her *maman* about it. Marie-Elise's answer was succinct. "Is Faulk not gentle with you? Is he not loving in bed? Is he not your husband? Then cease looking for trouble where trouble does not exist."

Eva was of the same opinion.

Nadine agreed with them, yet her emotional side swelled with insecurity.

And Judith's irksome presence did not help.

By the end of that sennight all of the guests had already departed with the exception of the Heathbornes.

"I am most impressed with what you have already accomplished," Lord Heathborne told Faulk at supper that eve. "Two scores and ten men is a good count."

"Not nearly as good as the king wishes, though," Faulk said.

"I shall endeavor to recruit for the king in Londontown," Lord Heathborne offered.

"I would be thankful for your help but expect no great results. Remember our meeting at your manor. Lords are somewhat parsimonious concerning the sharing of their men."

"I shall like to try, though."

Faulk nodded his head. "And I shall make sure King Richard is aware of your efforts."

Looking pleased, Lord Heathborne smiled. "Then my daughter and I would like to take our leave of you on the morrow."

"So soon?" Faulk asked politely.

Nadine choked on the wine she was drinking. Faulk turned a worried gaze to her. With effort she caught her breath.

"We would not like to overstay our welcome," Judith said.

A little too late for that, Nadine thought.

" 'Twas a pleasure to have you both here," Faulk said.

"Mayhap you and your lady wife might come visiting soon?" Lord Heathborne asked.

This time Judith choked.

Faulk raised an eyebrow. "Mayhap we should water the wine down. It seems to disagree with the ladies."

Nadine said naught. Entertaining Judith had been a task she had neither relished nor could have relinquished. Thus, the morrow could not arrive soon enough for her.

Resolved to avoid the spectacle of Faulk and Nadine basking in each other's company, Judith excused herself and retired early to her bedchamber.

They would depart on the morrow, and not a day too soon for her. Judith could not wait to return to Londontown.

At least there she could find male companionship with no trouble. Her forced celibacy had not agreed with her at all.

She was bored. Apart from her daily riding, and one hunting party, there had been absolutely naught to do. Even taunting Nadine had lost its charm, for the lady seemed very assured of herself. Judith had enjoyed best when Nadine knew not who she was.

Besides, in over a sennight she had uncovered naught she could use against the Saint Nadine. What a bore! She would have to forfeit her desire for revenge.

In passing Nadine's bedchamber Judith noticed the door half-open. She knew Nadine was at the great hall, therefore she made no effort to hasten her steps.

" 'Tis not surprising my Lord Faulk declares not his love for our Lady Nadine."

Interested, Judith halted immediately. Peeking inside, she saw Mildred and Marie-Elise tidying up the bedchamber and conversing. Quickly she moved to a spot where she could eavesdrop without being seen.

"Lord Faulk was deeply hurt by his first wife, Elizabeth," Mildred continued. "I should think he cannot even speak the words."

" 'Tis always a curse for the second wife," Marie-Elise said. "If the first wife was wonderful, then the second wife can never measure up; if she was awful, then the second can never prove to be any better."

" 'Tis more than that. Elizabeth's betrayal was beyond redemption and cut deep into my lord's heart." Mildred lowered her voice, and Judith had to strain to hear the rest. "Elizabeth tried to foist a child sired by another man on my Lord Faulk. And she almost succeeded. He was devastated when he learned the truth."

Judith remembered hearing of Faulk's first wife's death at childbirth, yet she never knew the child was not his. What would Nadine think of that?

Marie-Elise gasped. "Surely he doubts not that the child Nadine carries is his."

Nadine was enceinte?

"He knows 'tis his," Mildred said. "The prophecy foretold it."

"Prophecy?" Marie-Elise asked.

"The same prophecy that foretold Nadine's coming," Mildred explained. "Lord Faulk was told in what manner she would come to him, what she would look like, and most important of all, it warned him that she would be the only woman capable of bearing him heirs."

"The only one? Surely there must have been other women in his life. You say Lord Faulk has not one bastard child out there?"

"None. He is too honorable of a man to abandon his own blood. Nay, Nadine is the only one who can give him his heir. There is no doubt in my mind about that, nor in Lord Faulk's mind, I am sure."

"Mon Dieu!" Marie-Elise sounded shocked. "Faulk told Nadine he would have her and no other. 'Tis obvious now what he meant."

"I believe 'tis how it began," Mildred hurriedly added. "Yet I know my lord Faulk values Nadine above all else. He needs time to accept his own feelings for her."

Marie-Elise sighed. "Then we must afford them the time to come to an understanding on their own."

Mildred agreed.

Smiling broadly, Judith left her hiding place. At last, revenge was at hand.

The world was a wonderful place! Her dream of a fairy-tale romance had come true.

If only . . .

Nay, Nadine decided. She was not going down that road again. Faulk would declare his love when he was ready. And she would be patient and wait.

Furthermore, Judith would depart this morn.

Oh, life was wonderful!

With a smile planted on her face, Nadine opened the door of her bedchamber, ready to descend to the great hall to break her fast. Judith waited just outside the door, her hand raised as if she had been about to knock.

"My lady Nadine. I wish a word with you, if you will."

Nadine decided to disguise her aversion for Judith a few moments longer. After all, the woman was about to depart. "Please, enter."

Holding her breath against the nauseating lavender scent—she would forever dislike that fragrance—Nadine watched Judith sashay inside her bedchamber.

"I realize there has been some bad blood betwixt us." Judith stopped by the bedpost, taking in the tangled sheets, then lifting her gaze to Nadine. "Before I depart, in spirit of reconciliation, I wish to offer you my good wishes for a happy and fruitful life."

Nadine eyed Judith suspiciously. What was she up to now? " 'Tis a kind gesture. Thank you."

Judith took a few steps away from the bed, inspecting the bedchamber with her gaze, lifting a cloth here, straightening a cup there. "Lord Faulk is indeed a fortunate man," she said. "To have found you, that is."

"I believe I am the fortunate one."

"A match made in heaven. The handsome, honorable Faulk Brookstone weds the beautiful Nadine du Monte, the only woman who can bear him heirs."

Unease seeped into Nadine's heart. " 'Tis my duty as his wife."

"A duty blessed by a prophecy." Judith smiled as if she knew something Nadine did not. "I must confess Lord Faulk's preference for you over any other willing lady of the realm puzzled me. That is, until I learned of the prophecy. Then all the pieces fell into place."

Nadine knew of the prophecy that foretold her coming.

Faulk had told her, and she herself had spoken with the witch who confirmed Faulk's words that they were indeed destined to be together.

What was Judith implying?

"Speak your mind, Judith. I dislike riddles."

"Surely you know of what I speak. The prophecy that foretold you as being *the only woman* capable of bearing Lord Faulk's heir? And we all know how utterly important an heir is to a man of his position. Now I understand why he would have you and no other."

Nadine froze in place. *The only woman? Mon Dieu*, was that the reason Faulk had wedded her? Solely to provide him with an heir? An heir no one else but she would be able to give him?

The truth weighed heavily on Nadine's heart. She remembered Faulk's insistence that she was *enceinte* even before 'twas possible to know for sure. His obstinacy in wedding her at all costs. His apparent disregard for her wealth. He cared not. All he ever wished from her was an heir, and she was on her way to giving him what he wished.

"If I were you," Judith continued, "I would not hasten in fulfilling the prophecy, thus rendering myself unnecessary too soon."

Pain weakened Nadine's limbs, filled her body, compressed and tore her heart into a thousand little pieces. Faulk wished not to speak of love because love had never been a factor in his decision to wed her.

He would have wedded her no matter what.

With extreme effort Nadine schooled her features. "I appreciate your suggestion, Judith, but you are not me, are you?" She managed to smile while nonchalantly lowering herself to a chair. "I am the chosen one. The one Faulk wedded, and I am thrilled with the prospect of gifting him with his most cherished wish. I shudder to think of all the unfortunate young ladies forced to wed decrepit old men. . . ."

Judith shifted on her feet. Had her jab hit the target? Nadine was pleased with Judith's discomfiture. She deserved much more.

"Do as you please." Judith moved to the door. "May your good fortune never cease."

"May you be as fortunate as I am."

As soon as Judith left, Nadine's mask of bravery collapsed. All her dreams, all her joy, were built on a lie. The greatest love she thought she had found with Faulk was naught but a pipe dream. He did not love her. He had wedded her for the heir she could give him. Would he set her aside after she birthed his heir? Did it matter? If Faulk could not give her his love, she would not want to remain with him.

Faulk's eyes were on his guests as they crossed the gates of Whitecastle on their way out, but his thoughts were somewhere else. He grinned, remembering the incredible eve of passion he had spent with Nadine. Never had he experienced such depths of pleasure with any other woman. She had crawled under his skin and he could not get enough of her.

As soon as the gates closed, Faulk turned to Nadine and took her into his arms. His lips grazed hers. The taste of her, the smell of her inflamed him. He wanted her again.

Nadine surprised him by taking a step backward and away from his embrace.

"Is something amiss?" he asked.

"I do not feel well." She avoided his eyes.

"What ails you?"

She said naught, but her pained expression alarmed him. Had he hurt her last eve? Guilt stabbed at him. He had taken Nadine repeatedly. At times, almost roughly. Yet she had not complained. On the contrary.

God's teeth! He was a man, not an animal. He could control his lust. She had only to say so.

Could he have harmed their baby? The dismal thought took hold of him.

"Is it the baby?" he asked. What had he done? "I want you abed, immediately. I shall set the servants at your beck and call. I do not want to see you on your feet again until you feel totally well. You must think of the baby, Nadine. You must rest. Where is Marie-Elise?"

He knew he was babbling, but he could not help it. An *enceinte* woman was a mystery to him. His only experience had been with Elizabeth, and she had died in childbirth!

His own mother had fallen into sickness after his birth.

God's teeth! He could not allow that to happen to Nadine. She was too important to him.

Because of his heir?

Aye, his heir was of the utmost importance to him. Yet Nadine's presence, her feminine strength, her passionate nature complemented his life. He could not part with her.

Suddenly realizing Nadine had left him alone at the hall's entrance, Faulk marched inside in time to see her dash up the stairs.

"Nadine," he called out, but she ignored him.

"What the hell?" Faulk took the stairs two steps at a time in her pursuit. He found her in their bedchamber.

"You must never take the stairs again in such a haste, Nadine. I cannot even fathom what would happen if you fell—"

Faulk halted, tension gathering at his shoulders at the sight of the pain and anger etched on Nadine's face. Her silence enervated him. He was used to a talkative, rather plain-speaking Nadine. He knew not how to deal with this tongue-tied Nadine.

"Did I hurt you last eve?"

Silence.

"If I did, I shall keep my distance. I wish not to harm you or my heir."

"And we all know how important an heir is to you, do

we not?" she hissed, turning her back to him.

Befuddled, Faulk stared at her back.

Marie-Elise dashed in at that moment. "Nadine, are you ill? A servant warned me—" She halted, sensing the tension in the air. "Is it the baby?"

"Is that all everyone can think about? The baby?" Nadine shouted, whirling around.

Startled, Marie-Elise and Faulk exchanged a wary look. "*Enceinte* women are somewhat unpredictable," Marie-Elise said.

"So I see." He took a step toward Nadine. "Do you begrudge my wanting an heir?" God's teeth! Would Nadine deny him his most cherished wish?

Slowly she shook her head.

"Then I understand you not." He glared at her. "What is it you wish from me, Nadine?"

She turned longing eyes to him. "I want you to . . ."

Faulk's heart thundered. Would she demand his love?

". . . care."

Relief washed over him. That he could do. "I shall cherish, protect, and care for you, Nadine. Doubt it not." He reached for her, but Nadine avoided his touch.

With his temper about to flare, Faulk pivoted and marched out of the room. He knew not what to make of Nadine at this moment, and he cared not for her demeanor.

God's teeth! Would his life with Nadine be ever peaceful?

Chapter 24

FOR A MOMENT Nadine had been about to beg for Faulk's love, but the panicky look on his face changed her mind. There was no point in seeking love where love did not reside. Love could not be commanded at will. Love was a feeling so intense it permeated, it dictated, it transformed one's life. But it did so of its own accord.

Knowing that did naught to assuage Nadine's pain.

"What happened?" her mother asked. "What was that about?"

Nadine sighed. "This morn I learned I am naught but a breeding mare to my husband." The painful knowledge tore at her.

"I hope the choice of words is yours and not his."

"Lord Faulk is a man of few words, *Maman*. He speaks only that which suits him." Nadine strolled to the table and picked up the dagger Faulk gave her. She had been so happy with his gift. So thankful for his understanding and acceptance . . .

"If not from your husband, then how did you come by this brilliant conclusion?"

Nadine set the dagger down. "Lady Judith—"

Marie-Elise threw her hands in the air. "Say no more. *Ma petite fleur*, look at your source. From what you have told me about this lady, 'tis obvious she holds a grudge against you. You cannot put faith in her words."

"I agree Judith is not trustworthy, but she spoke the truth."

"That Faulk wed you for the heir you carry?"

"Aye."

"So what if 'tis true?" Marie-Elise insisted. " 'Tis his right and your duty as his wife."

"That is not the point, *Maman*." Nadine began pacing the room. "There is a prophecy that foretells I am *the only woman* who can give him heirs. Of course, he would wed me; he would have wedded Medusa herself if she could bear his heir."

"Then 'tis fortunate for both of you that you are the chosen one."

Nadine faced her mother. "This is not amusing."

Marie-Elise walked to her daughter and touched her face in a gentle caress. "Why are you so angry, *ma petite fleur*? Is it because Faulk did not tell you about the prophecy? Or because you think he had no choice in wedding you?"

"Faulk told me about the prophecy when we first met," Nadine begrudgingly recognized. "Yet he failed to mention I was the only woman who could bear him heirs."

"Is it not implied?" Marie-Elise shrugged. "After all, it stands to reason that if you were destined to wed him, you were also destined to bear his heir."

Her mother's thinking annoyed Nadine, especially because she could find no fault in it. 'Twas obvious the importance of an heir to a man like Faulk. She could understand that. She could live with that. What made her heart ache was that he had not chosen her, therefore did not love her.

Her beautiful dream of a perfect love was only that—a dream.

"The thought that Faulk returns not my feelings tears me apart," Nadine cried.

Marie-Elise took her daughter into her arms. "Lord Faulk cares for you. He just admitted it moments ago."

"I do not want care, *Maman*, I want love." Nadine fought the tears springing up in her eyes.

"Love has many different faces," Marie-Elise insisted. "Wait and see what shall happen. Do not be hasty. Is not your love strong enough for the both of you?"

Was it? "What if he sets me aside after the baby is born?"

"He shall do no such thing."

"Can you guarantee it?"

"There is no guarantee in life, Nadine. And I should know that better than anyone. However, let me remind you that your lord husband has already obtained what he wished from you. You carry his heir and he knows it. There is surely no need, past the consummation of the marriage— which has already happened—for him to continue to bestow his attention on you on the marriage bed."

"I am his wife, surely he wishes to exercise his husbandly's rights."

"He also has lordly rights over every wench in this castle. And I am certain they would be more than willing to serve him. Yet he chooses to come to you. I say he cares for you more than he wants to admit."

But would Faulk ever care enough to love her?

"Marie-Elise told me you wish to speak with me?" Faulk stood at the door that forenoon, staring at Nadine with caution in his eyes.

Nadine nodded.

He reached her in two long steps and, clearly uneasy, shoved a bunch of wildflowers at her. "She also told me you would like these."

Nadine's heart lurched. *Mon Dieu*, but she loved him!

She knew her mother had probably picked the flowers and given them to him, and yet . . .

"Thank you." She took the flowers from him, and his fingers touched hers. A shudder ran through her body.

She pivoted, trying to hide her emotions, taking her time to arrange the flowers in a pitcher of water. She refused to be like a lovesick puppy begging for Faulk's attention. There were new parameters to be established betwixt them. She just had to learn not to expect the impossible. No more dreaming for her.

"I apologize for my behavior this morn." She began to mend the gap that separated them. "*Maman* must be right, *enceinte* women behave in an erratic manner. I shall endeavor to control my emotions." She spun around to face him.

He strolled to her side. "It has been a trying time for you. What with your loss of memory, Roland's treachery, the move to Whitecastle . . . Life shall resume a more leisurely pace from now on."

Nadine nodded, her throat constricted. She wished him to take her into his arms, but he stood towering above her, his arms alongside his powerful body, making no move to embrace her.

Mon Dieu! This morn she had awakened thinking the world a wonderful place, then suddenly her world had collapsed in disappointment.

Faulk took a step backward. "If it pleases you, I shall move my belongings to another bedchamber."

"Nay," Nadine reached for him but stopped before touching him. "I mean, there is no need for that. I shall be fine."

He grinned. Relieved? Nay, she was just seeing what she wished to see. He touched her chin, turning it up to him, then kissed her lips tenderly.

Mayhap her rose-colored dream would not come true, but she could create a good life with Faulk. Her destiny was in her hands. Nadine pushed the pain away, deciding not to dwell on it, and parted her lips to him. Faulk accepted the invitation without hesitation, and gave her what was within his capabilities—his passion.

The ax fell down on the tree trunk with a thud. Bark and splinters flew in all directions. The pile alongside Faulk rose steadily. Needed hardwood was not the reason he was whacking at wood. Wielding the ax in such a manner was good exercise to his arms and spared him the need to concentrate as when he practiced with his sword.

It unfettered his mind to think.

Two full moons had gone by since he had met Nadine, and his life had never been the same since. Her odd behavior—the incomprehensible words, the unanswered questions, and her unwillingness to commit to him—had thankfully ceased since she had recovered her true identity.

His golden beauty had brought the brightness of sunshine with her presence in Whitecastle. The castle truly deserved its name now. Its whitewashed walls—Nadine's suggestion—gleamed blindly in the sun, the hall's rushes were changed almost as frequently as Nadine enjoyed her baths, and there were flowers everywhere.

Faulk had grown up amidst a string of stepmothers after his own mother had died, with only Mildred to care for the castle and him. Yet Mildred had never had the authority, or the desire, or even the imagination to turn a castle into a home.

And neither had Elizabeth.

But Nadine had taken upon herself to set things aright.

The object of his thoughts ambled inside his line of vision. Faulk leaned against the ax handle and watched Nadine meander away to the garden she and her mother were renovating—the garden that had belonged to his mother and that after her death had fallen to ruin.

Faulk was content with the state of his affairs. The reparation of the castle's surrounding wall had just been finished, his small army was growing steadily stronger, and Nadine had made his castle a pleasant place to live.

All was well. Then why did he have this feeling something was amiss?

He gazed at Nadine again, who continued on her trek without seeing him, and an uneasy feeling washed over him. He had been thankful when Nadine had stopped speaking of love to him, and even more so, that after their only altercation—once they were wedded—she had not turned him away from their marital bed.

There was genuine passion betwixt them.

And yet . . .

Nadine had changed. She was more controlled, a little more distant than the Nadine he had known. Mayhap 'twas as Marie-Elise said. *Enceinte* woman were a difficult lot. Last eve, after they had just made love, before he could even recover his breath, Nadine had asked him of his plans for them once the baby was born.

The question came out of nowhere, yet he sensed it must have been on her mind for a while. Could she be afraid he would set her aside? It made no sense to him, for he never even hinted at such.

Having no idea of what to say, and with no interest in pursuing such a serious conversation, Faulk simply said, "I think we should immediately begin working on the next baby."

Nadine fell into tears. He had no idea why such words would upset her.

"I promise to wait until you feel up to it," he amended, trying not to upset her further. And then she did the unpredictable again. She flung herself into his arms and kissed him repeatedly, passionately, and aye, joyfully.

They had ended up making love again and fallen asleep into each other arms.

Heat filled Faulk's loins at the memory, and he followed Nadine's retreating form with longing. Aye, their passion was truly great. Would that be enough for them?

"Has the lady finally conquered your heart of stone?"

Faulk shot a swift, disapproving gaze to Robert, then returned to the ax wielding. Robert had been dropping hints about Nadine these past weeks, but now he seemed determined to be more direct. Faulk did not welcome Robert's intrusion on his life. "You seem rather preoccupied with matters of the heart."

Robert shrugged. "There is naught amiss with sharing tender feelings for one's wife."

Faulk cocked his head. "Is there a point to this conversation? Or are you just dodging your tasks, mayhap saving your strength for those *tender feelings* later this eve? Here"—Faulk hurled the ax to Robert—"give your tongue a rest and exert those arms."

Nonplussed, Robert grabbed the ax and took his turn splintering the tree. "Lady Nadine is not Elizabeth, Faulk. She deserves your love."

Love! Faulk yanked the ax from Robert with a humph. Why was everyone obsessed with love? And Robert, too? God's teeth!

Faulk heaved the ax in the air and let it fall heavily on the tree. "From distrustful to champion," he muttered. "What brought this change of heart?"

"A favor received is a favor owed."

"What manner of speaking is this?"

"I speak as your friend, Faulk. Grant your lady wife what she so desires or risk losing her."

The forgotten words of the prophecy returned to haunt Faulk. *To keep her you must find love in your heart, for love is the uniting thread betwixt you.*

"You speak nonsense." Faulk ignored the foreboding chill on his spine. "My lady wife desires naught I have not already given her."

Robert shook his head. "If you think thus, I shall speak no more."

"Do I need your wise counsel I shall ask for it." Faulk stalked away. "Do you need me I shall be at the lists!" he shouted over his shoulder. Now he needed an activity that would occupy his mind, for he did not wish to think about losing Nadine.

The life inside Nadine began taking form, filling her with its presence, its love, transforming her yet again, giving her life new meaning.

She busied herself with improving Whitecastle and resurrecting its forgotten garden, while Faulk engrossed himself with the task that consumed most of his waking hours—the training of the king's men.

Nadine admired Faulk's stamina. He was the first out at the lists in the morn and the last to leave in the eve. Naught kept him away from his duty.

Many a time she watched him practice, brandishing that sword of his as if 'twas light as a feather. She knew 'twas not. She had tried to lift it once, and even using both hands she had struggled. Amused at her efforts Faulk had told her to stick to her dagger.

Nadine agreed with him. War was Faulk's business, and training men one of his finest skills.

One of them.

Despite the fact her body changed from a trim figure to a mountain site in no time at all, Faulk still desired her with the same intensity and passion.

Passion and companionship were not an undesirable lot in a marriage, yet Nadine had to exert a great effort to suppress her longing for love.

A few weeks before the Channel became impassable, Faulk sent Robert and Eva to Rosemanor, where they would remain until a new Castellan could be appointed.

At Yuletide joyous memories of Christmas past filled Nadine with melancholy, and an overwhelming desire to see Rosemanor again.

When tidings of Eva's pregnancy reached Whitecastle, an absurd feeling of envy overtook Nadine at the thought of Eva's child running within Rosemanor's beloved walls, playing hide-and-seek in its garden, as Nadine had done as a child.

Chiding herself, Nadine refused to dwell on those thoughts. After her own child was born—and her *maman* had told her it could happen anytime in the next two turns of the full moon—Nadine would return to Rosemanor for a visit. The thought of walking through Rosemanor's gardens cradling her child in her arms filled Nadine with joy.

The following days Nadine spent lounging near the hearth sewing little garments for her baby, and the nights blessedly warm in Faulk's arms.

Then, one morning, almost a month later, Nadine was quietly embroidering a tiny shirt for her baby, sitting in front of the hearth in her bedchamber, when her head began to buzz and the room to spin.

Frightened, she tried to rise, but 'twas as if she were nailed to the chair. Nadine tried to scream, but her voice did not come out. She clutched her belly and closed her eyes for a moment, willing the panic to disappear, but when she opened them again, she thought she would swoon with fright.

Nadine found herself in the suffocating little room of the gypsy of the future. Stunned, she stole a glance over her shoulders and saw Denise standing behind her, giving her an encouraging look.

Sacré Coeur! 'Twas all Nadine could do not to faint. She had all but forgotten her life in the future. And now those memories came crushing down on her, wreaking havoc with the serenity of her life. Nadine rebelled against them. She wanted naught to do with the future. Her life was now, in this time.

But the future refused to disappear in a puff of smoke as she wished. The clear image insisted in remaining a part of her. The gypsy's last prophetic words echoed in the room. *Beware of water. As it can bring you happiness, so it can take it away.*

And then, as swiftly as it had come, the vision disappeared.

For a long time Nadine sat, terrified, unable to move, unwilling to accept the terrible fate waiting for her. Tears ran down her face. Tears of fright, of anger, of denial.

And when she had wasted all her tears, Nadine inhaled deeply, caressing her swollen stomach. A deep, primitive strength filled her. She had accepted this medieval life. She had married Faulk as it was foretold. She was about to deliver their child.

To Nadine, the future did not exist. And she would make sure it remained that way.

Still, more prophetic words danced in her mind. *Do you take what fate offers you, you shall not be able to leave until the time of the new birth. And by then you shall have to fight to stay.*

Sacré Coeur! Would she be whisked back to the future after her baby was born? Was that the true meaning of the prophecy?

Mon Dieu! Nadine prayed. *Do not let it end this way.*

Nadine hastened across the bailey toward Whitecastle's gates, keeping to Faulk's back while he trained with his men. Once outside, she rushed past the bridge, down the hill, and into the woods.

There was only one person who would have answers for her. And that person was the witch.

"Do you seek me?"

Nadine pivoted. Relief washed over her at the sight of the witch. How did she do that?

"I must speak with you," Nadine said. "'Tis most important."

"I know your doubts."

"Then you must have answers for me."

The witch shrugged. "Some."

Nadine was tired of enigmas and puzzles and subterfuges. "You know where I came from." It was a statement not a question.

The witch nodded.

"Am I to go back?"

"Only you can decide that."

"You say 'tis my choice?"

"I told you once, I tell you again. The water has brought you here, the water can take you away."

Frustrated, Nadine sighed. "I have been through the Channel twice and naught happened."

"Both times you carried Lord Faulk's heir in your womb. Until the baby is born, naught shall happen."

Instinctively Nadine embraced her stomach, as if by doing so she could protect her child of the hovering menace. "And after?" The question came out in a whisper, so frightened she was of the answer.

"Wherever the baby is born, there must you remain."

Sacré Coeur! She would never see Rosemanor again. Never see her child roaming about the same places that brought her so much happiness. Never return home.

As if reading her mind, the witch said, " 'Tis a small price to pay for your happiness."

Aye, Nadine thought.

"I warn you, my lady. Under no circumstances should you cross the Channel again. Your time is near. If you remain in England, all shall be well."

Relieved to finally have control over her fate, Nadine made the final decision. She would gladly give up Rosemanor and never leave these shores again if she could have Faulk and her baby.

Upon returning to the castle, Nadine found Faulk at the hall with a visitor. She joined them. Faulk had a parchment on his hands. He raised his eyes to her.

"The king wishes his men immediately."

"I thought 'twas too early for travels across the Channel."

"Evidently our king is encouraged by the early signs of spring and has decided a journey across the Channel is once again viable."

What could she say? "Are the men ready?"

He nodded, but something on his face told Nadine there was more to the missive than what he had told her.

"Richard demands I deliver the men in person," he said abruptly.

Sacré Coeur! "Why? Why does he wish for you to go now? Now of all times?"

" 'Tis not up to us to question our king's orders."

"But the baby?"

"I vow to return in time for the baby's birth."

"What if something happens to you?"

"Naught shall happen to me. I shall not be in battle. Richard just wants to make sure the men are delivered safely. I shall return as soon as possible."

Nadine heard Faulk's assurance. How come she did not feel reassured?

Chapter 25

*F*AULK WAS DYING!

Nadine's vision blurred. As the world swirled around her, she sank down on the chair, the parchment clenched in her hands, the bloodied ribbon—the ribbon she had wrapped around Faulk's forearm before he departed for France—entwined around her fingers.

Mon Dieu! It could not be true. Surely she had misread it. Nadine took a deep breath, trying to control the desperate beating of her heart, then slowly smoothed the crushed parchment.

Her gaze glided over the words. The second reading changed naught. The horrifying tidings remained etched on the page. Faulk, her Faulk, was dying.

"There must be a mistake." She refused to believe it. "Have you seen him?" she asked the messenger—a man who had trained with Faulk and had left with him for France. "Surely his injuries could not be that serious."

The man shifted uneasily on his feet. " 'Tis a mortal wound, my lady. He cannot be moved, but he is conscious. *Was* conscious when I left," he added.

"What happened?" Marie-Elise dashed into the great hall. Her gaze flying from Nadine to the messenger.

In shock Nadine said, "Faulk is . . ." Her voice faltered. "Faulk is wounded, mortally wounded, and calls for me."

"Nay." Marie-Elise's hands flew to her mouth. "*Mon Dieu!* That cannot be true."

The tears that had swollen behind Nadine's eyes now cascaded down her face. The love of her life, the father of her child, lay wounded somewhere on French soil. His precious blood seeping the life away from the powerful, cherished body.

"Nay!" Nadine cried, sweeping a hand in front of her eyes, as if by doing so the image would disappear. Faulk could not die. She would not let him die. By all that was sacred in this world, she vowed to go to him and bring him back.

Oh, how she regretted not knowing much about modern medicine, but surely even her limited knowledge might be of help. Besides, she would ask her mother to pack every salve, potion, and herb available at Whitecastle.

With strength born out of desperation, Nadine rose. "Can you take me to him?" she asked the messenger.

"Aye, my lady. There is a ship waiting for you."

"Nadine, you cannot possibly travel in your condition," Marie-Elise said. "Think of the baby. You are less than a full moon away from delivering it. You cannot risk his life and yours, too!"

"Faulk calls for me, *Maman*. I must go to him." Nadine sidestepped her mother and trudged to the stairs. Her swollen body weighed her down.

"By the time you reach him, it might already be too late," Marie-Elise insisted, following Nadine up the stairs. "Lord Faulk would never put you and his baby in such danger."

"But he has asked for me, *Maman*."

"You cannot ride," Marie-Elise pointed out. "How are you to reach the ship? On foot?"

"If need be, but a cart would do as well."

"A cart is worse than riding a horse. 'Twill shake you

until your teeth rattle. It shall harm the baby. Besides, spring has not yet arrived. Though mild, 'tis still winter out there. Nadine, you cannot cross the Channel in your condition."

Nadine halted on the landing at the top of the stairs, and turned to her mother. "I realize 'twill not be an easy journey, but what choice do I have?"

If she did not go to Faulk and he died, she would never have a chance to tell him how much she loved him. All these months she had suppressed her love, had played the part of a woman in control of her feelings, so she would not be hurt for not having her love returned as she wished. Yet, in his own way, Faulk had loved her. He had given her all he could give, his passion, his respect, his caring. She was the one who had held back.

Sacré Coeur! What would she do without him?

Wherever your baby is born, there you must remain. The witch's words weighed on her decision.

Crossing the Channel so close to her due date, she might never be able to return to England. Yet, without Faulk, what was England to her? Naught. But what if he survived? What if she could not move him until he was in stable condition? Her baby would surely be born by then, and she would lose husband and child.

"Nadine, you must listen to me."

"No, *Maman*, you listen to me." Nadine faced her mother. "If you had had the chance to go to *Papa* before he died, to help him, to tell him how much you loved him, would you have gone?"

Nadine's words floated in the air like a blanketing fog, until there could be no denial of their truth. Marie-Elise's blue eyes filled with tears. Realizing she would not dissuade Nadine, she nodded. "Take care of the packing," she finally said. "I shall speak with Sir Garrett about an escort to France."

• • •

They left that same morn. Displeased, Sir Garrett had tried to convince Nadine of the folly of such perilous journey, yet Nadine would not be dissuaded.

She only hoped she would not be too late.

Stop thinking like that, she chided herself. Faulk would be alive, he would survive. He would see the heir he so longed for.

Nadine, Marie-Elise, and Mildred, who had insisted on accompanying them at hearing the horrifying tidings about Faulk, bundled together on a small, uncomfortable cart pulled by a horse. Nadine had insisted on that. The customary ox would take forever to travel betwixt Whitecastle and where the ship was docked, and Nadine had no intention of delaying her journey one single moment longer than necessary.

At dusk they arrived at the small fishing village near the Channel. The women settled into a small hut for the remainder of the night. The men camped outside.

At dawn they boarded the ship. So worried was Nadine that for the first time she did not panic at the sight of the Channel. Besides, naught would happen to her until her baby was born.

As Sir Garrett and his men settled their horses, the ship's crew prepared for departure, and Nadine and the women rushed into the small cabin. Soon the ship was on its way.

"How long till we reach France?" Mildred asked, sitting by Marie-Elise's side as Nadine paced, and breaking the heavy silence reigning in the room.

Much depended on the wind, the weather, the condition of the roads once they were ashore, the position of Richard's camp. "Too long, I am afraid," Nadine said.

"I took care of him, took him to my own breasts," Mildred whispered as if to herself. "I saw him grow from a baby to a boy to the fine man he became."

Marie-Elise patted Mildred's hand. "Faulk is a strong man, he shall survive, I am sure."

Aye, he would survive, Nadine thought. *Mon Dieu, do not let him die!* she prayed nonetheless.

Silence fell again in the small cabin. Each woman lost in her own thoughts, with her own prayers, and her own fears.

" 'Tis cold here," Marie-Elise suddenly complained. "They should have already brought our trunks to us. We need blankets."

"I shall see what is keeping the men," Mildred said.

"I will go with you," Marie-Elise offered.

Blankets would do Nadine no good. The sun itself, if fallen on her, would not warm her heart. Yet she understood the women's need to occupy themselves. Alone in the cabin Nadine fought her despair.

Her back began to ache. It happened often now, and Nadine took the vacant cot, lying down on it. Her eyes closed. She thought she was falling asleep when she heard a scuffle outside her door.

Startled, she half rose. Grunts and clashing swords soon followed. Alarmed, Nadine reached for the dagger Faulk had given her, and rushed to the door as it opened with a crash, hitting her hand and casting her dagger to the floor. She staggered back, her ungainly form making it difficult to balance herself. She twisted her body, avoiding falling on her back, falling on her knees instead. She spotted the dagger on the floor near her hand and reached for it. A foot stepped on it.

"I see you still enjoy playing with knives. I have already advised you to cease this most dangerous practice."

Mon Dieu! It could not be. Nadine's heart thudded as her gaze followed the length of the booted foot, up the leg, and finally the face. The detestable, frightening face of Roland.

He smiled down at her. "So, we meet again, my sweetest." He bent down and picked up the dagger from under his boot, then took Nadine's arm to help her rise.

Nadine shook free of his hold, but, unbalanced, fell backward. Gracelessly she struggled to her feet. In disbelief she glared at Roland. "What do you do here? What did you do to Marie-Elise and Mildred?"

"They are in good hands, worry not."

"Where you are concerned, there is always reason to worry." Despite her bravado, Nadine's knees turned into pudding knowing she was at Roland's mercy. And Roland had no mercy. "I hoped never to see you again."

"You wound me." He pointed to his heart.

"I very much doubt it. You have no heart." Nadine stole a glance at the half-open door. The sounds of battle filtered through the aperture.

"Expect no help, my sweetest." He stepped betwixt Nadine and the door. "Your men are occupied at this moment, and Faulk, your eternal rescuer, is dying somewhere on French soil."

His derisive laugher filled the room, piercing Nadine's heart. "Alas, how I wish it to be true."

What did Roland mean? Hope unclenched Nadine's heart. Could all be well with Faulk?

"Such an expressive face! You need not utter a word, and I know what is in your mind." He took a step toward her. Nadine backed away, until her legs hit the cot. She could retreat no farther.

"I hate to be the messenger of such tidings, but your Lord Faulk is alive and well, possibly availing himself of the camp whores, since his lady wife is so obviously bloated with child." He raked Nadine's body with a hungry gaze.

Faulk was alive. Relief and joy filled her up. Yet if he was alive, then . . . Anger overtook Nadine.

"Aye. 'Twas a ruse I used to get you out of Whitecastle. Was it not clever?" He traced a finger along her cheekbone. Nadine slapped his hand away. "With your dearest Faulk being as elusive as a cat, nine lives and all—"

In that Nadine agreed with Roland. Faulk was indeed like

a cat. A lion, in fact, just like the one on his banner. Strong, fiery, powerful, graceful as any feline. And if Roland was telling the truth, he was also alive.

"—I decided that if I cannot get him directly, then I would get him through you."

Roland's menace crushed her joy. "Are you not satisfied with the level to which you have already sunk? Must you continue to besmirch this poor soul of yours? Is there not an ounce of honor in your despicable heart?"

"Bah! Honor. Such an overrated trait. Honor, my sweetest, shall be your Lord Faulk's downfall. After I finish with you—and I intend to be very thorough—I shall send you back to him, and honorable man that he is, he shall take you back, disgusted as he might be at what I have done with you." Roland laughed.

Nadine swallowed hard at such a monstrous thought.

"And you," he continued. "You shall cling to your honor and fight me all the way, therefore paying a much higher price than if you just submitted yourself to my demands."

Bile rose in Nadine's throat.

But Roland was not finished yet. "Honor was also your father's downfall. In insisting on persecuting me in the name of honor and truth, he signed his own death warrant, forcing me to arrange his early demise."

Roland had killed her father? Her honorable, gentle father? "Nay!" Nadine wailed, lunging against Roland, hands balled up into fists. She hit him with such a force, he swayed on his feet, yet not hard enough to topple him over.

He caught her by her wrists, laughing at her, as if her pain amused him. Incensed, Nadine kicked him in the shins. In response he hurled her onto the hard cot, where she fell unbalanced and hit her head on the wall.

"By fighting me you make it harder on yourself," Roland said, rubbing his shins. "Your fate was sealed when I recognized you in Londontown. Had my plan worked then, you would now be my wife. And I would not need to go to all this trouble just to possess you."

Rubbing her head, fighting the ringing in her ears, Nadine scooped to the edge of the cot. If she kept him talking, mayhap she could distract him and escape. Better to face an entire enemy army, or the Channel itself, than this maniac.

"I was not aware you saw me in Londontown." Nadine slid farther from him.

"Do you recall a certain ambush on the road as you returned to Whitecastle from Londontown?"

"I should have guessed you were behind that, too." Nadine managed to keep the tremor out of her voice, though her heart thumped with fear.

Pleased, he hovered above her. "I had some help. The pretty Lady Judith wished you out of her way—"

Judith? Nadine was stunned. *The bitch!*

"—and I wanted Faulk out of the way, thus I manipulated the matter to my own interest. Pity, I entrusted the task to incompetent imbeciles."

With a swift move Roland jerked Nadine to him. "I am in control now, and I am no imbecile. I shall have you, Nadine, as many times as I so wish." He looked down on her distended belly. "And that shall not stop me." He kissed her in the mouth. A disgusting, punishing kiss, then he swirled Nadine around, pushing her against the cot.

Fighting for balance, Nadine braced herself, but Roland pushed her down, imprisoning her in an impossible position. A sudden sharp pain ran through her back, and a gush of hot liquid bathed her thighs. A moment later, a lacerating pain cut through her insides. Tears streamed down her face.

"Get off of me," she shouted.

Roland ignored her protests. "How does Faulk use you, Nadine? Is he rough with you? Does he take you from behind? Like this?" He thrust his body against her derrière. Fortunately, there were layers of clothing separating them.

Nadine's sobs closed up her throat. *Sacré Coeur!* Roland was beyond insane. She continued to struggle out of his grip, but in her present condition, her efforts amounted to naught. She had to get away from him!

In one supreme effort Nadine lifted her head and with all her might slammed it against Roland's face. He howled and let her go. She scampered to the door, but he quickly caught up with her, wrenching her back and throwing her against the wall.

She hit it like a rock and fell to the floor, disoriented. Her body contorted in pain and her head buzzed. She thought she would pass out. Fighting the feeling, she rolled into a ball, hands over her belly, back to Roland. She needed to be alert to protect her child. She felt his kick on her back, and for a moment Nadine thought the pain would kill her. Then she felt a sticky substance betwixt her thighs, and she did not need to look to know 'twas blood.

An immense sadness filled Nadine. The future flashed at her, but the future without her family was like death.

And Nadine would rather die than live without them.

The walls begin to swirl and her vision blackened. *Mon Dieu!* She prayed with the last remains of strength. *Do not let it end this way.*

Chapter 26

FAULK BROOKSTONE STOOD on the deck of his ship. The fog of dawn had slowly dissipated, and the sun rose proudly on the horizon. He was almost in England, and soon he would be reunited with Nadine. The king had been very pleased with him and had awarded Nadine's holdings to Faulk.

Rosemanor was a very wealthy estate with many tenants and farming land. In due course, Faulk would be able to recuperate his losses. He would also spend more time improving Whitecastle and its surrounding land.

A ship crossed his line of vision. Disinterested, he glanced at it, then turned his attention to the approaching shore.

The wind changed direction, and sounds of battle carried in the air. Surprised, Faulk looked back at the ship, noticing they were much closer now. He realized the other vessel was not moving very fast, and there was intense activity on the deck.

'Twas none of his affair. He wished to arrive ashore as soon as possible and return to Whitecastle, to Nadine, to his heir. He hoped all was well there.

Roland came suddenly to mind. Frustrated, Faulk waved the thought away. Roland would not dare attack Whitecastle, and he had not gone near Rosemanor, of that Faulk was sure. Yet, where was he? Was he still alive? Faulk wished he could put an end to Roland once and for all.

The ships drew closer, and a familiar banner on the deck caught Faulk's sight. Nay, he thought, many noblemen used the symbol of the lion.

Nonetheless he kept an eye on it. He was close enough now to make out the other symbol on the banner: the hawk kissing a flower.

God's teeth! 'Twas his banner.

He immediately ordered the captain of his ship to approach the other vessel. They were side by side now, and impatient, Faulk jumped into the cold water, followed by his men. With a few determined strokes Faulk reached the other ship and climbed aboard. His men followed him.

Faulk paused long enough to certify that Whitecastle's men were indeed in the full swing of a battle. Without further delay, Faulk joined the melee, descending his sword with lethal precision over his enemies. Whoever they were.

Sir Garrett howled at him. Accosted by two men he seemed to be trying to reach the ship's cabin. Faulk heart's stopped its beating. Foreboding congealed his veins.

Nay, it cannot be!

"My lord!" Garrett cried. "My lady Nadine!" he yelled betwixt gasps and thrusts of his sword.

Faulk fought his way to the cabin in time to see Nadine balled up on the floor and Roland on top of her. Fury blinded him. Jerking Roland back, Faulk hurled him to the wall. He fell like a bag of rocks. With the corner of his eyes, Faulk saw Marie-Elise and Mildred rushing to Nadine's aid.

He returned his attention to Roland in time to avoid the man's dagger from gutting him. Capturing Roland's hand with his, Faulk squeezed it until he heard the satisfying sound of bone breaking, and then he pummeled the vermin's face until blood gushed out, staining his hauberk.

With one well-placed fist into Roland's stomach, he felled the man to the floor in a heap of moans. Faulk reached for his sword and skewered Roland through like the animal he was.

"Too swift a death for you," Faulk spat before turning to Nadine.

"There is so much blood!" Marie-Elise cried. "*Mon Dieu*, how could Roland do this to her?"

With his heart breaking, Faulk knelt down beside Nadine, who lay unconscious on the floor. Crimson blood stained her gown contrasting with the paleness of her face. God's teeth, he had not arrived in time!

For the first time in his life, Faulk was truly frightened. Hesitantly he laid his ear to her chest. "She's alive," he said, relieved.

"Of course she is alive," Marie-Elise retorted. "Nadine cannot die. She shall not die."

With infinite gentleness, Faulk picked Nadine up and laid her on the cot. He knelt beside her. As he caressed her hair, he noticed a crimson streak staining the beautiful golden strands.

"Damn you, Roland. Damn you to hell!"

The ship lurched and began turning. Sir Garrett showed his face at the door.

"We return to England, my lord."

Faulk nodded, but his attention was on Nadine, who trembled like a leaf.

Marie-Elise laid her cloak over Nadine, then lifted Nadine's gown and her legs.

"I see the baby's head," Marie-Elise said.

"I have water and cloth." Mildred set the bucket on the floor and knelt down beside Marie-Elise.

"What can I do to help?" Faulk asked.

"Pray," Marie-Elise said. "Pray hard and long."

And so he did. Faulk prayed every prayer he knew, and begged succor of every saint known.

Nadine drifted in and out of consciousness, and her moans pierced Faulk's heart. When would this cease? If only he could suffer Nadine's pain for her. . . . He had seen many men lose limb and life in battle, and yet Nadine's pain tore him apart.

Oh, God! Do not take Nadine away from me!

"She has little strength left," Marie-Elise whispered, tears flooding her eyes as she stepped to Nadine's side. " 'Tis a big baby. She will not be able to deliver it on her own. We must help her."

He had done this to her. He had sought her, and hounded her, and seduced her. In his zeal to fulfill his vow to his father and make a prophecy come true, he had pursued Nadine until she had surrendered. And now, now she might die because of him.

Guilt filled his heart.

Marie-Elise bent over Nadine. *"Ma petite fleur,"* she called. "Do you hear me?"

Nadine fluttered her eyes open.

"You must push your baby out," Marie-Elise instructed.

Nadine moaned, closing her eyes.

"Nadine," Marie-Elise called again until Nadine stared back at her. "Take a deep breath, then push."

With a groan Nadine did as she was told.

"Again."

Still, it was not enough. Marie-Elise climbed on the cot.

"What are you doing?" Faulk asked, ready to haul Marie-Elise from his beloved.

Marie-Elise glared at Faulk. "If this baby does not come out soon, Nadine will die."

Faulk saw the desperation and urgency in Marie-Elise's eyes, and he shuddered in response. Marie-Elise would never harm Nadine—of that he was certain.

"What will you do?"

"I shall knead her stomach, thus helping the baby out."

"I shall do that."

For a moment, Marie-Elise hesitated, then she stepped down. Faulk lifted Nadine, settling her upper body on his lap.

" 'Tis almost over, my fair lady," he whispered in her ears. "Just a little while longer."

He looked at Marie-Elise, who had returned to her position at Nadine's feet, and she nodded at him.

As Faulk gently kneaded Nadine's stomach, Marie-Elise urged Nadine to push. Nadine weakly complied, and then, with one last push, a baby came out in a gush of blood and water.

" 'Tis a boy!" Mildred cried. His wailing filled the cabin.

Mildred cut the umbilical cord, and Marie-Elise swaddled the baby, then brought him to Nadine.

At the sight of her son, a tear fell from Nadine's eyes. She smiled, then went limp in Faulk's arms. Her face turned the palest of hues, and her shallow breathing all but disappeared.

"Nadine?" Faulk called, but Nadine did not answer. In desperation, he hugged her to him. "Do something!" he ordered Marie-Elise, who, hugging the baby in her arms, burst into tears.

"Mildred?" Faulk called, but Mildred, too, stared at him as if naught could be done.

Nay, Nadine could not die. He could not imagine his life without her smile, her spunk, her presence. He needed her.

To keep her you must find love in your heart, for love is the uniting thread betwixt you.

God's teeth! He loved her. He had loved Nadine all along.

The realization struck him like a lighting bolt.

"Do not dare die on me, Nadine. I need you. Do not leave me, I beseech you."

"She cannot hear you, my lord," Mildred said.

"She might," Marie-Elise said. "She loves you, Faulk. Only you can bring her back. You and God."

Dear God in heaven, Faulk prayed silently. *I beg you to save Nadine's life. I offer . . .* What could he offer God for such a great gift? His life? He would, but he wished to be with Nadine. To be with her for all time, to cherish her, and honor her, and love her and their son.

If not his life, what could he offer?

Dear God, I vow to love Nadine for the rest of my life, yet I shall never touch her again with lust in mind. I offer a life of celibacy in return for Nadine's life.

"I love you, my fair lady." Tears filled Faulk's eyes. He caressed Nadine's beautiful golden hair, longing to see her eyes open, to hear her melodious laugh again. She could not die. "I love you, Nadine. Come back to me, my fair lady."

Nadine drifted between the reality of an excruciating pain and the numbness of a lost soul. Her body was not hers to command. Her mind played tricks on her. She could swear she had heard Faulk telling her he loved her.

'Twas surely a dream! But what a lovely dream.

She tried to open her eyes, but her eyelids felt glued together. A tremendous dizziness threatened to overpower her. Her head buzzed with a distant sound. And in the midst of this chaos, a vision of the future came to her. A huge ferryboat, whose horn blasted as it sailed away on the Channel. She was on board, looking over the water. Floating over it.

The water brought you here, the water can take you away. The words chanted in her mind.

"No." Nadine rebelled. She would not leave Faulk. He was not dead.

"Do not dare leave me, my fair lady! Come back to me."

Faulk's words pulled Nadine from the enveloping floating sensation. She forced her eyes open. His face was bent over her. His brilliant eyes shone with tears. For her?

She wanted to tell him she loved him, but the words would not come out. A sharp pain almost doubled her over.

"Faulk," she whispered as the pain receded.

"Aye, my love. I am here."

He flashed that boyish smile of his, dimple and all, and Nadine's heart swelled with love. She tried to touch him, but her arm felt as heavy as lead.

"I love you," she said, and an incredible peace filled her, but then she felt the pull again, the water calling her. Another sharp pain doubled her over.

" 'Tis the afterbirth," she heard Mildred say. " 'Tis almost over now."

Almost over!

"*Ma petite fleur*, you must fight." Marie-Elise approached with a baby in her arms.

Her baby! Tears cascaded from Nadine's eyes at the sight of such an angelic face. Her gaze strayed from her son to Faulk.

"Behold your son," she whispered. " 'Tis my gift to you."

The pull was stronger now. Nadine felt the undulation of the ship as her eyes closed of their own volition.

She heard a hundred voices calling her name. *Ma petite fleur!* My fair lady! Lady Nadine! They echoed in her head, urging her to fight, holding her back from the levitating feeling that would steal her away from all that she loved.

"I love you, Nadine," the words seeped through the fog of her mind. "Do not leave me."

'Twas Faulk. Faulk was professing his love. *Mon Dieu!* She had not dreamed.

Nadine struggled to open her eyes. When she did, she saw Faulk's tears falling silently on her. 'Twas like a fresh spring shower bringing life to the earth.

Water. She must get away from the water.

The ferryboat's horn sounded again.

"Faulk . . . Take me away . . . from here," she whispered with the remainder of her strength. She must make him understand. *The water has brought you here, the water can take you away.* Would he remember?

Bewildered, he stared at her. "What?"

"Take me away . . . water . . . the witch . . ."

Comprehension suddenly stamped on his face. *He understood.*

Faulk took Nadine into his arms.

"My lord, do not," Marie-Elise pleaded. "You shall hurt her."

Ignoring her, Faulk rushed out onto the deck. The ship had already docked. Sidestepping his men, Faulk dashed on until he was on solid ground.

Instantly Nadine felt some of her strength back. She had won. Love had won. The future was no more. Her life was about to begin.

She lay her head on Faulk's shoulders and whispered in his ears, "You did say you love me, did you not?"

His thunderous laughter resonated in the open air, filling Nadine's heart with immeasurable joy.

Epilogue

"I STILL THINK that forcing Judith to wed was not punishment enough for her evil deeds," Marie-Elise said.

Nadine shifted her baby from one breast to the other. "Ah, but to wed the meanest, ugliest man alive was. Besides, 'twas a difficult decision for Faulk. Lord Heathborne has been friends with his family for years."

"That did not stop his daughter from her traitorous acts."

"True, but wedding below her station and to a man who shall not condone any capriciousness from her is punishment enough."

Nadine held her baby over one shoulder while making circular motions on his little back. A huge burp filled the room.

"Good boy." Nadine smiled. "Is he not the most wondrous thing you have ever seen?"

"Aye, babies are wondrous." Marie-Elise took her grandson in her arms, so Nadine could rearrange her clothing. "Your friend Eva should have hers soon."

Nadine nodded. She missed Eva, yet knowing that she and Robert were now taking care of Rosemanor placated Nadine's worries. One day, when her son was a grown man, mayhap he might wish to take over his grandsire's holding. That would so please her.

"Are we ever to return to Rosemanor?" There was longing in Marie-Elise's voice.

"You may return whenever you wish, *Maman*, but I shall never cross the Channel again." She took the baby from her mother and lay him down for a nap.

"I understand you not."

Bending over her son, Nadine watched Roger fall asleep. Pride and love filled her heart. "I shall never tempt fate again, *Maman*." The decision was deeply rooted in her soul. She could not even explain exactly why, yet she knew she would never return to Rosemanor. "I have all I wish here. My mother, my son, and my lord husband."

She kissed her baby, then turned to the door. "And speaking of husband, I believe 'tis time I speak with mine on an important matter."

As soon as Nadine stepped out on the bailey, a shadow crossed over her path. She lifted her gaze to the sky, and for a moment, an absurd image of a flying device crossed her mind. She shook her head. 'Twas only a huge bird gliding over her head. What else could it be?

She was just overwrought. Two full moons had passed since the birth of her child, and for a fortnight now she had been ready and willing to welcome her husband back to their marital bed. Yet Faulk seemed reluctant. She tried all she knew to entice him, and still he denied her.

Well, she would have no more of that. Having almost lost him and everything dear to her, Nadine would never take life for granted again. If Faulk had ceased to desire her, he best have a very good explanation.

With sure strides, Nadine approached the place where the men trained.

"Faulk," she called, halting a few feet away from him. She did not want to risk getting slashed by his sword.

He flipped a glance at her. "I am training, Nadine."

"I know, but I must speak with you."

"Later," he said.

She would not be dismissed. 'Twas too important of a matter. "I must speak with you now," she insisted.

"I said later." He did not even look at her.

Incensed, Nadine withdrew her dagger from the special pocket on her sleeve and sliced it through the air, hitting a tree near Faulk's head. Then she turned around and sauntered back to the great hall.

Stunned, Faulk pivoted and glared at her retreating form. The blade had missed his ear by an inch. What the hell was amiss with Nadine? As if he had to ask. She had made it perfectly clear for the past fortnight, and he had died every time he had to deny her.

Yet a vow to God could not be so easily disregarded. God had kept his part, and so would Faulk, even if it killed him. And by the looks of it, Nadine was pretty close to murdering him.

Still, he could not allow his lady wife to challenge him in front of his men. He had to find a way to stop Nadine's overtures. God's teeth, he did not know how much longer he could withstand his hunger for her.

He found her at the hall, sitting demurely with her embroidery in hand. He knew better than to trust such a domestic scene.

He set the dagger on the table. "Nadine, I have duties to perform. I must train my men so that they are able to defend this castle and your life. I cannot be at your beck and call."

"You also have a duty to your wife."

"I know not what you speak of, and I have not time to dally about." He pivoted, intending to leave, for he knew exactly what duty Nadine spoke of.

She ran past him and blocked his way. "Nay. You are not avoiding me."

He ran his fingers through his hair. He should have

known Nadine would not accept his word without an explanation. Yet at the time he had made his vow of celibacy to God, he had not pondered on Nadine's reaction. God's teeth, he had been begging for her life!

"I have a question for you."

Here we go.

"Do you love me?"

The thought that he had almost lost Nadine tore at his heart. He could not fathom life without her. But how was he to reconcile the love in his heart and the hunger in his body?

"You know I do." He could not lie to her, could not hurt her thus. Besides, he had vowed to love her for all time.

"Then why do you refuse my love?"

"I do not refuse—"

"You most certainly do."

Faulk groaned. "I know not what you mean. Have I not honored you? Cared for you? Provided for you? What do you want from me?" He rushed past her. He could not stand her loveliness.

"I want your love!" she shouted.

"You have that."

She came to be in front of him again. "I shall be blunt, Faulk. I want you back in my bed."

He had lost the battle. "I cannot," he whispered, the words burning his lips.

"What do you mean, you cannot?" She raked his body with her gaze, and Faulk all but exploded. Her gaze flew up to his face. "It looks to me you can but wish not."

God's teeth, he had to tell her. He could not let her think he did not desire her, did not love her. God only knew what thoughts were going through her mind.

Faulk let out a frustrating breath. "The truth is that I made a vow to God never to touch you again."

"You *what*?"

"You were dying. I knew not what to do. So, aye, I

begged God for your life, and in reparation I offered a life of celibacy."

"You had no right to make such a vow. 'Tis not only your celibacy we speak of, 'tis also mine. Or are you considering allowing me to take a lover?"

"You are my wife. You shall know no other man." God's teeth! Only Nadine would dare say such a thing to him.

"Then you best come back to me lest I entertain the idea."

She spun around and left Faulk standing in the middle of the hall, mouth agape in stunned surprise, and hands clenched in fists in utterly frustration.

" 'Tis a pleasure to join my lord and his lady wife again so soon after the baptism of your son. Is this a special occasion?" Father Anselm asked over supper that eve.

"We need your wise counsel, Father," Nadine said.

Guessing Nadine's intentions, Faulk interrupted. "I gave you not leave to discuss this matter."

"Father Anselm may be able to help us."

"The matter is settled, Nadine. I shall not bargain my vow to God."

"Well, you should have thought about that before you made this incredibly selfish vow."

"my lord, my lady," Father Anselm interrupted. "What seems to be the trouble?"

"The trouble is—" Nadine began.

"There is naught you can do about it, Father. I apologize for my wife's impetuosity in bringing such matter to you." He glared at Nadine.

"—my lord husband has broken his wedding vows to me."

"What?" He would kill Nadine, Faulk thought.

She stared him squarely in the face. " 'Tis true. When we wedded, you made your vows to me. Well, you have broken one of them."

"Nadine, I warn you . . ."

"You have," she insisted. "Do you recall 'With this body I thee worship'?"

Faulk groaned. He seemed to be doing a lot of that lately. He rose. "This conversation is over. My lady wife, retire to your bedchamber."

Nadine jumped to her feet. "I think not." She turned to the priest. "Are you or are you not God's representative on earth?"

Taken by surprise, the priest stuttered, "Aye."

"When a man makes a sacred wedding vow to a woman," she continued, "he also makes it to God, does he not?"

Father Anselm cleared his throat. "Aye," the monosyllable came out in a hushed tone.

"Then when he breaks it, he also breaks it to God, is that not right?"

The priest nodded.

"Then he cannot in one breath vow to worship a woman, and in the next vow never to touch her again. Can he?"

"Nay, that does not seem possible."

She turned to Faulk. "There you have it."

Faulk sank down on his chair. God's teeth, according to Nadine he had not only broken his vow to her, but also to God when he had attempted to save her life.

"My Lord Faulk, is there anything you wish to tell me?" Father Anselm asked.

"Like a public confession?" Faulk asked. The entire castle folk seemed to be at the great hall, hanging on every word spoken. From serving wenches to knights to Mildred and Marie-Elise. Even the dogs lay alert, their ears pinned up.

Faulk fixed a piercing glare at his men, and they—edgy at his constant foul mood of late—stood in unison and left the hall without a protest.

Mildred shooed the servants out. And Marie-Elise followed suit.

When they had all left, Faulk said, "Nadine was dying, and I made a vow of celibacy to God for her life."

"Lady Nadine has a point, my lord. Your marriage vows are sacred."

"Ha!" Nadine shot him an "I told you so" look.

"However"—the priest turned to Nadine—"Lord Faulk made his second vow in good conscience and cannot in good conscience ignore it."

Faulk returned Nadine's "I told you so" look, though he knew if he won this argument, he would be the greatest loser.

"Surely, there must be a satisfying resolution to this matter?" Nadine asked.

Father Anselm drew his palms together in a prayer. He closed his eyes and for what seemed an eternity remained silent. Faulk and Nadine stared at him, anxiously awaiting his response.

When the priest next opened his eyes, Nadine and Faulk jumped in their chairs.

"God would be best served if our Lord Faulk upheld his vow," Father Anselm said.

"Which one?" they asked in unison.

"When our lord Faulk made his vow to God, he was granted his wish—his wife's life. Therefore a restitution is in order. A penance in accordance with the gift received. Therefore I ask, what is Lady Nadine's life worth to you, my Lord Faulk?"

"Everything."

"Precisely. I propose, in thanksgiving to Lady Nadine's life, you build a chapel at Whitecastle, where you can praise and honor God daily for the rest of your life for his immense generosity."

Relief washed over Faulk. Dear Lord, he could do that. "I shall do so."

"And, in accordance to your own desire, I shall further

propose that there must be no marital relations betwixt you two on the day of our Lord—Sundays."

"I can live with that," Nadine whispered.

"And so 'tis ordered. My Lord Faulk, you are relieved of your vow of celibacy."

Faulk and Nadine turned to each other.

"What day is today?" Nadine asked, mischief already brightening her golden eyes.

Without a word Faulk took Nadine into his arms and carried her to the stairs.

In her ears he whispered, "Thank God 'tis Friday!"

ACKNOWLEDGMENTS AND THANKS

To my critique partners and friends extraordinaire Maureen Krail, Elizabeth Laiche, and Kathleen Nance, for giving so unselfishly of their time, their talent, and their friendship.

To SOLA, the Southern Louisiana chapter of Romance Writers of America, for giving me the tools to learn more about the craft of writing.

To my family in Brazil, and especially my mother, for always believing that I could realize my dream.

And last but certainly not least, to Dale, my husband, and Andrew, my son, for their understanding, support, and love.